IN THE POWER
OF THE GODDESS

The dragon was awakened by hunger. A genuine famishment that threatened to set flame to his breath. By the old gods of dragonhome, he swore he hadn't felt such a need for food in months.

His next discovery was even more unpleasant. He was tied up with massive ropes; indeed, they were nearly the size of cables. His arms were pinioned to his body, as were his legs and tail. Even his neck was roped and held down to the floor. No matter how he struggled, he could not break his bonds, although he rolled about on the floor and struck wooden pillars on either side.

Bazil began to bellow. At his fifth bellow, the doors opened and men with spears pushed in. But instead of bringing him food, they came to torment him. And this indignity was only the beginning. For atop the great ziggurat of the Goddess, beneath which Bazil was imprisoned, preparations were underway for a great magical work. But magic demanded a sacrifi~~~ and a work of great mag~~~ est sacrifice of all. . . .

If you and/or a friend would like to receive the *ROC Advance*, a bimonthly newsletter featuring all the newest and hottest ROC books and authors, on a complimentary basis, please fill out this form and return it to:

ROC Books/Penguin USA
375 Hudson Street
New York, NY 10014

Your Address
Name _____
Street _____ Apt. # _____
City _____ State _____ Zip _____

Friend's Address
Name _____
Street _____ Apt. # _____
City _____ State _____ Zip _____

A SWORD FOR A DRAGON

by
Christopher Rowley

A ROC BOOK

ROC
Published by the Penguin Group
Penguin Books USA Inc., 375 Hudson Street,
New York, New York 10014, U.S.A.
Penguin Books Ltd, 27 Wrights Lane,
London W8 5TZ, England
Penguin Books Australia Ltd, Ringwood,
Victoria, Australia
Penguin Books Canada Ltd, 10 Alcorn Avenue,
Toronto, Ontario, Canada M4V 3B2
Penguin Books (N.Z.) Ltd, 182–190 Wairau Road,
Auckland 10, New Zealand

Penguin Books Ltd, Registered Offices:
Harmondsworth, Middlesex, England

First published by Roc, an imprint of New American Library,
a division of Penguin Books USA Inc.

First Printing, April, 1993
10 9 8 7 6 5 4 3 2 1

 REGISTERED TRADEMARK—MARCA REGISTRADA

A SWORD
FOR A DRAGON

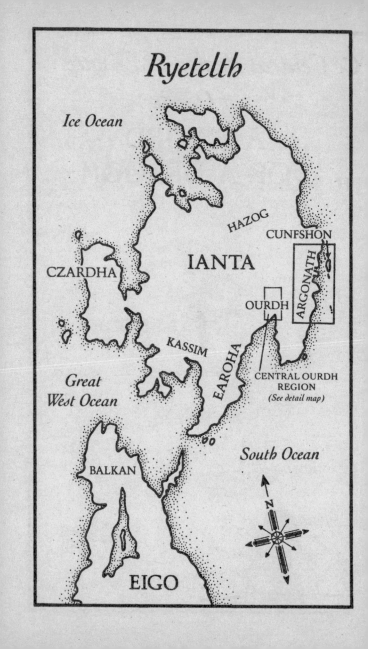

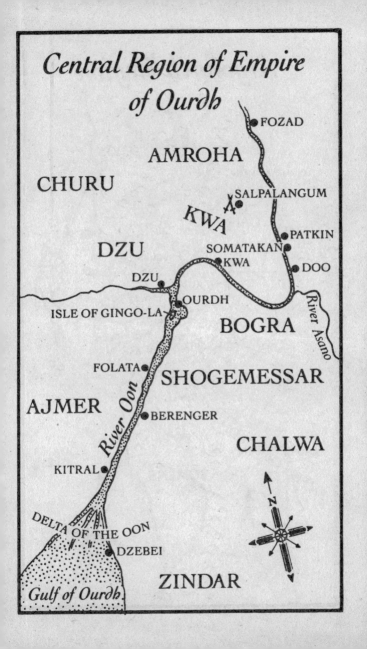

PROLOGUE

It was when the bishop found a dead child talking to him, just before a funeral service in the House of Auros in the city of Dzu that he knew he could not escape.

At night the eyes bore into him, like lancing points of fire from the dark. His allegiance was demanded. His beliefs made a mockery of. A voice whispered in his dreams.

And it was true, and he knew it. His faith was gone. There was no Auros, no benevolent center of the world. Even the House of Auros in tumbledown Dzu was a fraud. It was, in fact, the ancient Temple of the serpent god, Sephis. It had been turned over to the priests of Auros a few centuries before, when Sephis lost his hold upon Ourdh and the tyrant rule of Dzu was thrown down.

But the bishop of Auros in Dzu had dabbled in the Dark Arts. He had delved in the black books of the Masters. He had begun experiments. To escape censure from a disastrous situation involving a monkey, a highborn young woman, and an attempt to exchange their consciousnesses, he had taken a terrible oath to the mystery man who had saved him from disaster.

Now they had come to him for their payment.

The dead child refused to be buried. It lingered in the bishop's chambers.

"They are waiting for you," it announced. It lead him to the front door of the Temple.

The skull-faced man who called himself the high priest, Odirak, was waiting, accompanied by a man hidden in a voluminous black cloak. Behind this figure came a girl of perhaps seventeen years, wearing nothing but a cotton shift. She was slack-mouthed, benumbed by an enchantment.

The bishop let them into the House of Auros and then opened the heavy gate that shut away the basement. They went down into the great chamber of the pit, and the man in the cloak pulled back his hood. The bishop quailed. The man's face ended at the nose, all below was a glistening expanse of horn. The pale, naked scalp rose above eyes that were like windows onto a place of fire.

The dead child giggled, and the bishop's skin crawled.

The bishop knew that this was a Mesomaster, most powerful of all the acolytes of the Masters themselves. Never had the bishop dreamed that he might come to this pass.

With harsh phrases of power, the thing summoned a Black Mirror out of nothingness. It hung there in the air, a gleaming circle in which the grey shining backwash of chaos surged. At the Mesomaster's command, the mirror floated downward and arranged itself at knee height. The girl lay down, her eyes, mercifully, were quite blank. The dead child held a razor in its hand.

The bishop thought back to his disastrous experiment. What a fool he had been! Once again he wondered if he had been guided to the black arts, whether the enemy had known of some weakness in him that could be worked on to finally trap him.

The dead child slit the girl's throat, and tilted her head to spread her blood across the non-surface of the Black Mirror. It smoked and stank, and while it smoked the Mesomaster recited a terrible chant.

Something coalesced in the darkness within the Black Mirror. Surrounded in a halo of fractionalized sparks, the thing grew larger. Twisting motions writhed in the clouds of chaos.

The Mesomaster stepped back. From the mirror there came a gush of a thick green vapor that spilled out and rolled across the floor of the pit like a liquid, slowly filling it to knee height.

Light blazed suddenly from a point within the vapor. Something began to rise out of the vapor and take solid form. It was a dark green at first, but slowly it became golden and the surface took on a pattern of scales.

At length a great golden serpent coiled upon the floor and looked down upon them with huge expressionless eyes like portholes into nothingness.

The god Sephis was reborn, a malacostracan demon from another, darker world.

CHAPTER ONE

Dragoneer First Class Relkin of Quosh could think of many better ways of spending a precious four-week leave, but he had made a promise to his dragon. And so he found himself in a chill spring downpour, standing under a twisted pine tree on the slopes of Mt. Ulmo, staring out over an alpine meadow that was cloaked in cold fog.

It had rained for days. Relkin was damp, even under his Kenor freecoat with its thick waxed outer surface, which was proof against any single rain. He sighed audibly.

A tall, dark mass was visible in the meadow, a dragon, also in rain gear, with a waterproof mantle pulled around his neck keeping off the worst of the downpour.

They had been there for hours—the whole day to be precise, not to mention the day before and the day before that. In fact, they'd been coming to this forlorn spot for a full two weeks, and apart from the very first day, it had been just like this, cold, wet, and absolutely miserable.

There'd been nothing to eat but cold jerky and oats for a week, no company except a sulky dragon, and not even a fire since everything in the woods was soaked through and beyond the powers of even such a good fire starter as Relkin Orphanboy.

Worst of all was the knowledge that with a four-week leave, they could have gone much farther afield,

perhaps all the way back to the coastal cities, where
Relkin could have solved his biggest problem. Since
he was under the age of sixteen, he was too young to
be let into the military brothels, and General Paxion
had made the morals of dragonboys and young soldiers alike a priority of his stewardship of Fort Dalhousie. Free-lance trollops caught working outside the
legal brothels were likely to get military justice, which
had just about eliminated them from the district. Thus
almost all opportunities for a fast maturing dragonboy
to learn more of the mysteries of sex had disappeared.
Of course, there were girls in the town, on nearby
farms, and even in the fort, but their parents would
not have them mixing with dragonboys, oh no, not for
a moment. Dragonboys were all orphans, the dregs of
the coastal cities, and who wanted such landless trash
mixing with one's daughters? Not the good citizenry
of Dalhousie, that was for sure, even though those
same good citizens depended on the courage and te-
nacity of those very same boys in battle.

A quick trip to the coast, to Marneri or even Talion,
would have made all the difference. They could have
taken a riverboat to Razac and then gone down the
coast road. He could have done something about this
obsession with the opposite sex, and they could both
have enjoyed some warmer weather for a week or
two, which would have made a fine antidote to the
long hard winter they'd endured while attached to the
87th Marneri Dragons out at Fort Kenor.

Situated on the north flank of Mt. Kenor, overlook-
ing the great river and the western plains, Fort Kenor
was easily the least comfortable of all the forts in
Kenor. The winds that ripped down the Gan from the
High Plateau of Hazog were cold enough to go
through two wool shirts and a freecoat with a fur
lining.

But a promise was a promise, and dragons possessed keener memories than either men or elephants,

so there was no getting out of it. And so he was here, watching a cold, wet, sulky dragon standing out there in the meadow waiting for the love of his life to fly in.

And, of course, there was no sign of her, nothing to indicate that a silky green dragoness was coming to this meadow high above the forest of Tunina.

Relkin had heard the story many times, of course. Whenever Bazil had had a barrel of beer or two. So he knew that on this very spot, Baz had fought the mighty wild dragon, the Purple Green of Hook Mountain, and won the favor of the green female. And that Baz was by now the male parent of one or more young dragons, crossbreeds between the wild and the wingless wyverns of Argonath. And finally that the lithe green female would return to meet Bazil when the young ones were hatched.

Alas, the wild female dragon had not come, and it didn't look as though she was going to appear. Relkin would have a grouchy dragon on his hands for weeks to come. He sighed. It was enough to make a young man want to scream.

He looked up and noticed that the murk was darkening. The rain was falling more heavily than ever. He knew they'd never get a fire going, just another cold meal and then spend another miserable night sleeping under a rock overhang.

The big shape moved. Relkin shifted position. His right leg had almost gone to sleep. He shook it to dispel the pins and needles. Baz was giving up for the day. Relkin thanked the old gods and then reflexively begged the Great Mother's pardon. Relkin was hopelessly mixed up when it came to religion.

The dragon's demeanor was subdued when he drew close. "She will not come, I know this now," he said in a mournful voice.

Relkin kept quiet. It was better not to say anything. The dragon put out a huge arm and rested a well-trimmed set of claws on the boy's shoulder for a moment. A light touch, remarkable in a two-ton beast.

"Agh, it is all a waste! I am sorry boy, I one foolish dragon. She will not come."

Relkin continued to keep a diplomatic silence, and together they groped their way back through the sopping wet woods to the overhang.

Woods rats had found their food. The jerky was ripped to pieces and scattered. The oats and wheat biscuit had been gnawed and ruined. Worst of all, the pot of akh had been licked completely clean. Relkin salvaged a few fragments for a meal. The dragon ate a pound of unspoiled oats and the rest of the jerky. Neither did much to stave off the pangs of hunger.

It rained all night.

In the morning, it was still raining and colder than ever. Relkin awoke and found Bazil already up and working on the edge of his new sword, a military issue blade with no name, just the number six hundred and twenty-seven.

"It is over," he said with a dragon finality that was absolute. "We go back today. I will come again next year. If she lives, then I know she will come then."

Relkin shivered. "Next year? You want to come back here and do this again?"

"Boy not have to come! Dragon come alone!"

"It might come to that," muttered Relkin, though both knew he would never let his charge out of his sight for so long.

Bazil finished with the sword and held it up, rain splattering off the blue steel.

"Bah, this sword is clumsy, stupid. I do not want to fight with it."

Relkin had been hearing complaints about the sword, a straightforward military blade, almost eight feet long, ever since it had been presented to Brazil the previous summer.

For months, in fact, Relkin had been secretly saving

silver to buy his dragon a new and better blade, but the cost was enormous. Such a weapon represented a year's salary, and Relkin had a long way to go before he could approach one of the armorers at Fort Dalhousie and make a downpayment on one of the lovely blades that hung at the rear of their shops.

Bazil stood up and swung the sword, the steel whistling through the air and slicing off the tops of a couple of unfortunate saplings. With a final grumble, he sheathed the blade and picked around in the remains of the oat sack for a handful of grain.

In a sullen mood, and with bellies rumbling from hunger, they descended the hemlock-clad slopes of Mt. Ulmo. At the river Argo, which had risen to a torrent because of the incessant rain, the only ferry was reluctant to cross to the small town of Sutsons Camp.

They had to wait on the north side of the river, where there was nothing except a few battered huts used by local fishermen. They were fortunate in one thing: there were some fishermen there who'd had a reasonable catch the day before. So while they spent another miserable night, Relkin inside one of the verminous, smoky huts and Bazil bivouacked under a fishing boat pulled up on the shore, they at least had several quarts of a hot fish stew in their bellies.

The following morning, the rain gave up at last and was replaced with a freezing wind from the northwest, "Hazog Breath" it was called up on the cold-stone ramparts of Fort Kenor. Relkin and Baz waited disconsolately, sitting in front of a small fire. At lunch, they bought more fish soup from the fishermen. It was considerably thinner than it had been and did little to appease their hunger. Relkin was so subdued by cold and hunger that he scarcely argued with the fishermen about the quality of the soup.

The afternoon wore on, cold and colder. An occasional dark cloud flew past. The river continued in spate.

Then at last, just before dusk, they spied a sail and soon afterward cheered the arrival of a large trading boat, the *Tench,* captained by one Polymus Karpone.

Dragon and boy signaled frantically to the trader, and she set her sails to come around and fight the current, cross the stream, and pick them up.

The *Tench* was a two-masted brig with a shallow draught and a mobile keel. She was purposely built for the river trade and able to get in close to almost any shore.

Her captain was a bald, full-bellied man who wore a weathered suit of black fusgeen. His ruddy face was creased, and he most often had his pipe protruding from the corner of his mouth.

"What accommodations have you for a dragon and a dragoneer?" asked Relkin when they'd been hauled aboard.

'You can have the front quarter of my forward hold. It's a little tight, but it's warm down there and it's dry. Plenty of hay. We've taken dragons before this. Where are you headed?"

"Port Dalhousie."

"Well, that'll cost one silver groat apiece . . ."

"Two groats! To get from here to Dalhousie? That's extortion! One groat will suffice."

"One groat will buy only the cold collation, which is essentially bread."

Relkin scowled. "What are the hot items on the menu?"

"There is a venison pie, we took on several of them at Argo Landing. And there is the fish chowder, our chef is an expert on the chowder."

"Forget the chowder, we have eaten little but chowder for the last day or so."

"Then it must be two groats. A dragon will eat one entire pie, not to mention dumplings."

"Do you have akh?"

"We have the best akh from Jemins and Sveet, who are famous for all their bottled sauces. You must know the name."

"The dragon is fond of akh, especially on the dumplings." "He can have all the dumplings he wants, but it must be two silver groats. One of those pies is a penny's worth on its own."

Relkin looked to Bazil who shrugged. The captain opened the hatch above the galley a crack, and a waft of hot air carried the delicious smells of venison pies baking in the oven. Bazil groaned.

Relkin heaved a vast sigh. "Very well. It is far too much, but we are too tired to argue. Two groats it is."

The *Tench* pushed off and moved swiftly downriver. Bazil shed his mantle and cape, and Relkin got out of his wet clothes and put on slightly drier things from his pack, an undershirt of Marneri wool and some brown breeches. Then he went in search of hot food.

In the galley, Relkin found a little man with a monk's tonsure and a suit of coarse brown wool sitting on a bench eating a plate of dumplings and sauce. His trousers ended above the ankle and his feet, protected only by skimpy sandals, seemed blue from the chill winds that whipped around the deck. He seemed oblivious to the chill, however, happily murmuring to himself as he ate.

When Relkin asked for more akh on Bazil's pail of dumplings, the man with the tonsure looked up with immediate interest.

"Excuse me young fellow," he said. "Is it customary for people to eat akh in this province?"

The man had a curious accent, Relkin could not place it at first. And it was an outlandish idea, akh was a compound made of the hottest peppers, the strongest garlic, and a brew of aged fish stock. In

Relkin's experience, it appealed only to dragons and wood rats.

"Not at all, sir monk. I take the akh for my dragon."

The monk's eyes grew round. "Dragon? You are a dragoneer then. I am very pleased to meet a dragoneer. I have heard much of their prowess."

Relkin held out a hand. "Dragoneer First Class Relkin of Quosh, at your service sir monk."

The little man had a firm grip and beady, blue eyes. "I am Ton Akalon, from the Isles of Cunfshon. I am working for the Soil Survey."

Now it was Relkin's turn to be surprised. The little man had come all the way from Cunfshon! That explained the odd accent. All the way from the fabled Isles of Cunfshon, with their witches and cities of ancient stone.

"And is there a dragon on this ship then?" asked the surveyor.

Relkin came out of revery. "There is Sir Ton. And I am his dragoneer."

"Ton, please call me Ton. I would love to meet a dragon. Of course, one has read all about them, but I have never had the opportunity of actually seeing one in the flesh."

By now, Relkin had collected a trencher of pie, plus the pail of dumplings and akh, and a shoulder sack full of hot bread.

"My dragon would be honored to meet you, too, Sir Ton."

"No, just Ton. I am not a knight of the empire, and I doubt that I ever shall be. I am not a military man at all. My specialty is soil."

"Soil?"

The little man's eyes seemed to light up at the word.

"Yes, I am conducting a survey of the soils in Kenor. There are several highly fertile basins, over limestone, with good deep soils. The empire is considering making a considerable investment in these areas. Food is a great trade weapon you see. Once Kenor begins exporting grains in quantity, the empire will be able to vastly increase its effectiveness in the diplomatic arena."

"Food is a weapon?" This idea was new to Relkin.

"Yes, I'm afraid so. And I see your dragon likes plenty of it." Ton indicated the pail of dumplings, slathered in hot reeking akh that had been set out for Relkin.

"Here, I've finished my own. Allow me to help," said Ton Akalon, who picked up the heavy pail of dumplings and waited for Relkin to show the way. Relkin could detect no malice in the man, and his garb was too humble to be that of an enemy. One problem the enemy always had was that their agents did not care to pass as poor simple folk. Relkin recalled the aura of menace that had surrounded the evil Magician Thrembode when he had come to disable Bazil at the Dragon House in Marneri. Ton Akalon had no such aura, in fact, he seemed utterly harmless.

Bazil as not in a good mood, but at the sight of dinner, his eyes lit up to something like their normal brilliance.

"Baz, this is Ton Akalon from Cunfshon. He's never met a dragon before."

Big black eyes examined the surveyor.

"I am Bazil of Quosh. This is my dragonboy, Relkin. I have few complaints with him."

"The dragon is sulky at the moment," Relkin whispered to the surveyor.

Bazil snorted with derision, and ate.

"I am honored to meet you Sir Bazil. I have heard much of the dragons of Argonath," said Ton Akalon, "but of course we do not see them very much in Cunfshon."

Bazil swallowed a loaf thickly slathered with akh. Cunfshon?

"And what brings a man of Cunfshon all way to Kenor?" He asked, helping himself to a "nibble" of the venison pie that was six inches to a side.

"I am assisting the agricultural effort in Kenor, Sir Brazil. In particular, I am searching for places that might suit intensive grain farming perhaps."

"Aah. And have you found such places in Kenor?"

"Oh, indeed, Sir Dragon. However, I expect to find the best conditions in the South, in Monistol and Tuala."

Relkin returned with a foaming pail of ale. He drew off a cup for himself and a cup for the surveyor, and then passed the pail to Baz who took a long, deep draught.

"I have been telling your dragon about my mission. I hope to confirm our suspicions concerning Tuala and western Monistol."

Relkin's ears pricked up. Like anyone else in the frontier, he was always interested in good land. One day, years in the future, he and Baz would be mustered out of the legion and given land to farm.

"Oh yes, and what do you suspect?"

The surveyor's eyes lit up, the bony face became animated for a moment, and then he grew guarded.

"Well, all I can really tell you now is that Tuala will be a great place for the farmer. The survey's a secret until it's published of course, but I doubt there's any harm in letting you know that much."

"Around Lake Tua then. Well, it's not easy to get there. There's no direct river route."

"The Tuala road from Fort Redor will be the selected pathway for trade," said Ton Akalon with the assuredness of the high-level bureaucrat. "I believe it has been extended now to Lake Tua itself. In time, it will be upgraded to a plank road. The traffic will make fortunes for those who can supply good mules and wagons. Yes, there will be a bright future in the Tua basins."

Relkin chewed and swallowed. The pie was devilishly good.

"I've heard great things about wheat farming in the Esk Valley."

Ton Akalon frowned. "Ah yes, the Esk. Much have I read about the beauties of the Vale of Esk. But those soils are too light. My predecessor, Acultax, wrote extensively concerning the Esk Valley. In ancient times, before the fall of Veronath, it was a famous place of vineyards and orchards. Now I'm afraid they are exhausting the soil there. It will be wasteland, all gone back to scrub forest and broomesedge within twenty years if they continue this way. You mark my words."

Relkin smiled, he most certainly would. On his internal ledger, the very name of Esk Valley was being erased, while that of Tuala was burning bright.

Relkin had many questions about the fabulous Isles of Cunfshon, and many misperceptions that Ton Akalon did his best to correct. Quite soon, however, the food and the ale on top of it worked its own magic. Brazil's huge head dropped first, but Relkin soon yawned and slid down against the wall to a more comfortable position. It had suddenly become very hard to keep his eyes open. The surveyor noticed that his audience was asleep and jumped to his feet.

"Ah me, I've been running on again. I'm afraid it tends to happen. Get a lonely old surveyor drinking ale, and he can talk all night! I can see you're ready to sleep, good sirs. Thank you so much, an honor to have met you."

Snores were the only response. Ton Akalon finished his cup of ale, slipped out the door, and went back to his own cabin where he wrote down this first encounter with a battledragon team, in his travel journal. A journal that already covered sixty pages of close-written lettering in his immaculate hand.

The dragon was a great brown-green beast with occasional pale nodules on his underside and larger scales on his upper surfaces. His eyes were black, and most unquestionably filled with intelligence. The mouth, like a crocodile's almost and just as capable of swallowing immense quantities of food. Ton Akalon thrilled as he relived the moment. And the dragonboy was almost as remarkable. A youth of sixteen or less, but with the manners of an adult and a certain hardness around the mouth that betrayed experience of war. He wore weapons, as casually as children in Cunfshon carried hoops and rubber balls.

Eventually Ton Akalon grew sleepy and slipped into the blankets on the bunk and slid into a comfortable, deep sleep.

The *Tench* moved swiftly downstream and within a couple of hours came into its next stop, the small town of Long Lake, which was visible in a straggle of yellow lights along the dockside.

No sooner was the *Tench* snugged alongside the dock, when a disturbance broke out on the loading platform. A large full-bellied man in the uniform of a regimental commander forced his way through the crowd with bellowed oaths and curses. Accompanying him was a hefty man in black fusgeen with the glint of chain mail at neck and wrist. The presence of this man produced an avenue for the fat man with the loud voice. A few moments later, he stood on Captain Karpone's poop deck.

"Who is the master of this ship?" he demanded, and pounded on the deck with his heavy cane to emphasize his words.

Captain Karpone leaped forward.

"I am, good sir, Captain Polymus Karpone at your service. And may I ask you please to stop striking my deck like that, you're liable to wake every passenger."

The man did not seem to hear, and he continued lifting his cane and thudding it down as he strode about the deck.

Karpone seized the man's arm and restrained him. "Stop!"

"What? Stop what?"

"The deck, sir, pounding on it." The man stared down at the deck, then swung back to glare at Captain Karpone.

"Nonsense! I am not pounding! Anyway, I need a cabin, in fact, I require your largest cabin, at once. And I will need plenty of space in your holds. I have luggage. My guard will also require a cabin."

Karpone put his hands together and gave a whistle.

"Well, good sir, I am afraid that my cabins are all occupied. I've even rented out my own. However, I do have space in the hold. You'll have to share it with a dragon and a cargo of ax heads, but there's room down there for plenty of luggage."

"Impossible," roared the man. "Now listen to me carefully. Unless I have a cabin at once, I will put this ship under military command and satisfy myself." The man was pink and fat, and his pale hair was worn in curls. When he spoke, his jowls shook along with his curls.

"But, sir," protested Karpone, "all my cabins are full. I cannot just pull a passenger, a paying passenger from a cabin to suit you."

"I am a full commander, Eighth Regiment, Second Legion. It is imperative that I reach my command by tomorrow. That means I must get to Dalhousie, do you understand? Imperative. Military matters of the utmost importance."

"Well, good sir, of course, but this is not a military vessel, and under the laws of Kenor the military may not commandeer my ship without a hearing before a magistrate."

"What? Are you mad. Do you require a dip in the

river? Any more impertinences from you, sir, and Dandrax here will toss you over the side."

Karpone sighed inwardly. He desperately wanted to boot this fat popinjay's fat behind, but he dared not. Dandrax was young and fit, and clearly well used to his weapons.

"Well, good sir," Karpone rubbed his hands together, neither he nor his crew wanted any trouble. In truth, they were all getting on in years and well past their fighting days.

"The name is Glaves, Captain, Commander Porteous Glaves of the Eighth Marneri Regiment."

The commander was clearly much impressed with his title.

"Yes, uh, Commander."

"And I insist on a cabin, the very largest cabin. And bring me some hot food. At once!"

"As I said . . ."

"One more objection and I put this ship under military authority, do you understand?"

Karpone looked again at the heavyset thug who grinned back at him.

Karpone suppressed his fury with a little groan. He'd had high-handed officers aboard the *Tench* before, but no one quite like this. He had no idea what to do.

"I . . ." Karpone stood irresolute.

"Bah," snorted Glaves. "Take control Dandrax, find me a cabin."

The captain yelled in outrage and moved as if to draw his dirk, but he found a sword point pressed lightly against his throat.

"Wouldn't do that if I was you," said the thug.

A few minutes later, the surveyor, Ton Akalon, was picked up bodily and hurled from his cabin. His notes and satchel were tossed out to him. Commander Glaves took up residence with the dour-looking Dandrax standing outside the door.

Captain Karpone withdrew and met with his crew. They muttered together for a while and finally agreed there was nothing they could do that was worth doing. Nobody was going to get himself killed over it.

Ton Akalon dusted himself off and packed his notebook into his satchel. He inquired of the captain what might be done and where he might sleep. Humiliated, Karpone refused to do anything. It was up to the surveyor himself to take steps.

"Don't you have spells, magic powers? Turn the guard into a frog, and we will happily squash him flat. But as it is now, we are but four old men and he is young and strong. Someone would be killed."

The surveyor lacked such powers, and thus had to content himself with taking a corner of the forward hold.

He found the dragon and dragonboy fast asleep, snores rattling off the bulwarks. He marveled at how well they slept as he sought out an empty spot. In the dark, his foot caught on the dragon sword, and he fell over.

Relkin awoke at once, dirk out, eyes seeking in the darkness. He noticed movement in the hay and called out a challenge.

To his surprise, it was the surveyor from Cunfshon sprawled in the hay.

"Excuse me, my good friends, I was searching for a place to sleep, and in my clumsiness, I tripped over something."

Relkin by now was suspicious of the little man.

"I thought you had a cabin, Sir Ton." Relkin lit a lamp, and by its light he noticed that the slightly built surveyor was bleeding from a cut above the right eye and that his coat was torn.

"What happened?"

Ton Akalon briefly described the loss of his cabin.

Relkin frowned. "That seems quite unreasonable. What did Captain Karpone say?"

"Alas, the man is a commander in the legion, and with his henchman at his side, he is too formidable for either myself or the good Captain Karpone."

"A commander did you say?"

"A certain Commander Glaves, of a regiment in the Second Legion."

Relkin whistled. He and Baz were about to be assigned a new regimental posting. He hoped the old gods were still working for him.

"If it's a commander, then there's not much to be done about it I'm afraid."

Ton Akalon agreed with this assessment. Then he brightened, "I'm sure the commander will be leaving the ship at Dalhousie. I'm going all the way to Fort Redor, so I will regain my cabin very shortly."

Relkin gave a shrug and settled back to sleep. The dragon had awoken but had only slit one eye open, it was already closed again.

It was still dark several hours later when the *Tench* put in at Port Dalhousie. There was only the single light on the end of the Dally Point to guide them in, but Polymus Karpone had sailed these waters all his life.

With a rattle and a crash, the gangways were set down. A gang of workers in freecoats and thick-furred hats started shifting a cargo of molasses in eighty-gallon barrels to the dock.

Relkin awoke. The ship's motion had ceased.

"We're there." He shook Bazil's heavy head and scratched the dragon behind the ears.

"Still dark."

"Yes, but we're here. I think it might be better for us to get ashore before anyone else."

"Good thinking, boy. We get back to the fort and be in time for breakfast!"

"Now, why didn't I think of that?" muttered Relkin, for whom military food was a humdrum experience.

The dragon was astir. The surveyor woke up shortly,

blessed them, and wished them well. Then they left him and went up into the town of Port Dalhousie, a stretch of ten blocks with cobbled streets and solid structures of timber and stone.

It was the hour before dawn and apart from a few town cats, nothing was astir. Relkin and Baz made good speed up the road toward the fort, which stood on a rise above the point, where it dominated all the land around from its earthwork and timber towers.

They were about halfway when they heard a distant uproar from the town. Looking back, they perceived a struggle in progress on the dockside. A powerful voice was shouting above the others. They could clearly hear such phrases as, "refuse to pay," "filthy verminous tub," "I'll be damned if I do."

Relkin whistled. "I wouldn't want to be in Commander Glaves's regiment."

"Loud-voice fool if you ask this dragon."

"I was just thinking that myself."

They went on up to the gate house above.

CHAPTER TWO

Relkin was received in the gate house by a lieutenant still rubbing sleep from his eyes.

"Right," grunted the officer. "Who are you, which ledger?"

"Dragoneer First Class Relkin of Quosh, 109th dragons. And outside is the dragon they call the Broketail."

The lieutenant's eyebrows rose.

"The one that brought down the fell Doom of Orgmeen?"

"The very one."

"Well, well, I suppose we're honored then. And you're due here today?"

"Yes, sir."

It was clear that this officer wasn't going to extend any respect to a dragonboy, even if that dragonboy was a Dragoneer First Class. Relkin was used to this sort of thing with young officers in the infantry, he paid it no mind.

"Green ledger then." The officer flicked it open and ran his finger down the list. Then he closed it. "Right," he continued. "You're to report to the Eighth Regiment. The 109th dragons have been reconstructed as the dragon force for the Eighth."

Relkin was half surprised. He'd almost expected the number of the squad to be retired. There'd been seventy percent casualties among the dragon force. Only Baz, old Chektor, and Vander had survived, and

Vander had retired from active service because of his wounds.

"You're billeted in the East Quarter. There's a dragon hall. They'll give you refectory tickets there."

The officer turned around suddenly. "And, oh yes, there's a package for you. In the lockup."

"A package?"

"I don't know if you can carry it. It's damnably heavy. We had a hellish time getting it in there off the wagon."

His interest piqued, Relkin went over to the door of the lockup where packages and mail were stored for legionaries.

The clerk was only just putting his post together, but the package was clearly leaning against the back wall. It was a great sword, wrapped in a bolt of white cloth, tied with red ribbons, and sealed with wax. Clearly it was a dragon sword.

The seal bore a simple "L" upon it, and Relkin knew at once that this was the work of the lady.

He hefted the thing, lifting it away from the wall for a moment. It was heavy, indeed, as heavy as Piocar, Bazil's first, beloved blade. In fact, he could barely get it up onto his shoulder, but when it was balanced, he bore it quickly down the stairs, past the startled lieutenant of the Watch and out to his dragon.

Baz's eyes lit up like lamps, and his bag tongue flicked in and out in an involuntary lick of excitement. He clutched uselessly with his big forehands over the wrapping, so Relkin cut the ribbons and unwound the cloth. Before he was finished, the dragon lifted the sword from its scabbard and held it up into the light to examine it.

It had a chilling beauty, this shimmering blade of fine steel almost nine feet long and nine inches across at its widest point. The design was simple, a straight blade tapering toward the point and a black metal hilt with a wraparound guard. The only embellishment was a snarling steel cat's head on the end of the pommel. There was a letter addressed to Bazil of Quosh. Relkin opened it.

" 'To Sir Bazil of Quosh,' " he read. " 'This sword is for you, and is named Ecator for a friend who gave his life so that ours might be saved. He was a terror to our enemies. His spirit now inhabits this steel and, with your help, he will continue to harry them.

    With all due regard,
    Your friend
    Lessis.' "

Relkin shivered involuntarily. He remembered Ecator alright, the meanest-looking tomcat he'd ever seen, with eyes of yellow fury and a horde of rats obedient to his will. There were things that had happened in Tummuz Orgmeen that Relkin tried not to remember, and Ecator was one of them.

Bazil whipped the huge sword around in the air making scything sounds that caused Relkin to duck.

"Baz, you'll kill someone . . ."

The dragon was murmuring happy thoughts to himself in dragon speech, but he stopped when Relkin finished unwrapping the scabbard, and with a grunt of approval, he picked it up and looked it over. It was simple in design, plain steel wrapped in black leather, with brass fitments for the shoulder belt. The only decoration was another steel cat's head in profile placed near the hilt guard.

"I like this sword, it will fight."

He flicked the blade up and then turned it expertly in his hand and sheathed it.

"The lady kept her promise," he said with great satisfaction.

With a suddenly euphoric dragon tripping along beside him, Relkin made his way through the camp to the West Quadrant. It was just before reveille, and the camp was astir with early risers. The fort was laid out as a square, 350 military paces on a side, with towers at each corner and above the two gates, which were set on an east-west axis connected by the main street. To either side of the central street were the four "quarters." "Lines" of large and small tents filled the quarters. Among the tents, most of which housed ten soldiers apiece, there were the bigger, timber structures built for dragons.

The East Quarter was like the others, and its Dragon House hulked up in the center. Inside there were rows of capacious stalls, each equipped with a rough-hewn timber crib for a dragon. The doors were covered with wool curtains dyed in Marneri red and blue. Two units were currently sharing the place, so it was full. Big dragon heads poked out of the stalls as the broketail went past. Dragonboys scurried in the spaces between to pass the word.

A man in dragoneer uniform appeared. Relkin saluted and reported for duty.

"At ease, Dragoneer Relkin. I am Full Dragoneer Hatlin, in command of the new 109th. I would like to welcome you and the broketail dragon back to the 109th on behalf of everyone. I would add that I was honored to be offered this command. Like everyone else, I was overwhelmed by the accounts of what you fellows achieved at Tummuz Orgmeen."

"Thank you, sir," said Relkin.

Hatlin smiled thinly for a moment.

"Alright Dragoneer Relkin. You'll find I am a fair man, but a man who likes to see the rules obeyed. I take a dim view of stealing and cheating and the like. Play straight with me, and we'll have no problems."

Hatlin exchanged salutes with Bazil and directed them to a stall.

Dragonboys wore clogs in the Dragon House, and now clogs thundered on the cobbles as a mob of boys in blue jackets and red wool caps swarmed about the entrance of their stall.

Relkin pulled the curtain shut, took a deep breath, and then slipped outside for a moment where he announced to the throng that the broketail dragon would meet them all, but one at a time, later in the day, when they'd all had some breakfast. Then Relkin introduced himself to each in turn, and shook hands. There were a lot of new faces and names to remember.

Among them was one familiar face, Mono, old Chektor's dragonboy and the only other active survivor from the old 109th fighting dragons.

With a cry of joy, Relkin and Mono embraced.

"It is incredible that you survived!" said Mono, a tall dark-haired fellow with the looks of the South, where the sun shone on olive groves and vineyards. "When we saw you march off into the Gan from the river, we were sure we'd never see any of you again."

"Well, you almost didn't. It was a damned close thing. How is Chektor?"

"Good, his feet are healed from the summer campaign. We had a quiet time here all winter. How was Fort Kenor?"

"Bitter! By the old gods those winds off the Gan can freeze you to the bone!"

"Well, we're in for a warm summer. Have you heard?"

"Heard what? I just got here, I haven't heard anything."

"The civil war in Ourdh is going badly for their emperor, so an expeditionary force of two legions is being sent to help prop him up on his throne."

"And?"

"And the Eighth Regiment is going."

"Relkin let out a whoop and tossed his black Kenor rain hat into the air.

His visions of Tuala province and its good limestone

soils faded away, and were replaced by vistas of ancient Ourdh and its sly, sophisticated people in their huge cities.

You could buy anything you wanted in Ourdh, it was said, as long as you had the silver.

"Then we'll be going to the great city?"

"Why not?" Mono wore a slow smile.

"By the gods, there are women in Ourdh! Such women as we can scarcely dream of."

Relkin suddenly became aware of an audience of intent young faces, junior dragonboys all around. He clamped his mouth shut. He'd already said too much, and his words would be spread around in no time. He didn't want Hatlin coming down on him for affecting the morals of the young ones.

He clapped Mono on the shoulder.

"To Ourdh. Who would have imagined?"

In truth, Relkin did not mind in the least exchanging farmsteads for folly. It seemed a heaven-sent opportunity.

Had his luck changed when he invoked the old gods? Was that a sin? Would the Great Mother be frowning at him? And what if she was, if the old gods were on his side? Relkin had always had a hard time sorting out the gods and the goddess.

To Ourdh! Anyone could get what he wanted in Ourdh, everyone knew that. The place was the flesh-pot of the continent.

He wanted to jump in the air and kick his heels but dared not in the presence of all these young junior dragonboys, fresh out of the cities and not yet blooded in battle. He was a veteran and expected to set a sober, mature example.

A sudden heavy grunt turned his head, and he saw a huge brasshide dragon standing there on all fours.

With a glad cry, he hugged the monster's thick neck. "Old Chek, I'm so glad to see you."

"Ha, you so lucky to see me. Very lucky. By all

rights your bones should lie in Tummuz Orgmeen. Where is the broketail one?"

The curtain was pulled back, and Bazil emerged at the sound of a familiar dragon voice. The boys stared up in awe.

"Broketail, good to see you again. We the only ones left."

"Chektor."

The two dragons shook forehands together for a moment.

"I heard about Nessessitas, very sad. I very angry."

"I killed the one that did it. He did not live long to enjoy his triumph. Troll with sword, a new thing, much quicker than the older kinds. It surprised her, cut her knee. She could not move."

Chektor snapped his big jaws shut.

"They say we kill trolls again soon. I will kill many for her." The great beasts clasped forehands again and slipped into dragon speech as they entered Brazil's stall and drew the curtain once more.

Mono continued to introduce Relkin to the new dragonboys in the unit.

"Shim of Seant, he tends the brasshide, Likim." Shim was a slim, pale youth with silver hair and strange, almost colorless eyes.

"This is Tomas Black Eye, who has Cham, a leatherback from Blue Stone." Tomas wore a patch where he was missing an eye. "Solly here has Rold, a brasshide from Troat." Relkin shook hands and slapped palms.

A tall, sullen-faced youth was next. Mono grew quieter.

"And this is Swane of Revenant, he tends Vlok, another leatherback, a veteran from the 122nd, who've been broken up."

A veteran? From a disbanded unit? Questions filled Relkin's thoughts.

"Glad to meet you," said Relkin.

"Likewise I'm sure," said Swane with a surly expression.

"Your unit was broken up?"

"Three drags down with foot disease, the white rot. One lost to a fall on a patrol on the Argo, and one retired with incurably bad knees. Then they broke us up, never gave us another chance."

"I'm sorry."

"You had it rough, too, I hear," said Swane of Revenant. Relkin looked up at the taller boy.

"Something like that," he said.

"Incredible stories they told about it all. I expect you'll fill us in on what it was really like."

Relkin watched Swane's departing back and felt sure he was going to have trouble with that one. He wondered what Vlok himself would be like.

CHAPTER THREE

The next day dawned wild and windy, with grey clouds hurrying southwards. A chill north wind whistled around the timber buildings and flapped the tent walls. Inside, men stayed close to the braziers and put on the thick winter clothing of Kenor.

After breakfast, just as he was settling into a full inspection of all their weapons, Relkin received a summons from no less a personage than General Paxion, the commanding officer of the fort. With a groan, Relkin abandoned the spread of swords, knives, maces, crossbow and arrows, and searched out his uniform.

Once he had on his Marneri blue coat and his red wool cap with the badge of the 109th polished bright, he made his way to the general's office in the Rivergate Tower.

The interior of the tower was warm, smoky, and crowded with civilians who had business with the military supply. On the third floor were guards who let Relkin pass after a cursory inspection of the summons.

Shortly, he found himself in a big room with a long table down the middle and a thick Kenor shag rug on the floor. A fireplace dominated one side of the room, and the fire was well stoked up.

The general rose from behind a pile of scrolls and gestured with a pen for him to take a seat close by.

"So you know how to salute, a rare art for a dragonboy in my experience."

Paxion was a gingerish, red-haired man of large form and vigorous disposition. A formidable fighter, he'd served ten years in the line with the Second Regiment of the First Marneri Legion.

"Welcome back to Dalhousie, young Dragoneer Relkin. From all accounts you acquitted yourself well enough to win a dozen decorations in the affair at Tummuz Orgmeen."

Relkin kept as still as possible.

"In fact, I happen to know we'll be pinning a Legion Star on you in a day or so. I had the order back from Marneri the other day. There's been some debate over the matter apparently."

The general smiled, not unkindly. "There are those who believe a Legion Star should not be given to a dragonboy. But I am reliably informed that your case was taken up by some powerful people, and that in the end this made the difference."

Relkin tried not to smile, or nod, nor anything. A Legion Star was a higher honor, rarely given, and then only for extreme acts of personal bravery.

The Lady Lessis had remembered him as well. First the sword Ecator and now this. His heart swelled with pride, but Paxion was watching him closely, so he struggled not to show any emotion.

The general nodded after a moment, and smiled.

"A cool customer, that's what they told me." He pushed back from the table.

"A dragonboy with a Legion Star, the first in history and he doesn't utter so much as a peep. Well, that's not why I wanted to see you. We have a problem."

"Sir?"

"The wild dragon, the great one that came back with you from Tummuz Orgmeen."

"The Purple Green of Hook Mountain."

"The very one, he was billeted here for the winter.

I don't know why, it was pretty unsuitable. Just about ate us out of house and home."

"We never would have survived without him at Tummuz Orgmeen, sir."

"Yes I know, a formidable ally but an enormously hungry one."

Paxion rubbed his chin. "By the breath of the mother, it was a beeve a day to satisfy him sometimes."

Relkin nodded. Dragons had prodigious appetites, especially when they were active.

"Well," Paxion spread his hands and laid down his pen. "The long and the short of it is that the dragon found it too confining here, and he wandered away about two months ago. He was said to be hunting in the mountains. Then we had a lot of complaints from the elves of Tunina. They said he was frightening the game in the forest and making ordinary hunting impossible.

Then we had a panic up around Argo Landing, some sheep went missing and a shepherd claimed he was chased through the woods by a monster. A week or so later, we heard that he was in the woods along the Dally."

Paxion sighed. "And two days ago, a farmer came in and reported that half his dairy cows are missing, and that something is moving around in the woods south of here."

Paxion's face settled into a grim expression.

"We can't have that. It has to stop at once. But I don't want to confront the dragon. I understand he is wild, unused to the ways of men. I also know he must be a fearsome foe, but he can be killed and if we have to we will."

Relkin waited for the other sandal to drop.

"I want you and your dragon to go to him. Persuade him that he cannot remain in Kenor."

Relkin nodded. Bazil knew the wild one better than anyone. It was best that he take this message.

Paxion stood up and pointed to a globe.

"He must go north, boy, and soon. Already I hear rumors that free-lance hunters are chasing silver bounty to bring in his head. We have to stop that, too."

"Yes, sir, I agree completely. We will go at once."

"Good luck, young man, and report to me immediately upon your return."

Two days later, they tracked down the great beast to his lair in a cave on a farm on the west side of the river Dally.

The farm buildings had been battered, and the farmer and his wife had only just escaped with their lives after the farmer jabbed a pitchfork into the Purple Green while it was sleeping. The angry farmer and his terrified family were down in the town of Dalhousie crying their woe to all and sundry.

When they came upon him, the great Purple Green was sleeping. Awoken by the sound of Relkin's whistle, he emerged from the cave ready to kill anything that stood in his way.

But the fury died in the enormous eyes as they beheld Bazil and Relkin. The neck spines deflated and the huge muscles of thew and shoulder relaxed. The forked tongue tasted the air.

"Hail!" he bellowed.

The Purple Green had learned a little of the human speech since the fighting at Tummuz Orgmeen, but he did not care to use it much. Now he addressed Bazil in archaic dragon speech.

"Hail to thee, broken-tailed one. Welcome to my hunt! Together we shall course far and wide, and take only the very best for our sustenance."

Bazil stepped up and clasped forearms with the Purple Green. The wild dragon was still much larger than the wyvern, but the marks of starvation were on him. Relkin could see the ribs showing.

"Hunting not so good, especially around here," said Bazil.

"Hah! And how would you know, you who eats noodles."

Relkin looked up at the word "noodle," for which there was no equivalent in archaic dragon speech and which cropped up quite clearly in the midst of the general sibilance and guttural growling.

Bazil hissed lightly.

"There is no game here," he said, "except animals that belong to the humans. If you eat those, you will force the humans to kill you."

"They would not dare! I will kill them! And how is it that they dare to claim ownership of any animal?"

Bazil shrugged. "I know no answer to that, but I do know that they will kill you. They will come with clever traps and snares and poisons. Perhaps they will simply shoot you with so many poison arrows that you lose control of your limbs. Then they will cut your throat and take your head."

The Purple Green shook his head in denial, but there was a desperation there that told Baz that the wild one understood how hopeless his position was.

"You must be honest with yourself," said Bazil. "I know that your wings did not regain their strength, despite the magic of the lady."

"They regrew, the wounds are gone, but you are right, they have no strength, I cannot fly."

Baz held the other's gaze.

"Then you can barely hunt at all. You are a great dragon, you cannot hunt like a cat, you are no lion, all creeping and hiding and sudden pouncing. You must fly and then swoop down, that is the way you hunt."

The Purple Green's facade collapsed.

"It's true, I have eaten nothing but bears and one sick old elk. I am not fast enough."

And that was it, as a four-ton carnosaur with a top

speed of fifteen miles an hour, he was outclassed in an age of swift-moving mammals.

"That is not all you have eaten."

"Ach." The Purple Green hung his huge head. For a long half minute he looked away hissing to himself, then spoke wearily.

"It is true. But I do not understand how one animal can own another and declare it to be only his. All animals belong to the hunter that can overpower them and devour them, and to no one else excepting their mothers."

Bazil agreed, in principle. "Yes. That is how it should be, but in these times it is not. The enemy of the humans is the same enemy that destroyed your wings. The same that took you captive in the evil city."

The Purple Green bristled again.

"We have to live with the humans now. If we do not, they will kill us, do not doubt that they have the power. You know that. You have seen how they are."

"So many, they swarm over the world."

Bazil shrugged. "It is said by some that this is the end of the age of dragons, that eventually there will only be humans. That is why there are so many of them."

"There are none in Dragon Home. If any go there, they are soon devoured."

Bazil hissed again, pleased to hear that there was one part of the world still where dragonkind served itself and not the human race.

"But here, they rule. So it comes to this, my great friend, either you must leave this land and go north, or you must change your way of life completely."

"I will go north, and I will starve to death."

Baz nodded and then fell silent while he thought for several minutes. Then he walked off a ways with Relkin.

"The wild one will die on his own. He cannot hunt properly, just as we feared."

Relkin sighed in sorrow. They owed much to the great Purple Green. Then Bazil stunned him.

"What would the legion say if wild one join us in the 109th?"

Relkin sucked in a breath. Life, which had seemed so simple so recently, now seemed a lot more complicated.

"Well," he gulped. A wild dragon in the line of battle! "Of course, that's brilliant. Except that he's completely wild and he doesn't know how to fight with weapons."

"I know, but we train him. I already teach him how to hold a sword and a shield, back in evil city."

"Train him? Who will be so bold, not I. One argument and he'll eat me. I know him, he's eaten human before this."

Baz chuckled and hissed.

"Not bad idea, I think sometimes."

"Yeah, well remember the goose that laid the golden eggs. You eat one dragonboy and you never eat good food again. You have to eat nothing but wild meat."

"Dragonboy not taste as good as roast goose either."

Relkin hesitated. Bazil was right, it was the only fit solution. Bazil would have to train the wild one, and everyone else would have to learn to be very careful when they were around him.

And there was a plus side. The Purple Green was as big as the largest of their brasshide wyverns, but he was appreciably quicker than any brasshide. When trained, he would make a formidable tenth dragon for the squadron.

Relkin agreed. Baz went back and put it to the Purple Green.

"When they destroy your wings they change your

life. Even if you could live long enough to return to Dragon Home, you would starve to death there. But there is an alternative. Come back to fort, join legion, and fight with us. That way you will have the chance for revenge on our enemies. And remember, they always feed dragons well."

"Yes, but on noodles? I am not like you, I cannot get by on anything but meat."

"They will give you some meat, but you will have to get used to noodles. You must try akh again. Akh make anything good to eat."

"Disgusting stuff, I do not understand how you can eat it."

Bazil hissed again, slightly perplexed. Dragons were not the best at gentle persuasion, and akh was wonderful.

"Look, my friend, I can see your condition. There will be a lot more meat in the legions than there will be for you outside in the wild. If you eat their cattle, they will come to kill you."

"Let them try." The spines bristled.

"They will poison you. They will harry you in their hundreds, and they will fill your hide with arrows, and eventually you will succumb.

The Purple Green grew still. The wingless one was right, and such a death would be useless and degrading. He had spent weeks in hunger, and there was no doubt about what would happen to him if he went north.

He gave a huge sigh and gave in.

"I will try. You will teach me how to fight with the weapons of the humans."

"We will teach you, and you will be able to kill a great many of the enemy."

"I would like that."

And so they left the cave and returned to the fort.

Relkin's request produced complete consternation at first, but as Relkin pressed the point, people came around to the idea. They were always short of dragons, and once trained the Purple Green would be a tremendous military asset.

"It's most irregular," said General Paxion. "But Dragoneer Hatlin is for it, and we have a long campaign season ahead of us. We need every dragon we can get. But he'll have to eat like the rest of the dragon corps, he cannot dine on cattle anymore."

Relkin promised to handle the dragonboy chores associated with the wild one to begin with while a new dragonboy was summoned up.

General Paxion signed a special order and away went Relkin to celebrate. The general returned to his study of the map of the Empire of Ourdh, an ancient realm built on irrigation of the lower courses of the great river Oon. The "well-watered land," as they called it, had been a center for civilization since the Dawn Ages. Now it was an empire in the balance where a bloody civil war was raging. A civil war that was too important for the Argonath to ignore.

CHAPTER FOUR

While work intensified on the fleet of rafts that was to take them down the great river, the legion sorted out its equipment and drilled, regiment by regiment.

The 109th Marneri Dragons now got their first look at the Eighth Regiment and its new commander at a full regimental parade.

It was a brisk day, with a chill wind from the north coursing over the parade ground as the regiment formed up in squads and then centuries with the dragon force bringing up the rear.

The drums thundered and the pipes blew fiercely as the regiment went through its paces, rather clumsily, it must be said. The men were hesitant, unused to drilling as a regiment. The Third and Fourth Centuries actually got mixed up and made a devilish mess of things.

The new commander was mortified. He had a loud voice and no hesitation in deploying it to curse the sloppiness of the men. The sight of the worn uniforms on a few veterans, drafted in to give the Eighth a stiffening element, drove him to a most powerful passion.

The lieutenants and corporals were all nervous as cats, giving their men venemous looks as the commander rode up and down the ranks and criticized the lines, the squares, the dressing, indeed, everything that he saw.

The ways of frontier soldiers, he informed them were not good enough for Porteous Glaves. He had come to the frontier to instill into his men the virtues of the coastal cities, diligence, obedience, loyalty, and an appetite for hard work.

Of course, the men of the Second Legion, to a man, were from the coastal provinces, mostly from Aubinas and Seant. Which was where the surplus population was in the lands of the Argonath. The free folk of Kenor were farmers, mostly men who had served in the legions and were now reservists. And so the commander's references to them as frontier slops and "woodsmen" who were going to be taught how things should be done properly, fell upon incredulous ears. They weren't woodsmen, they'd all been to the big city now and again. Their faces went white with rage.

It got worse. It was announced that until their drill improved to the point where Commander Glaves could feel proud of them, they would drill every day and they would drill while wearing the hated neck "cuff," a four-inch-wide collar of stiff leather that went around a man's neck and forced his head back and his chin up and out. It had once been a punishment in the Kadein legions, but had more recently become a thing for display by a few crack regiments of Kadeiners. They received bonuses from wealthy men who identified with the regiments and were given honorary captaincies in return for their gold. Men wearing the neck cuffs and drilled to perfection made a fine sight with their heads tilted back and their spears and shields gleaming. Just the sort of backdrop aspiring young politicians required to show well in front of the ladies of Kadein.

The Marneri legions regarded the cuff as humiliating and barbaric, something from the ancient days of Veronath, when soldiers were often slaves.

Nor were the 109th spared the lash of the commander's tongue. He found the dragonboys a complete, disgusting mess. Their uniforms were dirty, patched, or incomplete, or all three at once. They wore nonregulation items of dress and weaponry. Their dragons seemed uninterested in the drills, and dull and listless during the right dress.

The commander warned them that their discipline would have to improve many times over.

Eventually, in complete gloom, the Eighth Regiment broke up at the end of the parade and wandered back into the lines of listless groups.

For Relkin and Bazil, the gloom was compounded by dread. The new commander was none other than the pompous idiot they had heard on board the *Tench* just a week or so before.

Relkin spent a sleepless night running schemes through his head for escaping from the 109th and the Eighth Regiment. Nothing occurred to him that seemed promising.

The next day dawned cloudless and sunny. The chill north winds were replaced abruptly by a balmy breeze from the east. That was the pattern of spring in Kenor, where winters were cold and summers hot. Spring was violent in its moods.

At noon, the entire legion paraded for a medals ceremony, filling the fort's parade ground with men who were suddenly sweating in their dark blue winter coats.

General Paxion gave out seven Combat Stars to men who had been wounded in sundry small actions over the winter. Then there were three Regimental Orders to be given to men of long service and distinction, sergeants close to retirement. And finally there was the matter of a single Legion Star to be given to a dragonboy in the 109th Marneri Dragons.

The ceremony was not a long one. The Combat Stars were presented, then the Regimental Orders. Here, things bogged down a bit as each sergeant gave a short speech and thanked his friends for their help over the years.

At last it was over, and Relkin was called out of

the ranks. He saw Glaves glance at him and then look
away with no change of expression. On the stand Relkin saluted and stood still while the star was pinned
on him and the general made a short speech. Then
with his heart thumping with pride and nervousness,
he returned to his place while the drums and pipes
began and the legion paraded past the commanders
and General Paxion and then out of the parade
ground where they broke up and made their way to
the lines.

Relkin, however, did not head for the East Dragon
House. He had been invited to take luncheon with
General Paxion's wife and the other ladies of the fort,
mostly the wives of the senior officers. It was going
to be an ordeal he was sure, but the food would make
up for it, with any luck at all.

Accordingly he made his way to the tower in the
south corner where General Paxion had his quarters.
On the uppermost floor there was a large room, white-
plastered and floored in oak. On the walls were paintings
of the Paxion family and a vast landscape of Kadein
by the great painter, Molla. In fact, the only thing
that betrayed the fact that this room was in a frontier
fort were the windows, which were narrow and easily
defended.

There was quite a crowd, most of it gathered at the
stand-up buffet at one end of the room. Relkin noted
the other medal winners of the day, who stood out as
pillars of blue and brown leather among the billows
of satin and lace that the ladies wore in imitation of
the fashion of Kadein.

Among the matrons of mature years were several
of their teenage daughters, who were enjoying the
break from the monotony of education and sewing.
The standout of this group was General Paxion's
youngest daughter, Kessetra. She wore a yellow satin
gown, cut tightly to her figure. She was a red-haired

beauty, with lush lips and green eyes in which swirled endless patterns of coquetry and manipulation.

All the young ladies made a great fuss of Relkin once he was identified, surrounding him in a sea of fans, curls, and satin. He was implored to tell them tales of the city of Tummuz Orgmeen. What were the evil women there like? Were there courtesans who really wore the skins of dead men, tanned like leather?

Struggling to retain his natural modesty, Relkin succumbed and told of the deep, dark tunnels and the slave pens for captive women, chained in the imp-bearing chambers.

The girls shuddered and squealed in horror and pressed for more details which he would have provided but for the arrival of Lady Fevill, the adjutant's extremely ample wife.

"Now, young man," said Lady Fevill, as she tugged him away from the girls who groaned in disappointment, "you must spend some time with the older women in the room."

She introduced him to a circle of her friends: Clevilla Hooks, wife of the captain of the First Century: Faja Rinard, whose husband led the Second Century: and Edyth Alexen and Alys Wulnow whose husbands served in the Second Century.

They, too, wished to hear personally of the horrors of Tummuz Orgmeen, so he described the slave market, with men and women in chains, with the marks of the lash and the brand on their skins. They listened in fascinated horror, and whenever he paused for breath, they fluttered their fans and exchanged exclamations.

At length, however, they tired of him and returned to full-strength gossip, leaving him free to turn his attention to the excellent buffet.

He had barely helped himself to some sillabub and

a plate of quibini and samosas when a vision in yellow satin appeared beside him.

"Hello, we didn't meet before, there was too much of a crowd. My name's Kessetra Paxion, you can call me Kessi."

Relkin knew who she was, and he also knew that she was seventeen and no longer the child of her mother's imagination.

"I expect you're finding all this pretty excruciating, I know I am," she said.

"Well, the food is good."

"Not particularly. The chicken is overdone and the sauces are dreadful. In Kadein, they would hoot at it and demand that the chef be fired."

Relkin forebore to point out that Kadein was hundreds of miles away on the other side of the Malgun Mountains. This was Kenor, land of the rough-hewn and free.

"Come," she commanded. "Take me up to the top of the tower, we can take a turn there. It is such a gorgeous day. We should be able to see all the way to Mt. Red Oak."

Relkin gobbled down his quibini and escorted Kessetra to the top of the tower, which was opened up for just such sight-seeing. They emerged into the warm sunshine of a late spring day in Kenor and immediately felt refreshed. Relkin felt something glitter just beneath his line of vision, and he looked down and there was his medal, a five-pointed star of silver positively aflame in the sunshine. No more than two hundred Legion Stars had ever been made. This thing would set him apart from the others in the unit unless he was careful. He resolved to put it away and keep it hidden. It was an awesome responsibility. He was no longer Relkin Orphanboy, child of nature, dragoneer and adventurer. Or rather, he was those things, but he was something more. He was now a figure of legend, someone whose every deed would be scrutinized by thousands. He saw that the lady had done this to force him to take life more seriously.

"Now,' said Kessetra, "tell me all about yourself. Where are you from?"

She was ravishingly beautiful, Relkin found his head almost swimming with the allure and he barely mumbled a reply.

"Where's that?" she said, looking off into the distance and shading her eyes from the sun.

"A village in Blue Stone."

"A village in Blue Stone . . ." she murmured, and then she laughed. "I knew a boy from Blue Stone once." She spoke as if it had been decades before. "He was a count, a very silly one. He tried to hurt me."

"What happened?"

"I had to teach him a lesson about love . . ."

"Ah, love," said Relkin.

"Yes love, isn't it wonderful. To be so in love with someone that you can think of nothing but that person's desires and wishes . . ."

She leaned close to ensure that her perfume enveloped him. Her eyes gleamed dangerously.

"Have you ever been in love, Dragoneer Relkin?"

He blushed, for he had loved Lagdalen of the Tarcho. But he knew better now. He had learned one of life's sad lessons. Lagdalen was several years older than he, and from one of the greatest families in Marneri. Tarchos had even been kings of Marneri in the past. He had no family except for a leatherback dragon of uncertain temper.

And, of course, Lagdalen was now wed to Captain Hollein Kesepton, whom Relkin admired as a soldier and a man.

"I was in love once," he stammered.

The girl's lush red lips settled into a tiny pout.

"Oh yes, puppy love?"

Her petulance annoyed him, and he spoke rashly.

"Not at all, I loved Lagdalen of the Tarcho."

Kessetra laughed gaily and nudged his elbow with hers.

"And you, a dragonboy and an orphan from Blue Stone. You aimed high there." She giggled and glanced away at the horizon.

Relkin felt his dignity under assault.

"We served together at Tummuz Orgmeen. We were alone there, in the vaults of the Doom. She proved herself a true soldier of Argonath."

Relkin tried to imagine this spoiled young woman in those dark tunnels. It was impossible.

"Oh, how awful, I never want to think about that place again. I never look that way," she gestured toward the bleak plains of the Northwest.

Relkin would have liked to be able to forget so easily. His mouth settled into a grim line, and he fell silent.

They faced east and as predicted, the day was so clear one could see the Malgun Mountains, a row of distant dark smudges on the horizon.

She pointed to the southern peaks. "Down there is Mt. Kohon. Way past that lies my home, Kadein. Have you ever been there, Relkin of Quosh?"

"No Kessetra, I have never been to Kadein." She groaned and tapped her folded fan against her lips. Relkin imagined kissing those lips, they were spectacular.

"The city is so grand, so beautiful." She sighed and crossed her hands over her breast. "How I wish I was there, walking up Slyte Hill or riding down the Avenue of Oaks."

She sighed again. Stuck out here in this appalling frontier fort because her father had been denied the post of tower captain in Kadein City. Oh yes, she knew very well what had happened, even if Father refused to tell her a thing. He'd lost out to Major Steenhur, and they'd been posted out here to this wilderness of bumpkins and soldiers. The best years of her life were going by, and she was far from the grand salons and balls and parties where real life was going on!

"Have you ever wished you were in Kadein, Relkin of Blue Stone?"

"I will go to Kadein some day. I want to see all the world's cities. I have been to Marneri, of course."

"Marneri is a nice city. I was there several times when I was a little girl. I liked the white stone walls and the narrow streets. But it's so small compared to Kadein. Kadein is spread out far beyond its walls. Our house is on Slyte Hill itself, miles from the Old City."

"I'm sure it's beautiful."

"Oh yes, it is. So beautiful, to ride in the woods of the Surd now, and onto the park at Blue Fountain, that would be heavenly. You can see the king's new palace there through the trees. The buildings are exquisite, everything is done in tiles, white, blue, and scarlet on the roofs."

She sighed again.

"When you come to the city, Relkin of Blue Stone, you must be sure to call on me. I will take you around if you like. There's so much to see."

Relkin enjoyed a hollow laugh inside. He doubted very much that Kessetra Paxion would be that happy to see him if he actually did show up at the door to her family's manse on Slyte Hill. Nor did he think he would fit in very easily with the fashionable crowd she would run with in the great southern city of the Argonath.

That wasn't his world. He knew that. There was no place for him there unless he brought with him a fortune, and as yet he had failed to discover a scheme that would provide him with one.

The hour was sounded from the bell in the North Tower and the luncheon was over. Relkin escorted Kessetra back to the lower hall where she bade him farewell.

He went in search of more quibini, but discovered that the buffet had been cleared away and there was nothing to be had but hot tea and lemons.

With his already tormented imagination filled with visions of the lovely Kessetra Paxion, he headed for the East Quarter Dragon House.

CHAPTER FIVE

Each day's passing brought their departure to the southlands closer. There were a thousand things to attend to, and Relkin was frantically busy getting equipment repaired or reissued from the legion commissary. Not only did he have to get all of Bazil's gear ready, but he had to see to the issue of weapons and armor and general equipment to the Purple Green.

First consideration went to their weapons. The new commander was insistent that they carry all the required weapons in the legion regulations.

That meant they had to carry an extra tail sword for each dragon plus a pair of tail maces. Each of these weapons was large and heavy. The shield, four feet wide and eight deep, was made of steel bands in a lattice covered in thick leather, a sheet of hard wood, and then leather again. By regulation there had to be eighty steel studs on the front of the shield, but Bazil's had only sixty left when Relkin inspected it, so he joined the mob at the blacksmith's shop and ended up waiting on line for an hour.

And that wasn't the only smithy work that needed doing. In addition, there was the great dragon helmet, and the breastplate and the cuisses of steel to check for faults or uncomfortable dents. On Bazil's breastplate, there was a problem place where a troll ax had hammered a considerable dent the year before at the battle of Ossur Galan. That had to be welded again and patched with fresh steel. The forge in Fort Dalhousie labored day and night to keep up with all the work.

And, of course, new equipment had to be fitted for the Purple Green who was bigger all round than any wyvern dragon.

Finally, there were Relkin's own weapons, short sword, dirk, crossbow, and two dozen arrows. They were all in order. The sword had been sharpened at Fort Kenor and had seen no action since.

But the weapons were merely the first item on a long list. There were water bottles to check, spoons and plates to requisition—they were due for new ones—plus flint and steel for fire making.

Then there was clothing. The dragon wore a joboquin, a harness of leather, on which his armor attached through a dozen retainer bolts. Bazil's joboquin needed mending, which sent Relkin to the repair shop, while the Purple Green had to be fitted with an especially large joboquin.

In addition, Relkin took outlines of the Purple Green's feet and brought them to the sandal maker. Relkin explained that the Purple Green of Hook Mountain was likely to prove a tenderfoot once they got into lengthy marching. The sandal maker whistled as he stared at the specifications, for these would be the largest sandals he had ever made.

For himself, Relkin collected a new blue coat and bought a pair of breeches in dark grey fusgeen. He also purchased a wide-brimmed hat to keep off the fierce sun of Ourdh, and had his Kenor freecoat rewaxed against rain.

Then there were all the dragon care supplies. Relkin carried a bottle of linament, the Old Sugustus brand, plus a bottle of mineral oil and a bottle of "Stinger" antiseptic. These he kept in a wooden case that he'd bought years before in the province of Borgan. It was made of knapwood and was durable, but light. Inside the upper shelf, the case held a dozen swabbers, files and prodders, plus tweezers large and small, and a very valuable pair of stout scissors for clipping dragon nails. The mineral oil needed refilling, so he went to the commissary for more, along with a fresh flask of Stinger.

At the same time, he picked up a new blanket of grey wool woven in Cunfshon by the men and women of the Legionary Relief League of Defwode plus a pair of newly waxed wool capes for the dragons from the same source.

When it was all gathered together, both dragons and dragonboys had heavy packs. Relkin then discovered that the straps on his own pack were coming loose from the canvas, and so he set at once to repair it. Nothing was worse on a campaign march than having one's pack fall apart. Thus was a Dragoneer First Class kept occupied as the days flew by.

Meanwhile, Bazil had spent much of his time working with the great Purple Green in the ring. They had given the Purple Green the legion issue blade that Bazil no longer needed. Relkin had cut the wild dragon's talons and worked long and hard showing the Purple Green how to grip the sword handle properly.

The Purple Green had struggled at first, but as his proficiency grew he became excited by the power of the sword, and he put in long hours swinging at the practice butts made from thick sections of pine trees. Occasionally he actually cut one in half, something that only a few brasshides of unusual mass could do.

All the other dragons were roused to competitiveness by the sight. There was even some jealousy in the air. In particular, there was trouble brewing with Vlok, the veteran from the ill-fated 122nd dragons.

As the Purple Green became more familiar with the weapons of the dragon legionary, so Vlok's complaints grew louder. He questioned the wild one's ability to stand up to full-scale battle. What did wild dragons know of battle? What kind of trust could they put in him?

Some of the younger dragons showed concern. They

knew only practice battle and training combats. They had yet to face trolls and imps in massed array. For guidance, they looked to the veterans. Vlok's words had weight, even though he had seen little combat himself.

Bazil Broketail had seen his share of battles already, despite only serving for sixteen months in the legions. He knew how fierce and steady an ally the Purple Green of Hook Mountain would be, but he didn't want to jump on Vlok too soon or too hard. He understood that the other dragons, having seen no action, felt insecure. Vlok, in particular, felt he had to prove himself, to show that he was of the same veteran standard as Chektor and Bazil.

Vlok's ill temper produced some scrapes with one or two of the younger dragons who resented his critical ways, but these fights never went beyond some shoving and bellowing in the Dragon House. Much worse was the situation with the Purple Green who was not good at taking criticism from anyone. The Purple Green was building up to a challenge to fight Vlok.

Brazil counseled patience.

"You have not the skill yet to fight a one like Vlok. He is good with a sword, you are still learning. He would kill you easily. You know this is truth."

The Purple Green accepted this, but only with a great deal of further persuasion.

Bazil and Relkin feared the worst might happen at any moment. Dragoneer Hatlin was so concerned, he was thinking of trying to revoke the placement of the Purple Green in the 109th dragons.

It finally came to a head when Vlok was passing through the exercise yard where the Purple Green was practicing his defensive strokes with Chektor. Chektor was massive but slow, like most brasshides. The Purple Green parried the blows, but was forced back by Chektor's technique.

Vlok called out as he went by, "Look at him, he fights like a goose, walking backwards!"

The Purple Green looked up at this and roared, "Who calls me a goose?"

Vlok chuckled, "I, Vlok, do so."

"Then you die!" The Purple Green abandoned Chektor and rushed upon Vlok with a roar.

They collided, and the smaller dragon was bowled over. The Purple Green tripped over his feet, however, and crashed to the ground as well.

A shout went up, and everyone poured out of the Dragon House.

Vlok was up and had drawn steel. The Purple Green regained a two-footed stance, and they closed. Neither carried shield or wore armor, and as their swords clashed they grappled with the free hand.

Vlok knew better than to stay close to the wild one, the strength in those giant thews was far beyond that of a leatherback wyvern. He spun away and swung and cut and came in overhead. He was quick and agile for such a great beast, and the Purple Green's vast strength was rendered moot.

The Purple Green blocked and blocked, and then only just blocked the next overhead. The wild one was outmatched in sword fighting. Vlok went the other way and swung right and then overhand to the left.

The Purple Green tripped again going backward and fell, the last sword stroke barely grazing him across the shoulder.

Vlok prepared to thrust home his blade.

Another sword interposed itself, the gleaming white steel of Ecator, and Vlok found the broketail dragon standing against him.

This was a different kettle of fish, as some might say, but Vlok's blood was warmed, and he threw caution to the winds.

He lunged and swung and cut. Ecator met his blade each time in perfect defense and turned away his thrusts. Vlok grew wilder as his arm grew tired.

Finally he hurled himself forward and swung overhand again. He lunged too close, and as they met, Bazil punched him hard on the side of the head. Vlok fell back, stunned into semiconsciousness. For a moment, he wobbled until Baz whacked him lightly with the flat of his new sword and laid him out.

The Purple Green had regained his feet by now. There was a little blood on his shoulder. Bazil remonstrated gently with the wild one, who seemed crestfallen. Together, they picked up the fallen Vlok and carried him back to his stall.

Vlok's dragonboy, Swane, threw himself at Relkin as he approached. The two went down in a tangle of fists and struggling limbs.

Dragoneer Hatlin intervened after a few seconds and hauled them to their feet.

"Enough!" he snapped. "Vlok started the fight. We all know how unfair that would be since the wild one is not yet skilled with the sword. The broketail did well to stop it. You two are to end this feud, do you understand?"

Neither boy raised an argument. Both were puffing, red-faced, with smuts in their hair.

Swane went into the stall, and Relkin followed. The dragons crowded inside turned to them and hissed.

"Go away. We have to talk to Vlok alone."

The dragonboys withdrew and pulled the curtain. Behind them sibilant dragon speech began. It rose in volume occasionally when Vlok spoke, but it went on.

Hours later, Bazil and the Purple Green left.

Vlok, Swane, and Relkin met. Vlok said that there was to be no feud and no further fighting. Vlok admitted that he had been unjustly critical, that he had lost a fair fight, and it was over.

Swane and Relkin shook hands, and Relkin hoped sincerely that this would be the end of it.

That night the orders went out. The first units to board the rafts would be leaving the following morning.

A few minutes later, a man came riding up from the town bearing a message. As he passed the guard, he whispered, and the word went through the fort in a flash.

King Sanker of Marneri was dead. His daughter Besita would be crowned queen.

The news brought a sudden silence throughout the fort. Sanker was not much loved as a king, but he had reigned for a long time and his passing was sudden. Most people had known only Sanker as their king.

The news was especially troubling to Commander Porteous Glaves of the Eighth Regiment. That same day he had received a scroll from Marneri with bad news. His request for a posting to Kadein to command a detachment from the First Legion had been denied. He could not shift from unit to unit. He would actually have to go with his regiment into the war way down in Ourdh, hundreds of miles distant. Now came Sanker's death, and any chance of a plea to the king's ear was gone. Glaves had no connections with the new queen's inner circle. He felt doomed.

He opened a bottle of fortified wine and took a heavy swig. He was actually going to have to spend months, maybe years, marching with a bunch of smelly dragons and soldiers all over the southlands, and quite likely would have to go into actual battle.

This was not part of the plan!

He moaned. He thought of his plump-faced adviser, Ruwat. Ruwat had suggested this. For political advantage, Ruwat had said, a necessary thing if he wanted to advance. How was he to advance if he was fighting for his life in some savage hellhole in Ourdh? The whole thing had become a disastrous fiasco. His fingers clenched uselessly, how he wanted to get his hands around Ruwat's fat throat!

CHAPTER SIX

Behind its great walls and towers, the city of Marneri was decked in the color of mourning. Black flags fluttered from every spire and every topmast of the tall ships in harbor. After a reign of forty-five years, the old king was dead.

King Sanker had been an unhappy man, beset with vague fears and possessed by self-destructive passion for drink that had almost unhinged him in his final years. But he had been a good monarch, chiefly because he had realized his limitations and let his skilled advisers rule in his name. In this, he had made amends for the checkered career of his sire, King Wauk, who had involved himself in matters beyond his abilities with disastrous results.

And so they buried Sanker with honor and a thunder of drums. One hundred drummers beating a slow march led the column that included King Neath of Kadein along with five other kings, two queens, and one crown prince from the nine cities of the Argonath. Behind these glittering personages came the members of the great families of Marneri, lead by the royal Bestigari, with the Clamoth, the Andonikri, and the Tarcho following behind. Then came the clans from Exsaf, the Brusta, the Hawki, and the Rook, the great families that had come from Cunfshon to help win back the land of Argonath. And there were more, high families from all the great cities and from Kenor, with military men in the uniforms of the legions, and civilians in black with the white blaze of Marneri on the breast.

Then came a great throng of merchants, sea captains, landowners, and general businessmen, all in the same funereal garb with badges of the white blaze affixed to breast or hat.

Lining the way down Tower Street and Foluran Hill was the mass of the population, with country folk from Seant and Aubinas and Seinster and the Blue Hills, plus artisans and other workers from every town and city in the region.

Marching among the Tarcho clan was Lagdalen, now a veteran of the great war. She wore the black weeds and velvet hood and she walked without her husband, for Captain Kesepton was far away, attached to General Hektor's staff on the expedition to Ourdh. Yet Lagdalen of the Tarcho did not walk alone, for at her side was Lessis of Valmes, wearing a frayed and faded old black cloak and worn-down shoes.

Lagdalen was acutely aware of the great honor done her by Lessis, who was the ranking representative of the Emperor of the Rose and a Great Witch of power, the "grey lady," the same pale, thin woman of indeterminate middle age and calm expression, who had walked in king's funerals for five hundred years.

Lessis could have been walking in the front rank, with the king of Kadein, but instead she walked beside her former assistant among the Tarcho clan.

Lagdalen's father and mother walked just ahead of her, and her brothers and sisters walked beside and behind. All of them were very conscious of Lessis's presence and very proud as a result. Many were both envious of Lagdalen and slightly awestruck by her new status. Just a year and a half ago, Lagdalen was a humble novice in the Temple Service. She was said to be troubled, unlikely to rise very fast or very far. There was even some story about a dalliance with an elfboy. Suddenly she was proclaimed as a heroine fit

for legends, returned from the dread city of the enemy
in glory, and engaged to wed the heroic young Captain
Hollein Kesepton. They had duly been married a
month later, and she now tended their first child.

Her relatives, her elder sisters, her mother and father, her cousins, all were struggling to cope with this
change. They hadn't been used to giving her much
respect and now felt they had to. This rankled for
some. Lagdalen walked a field laid with snares and
pitfalls every day, for a careless word could start a
crescendo of gossip and rumor.

But Lagdalen's thoughts were far away from such
concerns. She marched the familiar streets, past the
quiet crowds, and her thoughts were mostly with her
baby Laminna, now in the arms of her wet nurse, in
their apartment in the Tower of Guard. Or with Hollein, out there somewhere in the vast interior of the
continent. She tried not to think too much about the
perils he might face. He was a full captain of the legion, and would serve at least eight more years, perhaps for the rest of his life. He might be killed at any
time. She had to accept that.

Through all this, she thought very little about old
King Sanker. It was true that he had been king all her
life and for a long time before that, but when she
thought of royalty in Marneri now she thought of the
new queen, Besita.

Lagdalen had come to know Besita very well in the
past few months, ever since Besita had returned from
the great hospital in Bea where the witches had labored to pull out the roots of the evil spell set into
her by the stone deity of Tummuz Orgmeen. Back in
Marneri, Besita had been surrounded at once by a
team of dedicated young men and women, including
Lagdalen, who worked to continue the princess's re-
covery from sorcery.

Besita was a queen with a great many problems
confronting her. She was not a hardworking person

by nature and had already discovered how heavy the burden of a royal person's working day could be. Now it would be ten times as heavy. Besita would have to apply herself, and this she would dislike intensely. It would be a constant struggle for her to keep her attention focused on important matters, but it would have to be done and done well, for her very life and that of the white city itself would depend upon her diligence.

Intrigues were thick on the ground around her throne. She was queen, but queen of a city divided by her succession.

Everyone had always expected her cretinous brother Erald to become king. Old Sanker had always hated his daughter and claimed her bastard. There were good grounds for such suspicions. Her mother, Losset, had had numerous public adulterous liaisons, until Sanker finally had her executed for treason. But Erald had been harmed even before birth when a desperately unhappy Losset had indulged in heavy drinking bouts in the royal apartments. As Erald grew older, he became a clear threat to the city, a degenerate with a taste for repulsive, cruel pleasures.

He had died mysteriously, six months before, and everyone knew that he had been killed by the witches. Thus did the empire prune and trim the family trees of the Enniad royalties.

Sanker, already a bitter man, became quite venemous in his last few months. Soon after Erald's death, however, his health began to break down for good. First it was his liver and then it was his lungs, and he fell ill with a racking cough.

The sisters took him to the Temple hospital eventually, but there was little that could be done. As he lay dying in their care, so his final efforts to have Besita murdered were discovered and the plots were smothered.

The king was dead, the queen now sat the throne of Marneri.

At the corner of Tower Street and Foluran Hill, the procession turned to the right and went down to the massive, squat shape of the Temple of the Great Mother.

The burial ceremonies were long, almost endless, or so it seemed to Lagdalen, but at last the king was buried, and a shout of "long live the queen!" went up. The shout was echoed and reechoed but without full enthusiasm, another sign of the questions hanging over the succession. The folk of Marneri were as yet unsure of their new monarch and uncertain of her legitimacy.

The alternative to crowning Besita would likely be civil war with the great families grappling for the throne. No one wanted that.

Still, people were unhappy. There was the uncomfortable fact that the new queen had succumbed to an unnatural glamour worked on her by the fallen Doom of Tummuz Orgmeen. The witches had cleared her, expunging the taint, or so they said, but could there be any doubt that she would be their creature now? Any independence the city might have enjoyed was surely in jeopardy. The cities were constitutional monarchies, but the power of the sovereign was still very great.

The Empire of the Rose was not an empire in the traditional mode. Little money flowed to the emperor from his subject satrapies. The empire had been created for the sole purpose of reversing the fall of Veronath and removing the demon lords who ruled in the Dark Ages. The emperor sought to guide the cities and the free colonies, not to dictate to them. At least that was what they were supposed to believe. But here they saw the naked hand of the witches of Cunfshon, the emperor's servants, manipulating the succession. It rankled in the city.

The ceremonies continued with the burning of incense and the singing of hymns until they rose and left

the Temple and dispersed outside leaving Sanker for
the history books.

Lessis took Lagdalen by the arm.

"Come, my dear, walk with me, I have things to
discuss with you."

They turned left and cut through to the Garden of
Maternity, strolling uphill toward the Tower of Guard.

"A bitter business this," said Lessis.

"The funeral, my lady?"

"No dear, the succession. We had to do it, poor
Sanker could not accept the necessity. He never recovered from what Losset did to him."

Lagdalen said nothing. Lessis had discussed the
state of Marneri's affairs with her before, but she had
not heard this particular admission.

"You killed him, lady?"

"Not as such, girl, but when we removed Erald, we
took away his last hope. His death came swiftly then.
Poor man."

Lessis gave a heavy sigh. "Over the years I have
had to shoulder the burden of killing many men and
women, you know that by now, and I think you understand the necessity for it."

Lagdalen felt those grey eyes on her, and she shivered, sensing the power in the other. Lessis shrugged.

"In my work, it has been a sad necessity far more
often than I ever dreamed of when I was young. I
have forgotten most of these people whom I had chosen to destroy, but Sanker I will not forget. I remember him as a terrified teenager at his coronation. His
father had dealt with him quite brutally all his life. It
was a wonder the boy was still sane, but he survived
and, in fact, he did quite well at kingship. It went to
his head a little perhaps, and he fancied himself a
great general of the armies, alas. When the last great
crisis broke, I was sent to force him to relinquish any
real role in the command of the legions. He hated me

for that. It ruined him in a way, but he never sank into real wickedness."

Lessis put her hands behind her back as she walked. Lagdalen knew the mannerism well and knew she was about to hear important news.

"But guilt is guilt, and I have more than my share of it. It comes with a life such as mine." Lessis looked up and smiled at her. "And when I see one such as you, my darling Lagdalen, I am renewed and ready to fight on."

Then the smile disappeared, and Lessis looked down again.

"We have a terrible fight on our hands right now. I must ask for your help. I sail on the tide for Ourdh. The situation there is growing quite desperate. The ruler, the Fedafer, is in a state of complete panic and is likely to surrender to his enemies through sheer intimidation. He is a weak man. But if the priests of Sephis get hold of him, they will make him a slave of evil and a servant of the dark forces."

Lagdalen was surprised. She knew very well that Lessis had a deep dislike of Ourdhi society, where extreme patriarchy prevailed and women were treated as slaves with few rights.

"As you might imagine, I do not want to go." Lagdalen did not doubt the sincerity in Lessis's voice. "But I must. And yet our affairs here in Marneri are entering a very delicate stage. Someone must watch over Besita. She is such a goose, as you well know."

Lagdalen nodded.

"But if she will work hard, she can be a very good queen. She needs someone to help her, to guide her, and keep her attention fixed on matters of state."

"Yes, lady, of course."

Lessis clasped her hand. "It is very good of you to take up this service when you are a mother with a newborn babe, and on behalf of the Office, I thank you. But now we must ask you to take even more of

the burden. You must take my place. You must be at
her side as much as is humanly possible, and you must
try to keep her steady somehow."

Lagdalen felt a pang of regret. She could not refuse,
but she wanted nothing more than to be with Laminna,
her babe of three months. Nor did she want to spend
time nursing a petulant queen with a horror of hard
work. But she knew it would have to be done, or
Besita might give in to a weakness and lose everything
in an afternoon.

"Yes, my lady."

"Thank you, child, I know what a sacrifice this is,
and again I must tell you how much I appreciate your
courage and your sense of duty. Things are moving to
a critical stage of our great enterprise. Our success at
Tummuz Orgmeen has given the Master's a shocking
defeat, quite unexpected. They have responded by un-
leashing this long prepared civil war in Ourdh. There
is a great evil at work there, and we must destroy it.
We cannot allow Ourdh to sink into the clutches of
the dark forces."

They came around the corner of the camellias and
passed the statue to the Fertile Mother.

A shadowy shape leapt out of concealment at the
base of the statue and slipped up behind them.

At the very last moment, Lessis sensed the man and
half turned, raising her arm. This saved her life for
his first blow was deflected off the bone in her upper
arm.

She gave a little cry of pain and shock, and struck
at the man with her fist, connecting just below his
Adam's apple, not enough to stop him. He swung
again, a professional assassin's stroke even as Lagdalen threw herself at him and rammed a knee into his
belly. In horror, she saw the black metal dirk sink
into Lessis's side.

Lagdalen's scream brought shouts from nearby.
Men in Marneri blue and red were on the scene and,

with a weird shriek of insane joy, the man ran at them and died on their swords.

Lagdalen knelt beside Lessis, who was unconscious. There was a pink froth on her lips, death seemed imminent. Lagdalen felt her chest constrict and her mind go black with panic, horror, and a vast wave of sorrow.

CHAPTER SEVEN

Word of the disaster was sent at once to Cunfshon on the clipper *Stormwind*. Even with every scrap of sail clapped on and favorable winds across the Bright Sea, the passage would take a week. In the meantime the witches on the scene in Marneri did their best to keep Lessis alive.

She was rushed to the hospital in the Temple and examined by the high surgeon himself. One lung was found collapsed and a major blood vessel cut. This had to be repaired manually, a task close to the limits of surgical skill in the Empire of the Rose.

As the high surgeon worked with needle and fine thread, the witches of Marneri struggled to build a strong spell that would keep Lessis's spirit within her body and prevent any further weakening of her hold on life. It was difficult. Lessis had lost a lot of blood and was very close to death. After eight hours of chanting and spell work the witches ceased. Lessis survived in a state approaching that of hibernation. She could be fed through a straw, and she continued to breathe, slowly.

Ten days after the *Stormwind* cleared the harbor bar, a white herring gull flew into the city and made its way to the roof of the Temple in mid-evening. There, it set down and raised an outcry of gull squall until the Mistress of Animals, Fi-ice, climbed to the high roof and spoke with it. The message she received electrified her.

At once, she sent couriers to the Abbess Plesenta and the Princess Besita. They were to join her in the chamber of the Black Mirror. A response was coming from Cunfshon. A Great Witch was coming in person.

At the bell announcing the fall of night, the three met by the mirror and formed the circle.

Princess Besita, soon to be queen, was terrified. Helplessly she had protested to Fi-ice that since she was to be crowned in a matter of days, surely she should not be risked at the Black Mirror?

Alas, replied Fi-ice, there was a shortage of witches or priestesses who were experienced in the opening of the mirror. Three were needed, and only Fi-ice, Plesenta, and Besita in all of Marneri at that moment were privy to the knowledge required. In this could be seen the malice of old Sanker, who had forced Besita to take this service, in the often remarked hope that something would snatch the "dollop of bastardy" in the dark and feast on it. And so Besita had more experience with the mirror than even Fi-ice, who was a Witch of Standing and who, one day, might even be one of the Great.

In the high chamber in the Tower of Guard, they joined hands, created the spell, and opened the Black Mirror. It came with a hot, terrifying hiss, like a stream of oil striking red hot metal.

Set into a slab of black stone there was now a window blown through the fabric of the world, gazing into the hotly energetic subworld of chaos.

There was a background of grey emptiness, the chaotic ether. Here slid tumbling, whirling shapes of clouds and tentacles. Here ruled the monstrous Thingweights, dread horrors of the dark.

Wherever mortal humans opened such mirrors or entered the subworld for the advantages of swift travel between places in higher worlds, they risked a fearsome death. Priestesses had been snatched from before the mirror, taken in the wink of an eye by a

Thingweight's tentacle flashing through into the high world of Ryetelth.

From the hot ether of chaos came a continual roaring sound, the surf noise of an ocean of molten lead that lapped on sands of iron. Hot red sparks snapped and popped from the mirror's surface. Suddenly Fi-ice sensed the traveler. She came a long way, and she came quickly. There was a tremendous power in the person making contact. Fi-ice marveled, there were but thirteen of the Great, and only ten who still served in Cunfshon. Who might it be? Sausun of the golden hair? Or Irene of Alaf, the great orator with ultimate powers of voice and control with voice? Whoever it was, she had fantastic strength in the astral powers.

An orange flash swept the mirror. The three women tensed. Then they saw tentacles of orange-yellow going away from them, heading on toward the traveler. An errant predator of the subworld, a small one, had sensed the oncoming traveler and swept in to investigate. It had missed the mirror.

They glimpsed for a moment a tumbling, tigerish thing the size of a sperm whale, with the texture of a storm cloud bolt past and on toward the traveler. Then it was gone, reduced to a dot in the distance.

From the distance there came a bright flash of scarlet, and a moment later the predatory thing came hurtling back, crumpled, crushed, virtually flattened.

Fi-ice drew a tiny breath and tried to concentrate on simply keeping the mirror open. The power in that flash had been enormous. As she'd suspected, the traveler was one of the most powerful of the Great.

But the flash of energy would not go unnoticed in the near regions of chaos. Like blood in the ocean, it would quickly attract much greater predators.

There began a faint, distant flickering of purple energies, far away, behind the traveler. Soon it looked like lightning flashes beneath a distant storm cloud.

"Hurry, Traveler, you are sourced by a Thing-weight," called Fi-ice with her astral voice.

Besita had tears running down her cheeks while she trembled and shook. The Abbess Plesenta was bracing herself, wide-eyed. This service at the mirror was getting to be too frequent. Only a year or so before they'd almost lost Lessis here.

The traveler accelerated and could be seen now, a tiny black dot hurtling across the spasm of chaos. But the faraway purple energies and the colossus that hung above them were coming much faster. Already the gross exterior shapes of the Thingweight were becoming clear, and the flashes from the energetic section were enormous, painful on the eyes.

White-hot spats of energy were now leaping from the surface of the mirror like silver salmon breaking from black water.

Outrigger tentacles, like hairs at this distance, were twitching forward. If one of them found the mirror, it would take them all in a moment and form a feeding siphon here. If undiscovered and not destroyed, it would suck the entire city into its maw through gross mental suggestion. They would go as helplessly as moths to a candle, sucked down one by one into the obscene palpations of the darkness, where their life force would be burnt in brief flashes of euphoria on the receptor surfaces of the Thingweight.

Besita was close to breaking point.

The onrushing monster was the size of a large mountain, perhaps more. The palps were thrashing with excitement, blips of white heat were spattering from the mirror's surface like water on molten steel. Besita started to scream and tried to wrench her hand free of Plesenta's, who held on with a grunt of effort.

Suddenly a tall woman of angular appearance wearing a black cloak stepped out of the mirror and stood on the dais.

With a gasp, Plesenta let go and Besita jumped

back, snapping the triune. The mirror closed with a final explosive crack of energies.

The three stood there for a moment, dripping perspiration and shivering from stark, unalloyed terror. The newcomer stared at them wordlessly. She was immaculate, her black velvet cloak and boots spotless, not a single black hair out of place.

Fi-ice went forward to greet the traveler. She knew at once who it was. There was no mistaking the black velvet garb nor the motif of silver mouse skulls on her hems and rings and even on the ends of the skewers that held her long black hair pinned back. It was Ribela of Defwode, the oldest of the old, the Hidden One, the Seeress, the Queen of Mice. There were hundreds of names for her, accumulated over six centuries of service to the Empire of the Rose.

Fi-ice was struck by how lean was the face and how intimidating were the slanted black eyes. Then Ribela put her gloved hands together and brought them up in front of her like schoolgirls before a beloved teacher.

"Thank you, Sisters," she said in a sweet, husky voice. "You behaved with courage, I shall commend you."

They followed as the Great Witch strode from the room. Along the way they collected Burly, the chamberlain to the dead King Sanker, and Lady Flavia of the Novitiate.

Both were stunned. Indeed, Burly was terrified by the sight of the woman. Ribela of Defwode had not been seen in human form in a hundred years. She was said to wage her war in other worlds, countering the efforts of the Masters of Padmasa to ally with other centers of the dark power.

And yet Ribela was here in Marneri. To Burly it meant that something truly terrible was happening.

At Lessis's bedside, Ribela immediately began to weave a Greatspell, sending everyone, Burly and Besita included, to fetch her the necessary ingredients.

Burly puffed down the hill to the harbor and ordered the fins of three mackerel to be cut off and placed in some paper for him. Then he half ran back up the hill to the Temple and skipped in like any twelve-year-old boy might.

He bumped into Plesenta, the abbess was dancing along with her skirts in hand and some twigs of liomel.

They gasped, self-conscious at last. What in the world were they doing, skipping along like this, the lord chamberlain and the abbess of Marneri's Temple?

They both tried to hold themselves, to come to a halt and resume their more natural gravity. Indeed, for a moment both thought they'd succeeded, only to find their legs still in motion. Together they ran up the stairs so quickly their hearts were thundering in their chests, and then they ran down the corridor and so to Ribela's side.

The room was filled with smoke. A small fire was burning on an altar slab. Standing at the head of Lessis's bed, Ribela was reading from the Birrak, forming declensions and foundations for the Greatspell work she was about to do.

Lady Flavia came in with a white dove and long shears.

Ribela worked on. The liomel twigs were burnt and filled the chamber with their sweet musk. The fins of the mackerel were burnt next and overlaid the musk with a fishy stench. Ribela droned on, her voice gradually building in power until she began to form complete volumes and shape them with *creata cadenza*. The great words of power boomed and hissed in the room. She cut the dove's head off and sprinkled its blood in the flames.

The sound of wings frantically beating for escape seemed to fill their ears, though the bird lay limp in Ribela's hand. Gradually the sound diminished. Ribela laid her hands on Lessis's forehead. Then she whispered something in her ear.

Lessis's eyes opened briefly. She managed a weak smile and then closed them again. Ribela bent to put her ear by Lessis's lips. Lessis whispered in the language of cats.

Ribela turned away and clapped her hands for the nurses to return to their posts. She stalked out of the chamber, and outside she turned to Fi-ice.

"Who is responsible for the surgical work on the Lady Lessis?" she said most directly.

Fi-ice was taken aback, struggled to reply, not wishing to damn the high surgeon.

'Come on, woman, out with it," snapped Ribela.

"The high surgeon, Carleso."

"Ah, so a man is surgeon here. Well, he is to be commended. Excellent work. Excellent. Tell me, how long has it been that you have allowed a man to be high surgeon here in Marneri?"

"Ah, a man?"

"Yes, a person of the male sex," said Ribela, as if she was speaking to a simpleton.

"I do not know, lady, since the city was founded perhaps."

"Extraordinary. Are you sure you can trust him? Men are so easily governed by their passions. I have found them generally unsuited for precise, consistent work."

Fi-ice remembered, Ribela was from Defwode, the most conservative and matriarchal canton of Cunfshon.

"Things are different here in the Argonath, lady. Men are fully equal in all things."

Ribela did not seem pleased with this idea.

"So I've heard," she murmured. A moment later, she drew Burly aside into an empty office and closed the door, leaving Fi-ice and Plesenta outside.

Burly was still breathing hard, and seething inwardly at the wound to his dignity. To make a lord chamberlain run up and down on an errand like that?

It was unheard of. It was abominable. He might have had a heart attack.

Ribela stood in front of him and held him with those terrible black eyes. There was no moving once they fastened on you.

"I must leave at once for Ourdh. The situation there is very dangerous."

The sooner the better thought Burly.

Ribela noted his sour expression.

"I apologize, my lord chamberlain. Lessis was so close to death, I dared not wait an unnecessary moment. I am grateful that you can still run so briskly at your age."

"Harrum, uhm."

"Sometimes, my lord, we find ourselves forced to take up duties far outside of our normal scope of operations."

Burly saw a flicker of warmth cross that cold, perfect exterior, the cheeks like white marble, the lips like metal painted glossy red. To Ribela this was a joke, she challenged him to laugh with her. After all, why should she be here? She had other work to do, work that Burly could not even imagine.

"I see," he murmured, "I think. But tell me, what brings the Queen of Mice to have such an interest in the civil war in Ourdh? The place has been run by pestilential rulers since time immemorial. What difference will it make?"

"If Ourdh falls to the forces of Sephis, then the Masters will be able to obtain an army of women for their breeding pens. Some women live long enough to produce twelve imps, one a month, in those pens. Think of an army of one hundred twenty thousand imps. We could lose Kenor, perhaps be forced back to the shores of the ocean."

Burly shivered. He could see swarms of the enemy, a foul horde marching beneath the banners of the skull and thorn-pierced heart, stretching from horizon to horizon.

"You conjure up a most terrible vision." He shuddered. "I pray that we can avert this."

"We shall, old Burly, we shall. And you must help us here by putting aside your feelings and helping Besita as she becomes queen."

Burly's hackles rose again.

Sanker was barely in the ground, where they'd put him, these witches. Burly was bitter for his old king.

"Come, old Burly, let go of the pain. We know your honor, and we respect you. Sanker did his best, but he could not be allowed to foist Erald on the city of Marneri. You know that."

Ribela had been enjoined by Lessis to "tread lightly, Sister, the people of Marneri are not like those of Defwode." Ribela struggled to "tread lightly." It was not in her nature, alas.

But her needs were simple. She would take Lessis's place and immediately sail for Ourdh. To assist her, she would require the services of the young lady of the Tarcho family, who had been Lessis's assistant until recently.

Burly pointed out that the girl was now the mother of a newborn. She would not wish to leave Marneri. He received a withering look from those dark, hypnotic eyes.

"I know," she said, as if addressing a dolt of barely human intelligence. "But the girl also knows her duty, and in this instance, duty that must prevail. Send her to me."

Gulping for air, Burly left the witch and sent a message at once to the apartments of the Tarcho.

Lagdalen received the message in the nursery where she tended to baby Laminna. The message was peremptory. She left the baby with the wet nurse and ran down the hill to the Temple.

In a modest office room on the third floor, she

found the Lady Ribela waiting, the Seeress herself, standing like a statue by a window.

The velvet cloak shifted.

"Thank you for your promptness, my dear."

"I require your assistance for the mission I must undertake since your mistress has been disabled."

Lagdalen swallowed, her heart suddenly leaden. Leave now? And lose Laminna?

The witch was staring at her with those extraordinary eyes. *She bewitches me,* thought Lagdalen. "I am given no choice . . ."

But there was no spell, just the steady gaze. Lagdalen knew her duty, she had learned well from Lessis. She would go. And yet she felt the most dreadful sorrow. She heard a keening cry, and realized only dimly that it was herself who made it.

Ribela's perfect marble face grew taut.

"It is your duty girl! You have served Lessis well and been commended. You have experience of these matters, and that will be vital. I cannot have someone who knows nothing of the ways of the enemy on this mission."

Still Lagdalen struggled. Laminna's infancy would be gone by the time she returned, she would lose that sweetest of motherhood's seasons.

Lagdalen could hardly find words. She was stunned, choked, horrified, and yet unable to say no.

She acquiesced and fled to sob uncontrollably over Laminna in her cradle. The nurse, Wessary, did her best to console her, but to little avail.

Her mother, Lacustra, became indignant on hearing the news and became determined to intervene. Loudly she proclaimed that the Great Witch was not to take Lagdalen from her babe. Lagdalen had already given enough of herself to the cause. It was not the place of well-born girls like Lagdalen to be exposed again and again to this kind of hellish danger.

Lacustra went to Tommaso Tarcho, the father of

Lagdalen. Tommaso agreed with his wife. His daughter was now a mother, her battles were behind her. He would not allow this abduction.

But Lagdalen pleaded with them to do nothing. Her duty was clear, she could not deny it. The Great Witch was absolutely right, Lagdalen had the experience that was needed.

"Though it tears my heart in half, I must leave Laminna to Wessary, my Wessie will take care of her. I cannot bear it but I must, and I will."

Tommaso drew back then from his daughter. He scarcely recognized this young woman as the child he had prayed for during her troubled adolescence. But listening to her tone of voice, he understood that her mind could not be swayed.

"You have the will of the Tarchos, that is certain" was all he said in the end.

Lacustra had more difficulty in accepting it, but at length she retired to her own parlor, where she wept and muttered about the disrespect done to her and her family by the Great Witches. Her daughter, taken twice by the witches and made to serve in fantastic, foreign places where death and danger lurked in dread diversity.

Lagdalen stayed beside Laminna's cradle for most of the night. Wessary packed together some clothes for the journey, with spare sandals, a dirk of Cunfshon steel, a broad-brimmed hat to keep off rain and sun, and a Kenor freecoat, freshly waxed and waterproofed. Wessary had removed the wool lining of the coat and replaced missing buttons and clasps.

Lagdalen left at dawn, wearing the dark brown freecoat and carrying a rolled-up blanket and a small pack. She boarded the white ship *Merkuri* and sailed on the tide, heading down the Long Sound, its destination distant Ourdh.

CHAPTER EIGHT

Under blue skies, the Marneri Second Legion drifted down the River Argo through mild spring days. Their long rafts were in the center of a fleet of barges and commandeered brigs and riverboats. The rafts each carried three hundred men or fifty men and their horses, or one hundred men and ten dragons.

The men were cheerful enough about the expedition, but their general was not. General Paxion was a bag of nerves and doubts. He'd spent twenty years running a fort. That was what he knew how to do. He was devoted to knowing the details and making skillful decisions about small matters. He knew every drunk and most of the thieves by reputation. He was able to maintain firm justice, fair discipline, and was generally well liked by the men.

He did not look forward to campaigning in distant Ourdh under a hot sun with flies and mosquitoes and sickness in the ranks. At his age, it seemed like madness.

Still, the orders had been direct and emphatic. Hektor wanted to Second Legion as quickly as possible, and Paxion was on the scene so he would take the command.

The orders had gone on to include voluminous preparations for fighting off an attack by river pirates, which swarmed in northern Ourdh and who had gone over entirely to the Sephisti. This had prompted many unwelcome thoughts. The Sephisti were said to be very numerous and fanatical to the point of suicidal martyrdom. Were they sailing south to catastrophe, to end trussed up and burnt alive as offerings to a dark satanic god?

Now, at the head of a legion sailing off into strange and dangerous waters, he felt terribly unsure. It seemed so unfair, that a good, industrious military career should be destroyed like this, for he doubted his ability to stand up to the pressures that lay ahead.

"You're past it, you fool!" he said to himself in the mirror when he shaved.

The men were much less stricken with gloom than their commanding officer. In fact, a majority were eager to see the distant cities of Ourdh, so enormous in both fact and legend, and perhaps to sample some of the pleasures of the fleshpots.

Life in Dalhousie and the rest of Kenor was life on the frontier. The men had mostly come from the older cities of the Argonath and remembered more civilized ways.

In the evenings, they gathered around braziers of coals and sang the Kenor song while passing a little surreptitious rye whiskey among themselves.

"Waking through the land of Kenor, free and strong and in our hands . . ."

In the dark, the yellow lanterns of the fleet stretched up the river like a stream of stars, and the voices of the men rang off the water and carried away into the dark.

General Paxion found it hard to sleep. He spent much of the night anxiously reviewing each light through the telescope to assure himself that all was well.

On the second day, the rolling hill country of the Middle Argo gave way to a flatter landscape divided by the river. To the south lay forests of oak, pine, ash, and hemlock. To the north, the forests thinned out quickly into the Gan, a vast steppe that stretched away into the north as far as the Black Mountains that bordered Dragon Home.

The villages of the Middle Argo petered out here, and at night there were few lights and very far between. Long after sunset, they entered the Baratan Swamps, where the river lost itself for a dozen leagues of small lakes and twisting channels.

The moon rose and with it came the sound of a million amphibians caught in the frenzy of early spring. The night resounded to their wheeps, whoops, stirrups, and roars.

The men found the racket painful after a while and turned in with much grumbling, but the dragons were most curiously affected by the sounds of their amphibian cousins. They drifted to the side rails of barges and rafts, and when all were gathered on one side the vessels would tilt and men would roll out of bunks and awake with startled cries of woe and fury.

The amphibious chorus continued unabated and in the hearts of the great wyverns some ancient chord was struck, and they remained awake, listening intently and occasionally muttering together in the ancient tongue as the fleet drifted through the dark bayous and open lakes.

Later, when the moon was setting, they left the swamps behind and the dragons returned to their beds in the center of the raft. Rafts righted themselves once again, men were pitched back and forth as before and a chorus of human complaint arose in the place of amphibian breeding uproar.

The next morning, they awoke to find the rafts approaching the smooth cone of Mt. Kenor, its crown still ringed with snow.

Bazil and Relkin had spent the winter in the fort that sat on the north flank of the mountain. To them the country here was all too familiar. To the north was the dun drabness of the Gan. They had crossed that land the year before, on their way north to the

city of Tummuz Orgmeen. Relkin had no desire to
see it again.

To the south were the new wheat lands of Kenor,
with isolated farms scattered through the broad-leaved
forest. Far away to the east loomed the distant hills
of Esk.

Signal flags fluttered from the fort and were responded to from General Paxion's cutter. Shortly afterward, Paxion put in at the landing beneath the fort
and met there with General Dausar. There was a message from General Hektor, who was now far to the
south of them in the land of the Tekatek Teetol.

Paxion was urged to hurry south as quickly as possible. There was a battle looming in central Ourdh. The
Emperor Banwi Shogemessar was leading the Imperial
Host north from the great city on the east bank. He
would cross over at Kwa and meet the Sephisti hordes
somewhere north of there on the west bank.

General Hektor was determined to get both of his
legions to that battle. He was convinced that they
were essential to the cause. He already feared for the
lack of morale in the Imperial forces.

General Dausar intimated that he thought General
Paxion was very lucky and that he, General Dausar,
wished he were going with Paxion and the fighting
Second. Paxion smiled and endured the handclasps
and wished inwardly that Dausar was going in his
place.

With heavy heart, Paxion reembarked and caught
up with the rest of the fleet, which had sailed past
Fort Kenor.

By midday, the Argo was merging into the mighty
Oon. The river had broadened now until it was half
a mile wide. A great flat stream flowing sluggishly
through complex channels braided by islets with beds
of rushes and sheets of waterweed.

Eventually they left the rushes behind and entered
the Oon itself, a mighty stream, surprisingly shallow

in places and running clear with snow melt from the High Gan. In contrast, the water of the Argo was dark, thick with material brought down from the forests. The water of the Argo was visible within the greater volume of the Oon for a long time after the confluence.

The great volcanic cone of Mt. Kenor began to recede. Far away in the uttermost west, they glimpsed the sparkle of the snow atop the mighty White Bones Mountains. And before them in the west was the empty Gan, a sea of grass that stretched away in all directions.

The river broadened, and they encountered contrary winds and their progress was slowed for a while to almost nothing. As the afternoon wore on, they saw a line of dark clouds appear on the northern horizon. The wind died, then shifted to the north and quite soon there came a chilly blast, a final lick of wintry air coming down from the uttermost north. The winds rose and became quite gusty within minutes, and Paxion ordered the fleet to make for shore at a desolate fishing hamlet in northern Teot.

There they spent the night. The next day was grey and cold, clouds hurried past overhead, driven by the north winds. The fleet reembarked and made good speed, surging ahead down the river with the winds from the rear.

All day the wind strengthened and grew colder. Black clouds appeared in the far north and hurried to catch up with them. In late afternoon there were cold showers, and then at dusk it began to sleet and it became intolerable to sit out on the decks of the barges. On the rafts the men huddled around braziers inside the tents and rough-hewn cabins.

The rafts were pitching and threatening to break up when at last General Paxion ordered the fleet to seek safety on the eastern shore, where the lights of a good-sized Teetol village could be seen.

Two scouts with good knowledge of Teot-Doshak and the other north Teetol languages went ashore. They made contact and presented gifts of ax heads and anvils to the village elders. the Teetol welcomed the fleet to enter the protected inlet that served the village as safe harbor for its fishing boats.

The men scrambled ashore and worked to square away the rafts and barges under the driving sleet. But with dragons to help, the heavy work was soon done, and they quickly pitched tents and lashed things tight. The Teetol womenfolk were rousted out and put to fetching firewood and water for the legion.

Paxion dug into his own purse for the gold to buy hot food. Teetol stews and goulash were famous, and the women of the village boiled up an enormous hot bully goulash that was eaten with the evening's noodles. The men used their own silver to buy mead from the Teetol brewer women.

Some Teetol men with daughters of the right age appeared and tried to sell them to the legionaries. General Paxion had been forewarned of the practice, which he forbade, and sent all officers around the tents to ensure that none of his men indulged in this shameful trade.

Some of the men grumbled at this prohibition, but after a while even they found contentment in the hot food and the generously flowing mead. They sang their songs and played mouth organs and mouth harps. The "Kenor Song" was sung over and over, along with "Longlilly La Loo"and "Over the Mountains."

General Paxion himself took a turn around the tents, pausing to sip a little mead with the men and to exchange some banter with the sergeants. Paxion called on everyone to remember that the Teetol were prone to a sense of having been wronged. When wronged, the Teetol fought duels. Their method of dueling was ancient and quite unlike that of the

Argonath civilization. Each opponent took up a long pole, weighted at one end. Then, taking turns, they would strike each other as hard as possible. It was considered cowardly to even flinch from the blow when it came to one's turn to receive. The challenger was struck first, of course, but the Teetol were inured to it, and it was rare that the challenger could be incapacitated by the first blow. Then it would be their turn to strike.

Paxion painted a vivid picture of this, aided by his memories of a time many years before when he'd seen a legionary embroiled in a dispute over the payment for the use of a Teetol daughter.

Paxion's words were taken to heart. The Teetol had a well-deserved reputation for fighting and ill-temperedness. They were excessively proud and fractious. The men stayed in their tents.

Meanwhile Commander Glaves of the Eighth Regiment sat in his tent shivering against the night chill despite the thick rug pulled around his middle. Glumly, he counted his sorrows until Dandrax returned with a pannier full of hot bully goulash. Glaves fell on the stew with little mews of ecstasy. It was spicy and rich and full of vegetables and chunks of elk. It was the first good thing to happen in days.

So far, Glaves had found the traveling conditions far from ideal. On the barge, he was confined to a humiliatingly tiny cabin, in which he could scarcely lie down let alone turn around. The food was boring, and the sound of the men singing, "moaning like useless milk cows," as he put it, set his teeth on edge every evening. Again and again, he felt the pain of deep regret that he had ever joined the legions.

His spoon scraped on metal. He looked up. Wearily, Dandrax responded to the call. When he returned with another pannier of the stew, Glaves ate it immediately. At length he was stuffed.

He lay back on his cot and groaned. He suddenly

felt nauseated. It was an old problem for him, overeating followed by feeling ill. There came a sudden spasm, and he lurched to his feet, staggered out of the tent, and made his way down to the riverside, where he vomited, making a mess of a pair of white wool knee stockings.

He stood there gasping and heaving.

The sleet had turned to snow, and the air was quite cold. The ground was starting to get a coat of white. The cold air felt refreshing, and Glaves took several breaths and began to feel a mite better.

He turned around and found a few Teetol men watching him, wearing nothing except breechclouts and their weapons belts. Some of them wore short-sleeves vests made of beadwork, but nothing that might serve to keep out the chill north wind. They stood barefoot in the snow, smiling.

"Damned savages!" he muttered, envenomed at the sight. "Don't have the sense to put their clothes on!" He turned to head back to his tent, but found a burly Teetol, two inches taller than himself and sculpted from ridged muscle, standing squarely in his path.

The Teetol man put a hand on Glaves's chest and stopped his progress. The fellow had piercing black eyes and skin bronzed copper from the summer sun while his skull was shaved except for a top knot that was stiffened with bear grease and stood up in a spike nine inches tall. He smelled of bear grease and leather.

"You call the men of Teut-a-Dok village 'savages'?" he asked in good, though accented Verio.

Glaves sucked in a breath. He'd never dreamed the damned Teetol could understand Verio.

"Out of my way," he blustered. "How dare you impede an officer of the legion!"

The massively built Teetol brave stayed where he was. Worse, he stabbed Glaves on the sternum with a stiff forefinger.

"I call you a dog-faced cur with the courage of a woman," he snarled.

Glaves stared at the fellow, astounded by this turn of events and quite appalled. The insult to his dignity was mortifying. He exploded in rage.

"Why you!"He felt the hot bully goulash rising thickly in his gorge for a moment.

Weakly he signaled to Dandrax to appear from the shadows.

The tall, hard-faced mercenary came forward.

"Slay that man," snarled Glaves thickly.

Dandrax hesitated, though his hand strayed to his sword hilt. There were a dozen more Teetol men, some with tomahawks in their belts, standing behind the one that had attacked his master. If he drew his sword, there would be a melee and he might well die here. Dandrax had promised himself that he would never die for Porteous Glaves.

"No, master," he said. "There are too many."

The warrior laughed in a loud braying tone and pointed to Glaves.

"Not only are you dog-faced but you have the heart of a chicken. You would have someone else to fight your battles for you. Chicken dog, I call you."

There were legionaries watching by now and more were coming. Glaves began to feel trapped in a particularly unpleasant nightmare. The huge savage was persistent.

"I challenge you chicken dog, you must fight me in the traditional way."

Glaves demurred. Dozens of Teetol men and youths had gathered by now. As the word of what was happening spread so the entire village began to boil with activity.

Alerted by a concerned lieutenant that had witnessed the scene, General Paxion himself arrived on the run. He was none too pleased with what he now discovered.

Paxion had already realized that in Glaves he had a vindictive oaf commanding an entire regiment. He cursed the new system that allowed wealthy men to buy into regiments. Men like Porteous Glaves did not belong on the battlefield. But the cities were desperate for revenue, and they would take it however they could raise it now.

"What is this all about?"

Glaves saw Paxion and his heart sank, but he grasped at the general as if at a straw.

"This fellow came up to me and struck me. My man Dandrax has been helping me hold them off."

Dandrax heard the sarcastic tone in Glaves's voice and ignored it. He only took Glaves's gold because there was so much of it. Someday he would ignore the fat fool.

The brave stood forward.

"He lies. I challenge him because he is a chicken-hearted dog, a cur that should be whipped. He insult the men of Teetol. He think no Teetol speak the tongue of the city peoples."

Paxion looked back to Glaves for a moment.

"What do you mean he insulted the men of Teetol?"

"He think that no one in Teuta village speak Verio. But I Fish Eye, I speak Verio good. Yes?"

"Umm, yes, you do. And what did you hear my officer say?"

"He say Teetol are witless savages to go in bare feet in snow."

"I see." Paxion turned back to Glaves. His anger mellowing into a warm anticipation.

"Is this true, Commander?"

Glaves frothed. "Absolutely not, sir, I am heedful of our orders to befriend the Teetol."

Fish Eye was laughing again. He bellowed out a stream of Teetol to his friends, and the crowd of men and youths erupted into widespread laughter.

"Well-done, Commander," murmured Paxion with

heavy-handed irony. "You've convinced them that Argonathi men have souls of craven curs, hearts of chickens, and heads of dogs. I don't know what you said, but I am certain that you said something. Fish Eye is a man of honor, he may be a little proud, but looking at him I'd say he has reason to be." Paxion shrugged. "You'll have to meet the man face-to-face unless you can think of something clever."

"Preposterous," expostulated Glaves. "My dignity as a commander . . ."

"Will be gone completely if your men think you are afraid to face this man. So will the honor of your regiment."

"I refuse."

"Then you will be publicly branded a coward."

Glaves swallowed. Total disaster; a taint of cowardice would doom his political ambitions. There was no way out.

As if in a horrid dream, Porteous Glaves found himself stripped to the waist in the driving snow while a six-foot-long pole was thrust into his hands.

Fish Eye stood a few feet away, surrounded by friends and supporters who were placing bets on how many blows it would take to knock down the fat fool from the city.

Fish Eye handled the six-foot pole with a cheerful informality that bespoke long use and much experience. It seemed to slice through the air like a live thing. Glaves was sure this was going to be one of the worst days of his life.

Now the troops were coming out of the tents to watch. It wasn't often they got the chance to see a senior officer get beaten to a pulp.

There was an air of barely restrained hilarity among the men of the Eighth Regiment. Since Glaves had introduced the leather neck cuffs, they had hated him passionately. He had also had two men flogged for having a sip of whiskey in their tent. It was a legal punishment, but unnecessary since neither of the men were drunkards. Their eyes shone with a peculiar luster now as they watched the preparations.

Dandrax gave him a swallow of whiskey. He coughed as it burned its way down, but it left him feeling a tiny bit better.

"You strike first, sir," said Dandrax.

Glaves took a deep breath. Of course, that was it, the way out. This simple savage had miscalculated.

"Exactly, exactly, good point. Hit the fellow hard enough, and he won't come back for more." Glaves practiced a few swings with the pole. It was dreadfully solid yet flexible, a terrible thing to strike a man with.

Fish Eye stood forth. "It is time, come out to face me dog-faced chicken heart." Fish Eye thrust out his chest and stood there waiting.

Glaves swung the rod a few more times then stepped up, gathered all his strength and lashed out. The thing whistled through the air and then with a solid smack it struck Fish Eye on the chest.

It was as if he'd struck a tree. Fish Eye barely blinked for a moment, then gave him a huge smile, raised a finger at him, and wagged it back and forth.

The Teetol erupted into roars of approval and laughter. Now they would see Fish Eye strike his blow. Fish Eye was famous in the entire region for his strength with the pole.

Fish Eye began taking a few trial swings with his own rod. Glaves's throat went dry.

"Stand straight chicken-hearted dog that serves women. Now you will feel the rod of Fish Eye."

Everyone was watching, even the general. His disgrace, his destruction was in full view.

Fish Eye stood closer and swung the rod in long whistling passes that made the hair stand out on Porteous Glaves's neck. Porteous started to tremble, he could not stand this. He was about to break and run, losing all respect forever.

He became aware that the crowd had quietened behind him. He looked back.

A huge form had shouldered through the throng and stood very close. Someone whistled.

He glanced up. A dragonboy was perched on a great dragon's shoulders, the boy's face was expressionless. Then, at last, as if in a dream Glaves saw the dragon's face, saw those immense eyes focused on him. His mouth was dry, the Teetol rod was whistling, he wanted to run, to hide, to go anywhere in the world but this terrible place, but the dragon eyes were on him and he froze in place unable to move, unable to even blink.

Fish Eye gave a little grunt, his rod flashed, and Glaves felt a thunderbolt strike across his upper chest.

For a moment he was numb, then his chest seemed to explode. He was conscious only of his feet leaving the ground. Helplessly he lay in the snow, struggling to breathe.

The watching Teetol, however, now gave up whistles of praise, for the fat Argonathi had taken the blow well, without flinching or blinking.

Fish Eye was disappointed, he had clearly hoped for a more humiliating finish to the bout. For if Glaves had flinched and then been knocked to the ground, then Fish Eye, the victor, would have been allowed to strike him once more, on any part of the anatomy he could reach.

Loudly he protested that he was certain the fat useless ass from Argonath had flinched. But the Teetol had been watching most carefully as was the custom, and they knew that Glaves had not even looked at Fish Eye as the blow was struck and flinched not an iota. In these things the Teetol were an honest people. Now they whistled their refusal.

Fish Eye swung his rod, shrieking through the air, but the Teetol whistled back their disapproval even louder.

"That's enough," said General Paxion. The men might enjoy the sight of Glaves being humbled, but to go further would be to humiliate the legion, and they would not stand for that.

Fish Eye was about to strike Glaves anyway when a great shadow fell over the scene, and the broketail dragon moved around the fallen commander and picked up the rod he'd dropped. The dragon examined the rod, then examined Fish Eye, and then swung the rod experimentally in the air.

He swung it again, and it blurred back and forth.

The Teetol all stepped back with a sigh and then a laugh. Fish Eye scowled briefly at being denied his prey, but then decided to make the best of it and pantomimed running back in great fear of the dragon.

Everyone roared at the joke, and while they were still roaring, Relkin and Bazil carried Glaves back to his tent and set him on his bed.

Glaves feigned unconsciousness and lolled back with his eyes closed and his mouth open breathing loudly. His chest was on fire. He'd probably broken half his ribs!

By the wicked old gods of Veronath, he vowed to someday get his hands around the neck of Ruwat, who'd suggested this mad idea in the first place.

He felt the dragonboy press a finger to his carotid artery and take his pulse. His face was wiped with a cool cloth and then his shirt was opened.

Glaves kept very still. The damned boy wanted to rob him! He would discover his mistake in just a moment. Glaves felt surreptitiously for his knife.

But Relkin merely wanted to check the commander for injuries. Carefully he felt for broken ribs.

There was a huge red welt right across the pectoral region. The Commander was going to have a painful bruise for a long time, but Relkin's sensitive fingers could detect no broken bones.

Glaves remained still, puzzled somewhat. The scurvy

dragonboy must be too stupid to even notice the purse of gold he kept on a leather belt inside his shirt. But no, he felt the boy find the belt and touch the purse.

He gripped his knife.

But Relkin did not remove the little bag of coins. It never occurred to him to even try. He had no wish to get a flogging, and stealing the commander's purse in this situation would guarantee it.

Glaves relaxed, even more surprised. The boy must be incredibly stupid. He was the same one that had been awarded a Legion Star. So this was the best the legion could offer. This is what it took to win the highest awards in the military. Glaves sighed with pity for the poor dolts.

Relkin refastened the commander's shirt and laid a blanket over him. Then he joined Baz who was leaning on his sword and conversing with a pair of legionaries. Together they strolled back to their tent.

CHAPTER NINE

On into the southlands went the legion fleet as the great river snaked back and forth in huge arcs across an increasingly flat, low-lying marshland. Occasionally they would see boats of Teetol make or the smokes of Teetol villages, but, in general, the land seemed as empty of human beings as it was full of wildfowl. Thousands upon thousands of ducks, geese, swans, and cranes filled the waters and the air. Occasionally they glimpsed herds of animals, wild auroch, water beast, black antelope. Once they saw a large hunting party of Teetol braves, in big twenty-man canoes with totems carved into the prows.

The Teetol saw them and stayed well clear, heading for the western side of the river.

For days it went thus, and then in a matter hours they crossed the boundary between the world of the Teetol and the ancient Empire of Ourdh.

First there were scattered villages, trading posts, rickety docks poking out into the river, and then quite abruptly huge watchtowers built of sun-dried-mud brick rose up against the sky. These great square towers, with battlements at the top, became a brooding presence over the river.

The landscape became a monotony of irrigation channels surrounding the sinuous windings of the river. Houses and farm buildings all made of mud brick began to appear and soon to crowd the riverside.

Everywhere they looked they saw the peasant

masses, the fedd, bent over their labors. On the backs of these masses, bound to the land by ancient laws of tenure, the dynasties of Ourdh had come and gone for thousands of years.

Here and there, prosperous towns and villages were painted white. Elsewhere they were in poor condition, with walls tumbling and weeds growing on them.

On the river there were small craft of many kinds. Later they began to see larger vessels, two- and three-masted ships, even deep-sea ships from faraway lands.

They passed their first Ourdhi city, ancient Forkono, a large place with many three-story buildings in the central district. Here as everywhere the dominant style was for mud brick with white-painted stucco.

And so it continued, through the great province of Usono and on into Sagala and eventually to Shekawat their first really large city. Here they saw the great temple pyramid, the Shekawata Puchin, which towered three hundred feet into the air and dominated the whole area.

Here they also saw a few deep-sea vessels, including a trader from Kadein, come to Shekawat to sell Kadein wine and take home sesame oil, hot peppers, dates, honey, and raisins.

The trader spoke of river pirates on the reaches to the south of them. "They're thick on the water like mosquitoes on a bog. Watch out for fireboats and sneak attacks at night."

At Shekawat, General Paxion found more messages from General Hektor bidding him to hurry. A huge battle loomed and the Second Legion was needed desperately.

The legion upped anchors once more and went on, leaving most of the men frustrated. They'd all been waiting for their first chance to take liberty in one of Ourdh's great cities. Shekawat was easily the size of Kadein itself.

But the men drew solace from the knowledge that

much greater cities lay ahead of them. In Ourdh, there were four truly great cities, each with more than a million people. Dzebei, Kwa, Patwa, and Ourdh itself. Their names were synonymous around the world for sophisticated vice and decadent indulgence.

However, the fleet made no more stops, although it did slow occasionally to pick up fresh water. They passed city after city, from the beautiful lacy towers and jade walls of Jumzu to the vast embankments of Zudein. The men could only stare at them and imagine the delights of the fabled fleshpots therein.

In between the cities, they saw vast ruins, major places of ceremonial built for forgotten gods now left desolate. Some appeared to be little more than eroded hills, the only eruptions on the otherwise flat landscape of the floodplain.

After they passed Zudein, they entered the heartland of the worship of Auros, the ruling god of Ourdh. Now each of the man-built hills was topped with a temple, dominated by a vast statue of Auros. Normally these were of the beneficient god of the harvest, a smiling, fat-bellied man who held calipers in one hand and a sickle in the other. These statues were laminated in gold leaf and glowed so in the sun that they were visible for many miles across the irrigated world of the Fedd.

Meanwhile the weather had become much warmer. In coming from northern Kenor, they had sliced spring to a week, for in Ourdh it was early summer and quite torrid during the days.

The men rolled up their freecoats and stowed away their winter leathers, switching to lighter linens and cottons. At night, the flames of sacred fires atop the ziggurats were visible over great distances. These lights could be seen in all directions, one after the other stretching away into the haze.

Sometimes at night they glimpsed the lean shapes

of river pirate galleys stealing softly toward them with muffled oars.

Paxion had ordered maximum vigilance, and at each such sighting his more maneuverable cutters turned and intercepted the marauders, driving them off with fire arrows and bolts from the big catapults.

By day, they saw craft by the hundreds, of all shapes and sizes, plying the water.

They passed mighty Fozad in the night, and for an hour the lights went on as they passed the suburbs stretched out to the south and east.

Then shortly after dawn, they rounded another great hooked sandbar crowned with scrub vegetation and found a party of officers from the Kadein First Legion awaiting them on the shore under a legion flag.

It was a place like any other here on the floodplain, where palm trees fringed the bank of the river. Beyond the trees stood villages and fields of irrigated wheat and barley. Donkeys could be seen in motion here and there among the working fedd.

The senior Kadeini officer approached in a small boat.

"Sub-Commander Vanute, First Kadein Regiment reporting."

Paxion returned the man's salute and received a letter from Hektor and an oral aside.

"Begging your pardon, sir, but the general, he gave me an extra message, just for your ear, sir, if you know what I mean."

Paxion drew the man aside.

"What is it, man?"

"Sir, the general said that if you don't get to him in time, he fears the whole thing will be lost and we'll be a bunch of silly buggers sitting out here completely surrounded by a hostile horde that will cook us over slow fires and feed our flesh to dogs. The war here is unbelievably fierce."

Paxion felt his mouth go dry. The worst nightmare

was coming true. This was exactly what he'd feared since the beginning of this whole mad venture.

He glanced at the letter quickly. He was instructed to head west at once, to meet with Hektor and the Imperial Army somewhere about fifty miles from the river. A vast horde of the enemy was striking eastwards, aiming to cut the Imperial Army off from its communications to the south. The emperor would be trapped on the west bank of the river, the Imperial Army would disintegrate and flee, all else would collapse.

"Sir?" the sub-commander was waiting for his response. He pulled himself back to reality, forcing the words out.

"Tell the general that we will be there, I don't know how, but we'll be there."

"Yes, sir. If you make a landing here and march directly west, sir, you will find him at a place called Salpalangum. A small city, very old. There's a ziggurat there that is said to be especially beautiful."

"At once then." Paxion gave the orders and the fleet put in to the shore. The men disembarked along with the cavalry and the dragon squadrons.

There was a great potential for chaos in such an operation, but the men of the Second Marneri were seasoned veterans now, and they did the thing quickly and efficiently. Within two hours the entire legion was ashore and marching inland. Paxion felt a certain degree of pride at the sight. He'd had this legion at Dalhousie for less than a year, but they'd absorbed the essential lesson of discipline in a military formation. With discipline and energy, a unit the size of a legion could maneuver as quickly as a unit one-tenth its size. With discipline and training, the legions of Argonath were worth ten times their weight in enemies, and they'd proved this again and again on the battlefield.

With a steady stride they went, heading down a

straight road to a certain battle and an unknown destiny. Five thousand men, six hundred cavalry, and one hundred and fifty dragons, a sight that brought a lump to General Paxion's throat and a crushing fear of failure to his heart.

He became obsessed with the need to show an example, and ran his staff ragged by riding up and down the columns every hour, letting everyone see the commanding officer. He kept up a constant flow of encouragement, praising the men's marching to their officers, and all the while pushing for everyone to hurry. Staff officers, scouts, and messengers were constantly riding back and forth, enhancing the atmosphere of haste.

The Eighth Regiment was nominally the last in line, but this was not a parade, and they had been one of the first to get ashore and so they were just behind the First Regiment at the front of the column.

The men were suffering in the hated neck collars, which chafed and rubbed the skin raw under the chin and beneath the ears. They were hideously hot to wear in these conditions, the tight leather seemed to constrict the throat.

But Porteous Glaves had ordered it, and for anyone to refuse to wear it would be certain to bring a flogging. Glaves had threatened this repeatedly while they were on board ship. When they marched, they were to wear the leather stock around their neck. It had been embossed with the mark of the Two and the Eight, and they were to show it off proudly. He would brook no discussion of it.

Still the men kept up a good pace, they were determined to show that the Eighth Regiment was no slouch, leather collars or not.

At the rear of the regiment, in front of the supply wagons and the medical team wagon, marched the 109th dragons. Relkin and Bazil had fallen into the steady pace quite easily, though not without the usual complaints from the dragon.

Bazil Broketail felt he had already done more than his share of marching for the legions, all the way to Tummuz Orgmeen and back, for instance.

If there was anything to be said for it, it was that at least the dragons found the road level and not too hard for the big callused pads on the soles of their feet. And they were rarely far from water. They crossed an irrigation-channel bridge every hundred yards or so and were able to cool their feet, although they were forbidden to drink the water for fear of disease.

The zone near the river was rich with orchards and many small fields of barley, but later the orchards were replaced with larger fields, surrounded by thorn-bush as well as palm. Villages of mud brick sprawled along untidy lanes right next to extensive pigpens filled with a multitude of small black pigs.

They passed a small tumbledown ziggurat that had trees growing on its crown. At the base were mounds of rubble, and among the ruins were hordes of starving children, outcasts from the villages. These children were thin, desperate, thievish in the extreme. Up and down the columns there were dozens of incidents as knives, plates, compasses, freecoats were stolen, angry oaths were heard, and running men pursuing the thieves became a common sight.

They entered a town, Aroshakan, and the people came out en masse to stare at the tall men with blond beards from the North as they went marching by. The crowds gasped at the sight of the horses, hundreds of them, and such fiery, tall steeds, quite unlike the little ponies and donkeys of Ourdh.

And at last there came the dragons, great lumbering brasshides, lean, long leatherbacks, shiny gristles, and angular hard greens. Great reptiles marching on all fours, bearing armor and swords strapped over their backs. From the lowly fedd to the aristocrats in their jade-inlaid coaches, all the people of the town made the sign of the smile of Auros, from the left breast to the right breast.

"Auros, protect me," whispered one and all.

Everyone knew that this was a certain portent of the return of the great serpent. Sephis the Terrible lived again in Dzu. The time of Auros was done. The time of blood had come again. It was fate and nothing could prevent it.

The columns of legionaries passed by and were soon gone, swallowed up in the immensity of the province of Kwa, heading west down the road to Salpalangum.

A messenger rode in shortly before nightfall, one Captain Kesepton from General Hektor's staff. He had an urgent message for Paxion.

"Sir, General Hektor's regrets, but will you keep marching tonight? It is the only way you can join him by noon tomorrow when he thinks you'll be needed."

Paxion read the message, which confirmed what young Captain Kesepton was saying. He wondered to himself what use his legion would be on the battlefield if it had marched all night.

Hektor suggested that he break for meals every four hours to keep everyone's strength up and to perhaps lift the men's spirits with measures of whiskey every so often through the night.

Captain Kesepton also warned that there were groups of marauding Sephisti irregulars in the country ahead.

Paxion stared off into the gathering murk. Already the fires were being lit atop the ziggurats. They seemed baleful, threatening sparks of red in an enemy haunted dusk.

CHAPTER TEN

Under a full yellow moon, they marched through a landscape scented with magnolia and almond blossom. Torches were raised onto the regimental standards to light the way, and as they marched, they sang while the drummer boys kept the rhythm fast.

Paxion kept doling out water to the marching columns. He understood how important food and water were for marching men and dragons. Every three hours, they halted for another quick meal and strong hot kalut.

After twenty minutes or so, Paxion had the drums going again and the men fell in and resumed the march, their teeth gritted against the soreness in their legs.

It had to be done, and they were the men to do it. No one should be able to say that the Marneri Second Legion had failed for want of heart. The feet went forward, and they reached deep into themselves and sang once more the "Kenor Song," and "La Loo La Lilly," and "Chops and Minstrels."

At last, dawn stole in on the east. Raucous guinea fowl announced the fact from hundreds of surrounding farms. Soon farmers setting off for their fields were startled to find the legion blocking the road as it tramped past, heading west.

Bazil had aching feet and poor old Chektor's feet were already inflamed. Mono was at work with poultice and blister sherbert every time they halted. But

Relkin was less concerned for Bazil than he was for the Purple Green. The broketail dragon had tough feet and strong legs. He weighed a third less than Chektor, a brasshide, and he had shown the year before that he could walk the length of the land. However, the great wild one had never marched anywhere before and with his great weight, twice that of a leatherback, he was putting tremendous pressure on his feet. Relkin had expected it, however, and had had made a pair of huge, fitted sandals for the wild one. The Purple Green had haughtily disdained them at the time.

Now his feet were sore and blistered. Relkin had already used blister sherbet to cool the sores and shrink them. In the raw places, he spread an ointment of honey and molasses that would kill any bacterial growth by dehydrating it.

Casually, as if offering any mundane piece of equipment, he brought up the sandals once more.

The Purple Green exchanged a long look with him. For a long second, Relkin imagined himself being seized and devoured in those heavy jaws.

"Hah!" a sudden dragon snort. "This is how you make the dragons slaves then? You are always offering your help, just as long as they fight for you."

"We fight for them, too."

The Purple Green snorted derisively.

"Bring me the sandals. I am accustomed to flying over the distances, not crawling along like this. My feet hurt too much."

Relkin was mindful of the immense loss of dragon dignity involved. He murmured, "I understand completely, be back in a moment."

Relkin slipped out of the ranks after requesting permission from Dragoneer Hatlin. He ran back along the column to the line of wagons carrying food and equipment. In the 109th equipment wagon was the wrapped pair of gigantic sandals that had boggled the mind of the sandal maker when he first asked for them. Now he staggered back, carefully put them under the dragon's huge feet, and did up the fastenings around the massive ankles of the dragon. The straps were all lined with rabbit fur to ease the chafing, but Relkin knew he would have to work hard with blister sherbet and lotion for the next few stops.

Then he went down to fetch the Purple Green an extra ration of water. At the water wagon, a horseman was drawing a ladle for himself. Relkin failed to recognize him until there was a sudden tap on his shoulder. He turned around to find a captain, with the red tabs on his lapel that marked him as a staff officer, standing in front of him.

"So now you're carrying a Legion Star, you don't recognize your friends anymore, eh?" said Captain Hollein Kesepton with a smile.

Relkin was so startled to suddenly find his friend and Lagdalen's husband here at the water wagon, he was reduced to babbling for a moment. Then he remembered to salute, and they shook hands. The captain slid out of the saddle and gave him a big hug and a shake.

"I should have known," said Hollein Kesepton. "Relkin and Bazil of Quosh would be sure to get themselves sent with the expedition. They couldn't keep you two away from danger no matter how they tried."

"Believe me, we didn't get any choice." Relkin shrugged. "But we're ready for them. What are they like, really?"

"The enemy?"

Relkin's nod brought a bitter smile.

"Well, they're very numerous and they care little for life. I have seen such savagery here, things that I hope I can learn to forget someday."

The captain seemed genuinely shaken. Relkin felt uneasy.

"The rumor is that we're going to be overwhelmed. And that the Imperial Army is no good."

Kesepton gave a harsh bark of laughter.

"Overwhelmed? What faint hearts are these? We have more than ten thousand from Argonath. We can hold any number of the enemy, even if they are more numerous than the stars in the sky."

Hollein drank his water.

"What about the Imperial Army, is it as bad as they say?"

"It's not good, but I believe General Hektor has a plan. Do not give up all hope yet. The general understands the true situation. Hektor is no placeman, he can fight."

"Tell the general that the 109th dragons are ready for battle."

Kesepton laughed merrily. "Indeed I will, indeed."

Relkin changed the subject. "But, Captain, what news have you from Lagdalen of the Tarcho?"

Kesepton grew somber. "Alas, very little. I heard that there has been a crisis of some kind in Marneri, and that Lagdalen had left the city and sailed south with a Great Witch from Cunfshon. A week ago perhaps, and where they are bound I know not."

"But the child?"

"Is with a wet nurse and its grandmother. The child will do well enough. As for Lagdalen, who can say? That work is always very dangerous as well we both know."

Relkin understood all too well. Accompanying a Great Witch on one of her missions was guaranteed to be dangerous work; both he and Hollein Kesepton had experience in such matters.

"And where are we going, if you can tell us?"

"There's no secret about that. We're marching to a city called Salpalangum in time to join Hektor and the Imperial Army for what I think will be a hell of a battle tomorrow. The city is about ten miles farther up the road here."

Hektor gestured. "The enemy is coming from the west, where they are strong. They're trying to cut the emperor off from Kwa, which lies to the south of here. We have to stop them."

"And they're fanatics who don't fear death?"

"There is a madness in them like nothing I've ever seen before. But they have no discipline in their formations, they charge like a crazed mob, and they can be handled like any mob. Give me two legions of good trained men, Argonathi men, and . . ." The Captain halted himself with a rueful shrug. "And you've got me babbling and all I'm drinking is water!"

Relkin's tub for the dragon was full now. With a heave, he got it up on his shoulder.

"For Argonath!"

"Alright, boy, may the Mother protect you."

"And you, Captain."

Kesepton remounted and wheeled away into the dark. Shortly afterward, he left the columns and rode ahead with a small escort seeking to make contact with General Hektor's forces. Behind him the legion marched, on legs that felt like wooden pins, through a gathering morning.

Past palm trees and ocher-brick villages, carp ponds and piggeries they went. Hours went by, and the sun climbed into the sky and became a blazing monster.

In the Eighth Regiment, debilitated by the hated neck cuffs, men began to fall at last. They were red in the face, bathed in sweat, breathing hard. When it came it was usually swift, and a man would abruptly drop in his tracks. The supply wagons were soon full of unconscious men. A few cavalrymen were carrying others over their saddles.

And then at last there were riders coming down the road toward them, and men in the uniforms of Ka-

deini Cavalry rode up. They brought another urgent
message from General Hektor, a command that the
Second Legion pick up its pace. The battle might
begin at any moment.

The drums began to beat, once more General Paxion roused himself and ordered tea laced with whiskey
given out to the men while messengers thundered up
and down the columns with orders.

On they went. In the Eighth Regiment the next man
collapsed after five minutes. Another went down a
minute or so later.

Paxion himself happened to be riding by when the
next man staggered out of the ranks and collapsed.
The general dismounted at once and knelt by the
fallen soldier. With a face suffused with rage, he rose
and ordered that the Eighth Regiment remove the
hated neck cuffs at once.

"Commander Glaves, I will speak to you, sir, instantly. Follow me." Paxion remounted and rode away
under a thunderous cloud.

The men fumbled at the fasteners with eager fingers
and a ragged cheer went up as they threw the hated
collars down into the dust. Then they picked up the
pace once more and caught up with the First Regiment
ahead of them.

After a while Commander Glaves returned, red in
the face and quite subdued. He resumed his position
at the head of the regiment without a word to anyone,
even Major Breez.

Now the column began to pass rear elements of a
huge army, the Imperial baggage train. A sea of tents
stretched along the road like a small city. The sides of
the road were congested with mules and small wagons
struggling to get by while the legion shouldered its
way through.

Troops of the Imperial Army became visible, men
of slight stature and nut brown skins, clad in white
pantaloons, shirts and conical hats set off with scarlet

sashes and round steel shields. These soldiers were seen in steadily increasing numbers on the sides of the roads. They seemed to lack military zest. Many carried no weapons.

A great mass of them was concentrated in one field as they went past. And then they saw the ziggurat, a small one of perhaps one hundred feet height, and beneath it the ocher-brick walls of Salpalangum.

Now they marched around the city, through suburbs of villas and gardens until they emerged onto a broad, open plain on the western approach to the city.

They found that they stood on a crescent-shaped plateau with the city in the center and the two horns trailing off westwards. On either side of them were vast numbers of Imperial soldiers in the white and the red, and then, ahead of them they saw the standards of the Kadein First Legion, and the regiments of Kadein soldiers in green coats and grey trousers.

The Kadeini greeted them with a thunderous cheer, and the men of the Second Legion returned it with one of their own that was just as loud.

At last came the order to halt. The men and dragons fell out and set to final preparations for combat. The question on everyone's lips was "where were the enemy?"

General Paxion rode up to General Hektor's headquarters, a white tent, set a little ways apart from a collection of huge red and purple tents that marked the emperor's personal headquarters.

Paxion found General Hektor standing bent over a table, a map spread out in front of him.

Hektor greeted him with a firm handshake and a gesture toward the map.

"Well done Paxion, a splendid piece of marching. The Marneri Second should be known henceforth as the "Iron Foots.""

"Thank you, General, thank you very much."

"Forty miles in a little more than twenty-four hours.

Excellent! Now I think we really might give our enemies a surprise."

"Shall I deploy to face attack?"

"Not just yet, the enemy has yet to show himself today. Yesterday they were demonstrating up and down on our front here, but today appears to be the calm before the storm. I expect our enemy is trying to sort himself out. Such huge numbers can make even the simplest maneuver chaotic."

Paxion breathed a sigh of relief.

"Then possibly we won't fight today?"

Hektor hunched over the map.

"Anything's possible, but I rather think he will attack today sometime. Look here, this is Salpalangum," he stabbed the map with a thick forefinger. "The emperor and his army are supplied from the south, from Kwa down here. The enemy are trying to cut off the communications with the south. They are very confident, and they know that the Imperial Army is shaky. If they attack here now, they can possibly take the emperor himself, and if they did that, they would win everything."

Paxion's face fell. "I see. I had hoped the men might rest a while before combat; they've given everything on the march."

Hektor nodded and chuckled. "You haven't been in battle for a while, eh, General? Once they smell blood and terror in the air, they'll find the strength. It's either that or death. It always amazes me how much energy men can find for battle when they must. Don't worry about your men. But pay attention here now, this is my plan and I will need your close cooperation."

General Paxion sighed inwardly. Bending close, he fought to overcome the fatigue and comprehend General Hektor's instructions.

CHAPTER ELEVEN

The Second Legion stood down in its position. The men dropped to the ground and most of them contrived to sleep at once. The plain was suddenly carpeted with prone forms except where the cooks started boiling up a fresh supply of Ourdhi kalut, the dark coffee of the southlands that was so vital to the legions. Elsewhere the surgeons were at work on the most severe exhaustion cases, and dragonboys ran up and down on errands of their own.

Beyond the prone figures of the Second Legion of Marneri were the ranks of the Kadein First Legion in their distinctive green shirts and grey breeches. They were standing to in loose rank while they drank hot dark kalut and discussed the coming battle.

On the other side, past a strip of clear ground began the formations of the Imperial Army, a vast mass of men in white with colored sashes denoting their regiments and brigades. There were thousands upon thousands of them, arrayed into the distance on both flanks.

Behind this huge army lay the ocher walls of Salpalangum, studded with turrets and towers. In front stretched a flat terrain, cleared of vegetation for a hundred yards before the first palm trees arose.

Here they would stand for the great battle. This was what they had come so far to find. And yet the significance of the event was not uppermost in the minds of the men and the dragons of the legion. Uppermost were concerns about their feet and their aching legs. That is when they remained conscious long enough to have concerns at all.

But for dragonboys, there was no rest. Dragons had to be fed, watered, and tended. Relkin ignored the pains in his own legs and rolled a water keg down the lines to refresh his pair of dragons. While they drank, he took a look at the Purple Green's battered feet.

There were blisters and a lot of sore places, but nothing was actually bleeding. The huge sandals had done their job. Feeling pleased with himself, he worked quickly with blister sherbet and some medicinal honey, then rubbed a toner cream into the massive, clawed reptile feet that had gone pink from irritation. The Purple Green meanwhile drank water in long, slow sips that took down about half a gallon at a time. Then he set the keg aside, closed his enormous eyes, and sighed in unmistakable contentment.

The broketail dragon noted the Purple Green's state of near ecstasy. "So my wild friend, welcome to the legion life."

The Purple Green's eyes popped open and narrowed. "We walk all night, and we have come the distance of ten wing beats. This is one terrible way to live."

"The boy is good, though. He knows how to work on a dragon's feet."

The Purple Green, in fact, had forgotten he even had feet. They had been very sore a few minutes earlier, and now he scarcely felt them. He looked up, but the boy was already gone, trundling the empty keg down the lines to the water wagon. It was a strange sensation to have someone who brought one water and tended to one's sore and blistered feet. Instinctively the Purple Green felt annoyance, his big forehands clenched. It would be good to fight soon. By the old gods of Dragon Home, it would be good to fight the enemy!

The other dragons were stretched out around them, Vlok and Chektor, and the young ones. It was a strangely peaceful sight.

"We will fight now?" said the Purple Green.

"We will fight," said Chektor with a sour grunt. Old Chek's feet were in bad shape now, but he knew there was no point in complaining about it.

"Good," said Vlok, always combative. "Where are the enemy?"

The broketail pointed out across the flat plain toward a distant windbreak of palm trees. "Out there."

"Will there be trolls?"

"No. At least that is what Dragoneer Hatlin says."

"Mmm." The dragons thought about this. With no trolls to fight, there would only be men or imps to face them. Men had little chance against a dragon unless they were well trained and armed with long lances. Imps would be driven at them in swarms seeking to overwhelm with sheer weight of numbers. The dragons had been trained in methods for dealing with both techniques.

Relkin meanwhile had returned the keg to the water wagon and gone over to the cook fires where he begged a cup of hot kalut.

The soldiers there were grumbling about their feet and their sore legs. Relkin had heard enough such talk so he left them and strolled over to the smith's fire, which was blazing high, while burly Cordwain, the smith for the Eighth Regiment, struck sparks from steel as he straightened spearheads on his anvil. Relkin stood there, sipped kalut, and watched the smith work, admiring his skill.

Suddenly he felt a sharp pain across his shoulder and spun about while his hand went to his dirk. A white carriage pulled by a pair of dainty white ponies had come to a halt behind him. A youth with golden curls sat on the driver's seat and made play with a long whip.

Relkin rubbed his shoulder and studied the youth. Nobody struck Relkin Dragoneer First Class like that and got away with it. This golden-haired coach boy would soon learn this.

The blind across the carriage's side window was pulled aside, and a young Ourdhi woman of aristocratic bearing thrust out her head. She wore a black velvet hat shaped like a small box, and a shimmering veil and a purple gown.

"You," she said in Ourdhi accented Verio, "the boy standing there drinking. Where is the headquarters of the Imperial Army?"

Relkin stared back truculently, disinclined to answer after being struck with golden hair's whip.

"That's a military secret, madam, and I can't be giving it away to just anyone who goes by, now can I?"

The woman stared at him perplexed.

"What is this? You won't tell me! Who are you, boy?"

"Relkin of Quosh, Dragoneer First Class, one hundred and ninth of Marneri, at your service, lady."

Suddenly she smiled, a not altogether reassuring sight.

"Well, Dragoneer"—the accent was very nasal but the command of the language was complete—"I am the Princess Zettila, and I have an urgent message for the emperor himself. Please help me now, and I will put in a good word for you at your court-martial. Because when I have finished reporting the disrespect you show me, I am sure you will be put on trial for your life."

Relkin shrugged. Maybe she really was a princess, maybe she could get him in big trouble, but he doubted it. He had done nothing wrong. General Hektor would pay no attention to such demands. Still, it would be better not to antagonize her any further if he could help it. Powerful people could sometimes be highly vindictive.

"My apologies, Your Highness. We've only just arrived here. We marched in overnight, and I had no idea that someone like yourself would be up here in our lines. Anyway, I expect that you'll need to turn back and go around the legion standard over there. I think the Imperial headquarters are in that direction." He pointed beyond the standards set behind the two Argonath legions.

The princess frowned. "Why should I not just continue in this direction, going through the ranks of these men?" she pointed toward the rows of sleeping soldiers of the Second Legion.

Relkin shut his mouth until his first reply was stifled. It was going to be difficult to keep out of trouble if he had to speak with this princess very long.

"One good reason for not going in that direction, Your Highness, is that it would take your ponies right past two squadrons of dragons."

Princess Zettila paled slightly at this news, then she leaned forward and spoke sharply to the youth in the driver's seat in Ourdhi.

"Aimlor, turn the coach around, we'll go back and get directions from someone less addled than this surly youth."

Golden Hair on the driving board made a face and began the process of shifting the ponies around within a confined space. Since Aimlor had not been chosen for his skills with horses, he soon made a hash of this complex maneuver. The ponies became quite boisterous. Aimlor cracked his whip and went red in the face, shouting at them to no avail.

Relkin glanced back over his shoulder and groaned. A huge, familiar form was lumbering down the lines.

"Aimlor!" he shouted in Verio. "Pull back harder

on the rein. Stop using the whip." He danced in front of the carriage waving his hands.

Aimlor understood none of this, and cursed him and struck at him with the whip. The princess leaned out of the carriage and screamed invective at him in Ourdhi.

Relkin could see the Purple Green getting closer, heading toward the water wagon for a refill. The ponies caught the scent of dragon and went mad. They plunged and kicked and shattered the front paneling of the little white carriage. The princess screamed as the carriage bounced backward and she was thrown to the floor.

Aimlor lashed out with his whip, striking the ponies again and again and whipping them into a further frenzy. They turned and began to run away from the dragons right past Relkin. He could see that they were out of Aimlor's control. Relkin dropped his kalut, vaulted onto the running board, and climbed up onto the driver's seat. Aimlor turned on him with a furious expression and yelled something in Ourdhi. With no further ado, Relkin lifted a foot and kicked him in the belly. Aimlor tumbled backward and fell off the carriage with a cry of woe.

Relkin took the reins and hauled back on them with a steady pressure. The ponies shook hard and heavy, but were unable to break his grip. Still they continued to try and bolt away from the approaching dragon. They bucked suddenly and the right-side pony broke his grip momentarily and almost got the bit between its teeth. Relkin was jerked up onto his feet. For a moment he hung there close to falling out, then he regained his balance and yanked hard on the reins, hauling the horses' heads around and forcing them to slow to a complete stop.

He held them for a moment and then let them out a little. They moved, but at a trot and no longer at a breakneck run. Behind them the Purple Green had

passed by en route to the water wagon seeking another keg of water. Disaster had been averted.

Eventually Relkin brought them to a walk and
rounded the legion standards, which were set up beside General Paxion's command tent.

Ahead lay the larger tent of General Hektor, another plain white expanse of canvas. Past that was the
Imperial headquarters, a cluster of purple and scarlet
tents, with waving golden pennons.

Aimlor ran up in front and caught the left pony's
bridle. Breathing hard, he threw Relkin a murderous
look.

Relkin pulled the ponies to a halt, tied the reins
off, and then stepped down and bowed with a flourish.
Aimlor faced him angrily, but, though he was the bigger of the two, he did nothing. There was that dirk,
and something in Relkin's steady gaze that deterred
Aimlor. Sullenly, Aimlor climbed up into the driver's
seat.

Relkin found the Princess Zettila staring at him with
a frighteningly intense expression on her face. She
pointed a finger and said two Ourdhi words, one of
which sounded like "ah-weez."

"Glad to be able to be of service, Your Highness."
Relkin doffed his cap, turned, and slipped away
through the small crowd of soldiers and camp followers that had formed around the carriage.

Aimlor whipped up the ponies, and they quickly
bore the princess away. There had been something
strange about the Princess Zettila's stare, an intensity
beyond normal. It left Relkin with vague uneasiness.

This mood was dissipated swiftly on his return to
his position, where Dragoneer Hatlin spoke sharply at
him about overstaying permission to be away from the
unit. Relkin tried to explain, but he soon saw that
Hatlin didn't believe a word so he gave up and lapsed
into silence. Hatlin left.

Bazil was full of questions. Who was the lady in the carriage?

"A princess," he grunted. "And she offered me the job of driving her coach and living a pampered life. But I said I could not accept since I had to take care of two dragons."

"Hah, so you thought you would be fertilizing royal eggs at night eh?"

"And why not?" Am I not from the village of Quosh?"

"Fertilizing the eggs is all you have thought about for half a year now. Maybe dragonboy have to leave legion and find a mate."

Relkin laughed. "Doesn't bear thinking about does it, not compared to taking care of a pair of cranky dragons."

"Hmmf. Purple Green has not complained about his feet for long time now."

"A miracle of planning."

Bazil's eyes lit up with amusement. "Good thinking with the sandals, I agree. Sometimes dragonboy do good."

"They're coming," said a voice to their right. It was Mono. Chektor stood on his hind legs and craned his neck.

"Boy is right. They come."

Relkin climbed up onto Bazil's shoulder and gazed out into the west.

Coming across the small fields, pressing through the palm groves was a vast mass of figures, all clad in black robes. Above their heads waved banners on which a golden serpent writhed across a black background.

To the horizon, the land was darkened with the enemy horde. A great mass of horsemen moved out from behind some palms to the left. Drums were thudding, and a shrill ululation from a hundred thousand throats filled the air. Even the ground began to shake under the weight of the approaching horde.

Dragoneer Hatlin was on their front calling out orders.

"Fall in!" was the cry throughout the regiments. "Prepare to receive the enemy."

Dragons and dragonboys hustled into position. Huge swords came out of the shoulder scabbards, and big helmets were strapped on. Boys slid arrows into their Cunfshon crossbows.

CHAPTER TWELVE

As the Sephisti horde emerged onto open ground under the serpent banner, so the air of crisis in the emperor's own tent rose to a fever pitch.

At the inner entrance, golden horns suddenly blew to announce the emperor's arrival. A small man weighed down by his troubles, the emperor wore a simple tunic of gold cloth and sandals of gold thread studded with emeralds.

The court stirred and rose to its collective feet. On the right were ranked the viziers, the monstekirs, the stekirs, and other nobles of the great fertile land. On the left were the eunuchs of the civil service and the high priest of Auros and the high priestess of Gingo-La.

In the center was the light wooden throne that was used by emperors of Ourdh on military campaigns. Around the throne were the inner circle: his sister Biruma, who was by title the Duchess of Patwa; then the high vizier, old Jiji Vokosong the Montzoon of Baharad; and last and least, General Knazud, commander of the Imperial Army.

Besides these three, set off a little distance was another, his aunt Haruma, the only one he could truly trust for she had no power of her own, no life outside his protection. Haruma was clad very simply, especially in comparison to the other three by the throne. She wore a simple green cloak and few jewels, all emeralds as befitted a member of the Shogemessar family.

The others, especially the general in his gold-plated armor, were blinding in their magnificence. The Duchess of Patwa wore a necklace of huge, square-cut emeralds, five gold chains, solid gold bracelets on both forearms, and rings on every digit studded with diamonds, emeralds, and sapphires—but no rubies, never a single ruby, garnet, or any reddish stone.

No member of the Shogemessar family would ever wear a ruby, of course, since rubies were the jewel of the old south dynasties from the province of Dzebei. The Shogemessar dynasty hailed from the eastern province of Patwara, where the Sunusolo,a tributary of the Oon, ran forth from the Malgun Mountains. Emeralds had been found from early times in the river gravels.

The high vizier, the Montzoon of Baharad, was closely allied to the Shogemessar family and thus wore many emeralds, especially the huge Star of Baharad, which glinted on his turban. He wore a yellow silk robe and scarlet platform shoes that elevated him half a foot into the air. The shoes, a hereditary perk of high viziership required that the high vizier be physically carried from place to place since walking was almost impossible.

The emperor, Banwi Shogemessar, took his place on the simple throne. A figure in simple grey robes, the Chamberlain Vixed, approached from the line of eunuchs on the left.

"Greetings, Your Majesty." The eunuchs prostrated themselves while singing the "Glory, Glory, Glory," as was prescribed in court protocol.

The emperor clapped his hands.

"Stop that groveling. The enemy is attacking! At any moment we may be in flight. There's no time for it."

"As you wish, Your Majesty," said Vixed, bowing

low and signaling the other eunuchs to rise from their knees.

Banwi Shogemessar, Fedafer of the well-watered land, lord of Heaven and Earth, golden emperor of ancient Ourdh, sat there trembling. In part, it was induced by fear, or rather total abject terror, and in part, it was caused by rage, over the bad advice he had been given by his advisers.

He was trying to keep his temper under control, and it was very difficult. His hands wanted to fly up and dart around on their own. He badly wanted to shout and scream.

The ground was shaking underneath them as the enemy tramped forward. If the enemy won, or rather, when they won, he knew what they would do to him.

That very morning, he had been told it all once again by the rooster's head that popped out of his breakfast egg and addressed him in fluent Ourdhi. He would be taken to the pit of Sephis and given to the reborn god.

"Brother, you seem pale." Biruma was leaning in toward him, her long nose seeming even more predatory than normal.

"Sister, we're trapped here by a hundred thousand religious fanatics who want my blood. Or worse." He glared at Penitem, the high priest of Auros.

The sight of the high priest brought the rage to the surface.

"Priest! It's your damned fault. You fools, you told me it was impossible, that the old god was dead. And like an idiot I believed you. Ravens talking to me from the window? 'Just black magic, Your majesty, don't be worried.' The dreams with the serpent? Take dream bane at sleep time, Majesty. Pay it no heed, there are just some very good magicians in Dzu. They will overreach and be torn down shortly, there is nothing to fear.' Well, damn you, there is plenty to fear now!"

Penitem, high priest of Auros, shifted uncomfortably in his place. It was true enough, he and his staff had done a perfectly miserable job of advising the emperor. They had simply not believed it possible. Under the rationalism of Auros, when all the worlds were measured correctly and justice was enthroned, it was impossible for there to be any other gods, only the so-called "goddess" of Gingo-La. To the Auroans, the worshipers of Gingo-La were really atavists, pagans worshiping the older pantheon of gods and mother goddesses. The priests of Auros maintained an amused contempt for all the rituals of the priestesses, and as for the doings in other lands, such things were either the work of black magic or simply laughable.

But now they had been driven to consider things they had previously thought impossible.

"We have consulted with the witches of the eastern Isles. They inform us that the so-called god Sephis is not a true god but is a high demon brought here from its own hellish plane of existence to reestablish the old cult of the serpent and to bring down the empire."

"To what purpose, man," snapped Banwi leaning closer.

"To enable the Makers of imps to buy women freely on our markets and breed them in the pens of Axoxo under the Doom of the White Bones Mountains."

"Yes, yes," said Banwi ill-temperedly. "So you've said before. But that wasn't what you said when we could still have done something about this. Now we're trapped here and we have to give battle and we may well lose. Our army is rife with defeatism and treason."

General Knazud struggled with his feelings. The Patwari gangs infested the supply system for the army, corruption was monstrous. The army suffered from shortages of everything.

"Sire, may I say something."

"Silence, General, do not speak. I can use my eyes. Our forces are riddled with fear, no, terror. They have heard that the old god is alive once more, and that in the end all the followers of Auros will go before the old god and be enslaved by its eyes. Any who resist will be slain."

The thunder of the enemy drums was getting very loud. Banwi turned anguished eyes to his aunt. She alone knew what had happened at breakfast. She alone of all these people could he trust.

"Aunt, what am I to do?" He wailed.

Haruma smiled and bent the knee slightly.

"My lord, you must resist the enemy, for he can be defeated."

"My army is weakened by fear. The men will break and run."

"Trust the Argonathi general and his troops, they will stand and fight."

"But there are so few of them. They will be overwhelmed. The Sephisti come in a horde ten times their number."

"The Argonathi troops are the better. They have their own cavalry, and they have dragons. You will see."

"I will see a lot more of what I saw this morning . . ." He turned away from Haruma in sudden anger.

What did she want from him? To give away his rule to the witches of the East? To allow them to penetrate Ourdhi society and overthrow the ancient order and elevate the status of women? He could not allow that. He could not trust these foreigners with their alien thoughts.

He banged his fist on the wooden arm of the throne. It was barely audible with the thunder of drumming outside.

"Somebody tell me something good . . ." he said plaintively. "I need some good news and I need it now . . ."

The grand vizier nodded and mumbled. General Knazud spoke up. "We have been joined by the other Argonathi legion. There are now two of them. They are positioned close by, in the center of our line."

Banwi scowled and turned away.

His sister caught his eye.

"Beloved Brother, the Princess Zettila has also just arrived. She requests an audience."

Zettila was back. Banwi stood up. Here was something at least to divert him.

"We grant this request. Show her to my tent."

General Knazud's face fell. Haruma groaned inwardly. Sister Biruma wore a gloating look of triumph.

There was a sudden commotion at the entrance. A guard put his head in and spoke to one of the chamberlain's staff. Word was passed forward swiftly.

"A messenger, lord, from the Argonath general."

Banwi waved for the messenger to be let in.

A young captain, with a dashing look to him, came forward and proffered a small scroll to the chamberlain, who conveyed it to the emperor.

"Translate," said Banwi, after a glance at the barbarous scrawlings in Argonathi Verio.

Old Vixed was fluent in Verio, as with many other tongues.

"Your Majesty, Banwi Shogemessar, Emperor of Ourdh, Fedafer of Fedafers, Light of the East, Fire of the North, He Who Rules the Reed Plains and terrifies the Teetol . . . etc. etc. greetings from General Hektor, who is pleased to announce that his legions are in position and ready to receive the enemy, who is in sight."

"Yes? That's all?"

"That is all, Your Majesty."

"Good grief, well, tell the barbarian that we are very pleased, and we expect them to die like heroes."

Vixed nodded, told the captain that the emperor was most pleased to welcome them to the field of heroic battle, and that he expected the heroes of Argonath to fight well.

Abruptly, the emperor rose from the throne, ending the audience. The golden horns blew, and everyone either bowed low or bent the knee, except young Cap-

tain Kesepton who merely bobbed his head, ducked
out, and raced to his horse.

The emperor went directly to his tent, ignoring the
sound of battle. Inside his tent, a vista of gold, red,
and purple silks, with white upholstered furnitures, he
threw himself onto a soft settee.

The Princess Zettila was waiting for him, kneeling
submissively with her head to the ground. He snapped
his fingers.

She looked up.

"I have learned much, my lord. There are spies in
your very household."

"Again! Damn Vixed, I told him to purge."

"Vixed is no longer capable of staying Biruma. She
has some information about him, something that she
is blackmailing him with."

Banwi sucked in a breath.

"You have proof of this?"

"No, Your Majesty, alas that is impossible. But I
have a source, a very good source."

He bent his head and indicated that she was to whisper only in his ear.

"What does Lopitoli intend?" he whispered harshly,
barely able to contain the rage that the merest mention of his mother's name brought on.

"She has placed Zanizaru in Ourdh. You are to be
poisoned when you next dine in Kwa. The arrange-
ments are all in place."

"Biruma?"

"Yes. She will doctor your wine when you are not
looking. She has a poison from Lopitoli that perfectly
mimics the effects of a heart seizure. You will fall to
the floor clutching at your chest, barely able to
breathe. You will expire there, and no one will be
able to point at Lopitoli. Then Zanizaru will be proclaimed and anointed."

"What counterstroke do you recommend?"

"Go at once to the city, take Zanizaru and cut off

his head. Show Lopitoli that her plots are penetrated. She will withdraw from the city for months, perhaps a whole year. In that time, you can regain control over the Shogemessar family finances. Then she will be helpless, for you can cut her out of your will."

Banwi chuckled.

"Ah, I like it. However, there is the problem of the Sephisti. What are we to do about them?"

Princess Zettila was finally at a loss.

"They cannot be defeated?"

"Unlikely." The emperor looked very grim. "They are about to destroy my army."

Princess Zettila became most anxious.

"Then we must escape, at once. Leave the field and ride south, get to Kwa tonight and cross the river. You can be safe in Ourdh by the day after tomorrow. And you can deal with Zanizaru."

The emperor had a strong urge to do exactly that and finally rid himself of his over-mighty cousin with his pretensions to the throne. Banwi had refrained from killing him before because of his fear of Lopitoli, and her enormous influence with the noble families.

But if he had real evidence that Lopitoli had conspired against him and planned to put Zanizaru in his place, real evidence, then he need not fear her retribution and he could strike back at last.

"The Sephisti will have the west bank, the Shogemessar will have the east," he said. "That is what I foresee."

Zettila nodded. "To have half the empire is better than to have none of it."

"I agree. Go now, fetch horses and a cavalry detachment, we ride at once."

Zettila paused at the door. "What about Auntie Haruma? Shouldn't we take her, too?"

"Yes, tell her to come here at once. Now hurry!"

CHAPTER THIRTEEN

The great Battle of Salpalangum was joined. A mass of perhaps one hundred thousand black-clad Sephisti fanatics crashed home against the sixty-thousand-strong army of the Emperor Banwi Shogemessar reinforced with ten thousand men and dragons of Argonath.

On the front of the Marneri Second Legion, there was now nothing to be seen but a forest of banners of the golden serpent writhing above the great mass of men in black with their round shields embossed with the serpent design. Their drums thundered constantly, and their shrill cries filled the upper register.

The legion tensed awaiting the shock while the Argonathi archers, men of Kenor for the most part, loosed salvos of arrows into the enemy host, dropping men by the hundreds, though it made no discernible impression on the onrush. And then the first rows of Sephisti soldier were upon them, whirling their swords above their heads and screaming in maniacal rage.

The dragonboys sucked in their breath with wonder at the sight of mere men, with little body armor, hurling themselves right at the dragons. The result was dreadfully predictable. The great dragon swords swung, hammering aside those of the strongest men and slicing through shields, armor, and anything else they met.

Very quickly the Sephisti began to pile up in heaps in front of the dragons. Occasionally one or two would slip through, but these were dealt with by the dragonboys and the dragoneers who were on them at once with crossbow and sword.

Against the swordsmen of the Second Legion, the Sephisti had little more chance. The men of Argonath fought as they had been trained. In this kind of battle, the power of discipline was overwhelming. The front man on the line wielded shield and sword. Behind him worked the second man with spear and javelin. The rectangular shields were designed with hooks and flanges on their edges so they might be locked together. As the enemy approached, the javelin men threw slender pilae made of soft iron, which sank into the shields of the Sephisti, then bent and made them unwieldy.

When possible, the Argonath front rank would lock shields with the men beside them, creating a wall of rectangular shields from behind which the spearmen could freely stab into the tight-packed mass of the Sephisti horde. Then the third or reserve line of legionaries would drop their own shields, put their shoulders to the front line as if they were in a scrum over a football, and help the front men to squeeze and compress the enemy on the other side of the shield wall.

And now the poor discipline of the horde worked its deadly affect, for more and more men came up at the rear and pushed forward, driving the men at the front into a dense mass, constrained by the shields of the Argonathi and unable to free themselves to fight. Virtually helpless, they were borne forward, tripping over the corpses of the men before them until they were offered up to the darting spears and stabbing swords thrust over the shield wall. Many would die with their arms pinned against their sides by the crush, no more able to fend for themselves than cattle in the chute to the killing floor.

The bodies mounted up in front of the Argonathi shields. And wherever a small break did open in that wall of metal, it was swiftly reinforced by roaming groups called the "pluggers." These were usually the strongest, heaviest men in a century. Their role was to get to any breach in the line and block it up quickly and efficiently.

Accompanying the pluggers were the archers, roving up and down the rear of the line, firing at targets as they presented themselves. The archers concentrated on enemy officers and horsemen, and took a deadly toll.

After about half an hour of this, the Sephisti horde opposite the Argonath line thinned out and then faded away, leaving an open space thickly carpeted with the dead and the dying. On either side of them the battle continued to rage, but on their front the legions were now given a healthy respect and two hundred yards clearance.

Like the other dragons, except the Purple Green who knew no better, Bazil Broketail did not enjoy this work. These men that he killed did not fight with much skill despite their passion. They were amateur soldiers. It was butchery. The Broketail almost wished there were some trolls on the field to give Ecator a proper workout.

Still, when men came at him with steel in their hands, he reacted as he had been trained. It was important not to let a man get inside your shield arm, that was the only real danger from a man with a sword. You kept him at bay with your own huge shield, and you cut him down with sweeps of the dragon sword. Men could jump almost three feet in the air to evade the sword, and they could crouch down to a little more than three feet. A sword swinging through at exactly three feet caught most of them.

Spears and lances were more dangerous. Here one had to take the shafts on the shield and then break them with the sword, since one could not reach the men behind them. Men without spears would retreat.

So Bazil had trained many, many times, and now he worked almost without thought. Ecator was a pleasure to wield, the balance reminded him of his old sword, Piocar, and there was an energy in the blade that seemed to make it much livelier than any sword he had ever wielded.

Back and forth he swung Ecator in a blazing net of slicing steel. No man could stand before him for very long at all, and few swords could parry more than a single blow from Ecator before shattering.

Occasionally a man's shield would stay the first blow, and then Bazil struck with tail sword over the shield or else kicked out with the talons on his feet to pull the man down and trample him.

Only a few got past the dragon. Relkin shot three who managed it and then finished them with the dirk. One of them came at him with the sword despite the arrow in his neck, and Mono ran in from the side to distract the Sephisti while Relkin slipped past his shield and struck up and in with short sword.

Relkin Orphanboy had become a soldier. He was no longer a youth from Quosh who sickened easily at such slaughter. It was his work. There was a grimness in his heart now, a band of metal that had been wrought by battle. And still there was something terrible about this.

Relkin felt as if he'd become a small cog in some windup killing machine, something inhuman that was formed from the disciplined work of ten thousand men and several hundred dragons. It had not always been so easy, nor so cold-blooded. He remembered the battle at Elgoma's Lodge in the winter campaign against the Teetol. That had been a very different kind of fight for a legion. The Teetol had learned from long and bitter experience not to engage blindly with a legion front. The Teetol fought with bow, arrow, spear, and short rushing charges at the flank of the dragon squadrons. The Teetol used ambushes and drop pits, giant snares in the forest to break dragon legs, fires set in summer heat in the thickets. The Teetol were still a dangerous foe, even for a full legion.

The horde of Sephis knew nothing of tactics, they came on as if by mere weight of numbers alone they could win victory, but, in fact, they were nothing but meat for the mincer.

With no trolls to stiffen their formations, the Sephisti soldiers could not stand against a legion with dragons. Once again the rule was proven.

It was not so easy, however, on either side of the narrow front held by the Argonathi legions. The Imperial Army was little better organized than the Sephisti horde, and considerably less enthusiastic for battle. At first they held and a confused melee broke out up and down the line, but as more and more Sephisti came up and began to break into their formations and to lap around the flanks, so the Imperial Army began to break down and run.

By that time, the soldiery of Ourdh had already been betrayed by all their leaders. First to abandon the field was the emperor, speeding away in a white coach with the Princess Zettila and an escort of shamefaced cavalrymen. Behind him came a torrent of carriages and gilded coaches as the rest of the court fled in panic.

At the sight of the Imperial Court seeking safety in flight, the senior officers, drawn from the ranks of the stekirs of the realm, also fled. Following them were the rest of the officers, nobles all with little in common with the fedd of the ranks.

For a while the ordinary men continued to fight, soldiers often will even when all reason for it has been lost. But without officers and under tremendous pressure from a fanatical enemy, they soon lost any cohesion they might have had and everything began to break down.

It began with a few in the rear ranks fleeing down

the road after the officers. Then came a trickle from
the central ranks, and then the fear took hold and
everyone still on their feet ran blindly away in panic.
Thousands sought safety inside the city of Salpalangum, but the gates remained shut.

Some of the Imperial cavalry units, the cream of
the army, held together and rode from the field in
more or less organized fashion, but most formations
broke down into mobs of scurrying fugitives running
as fast as their feet could take them toward the river
in the east.

In pursuit poured two rivers of men in black garb
that flowed around the Argonath legions like water
around a pair of square rocks. Once beyond the immediate battlefield, the enemy horde broadened out, by-
passing the shut-up city and heading eastwards.
Slaughter and looting began that would go on for
hours across the prosperous countryside of northern
Kwa. The Battle of Salpalangum was over, except that
the two Argonathi legions remained in the field and
under a calm set of orders began to transform their
dispositions.

The orders were received with little emotion by
most of the commanders of the regiments. Regiments
trained in flank maneuver were to move around line
regiments and take up flanking duties. Meanwhile the
line at front was to be shortened. The men, the dragons, everyone knew that they were preparing for an
attack of their own. Despite the vast numbers of Sephisti opposing them, the spirit in the legion soared.

Soared, that is, except at the helm of the Eighth
Marneri, where Commander Porteous Glaves received
the orders with anything but calm.

The Eighth was in the line between the Seventh,
who were skilled flankers, and the Sixth. This was
because the Eighth were a new unit and untrained yet
in flanking techniques.

Porteous Glaves, however, had seen the flight of

the court of Ourdh down the field behind him. Then
he had seen the flight of the Ourdhi generals and the
other officers, and finally he had watched with sinking
heart as the great mass of the Imperial Army broke
and fled.

The legions were now abandoned, completely surrounded by a sea of Sephisti fanatics. Glaves was filled
with rage and terror. He did not want to die here.
The Sephisti did horrible things to their captives. If it
looked like he was going to be captured, he must kill
himself and he wasn't sure he could actually do that.
On the other hand, he could not imagine enduring
extreme tortures. He ground his teeth and raged at
Ruwat, who had advised him to buy his commission
in the legions.

At the beginning of the fighting, Glaves had spurred
his horse up and down behind his men roaring encouragement to them and shouting insults into the enemy's
faces. He was determined to make a good show of it
and be seen by everyone in the legion to be in command and in full voice.

However, the men did their job with brutal effi-
ciency, aided by the indiscipline of the Sephisti mass.
There was nothing that was dashing or romantic about
this. The slaughter went on and on, blood flowed and
spattered high, and Glaves fell silent, disgusted by the
sounds of death and the morbid stench. Blood and
offal splashed up onto his trousers, flung back from a
dragon sword. More struck him across the side of the
face and down his shoulder. Revulsion turned his
stomach. He drifted back to the rear of the position
and sat his horse quietly with Dandrax at his side.
Occasionally he sipped water and winced when a
dragon blade made a spectacularly loud noise chopping through some hapless Sephisti.

Glaves struggled to think of some way out of this
trap. Flight seemed out of the question. Not only
would he be seen and condemned, but beyond the

legion's formation there was nothing but a great mass of Sephisti with packs of black-garbed cavalry dashing through ready to pick off someone like himself in a moment. Flight was out, surrender was impossible. There seemed to be nothing to do but to sit there, trembling, sweating, and praying for survival.

Then came orders from General Hektor, and the legion began to shift its regiments. The Eighth were ordered to hold their position and take over some of the line held by the Sixth, which was in motion around behind the Eighth, on its way to join the Seventh. Behind the Sixth came the Third regiment to further bolster the flank, and the legion became a three-sided weapon, a blade waiting to be hurled at the enemy.

Even before these maneuvers were completed, General Hektor had summoned the legion commanders to his tent. The general appeared very calm despite the disappearance of the vast Imperial Host. Once again Porteous Glaves told himself that he would never understand the military mind.

"Alright, gentlemen," said the general. "This is the situation. The enemy has lost cohesion, and most of his force is now chasing the Imperial rabble away towards the river. On our front there are perhaps twenty thousand enemy troops, perhaps less, and behind their center lies the headquarters of their army with their commanding officers. We will attack at once, keeping our front shortened to four regiments width, with flanks of four regiments and a central reserve of four regiments. Marneri Second will provide front and left flank, Kadein First will take right flank and provide the reserve. We will march at once!"

Drummers were sounding the signal, the silver Argonathi cornets blew, and the legions rose up as one and went forward at a steady trot across the open ground toward the center of the enemy mass, which lay about two hundred paces in front of them.

Arrows came whistling in among them, but the men

of Kenor were firing as they advanced, and their shafts were dropping the enemy's archers as fast as they revealed themselves.

Then came a surging mass of horseman, a cavalry charge. "Prepare to receive cavalry!" went up the shout.

Cavalry! They were going to be run down by masses of wild-eyed Sephisti calvary! Porteous Glaves felt his heart stop at the thought. He had read much concerning the new Talion tactics of heavy cavalry, and now was in total dread of being attacked by horsemen of any description.

To flee was impossible, to go forward was to accept death. Porteous saw arrows come hurtling toward him. He ducked and sobbed with fright. His horse shied suddenly, then his head bobbed up and there was a sudden thwack across his forehead as an arrow went skittering away. Stunned, he sagged in his seat and then fell out of the saddle.

His skull rang from the blow, but he was still conscious. He put a hand to his forehead, it was wet. He was bleeding. He stiffened with sudden hope. Perhaps this was the way to salvation? Perhaps the Mother had forgiven him his sins and was showing him the way? Porteous lay still. Dandrax leaped down to investigate.

"Be still, you fool, keep others away!" snapped Glaves from the side of his mouth. After a moment or two, he continued in a low whisper. "How much blood is there on my forehead?"

"Plenty. You need to have the wound bound."

"No, later. Now look behind us. Is the way clear for us to retreat?"

Dandrax looked back. The reserve regiments were passing them. General Hektor's staff was already ahead. Behind them were just the water wagons and baggage train, protected by a screen of pluggers and some units of Talion cavalry, ready to repel any marauders.

After that there was nothing, except the enemy dead and in the distance small groups of white-garbed men running away.

Dandrax looked to the front. The enemy cavalry were achieving little. They were not trained for a lances-down charge against a shield wall. Their horses were spooked by the presence of dragons.

"The enemy cavalry is breaking off and riding away. We can leave soon, master. Let the wagons go past."

Glaves lay there and stared up at the sky, which was so bright and blue and without a cloud. Salvation!

The wagons went by, Dandrax remained hunched over his fallen employer. A captain came by and detailed some men to stay with the commander and to bring him back to consciousness if at all possible.

Two hundred yards ahead of their prone commander, the Eighth Regiment hustled forward in the line, charging into the Sephisti center Guard, an elite unit of men selected for their strength and ferocity. The men of the Eighth had heard of Glaves's fall and their spirits had soared. Now they went in with a roar and were quite unstoppable.

The Sephisti Guard roared in its own challenge to the legion front, and swept forward with their swords high.

But now the legionaries threw their javelins, and the thin heads of the javelins sank home in the enemy shields once more. The javelins bent easily, but they were hard to pull out. A shield with two or three stuck in it was difficult to maneuver and easy to catch with the edge of one's own shield to open the opponent to a swift stabbing stroke of the sword, or to the stabbing spears and javelins from the men behind.

The formations came together with a crunch of shields on shields, but the Sephisti were already in confusion, and now the legions shattered the front ranks of the Sephisti Guards while the massed dragons smashed into the center and broke it asunder.

Beyond the shattered Guard division, there was a screen of cavalry and then the Sephisti high priests and their generals, who hurriedly mounted their horses in an attempt to flee.

The horses were unused to dragons, however, and were quickly panicked. Dragons and dragonboys ran through the disintegrating cavalry, dropping riders, knocking over horses, and breaking in at last on a group of terrified men on horseback who wore long black robes, golden fillets wrapped around shaven heads, and scarlet fetishes dangling from their belts. These men tried to spur their mounts to safety, but too late, for a wedge of Talionese cavalry had cut through on the right flank and swung in now to block their escape.

Relkin ran up behind a man of considerable girth astride a grey horse and vaulted into the saddle behind him. His dirk was against the man's throat. With a faint scream, the man threw himself from the saddle and lay writhing on the ground.

The broketail dragon stomped over and stirred the priest with his sword tip. The man came to his feet again with another shriek.

Two legionaries thrust forward, grabbed the fellow, bound his wrists, and lead him away. On his forehead was the prominent mark of the brand of the serpent.

Relkin dismounted and handed the horse over to a Talion trooper who took the reins and pulled it behind him to the rear. Relkin had his eyes on something else. There, behind a small black tent, a tall pole was thrust into the ground and atop it fluttered a special banner, in which the serpent god was worked in gold and red and surrounded with lettering in more gold.

"Their battle standard!" he shouted to Bazil. The dragon turned and waved his sword, and together they pushed their way through to the tent.

A handful of Sephisti Guards barred their way with drawn swords. Relkin put an arrow into one, and

Bazil engaged the rest. Steel clanged on steel as Ecator sliced and hummed through the air.

The last Guard toppled, clove neatly in twain. Relkin hauled down the Sephisti army's battle standard and tucked it away in his pack.

Then he vaulted up onto his dragon's back and took a look around.

The Battle of Salpalangum was over, at last. The Sephisti horde had broken up into a confused mass. The commanders, the generals, and their staff had for the most part been taken prisoner, and the center of the army was destroyed. The wings of the horde were still pursuing the remnants of the Imperial Army and were lost to any effective use for days, perhaps weeks. The legions held the field and remained intact. There had been very few casualties, morale was very high.

But General Hektor was not one to relax too far. He ordered that the position be fortified. A ditch was dug, stakes were set out, and a rampart was raised. Within it the legions stood down at last, while the moon rose into a night haunted with the cries of the enemy wounded, left dying on the field.

Hektor broke out whiskey and sent good measures around to every man. The Marneri Second were the most worn, and he allowed them the first sleep.

It was then that Commander Porteous Glaves returned to his men, brought in over his horse by Dandrax. His head was bandaged messily, there was blood all over him. Hektor sent his own surgeon to investigate while Dandrax set up a tent and put the commander to bed.

The surgeon found a long narrow cut across the commander's forehead, plus a large, purpling bruise. He reported that Glaves was very fortunate to be alive. "An inch to the right and it would have gone through the commander's temple." Hektor accepted this and put away thoughts of a court-martial.

Night fell across old Salpalangum just a mile away.

The city's lamps were lit one by one. In the legions' camp the spirit was high. Salpalangum would forever be known as a great victory. Best of all, the casualty list was short with less than a dozen dead, and the surgeon reporting no need for a single amputation.

Around the tents the men who were awake spoke animatedly, drank their whiskey ration, and sang a few songs. There was an excitement, a strange current of jubilation among them. They had performed the art of war at a level close to perfection. They had mown down the enemy as if they were corn. Exhilaration and pride leaped from eye to eye.

The dragons of the 109th, along with their dragonboys, slept through it all, too worn to do anything but fall down in their places and surrender to exhaustion.

CHAPTER FOURTEEN

Lagdalen of the Tarcho stood on the terrace on the top floor of the house of the merchant Irhan of Bea and gazed out at the enormity of the great city of Ourdh.

It was dark now, but the city was lit up with a million lamps. Great avenues like rivers of yellow lights stretching away into the heart of the city, where the towers of the Imperial Fortress of Zadul stood each with a powerful green lamp lit at its top.

Much closer, towering into the dark like a mountain, was the great ziggurat of Auros Colossus. High above at its peak, the statue of Auros Colossus was bathed in golden light.

The breeze was warm, and Lagdalen was wearing only a shift and a cotton skirt with sandals. The air brought odors of the city, jasmine from the gardens nearby, and ranker things from the west and the north, where the quarters were more crowded and poor. The southern warmth was a luxury for a girl from the northlands. She was conscious of the fact that she was a long way from home.

How unimaginable it all was for a simple Marneri girl. Why you could fit the whole city of Marneri inside the city of the Fedafer, which was merely a small section of the great mass of the city of Ourdh. Millions of people lived here, more than lived in all the Argonath cities combined.

Already she had seen sights she would never forget,

horrors she had been spared even in Tummuz Orgmeen, and things to marvel at, like the golden statue
of the goddess Gingo-La, which stood above her temple on the Imperial Avenue. She could see the statue
from where she stood, illuminated with a silvery glare,
glittering on a small pyramid set above the goddess's
temple.

She remembered how shocked she'd been when Ribela told her that there were no temples to the Great
Mother. It seemed unthinkable that the Ourdhi could
not understand that the Great Mother was behind everything, even behind their silly gods and goddesses.

The Mother was in everything. She was literally the
source of the substance of the world. Which was why
there were no statues of her, no idols in any temple.
She *was* the Temple in a way.

Lagdalen sighed. At another time, perhaps, she
would have been fascinated by it all. She would have
been thankful for the opportunity to see this and ex-
pand her understanding. But she was not; instead she
was perfectly miserable most of the time, thinking
endlessly of little Laminna with her laughing newborn's eyes. Was she well? Was she happy? Did she
miss her mother?

Lagdalen gave a small groan. Wessary was one of
the most maternal girls Lagdalen had ever known.
Laminna would be very well cared for. Laminna
would not even miss her true mother. By the time
Lagdalen returned to her baby, she would think that
Wessary was her true mother.

Lagdalen locked her teeth together. These thoughts
had to be banished. Someday, she rued, someday she
would bring her baby to see this place. Someday.

There was a sound behind her, and she turned. The
Merchant Irhan was striding ponderously toward her.

"How charming," he said. "You are enjoying the
view?"

"Yes, Merchant, very much."

"This is your first visit to Ourdh?"

"Yes."

Merchant Irhan puffed out his chest. He was a large, rotund man who wore simple caftan suits in dark colors, very much in the Cunfshon mode.

"I do hope you will form a good impression of the old place. We have nothing like this in our homeland."

She nodded. "Exactly what I was thinking myself."

"Ah, that breeze, that slight scent of corruption, the flowers of the garden, that is Ourdh to me. That and the great cooking on Hot Spice Street."

"Many people have mentioned that. I do hope we are able to visit it at least once."

The merchant's fat face broke into shock.

"Great Mother beside me! But of course you must go every night. The cuisine of the Spice Streets is the greatest of the world. Here they blend the sesame and wheat of the North with the olives, fish, and wine of the coast and the South. They add the tropical delights of Canfalon and the mushrooms of the eastern provinces with a dash of imported exotica from Eigo and the tropical isles. Ah, the Street of Spice. Believe me when I tell you that in Kadein there are only perhaps three restaurants that might match the first dozen or so here in Ourdh. We shall leave for one of my favorite establishments in one hour. To Endrydo's we shall go, an excellent place with a selection of wines that is quite enormous. How will that do? Will it suit, will it suit? By the Mother beside me, that will suit very well, I think."

He patted his capacious stomach.

"So, to Endrydo's. The baked duck and the falafel are wonderful. And you will love the spiced eels."

There was another sound at the door accompanied by a little tinkle. The merchant's wife, Inula, approached. On her square hat of black satin were attached several little bells that jingled constantly. She wore an evening gown of grey silk with satin shoes and hair raised in a fan around her head in the stiff, lacquered style of Ourdh. She descended on Lagdalen, took her hand, and squeezed it between both her own.

"My dear, it is such an honor to have you here. You are such an image of Marneri loveliness. Such freshness, such clear eyes. You are a living reproach to the jadedness of our lives here in this sinful old city."

"Lady Inula, it is I who am honored to be your guest."

"Why thank you, my dear. Do please remember me to your father, I knew Tommaso very well once. You know he spent five years in Bea when he was a young man."

"I will, lady."

Inula put a hand through her husband's arm and breathed in the spicy night air.

"Ah, the city, once it gets in your blood it's hard to ever let it go. Do you know on my last visit home, I felt quite unhappy? Bea is a small place, not even as big as Marneri. All those cramped little houses inside the walls, the closeness, the tightness. The smell of fish!"

She laughed. "We have become too used to this great city perhaps."

Lagdalen compressed her lips and spoke carefully. "But how do you cope with all the wickedness? We passed a slave market today. They were buying and selling people by the hundreds."

The merchant harrumphed. The Lady Inula spoke quickly.

"The ways of Ourdh are cruel. They are an ancient people, civilized when the lands of Veronath were still peopled by bears and wolves." She fluttered her hands.

"They have been this way for aeons. It's hard to understand at first, but you cannot escape the fact that under the cruelty, there flourishes a rich and vibrant culture. This is one of the greatest cities of the world. There are arts and skills here that are unknown elsewhere. You must visit the new exhibition at the Galleries of Palmook. The trompe l'oeil work of the new school of painters is absolutely wonderful. Amazing skill and very droll at times."

"And they leave the corpses of the condemned to hang on the gibbets of the Zoda," said Lagdalen.

Merchant Irhan gripped the rail of the balustrade and spoke in a calm voice as if reciting something he had said many times before.

"The Ourdhi believe that life means pain and sorrow as much as joy and pleasure. They believe they must celebrate all aspects of life. Even death. Their criminal justice system is brutal but effective. They pay for information, they investigate, and they convict. Those convicted of serious crimes go to the gibbet."

Lagdalen glanced down into the teeming street below. This was Kasfaar Street, a busy avenue for carriages, wagons, and a swarm of rickshas driven by slaves chained to their seats. Passengers in these rickshas commonly carried long, thin whips with which to urge on the ricksha men.

Irhan observed her for a moment.

"Ah yes, the ricksha system. Well, there you see the other chief aspect of their criminal justice system. Ricksha men are convicts of crimes of violence and thievery that do not merit execution. They serve their times between the shafts and are released, usually in much better physical shape than when they were first clapped into service."

Merchant Irhan seemed to approve of the system. Lagdalen was not sure.

"How do they know that the men are justly convicted, especially those who die upon the gibbet?"

The merchant laughed indulgently. "There are trials, there are courts. The thing is done officially. There is justice."

His wife gave a little snort and turned away. Lagdalen understood. Inula was not completely in agreement, but she would not contradict her husband. Her message was plain, though. There was justice and there was also corruption. Justice was muddied here by blood.

And here were the merchant and his wife, living in a house two or even three times as large as they would have had in Bea or Marneri. Four floors and twenty-four rooms, including a ballroom and heated bathing pools. It was lavish even to a Tarcho who had grown up in the best accommodations of the Tower of Guard. But for Irhan and Inula, it had become their way of life.

For this life they had abandoned their homeland, trading its austerity and purpose for a hedonic decadence. Irhan owned no slaves, or so he said. Inula claimed that the servants in the kitchens of the house were free, but Ribela had explained that they were bonded, part chattel, tied to the house itself. They were under threat of corporal punishment, and they were not paid above meals and maintenance or their part of the house. Lagdalen guessed that neither the merchant nor his wife were unduly upset by the notion of slavery. They had accepted the evil along with the great in Ourdh.

Suddenly she felt a familiar presence nearby, and she turned. Ribela of Defwode had joined them. Ribela wore her customary dark clothing, arrayed with silver mouse skulls.

"Lady," said the merchant, bowing. Inula bent one knee.

Ribela bowed politely in return.

"Brother Irhan, Sister Inula, a pleasant evening I believe."

"Most pleasant, my lady, and we thought we might

take you and Lagdalen to visit the Street of Spices, one of the wonders of the world. After your long voyage, you must be ready for some more interesting food."

Ribela's frozen visage cracked momentarily in a tight smile. The merchant's wife actually thought that the Queen of Mice was interested in what she ate, other than its nutritional qualities? She snorted, amused.

"Perhaps on another evening. Tonight, I am afraid we have work to do." Her gaze shifted to Lagdalen.

"We are expected at the palace. I wish to visit with the emperor. You will accomany me and take notes if required. Bring stylus and pad."

Inula was most disappointed. "Then tomorrow night perhaps?"

"Yes, perhaps, if we are still here." Ribela turned away with a tiny bow.

Merchant Irhan put a hand out to his wife's shoulder.

"Say nothing, madam," he muttered. "Say nothing."

Ribela and Lagdalen were gone.

"She is the Queen of Mice, dear, you must remember that. She is more than six hundred years old."

Inula nodded, "How could one forget? All those silver skulls. It seems quite barbaric somehow."

And Irhan pondered on the differences in which the world was seen by the Argonath and the Ourdhi.

CHAPTER FIFTEEN

The coach clattered smartly through the temple district on the Imperial Avenue. The traffic here was restricted to carriages and coaches, with just a handful of rickshas in the service of the administrative bureaucracy.

They passed under the mass of the Temple of Gingo-La, a mound fifty feet high and a half a mile long on which sat a small pyramid and a massive temple. Atop the pyramid glittered the statue of the goddess, who was depicted in flowing maternal clothing holding a baby in her arms.

Then to their left, they passed the much more massive ziggurat of Auros Colossus. Smaller temples and ziggurats lined the way, most of them devoted to one aspect or another of Auros. Auros Perfection was decorated in sea green tile; Auros Tranquility was a chilling white.

At last they left the temples behind and crossed the wide-open space known as the Zoda, "the open place" that served as parade ground and execution ground. Along the northern side of the Zoda there were rows of gibbets on which hung criminals slowly decomposing in the open air. Streams of ravens and carrion crows flocked in and out of that section.

Lagdalen glanced that way and then turned away with a shiver. Ahead stretched the great wall of the Imperial City, the city of the Fedafer, which was literally a city within a city.

The great Fedafer Gate loomed above them at last. A guard came forward and was fixed by Ribela's gaze. The gate was opened without further ado.

Inside, Lagdalen gazed at the seven palaces and the private temple to Auros, Emperor of the Universe. Every building was exquisite, even the barracks for the Fedafer's guard. Gardens lush with flowers, fruit trees, and topiary encircled the buildings. Great trees, already in flower, grew along the inner roads. Little carts, pulled by miniature donkeys, rolled along the roads, carrying shaven-headed eunuchs of the bureaucracy.

Finally they stopped outside the imposing gate of the Imperial Palace itself, a vast structure of white brick with towers and turrets in profusion above.

Inside, in a huge pale green entry hall with heroic paintings on a vast scale, they came to a stop by a red desk at which sat a eunuch in white robes with a polished skull on which a geometric pattern had been painted in red.

The eunuch avoided looking directly into Ribela's eyes, indeed he kept his head down, bobbing over his desk. He refused to look up at her at all. In his hand he held charms, and he mumbled charm spells to ward off the powers of the witch.

A messenger, a tiny little man, another eunuch in white robes, was sent through an inner door. The eunuch at the desk took out a pair of earplugs and ostentatiously inserted them.

Ribela sniffed.

They waited. Lagdalen could sense the mounting impatience in the lady. Ribela was not used to dealing with the world of men, she lacked the Grey Lady's skills in managing people.

They waited and occasional parties of eunuchs in the white garb of their caste would pass through the hall. At the sight of the Queen of Mice, they cast their eyes to the floor, put their fingers in their ears, and murmured prayers to Auros.

Ribela's anger was stoked further by these demonstrations. Lessis had warned her emphatically about losing her temper with the Ourdhi. "Men will react badly to such a display. You cannot win their hearts thus. Hear me Ribela."

Ribela had heard, but she cautioned herself that Lessis, in fact, had little experience with the Ourdhi. Lessis had never sought duty in the corruption of the southland. What the Ourdhi did in their festivals, especially those of the old river goddess Oona, horrified her too much.

The work of the Office of Unusual Insight in Ourdh had been carried out by others, by Vleda, Witch of Standing from Talion and Crissima, who was now Great Witch in Kadein.

So perhaps Lessis's advice about how to work with the Ourdhi was wrong. Perhaps more direct methods were necessary. Ribela glanced toward the eunuch at the desk. If those earplugs were removed, she could use her voice on him. He could be made to convey her directly to the emperor.

Lagdalen was looking at her. Ribela looked away with a stab of annoyance. The girl judged her by Lessis's standard the entire time. It was very difficult to follow in the Grey Lady's path, since Lessis of Valmes was the closest thing to a saint in existence. Ribela was not a saint; she could never stomach the way human beings mismanaged their affairs. It always made her want to shake them.

Now she, Ribela of Defwode, was supposed to wait here on the whim of this wretched little emperor, Banwi Shogemessar. She was supposed to wait, as if her time were not extremely valuable. She had left the entire Escopus project in the hands of her subordinates. Mother help them all if someone made any serious mistakes. She had to get back quickly. Already she had spent more than a week away from Defwode. She must finish this work and then return at once via the Black Mirror. That way she could be back in time to rejoin the Escopus project before the Solstice crisis.

Ribela looked back to the eunuch's earplugs. She itched to rip them out.

Lagdalen bit her lip.

A pair of double doors opened, and a small party of high officials was carried in in sedan chairs.

Exiting the chairs were two nobles with full heads of hair, long and unkempt. They wore elaborate garments of emerald green silk. With them were a pack of bald-headed eunuchs in white.

The eunuch at the table was bowing low before the new eunuchs.

"The Monstekir of Kwa and the Monstekir of Canfalon do greet you, Lady of the Isles," said one of the new eunuchs, who wore a purple cap on his shaven skull.

Everyone but the monstekirs now bowed low to Ribela.

Lagdalen was grateful that she had managed to learn so much Ourdhi in just the few days of their journey. Ribela had of course been the inspiration. Ribela had said that it was possible to learn much of a language in seven days if one applied oneself to the maximum. And Ribela had been right. They had spoken nothing but Ourdhi, and done nothing but studied it together every waking hour aboard ship.

"My dear, your mind is still young, still relatively elastic. You must stretch yourself, discover all your capabilities. You cannot know them until you seek them out."

Now Lagdalen found she could follow much of what was said and make deductions about the rest. It was amazing.

"We thank you," said Ribela. "Now, take me to the Fedafer."

The monstekirs twirled their batons and shook their heads.

"The Fedafer sent us to say that he is indisposed and must beg you to cancel your audience with him. Inquire tomorrow as to when a new meeting can be set up."

Ribela went rigid. Lagdalen tensed. One did not trifle with the Queen of Mice.

"In such dangerous times, it is sorrowful to hear of the Fedafer's illness. What is the cause? I am, of course, trained in the healing arts."

The monstekirs paled at the sound of Ribela's fluent but barbarously accented Ourdhi.

"It will not be necessary to trouble yourself," they said hastily. "The doctors have been working with the Fedafer for hours."

Ribela's eyes narrowed in puzzlement. "But only an hour ago my messenger brought me word that the Fedafer was ready to see me. How can this be? There is some inconsistency here."

The monstekirs squirmed. The eunuchs babbled among themselves.

Ribela's patience snapped, audibly. With a hiss, she took a deep breath. The eunuchs clapped their hands to their ears, but the monstekirs were too slow.

Ribela used a set of snap spells to hold them and murmured another small spell. Within a minute, they were all walking through the inner doors behind the monstekirs. The eunuchs trailed along behind muttering to themselves.

They proceeded through a series of rooms, each slightly smaller than the last and more like a jewel box.

Finally they stopped at a set of double doors with guards outside.

The monstekirs fluttered their hands and the doors were opened.

CHAPTER SIXTEEN

The Fedafer of Ourdh, lord of the well-watered land, master of the great river, provider for the mouths of the millions, favored first son of Auros, living consort of Gingo-La, august excellence of the south wind, bringer of rain, sower of seed, king of Ajmer, king of Bogra, king of Patwa, high lord of Shogemessar, Emperor Banwi the Great, was crouched, shivering with fear, on a blue silk couch in the apartment of his Aunt Haruma.

"What shall I do?" he begged.

Haruma looked at him with pity. Poor man, his nerves were disintegrating under the pressures. It had been coming for years, but the crisis had grown to such proportions that it was overwhelming him. Lopitoli knew this well and was playing to it. She knew her son's weaknesses.

"You must put aside your mother's plotting. If you catch Zanizaru, then dispose of him. You warned him after the last attempt, it is time the crocodiles feasted on Zanizaru. Lopitoli can be left where she is; without Zanizaru she has no heir to work with, not for a few years, until one of your younger cousins grows to maturity. In that time, you can prepare to deal with Lopitoli. At the moment, she is still too powerful."

"Bah! You say ignore her, but she is ignored at great peril. I know what she is capable of. There are so many tasteless poisons, including slow ones that take effect only after a day or more. My tasters are

no good against those, and Lopitoli knows them all.
Remember how my father died, he set himself against
her, and she killed him. Then she killed my uncles
and my brothers and Cousin Aloop. And you say ignore her?"

Haruma sighed. "Her position is not as strong as it
was, and you have the proof of Zanizaru's rebellion.
With a civil war on our hands, this is the very worst
time for a dowager empress to attempt such a thing.
You have the political advantage. The stekirs will all
follow you; she has isolated herself."

"Oh where is Zettila? Why is she not here?"

Haruma frowned. "Zettila plays her own game, you
know that. She is not necessarily to be trusted."

His face grew pinched with pique.

"I trust her, Aunt. She is precious to me."

"Just be careful, my lord, that is all I say." Haruma
knew that Zettila's extremism as a daughter of Gingo-
La had grown strong. Did the priestesses of Gingo-La
really have the best interests of the emperor at heart?

"My mother is the real threat!"

"You must concentrate on the enemy in Dzu, my
lord. They are more dangerous to you than anything
else."

"They can have the West. They can do what they
like as long as I hold the city and the East."

"But you are King of Ajmer."

"Bah! Nothing there but sand and flies. I will make
them a gift of Ajmer."

"But, my lord, why do you assume that they must
win? General Hektor defeated them at Salpalangum."

"Enough!" It was inadmissable that Hektor had won
a battle. The emperor had decided the battle was to be
lost, he had fled and his army had been beaten and fled
as well. It was not possible that that same battle could
then have been a victory, for the Argonathi troops.

"My lord, I am just your foolish old Aunt Haruma.
I want only what is best."

"You did not use to want anything, I preferred it that way."

"My lord, why will you not even listen to the things that General Hektor has discovered from questioning his captives?"

"It will be lies, woman. Don't you see that this is all a trick, a way to trick me out of what will be left to me. The Argonathi think they can take the East while the Sephisti take the West. They think they can leave me with nothing! But I see through their plot. They will not succeed."

Banwi's voice rose an octave.

"General Hektor marches on Dzu. He plans to be there before the enemy can mobilize to meet him."

"He will be taken and devoured by the serpent. I have seen this in my dreams."

Haruma rolled her eyes. How could the Argonathi general seize the empire if he was to be devoured by the serpent? Her nephew's wits are addled.

"My lord, your dreams should be heard by the soothsayer, why do you not go to her now?"

"She is an agent."

"Myela an agent? Of whom, lord? I have known her all my life, and she is trustworthy."

"My dream showed me that the foreigners will be destroyed. I will strike a bargain with the Sephisti. They can have the West, and I will hold the East."

Haruma felt despair grip her heart. How had Banwi wedded himself to this absurd conception?

There was a jingle at the door. A servant popped his head in and whispered to her. She nodded wearily.

"My lord, your cousin is here."

Banwi straightened up with a smile.

Princess Zettila fluttered in, and she was laughing.

"Oh, my lord, that witch was a sight. When the doors were opened and she walked into the empty room, I thought she was going to turn the monstekirs into dogs for a moment. I watched from the peephole

in the wall by the secret panel. She whirled and
screeched and uttered a thousand curses against your
name."

Banwi scowled. "Damn the witch! I will not see her.
They plan to depose me and take my throne, I will
not be fooled so easily."

Haruma sighed. Banwi was dooming himself. The
threat of Sephis was real, and Banwi was unable to
face the truth. Haruma wondered if she dared to approach the witch herself. Someone had to.

CHAPTER SEVENTEEN

By nightfall the following day, Ribela's messenger returned from General Hektor's army one hundred miles to the north.

Lagdalen received a summons to the balcony.

She found Ribela and a dirty-looking sea gull that was still getting its breath back after beating downriver against the wind all afternoon.

"There is news?" she said, at once hopeful.

Ribela looked at her unsympathetically.

"There is news, for you especially."

Lagdalen's heart thumped a little louder in her chest at that. What did she mean? Was Hollein alright? Did he still live? Had he been wounded?

Ribela soured at the expression on the girl's face. She wondered sometimes what Lessis had seen in this girl. At times she seemed most unsuited for the life of the Office of Unusual Insight.

"General Hektor is marching to Dzu at once. The enemy forces are disorganized and will remain so for days. By then he will be at Dzu, where we shall meet him and together destroy whatever this unholy thing is that the Masters have brought into existence there."

Lagdalen nodded attentively and took slow breaths to calm her racing heart. It was important to show no emotion, or else Ribela might not even pass on any news about Hollein. Lagdalen understood how Ribela despised human emotions.

Ribela stared at her for a long second, then relented.

"And a certain Captain Kesepton is well and unharmed. General Hektor made a point of adding this information. Considering that I never told him that you were accompanying me, the general seems very well informed, don't you think?"

Lagdalen flushed at the accusation.

"My lady, I have made no attempt to communicate with him."

Ribela smiled slightly.

"I don't doubt that, my dear, you understand the need for secrecy. But some chatterboxes in Marneri apparently do not."

"Yes, my lady." Lagdalen looked away, her thoughts far away with that captain of the legion, marching somewhere in the vast interior of Ourdh.

Ribela looked at the girl and felt a sudden stab of self-criticism. This was not something that happened very often. But at this moment, she felt that she was just a withered old hag who had forgotten how to be human. Here was this lovely young woman who had been torn from her first baby, whose husband was engaged in a great battle in an alien land, whose entire life had been turned upside down, and the Great Witch Ribela was utterly unable of feeling any sympathy. It was a wretched performance. Lessis would have handled it more skillfully.

"I am sorry, my dear, you must forgive me. I'm a little rusty on human relations these days. I've forgotten so much, you see."

Lagdalen held her tongue, not knowing what to say.

A messenger was announced by a servant. Ribela questioned him carefully and then admitted the messenger.

It turned out to be a woman in her late middle years, her body grown soft and quite plump from a comfortable life. She wore a veil and a full-length brown robe that covered every inch of her body and legs. It had a hood that swept up and covered her head.

Ribela sighed. This was the everyday costume of most Ourdhi women in public, unless they were slaves or prostitutes, and even most slaves wore the "garub" of Ourdh. Ribela was not accustomed to such extreme patriarchal social norms. Nor was Lagdalen who found it very strange. Here in Ourdh women were chattels not persons; it was unsettling.

The woman pulled aside the veil and the hood to reveal a fleshy face with thick lips and a broad nose. Her dark eyes were filled with a quiet wisdom that Ribela noticed at once. There was more here than met the eye.

"Greetings," said the woman. "I bring you word from a person with important information." The woman looked at Ribela beseechingly. "Perhaps for your ears alone, Great Witch."

Ribela gave a start. Who was this? How did they know so much?

"My message concerns the emperor."

Ribela had already reached this conclusion. This had to come from the emperor himself, or from his circle. Perhaps there was some explanation for the farce she'd been made to endure earlier.

"Who are you?" said Ribela in plain voice.

The woman licked her lips nervously. She was bad at dissembling. "I cannot say."

"Cannot or will not."

"Alone, only with you. It is not safe."

Ribela inclined her head to the door, and Lagdalen nodded and left without a word.

The woman took a seat on the terrace, near the edge. She waited for Ribela to join her.

"I am Haruma ba Shogemessar."

Ribela's eyes widened. So this was the emperor's trusted aunt.

"I see," she said. "Welcome then. And from whom are your messages from?"

"Myself. I did not want to arouse suspicion in your young campanion."

"She will tell no one of your presence here."

"I must try to explain the reasons for my nephew's discourtesy yesterday."

"Indeed?"

"The situation is confused. Banwi is under some kind of spell, I fear. He believes that the Sephisti will accept just half of the empire, and that they will allow him to keep the East. He sees plots and conspiracies everywhere. The Princess Zettila fills his ear with her tales of the family intrigues."

"As I understand it, he has good reason to fear his family."

"He eats almost nothing, he goes down to the kitchens in person to fetch bread and pickles. He never trusts any cooked food. He trusts no one, not even the tasters."

"This is not an enviable position to be in."

Haruma paused and took a deep breath.

"He will not see you. He thinks you will place him under a spell and engineer a takeover of his realm. He will not cooperate with General Hektor. He will do nothing against the Sephisti. I swear there is some sorcery at work."

Ribela had already made her decision in this matter. The sea gull's news would set her in motion now.

"Thank you, sister, for coming to tell me this. I will be leaving the city very shortly, and I will not make any further attempts to see the emperor on this visit."

Haruma's eyes clouded. "Oh, my lady, I wish you would see him. Someone has to break this spell that has him. He will not defend himself against the real dangers, he is obsessed with Lopitoli's plots alone."

"I cannot see an emperor who refuses to see me. I cannot do battle with the emperor's guards, I am but a single woman. I cannot see him. My time here is to be short. However, later perhaps, we will be able to investigate this sorcery you detect."

Haruma wanted to protest, but dared not. Ribela patted her hand.

"Thank you, sister, for your courage in coming here. I speak for the Emperor of the Rose in this, you will be remembered as a friend."

Haruma rose, resumed her head coverings, and left. Ribela meditated on the situation and attempted to divine the threads of the immediate future. It was time to investigate this thing in the city of Dzu. She had tried to identify it before from a distance and failed. As they were so close now, however, it should be possible to pierce the veils at last.

CHAPTER EIGHTEEN

The legions marched south for three days, swinging along at a steady pace down flat dusty roads through a landscape of palm trees, fields of wheat and mud-brick villages. Occasional vast ziggurats would loom above the plain and then be left behind. And everywhere around them they saw the peasant masses, the fedd, at work. Gangs of men dug ditches, single farmers ploughed with teams of bullocks, others traveled beside their donkeys, heaped with sacks of grain or bundles of firewood. In the villages swarms of ragged little children would follow behind the dragons with awestruck faces. Women peered out of the shadows or from the yards where they worked.

During the first day, they encountered evidence of the passage of the army of Sephis. Villages had been burned, fields scorched, and thousands of people set in motion, fleeing the devastation. On the second day, they glimpsed a few bands of Sephisti soldiers, all of which made haste to put more distance between themselves and the legions.

On the third day, they saw nothing but village after village with no sign of the enemy. Life here went on as it had for millennia, placid and eternal, blessed by Auros who looked on from the tops of the ziggurats.

The towns along the road increased in size as they proceeded south. It was apparent that they were close to a major city, which meant the great conurbation of Kwa.

Eventually the broad straight road became a street lined with buildings. Some of these buildings reached three stories in height. At noon, they passed an enormous ziggurat where a ceremony was in progress. A bull was sacrificed to Auros, and its blood cascaded down the stones of the temple ziggurat while brass horns brayed, flutes whistled, drums thundered. A crowd of men in white tunics covered one side of the ziggurat in dense profusion. They turned from the ceremony to stare at the Argonathi legions with slight surprise. Many Imperial Army formations had passed through here only a few days previously. They had become used to marching armies.

Then the dragons hove into view, and the men reacted with a collective gasp. Many came down to join the children in the road, following along, staring at the huge hulks of brown and green armor plate, as they swung along the road, eating up the miles.

An hour later, the legions paused for lunch. Fires were lit and the cooks made play with bread and beans, but were interrupted when hundreds of women emerged briefly from their kitchens with pots of soup, freshly baked breads, and even fresh brewed beer, which they distributed among the men.

It was a spontaneous display of the gratitude of the fedd for their salvation from the ravages of the armies of Sephis.

The men and the dragons ate colossal meals. General Hektor ordered extra-strong kalut to be brewed, but as soon as the word reached the womenfolk of the surrounding neighborhoods, a swarm of children were sent among them carrying gourds of hot kalut straight from the brew that constantly sat by the stoves of most Ourdhi households.

Recharged and refreshed, the legions resumed the march. In the distance now, off to their left, they could see the tops of the tall buildings in the central part of the great conurbation of Kwa.

The sight of the ziggurats and towers sent a new wave of jokes about the whores in Kwa through the ranks. Many a look of longing was cast that way. But the legion was marching around central Kwa, taking a road that stretched between two of the broad arms of suburbs that flooded out of the central district and up the radial roads. Between the radial avenues, the houses thinned out again, and there were extensive animal pens and manufactories.

By midafternoon, they began to notice the clouds in the far south. General Hektor had received a warning of rain from the weather witch. He tried to pick up the pace. He wanted to get his pair of legions well away from Kwa before nightfall. He understood the powerful temptations there would be otherwise.

The southern skies darkened swiftly and heavy storm clouds billowed up. Within two hours there began a drenching rain, accompanied by gusty winds.

They were still well within the suburban zone about Kwa, in a sector with many fine houses, surrounded by gardens and ornamental trees. The houses here were painted in many shades of sand and light ocher. Horse-drawn carriages were common on the side streets.

General Hektor cursed. This was not a good place to camp. There were men who'd be tempted to thievery. Others who would go absent to get to central Kwa and taste its pleasures. He would have to discipline men, there would have to be floggings. Hektor hated that side of the army life, but knew he would have to enforce the rules. The legions were held together by the rule book, and without it they were all doomed.

Talion scouts reported a nearby amphitheater of good size that would serve as temporary urban bivouac. Hektor sent out the weather witch, who spoke good Uld, the tongue of central Ourdh. The local authorities were found, and permission was obtained.

Two tired, wet legions marched into the local chariot racing arena and pitched camp. Hektor and his defense specialists went around the perimeter. There were a dozen entrances and exits, including subterranean ones used for dead animals and waste. It wasn't going to be easy keeping the men inside through the night.

Hektor and Paxion conferred. Paxion had long experience with such matters. He suggested that they issue a double round of whiskey. The men were exhausted after marching thirty-five miles a day for three days. Let the whiskey relax them, and they would sleep soundly soon.

Paxion's understanding of the men was correct. Only a handful of known troublemakers, two of them skilled thieves sent to the legions in lieu of long sentences on the prison island, tried to make it out. The rest sang some songs, laughed, chattered, and went to sleep in fine fettle with full bellies.

General Hektor breathed a huge sigh of relief.

"My thanks, General Paxion," he murmured. He straightened up. "General, I will ask you to take command for the rest of the evening. Major Breez has invited me and the surgeons to a meal in his tent. We have some things to discuss, and I intend to relax with a glass or two of Ourdhi wine. I'm told there are some good ones."

Paxion, though tired, was glad to be of service. Since the great victory at Salpalangum, he had been feeling old and useless. He was proud to receive General Hektor's trust.

Content with their preparations for the evening, neither man thought to look in on the dragonboys, who were too young to be given any whiskey at all. This was a mistake.

Indeed, as soon as the legions had finally pitched camp and settled down in the chariot arena, five particular dragonboys leapt into action with unusual zest.

Blister sherbet was applied to sore spots on dragon feet, and poultices and bandages were checked and changed. Food was brought for their giant charges, and each wyvern was given a cask of fresh brewed ale, donated by a local brewery. The beers and ales of Ourdh were justly famous, and dragonish mirth was soon making the ground shake. However, it was a short-lived thing since the wyverns were close to exhaustion. Soon they were snoring at the usual thunderous volume.

Five dragonboys gathered at the prearranged spot. The outer wall of the arena was old and pitted, an easy climb for nimble youths. Swane of Revenant went upwind of a pair of guards stationed to cover the southern quadrant of the wall. The others gathered downwind. Swane made a small fire from oily rags. The guards smelled smoke and went to investigate. Swane hid himself in a crevice in the wall.

The other four climbed over and made a swift descent. Then they waited by the foot of the wall in the shadows.

The guards investigated and found nothing but a few ashes. They sniffed around but soon gave up and went back to their post. As they left, Swane signaled and then started to climb down. When he was halfway down, the others stepped out and drew a blanket taut between them, and Swane jumped the last twenty feet.

The arena sat at a crossroads where the west trending road they'd marched along intersected a great radial avenue. This avenue was wide and packed with traffic of all kinds. It was lined with many shops and arcades, many of them still open, lit up with brightly colored lanterns of scarlet and green. On the pavements here were throngs of shoppers, including women, all of them clad head to foot in the traditional black garb. These were not the women the five dragonboys were interested in.

"Out for the night! Alright my boys, here we go."
Swane of Revenant claimed the leadership of the
group, basically because he was taller and more heavily built than any of the others. Tomas Black Eye,
who tended Cham, went along with Swane. Shim of
Seant, who tended Likim the big brasshide, accepted
Swane's leadership as well. Mono, who tended Chektor, was less acquiescent, and Relkin of Quosh went
his own way completely. He did, however, accompany
the others on his quest, driven by a desperation known
only to youths on the verge of becoming men. There
was always a slight tension between Swane and Relkin. Relkin had seen too much real combat to be
overly impressed with Swane's swagger. Relkin knew
that skill with dirk and sword meant more than brute
strength.

They headed down Sokwa Avenue into the heart of
the city of Kwa. Despite the drain of the three days
hard marching, they fairly skipped along the great
paved avenue, dodging wagons and gaggles of women
in black. Quite soon they found a side street where
several establishments that sold beverages and food
put out chairs and tables in the streets. The sound of
the wailing uinbor and the thudding zambala came
from darkened rooms filled with swaying men.

"Down here, this looks lively enough," said Swane.

The smell of hot kalut and the sour reek of stale
beer pervaded the air.

Inside the doors of the beer halls, they glimpsed an
atmosphere dark with smoke and they smelled the
reek of batshooba, a narcotic bush that was smoked
by the men of Ourdh. There were no women in sight.

For a moment the dragonboys were nonplussed.
Where were the famous fleshpots of Ourdh?

They slipped into an establishment that seemed less
smoky than the rest. Swane of Revenant negotiated a
round of mugs of a dark, heavy beer.

The dragonboys sipped the beer.

"Interesting," said Shim of Seant. "More bitter than beer at home."

"Ach, Seant beer is all piss. This is good, more like a Marneri beer," retorted Thomas Black Eye, who was always free with his opinions.

"I'll give you piss you one-eyed monkey."

"Enough of that," said Swane. "Look over there."

A heavyset man in a grey coat with jeweled rings on his fingers and a red velvet skullcap was passing through the tables, speaking to the men drinking beer. Their responses were cheerful, sometimes insulting, but the man took no offense. He laughed with them and moved to the next group.

Swane wagged a forefinger.

"That, my friends, is a pimp. Now we can see about what we came for."

Swane signaled the fellow. They exchanged a few sentences of Uld. The fellow instantly guessed who they were and soon understood what they were seeking. He emitted a short bark of laughter and mimed the counting of coins with a lascivious sneer.

They produced silver pieces minted in Marneri. The man tried two or three with his teeth and laughed again, then gestured that they should follow him toward the rear of the establishment.

Swane was already up on his feet. Tomas and Shim were quick to join him, then Mono. Relkin however stayed put.

"What's wrong wit' you? Afraid to get your wick wet?" sneered Swane.

"I don't trust that man, that's all. There'll be others."

"What's he say?" said Shim.

"I don't know, doesn't like this pimp we got."

"What's wrong with him?"

"Ask the Quoshite."

Shim looked over to Relkin. Relkin of Quosh was the one they all respected the most, but he was withdrawn, hardly friendly sometimes. It was difficult to know what to make of him. Relkin said nothing. Mono turned to him and shrugged. "You know there may not be another opportunity, my friend."

"There'll be another pimp."

Mono shrugged again and went with the others. They disappeared into the crowd. Relkin finished his beer alone and soon began to feel stupid for not going with them. What was the point of climbing down the wall after all? He hadn't come just for a beer. He wondered if he'd reacted that way because Swane had seen the pimp first. It was Swane's pimp, so he couldn't possibly like him. Sometimes Relkin wondered why it meant so much to him.

However, no sooner had he set down his glass then another pimp was beside him. This was a smaller man, with fewer rings on his fingers and a thin mustache. He wore a little square hat of some shiny black material and a black and gold gown.

"You are a visitor to the city?" he asked in a slightly singsong Verio. "You wish perhaps to sample some of the pleasures of life?"

Relkin nodded. "You speak Verio?"

"Yes, I trade for many years with Verio peoples. Come with me if you like a good clean girl, not a street whore, very clean."

Relkin licked his lips. This was what he'd come for. And still he felt a flicker of doubt. Then his resolve returned. He had to get this over with, it'd been driving him crazy for months. And in the legion there was damned little chance of meeting any girls.

"Come," said the man in the black box hat. "You are from the cold North. For a piece of silver, you may feel some of our southern warmth." The man smiled and gestured, "You are from the North, yes?"

"Yes, from Kenor."

The man nodded and smiled. "Yes, I know it. Very

cold." The man laughed, displaying teeth stained brown from batshooba smoke.

"But you come with me now, for I have a sweet girl who you will like. Cost only one silver piece."

"Marneri silver?"

"Yes, Marneri silver very good. One silver piece, you have good time."

"I have good time first and then silver piece," said Relkin holding up a single Marneri coin.

The man nodded, rubbed his hands together, and lead Relkin to a back entrance to the beer hall. They went down a narrow street with two-story buildings on either side. On the upper floors of these buildings were balconies on which sat young women, their faces and most of their bodies exposed. In the chambers behind the balconies, they practiced their trade and lived their sad lives.

Relkin gazed up at them, at faces like masks of beauty that appeared for a moment and then disappeared behind a fan. Bodies were contorted for his gaze, and mocking laughter followed when he blushed and averted his eyes.

The man showed him to a door, which opened at the knock. An older women conducted Relkin to an upper chamber, a door was opened, and he stepped within. A girl, no more than eighteen years, lay on the couch. She wore a flimsy robe belted at her waist.

He stared at her. A single silver piece didn't seem enough somehow. She was beautiful, with creamy brown skin, straight black hair that grew to her shoulders, and a sultry softness to her lips that seemed to beckon to him.

Relkin felt himself harden anew.

The older woman was smiling and nodding and pointing to the girl. Then she closed the door.

With a deep breath, Relkin strode over to the girl and sat beside her. She did not move and once more his doubts resurfaced, but he dismissed them, smiled ingratiatingly, and stroked her leg.

She shuddered, closed her eyes, and lay back with a little moan. It was not quite what he had been expecting.

"Hey, I'm not that ugly!"

To his surprise, the girl raised her head.

"You are from Veronath?" She said in fluent Verio.

"Veronath? No, girl, there is no Veronath. That died a long time ago. I am from Argonath."

"But you speak Verio."

"Yes, of course."

"Why are you here?"

"Here? Well, I . . ." suddenly Relkin caught himself. What was this? He'd come here for a whore. He flushed.

"I might ask the same about yourself."

"I am not here by choice." She shifted on the bed, and Relkin saw that she wore bracelets and that chains ran from the bracelets to the iron posts at the head of the bed. She was literally chained to the bed.

Relkin was appalled. This was definitely not what he'd expected.

"And I didn't want to go with Swane's pimp!" he said with a groan.

"What did you say?"

"Nothing. I, well, I'm with the legions. We're here to fight the Sephisti army, to help the emperor."

This was ridiculous, he couldn't rape someone who was chained to a bed. His desire had vanished.

"You are a soldier? You look a little young to be a soldier."

"Dragonboy, one hundred and ninth dragons, Marneri Second Legion." He said it with pride.

"Dragonboy? What does this mean?"

"I am paired with a dragon. I take care of him. We fight as a team."

"I have heard that dragons fight in the armies of the North, that they are very terrible."

"They are when they're aroused."

"And you have brought these terrible monsters to Ourdh?"

"Yes. We fought the enemy four days back, up north from here."

"And you defeated the enemy?"

"Big battle."

"Yes, that was what they were expecting when I was abducted."

"When you were abducted?"

Her lip curled. "Did you think I was some common street whore?"

"To tell the truth, no I didn't."

"Well, you have some wits at least. I am Miranswa Zudeina, and I am here because my evil, hateful aunt had me abducted. She wishes to steal my inheritance."

He sucked in a breath, astonished.

"My father died recently. He was a Dneej and a great merchant. He hated Aunt Elekwa. Some say she poisoned him. He would not leave her anything in his will. I would have inherited everything."

"Why should he leave anything to this aunt of yours anyway?"

"Elekwa is the first wife of the emperor's brother, and very powerful. We always believed that she poisoned my mother, she was jealous of her beauty."

"So you think she killed both of your parents?"

"Yes. My father could not hide his hatred of her."

"Hmm, sounds like your father bequeathed you a lot of trouble then."

She agreed with a toss of her head. Then she broke into tears. His heart was rent.

"And now," she sobbed, "now I am condemned to be raped here, over and over again for the rest of my life."

Relkin had never met with such outright injustice.

"I will not let it happen!" he exclaimed.

"You will help me?" She seemed surprised.

"Of course. We're going to get you out of here right now."

"The slave master will take you."

"He can try." Relkin pulled his knife.

"You will be castrated and sold as a gardener."

Relkin didn't give it a second thought. There was a single window in the room, and he opened the shutters. Below, there was a small courtyard with the backs of other buildings on the far side. There were several doors, some of them open.

"All we have to do is climb down and go out through one of those buildings."

"And then what? We'll be in the middle of Kwa, and you will be a thief. Thieves they sell in the slave market. I will be returned to the slave master, and they will beat me and chain me up again."

"No, we'll go to the legion and tell General Hektor. He will not allow this."

Her eyes came alive at this. "How far is it to your legion's camp?"

"A mile or so, we can be there in ten minutes if we run."

She licked her lips, looked to the door, and calculated that this was probably her only chance of escaping the horrifying fate that Aunt Elekwa had arranged for her. No one would ever find her here and with Daddy dead, she had no protector. She would stay here chained to the walls in Zedd's whorehouse until she was too old and worn-out to serve anymore. Then she would be sold to some other slave master and taken on the rural circuits to service old men in the villages.

"Let's go."

He levered away the links connecting the chains to the cuffs on her wrists.

"We'll get those off you once we get you to the camp."

Miranswa was an agile girl, and though not gifted at climbing, she managed well enough until they reached the ledge atop the first-floor window. She slipped and fell the rest of the way, landing by chance on some bales of hay stacked along the bottom of the wall.

Relkin was down beside her in a moment, and together they ran across the courtyard and darted into an open doorway. Behind them there came a hoarse shout of rage. Then they were plunged into darkness and found themselves inside a room thick with bat-shooba smoke. Men were sitting around small tables drinking kalut and smoking batshooba through large water pipes that gurgled.

At the sight of Miranswa, who wore only the silk robe provided by the whorehouse, the men jumped to their feet. Shouts of anger and astonishment arose.

By the time they reached the door, they were being pursued by a dozen or more men who bellowed as they came, enraged at this insult to tradition and taboo.

Outside in the street, Miranswa's clothing was just as problematic. In Ourdh, all women wore the garub in public and kept their heads covered. A woman wearing a silk robe tied at the waist and nothing else would be arrested and quite possibly hanged in public after a brief trial.

Relkin dragged her into a small, hole-in-the-wall shop that appeared to sell cloth. The owner appeared, a short round man with an oily smile. His face purpled at the sight of Miranswa, and then Relkin had his dirk up against the man's throat.

Miranswa found some black cloth, a fine woolen. A mark along the side denoted it as woven in faraway Cunfshon, by deft hands in old Defwode. Hurriedly she cut herself a large piece that she contrived to wrap around herself and pin together in front like a garub. She cut another piece and wound it around her head. For a veil, they took the man's handkerchief. Relkin dropped a couple of pieces of silver from his purse into the little man's nerveless hand, then they fled.

The shopkeeper had emerged from his shop and was yelling after them when Relkin waved down a ricksha pulled by a pair of men chained to the rail. Miranswa climbed aboard and shouted something in Ourdhi to them, and the men took off at a fast walk. Relkin crouched in the back next to Miranswa and looked behind them.

The shopkeeper and his fellows were standing in the midst of the avenue waving their fists, but no longer pursuing them.

However, Relkin knew, they would soon run into the pimp and his guards.

"We need to get out of this ricksha soon. Get another one. The pimp will be after us."

"No need," she said. And then she gave the ricksha men new orders, and they began to turn to the right and then entered another, smaller street, a narrow place running between rows of two-story mud-brick tenements. Miranswa turned them again, and they entered a slightly grander street.

Relkin was beginning to feel lost. There was no sign of pursuit behind them.

"Where are your friends?" she asked.

"The camp is in an arena, they use it for chariot racing." Miranswa conversed with the ricksha men and soon had them heading north along a small avenue lined with large three-story houses, some of which were surrounded by gardens brimming with flowers. Quite soon the walls of the arena became visible, and Relkin realized that he was going to be in a great deal of trouble. How was he going to explain this away? He'd be lucky if he wasn't flogged out of the legion.

CHAPTER NINETEEN

Porteous Glaves fidgeted in his tent. This night would be the making of him or the breaking. He had decided that there was no other way.

The moment of decision had come when General Hektor had refused his plea for compassionate leave and ordered him to remain at his post. There was a sloop, the *Ivory* from Talion, in the port of Kwa. It was heading back to the Argonath shortly. Porteous Glaves had hoped to be aboard when she left.

Glaves wore a massive bandage on his forehead where the surgeon stitched a long shallow cut. The surgeon had seen many such wounds. He remarked to General Hektor in Glaves's presence that normally men got up and fought on with blood in their eyes. With such a wound, they didn't lie prone on the battlefield until the fighting was over.

Hektor had turned to Glaves with brooding eyes and told him curtly to return to the Eighth Regiment. Glaves had made his decision then and there.

Glaves exhaled and poured another glass of the Ourdhi wine. His eyes fell on something, and he guffawed suddenly. No one would ever discover the truth, he'd make sure of that!

Leaning against the side of the tent was the captured banner. He'd had Dandrax bring it to him from the dragonboy's tent. Porteous intended to send it back to Marneri that very night with a long note attached that would explain how Porteous Glaves had personally captured the banner after leading a heroic charge that broke the enemy line and ended the battle.

His messenger would be the captain of the merchant sloop *Ivory,* which would sail within the hour and be in Marneri in a week.

Glaves poured more wine and rolled it around his mouth, savoring it. The local wines were very good, rich and fruity, with a degree of complexity. He wondered how General Hektor was enjoying the wine at his dinner with Major Breez.

Glaves was moved to chuckle at the thought. Soon, very soon he would be released from this mad adventure. Within days, he'd be on a ship himself and on his way back to a glorious reception as a war hero in Marneri.

There was a movement at the flap. Dandrax looked in.

"Visitor for you, master."

It was Captain Streen of the *Ivory,* a lean-faced fellow from Vusk.

"Commander, I will put in to Marneri for you within the week. Once we beat out of the gulf of Ourdh and get around the Cape, we'll be running in front of the wind the whole way."

"I am very grateful to you, Captain, as will be the people of Marneri to whom you will be taking this token or our conquest here in Ourdh. The morale of the city will be greatly improved, you can be certain."

"And I will be a gold piece to the better, correct?"

"Ah, yes, of course. You will go at once to Master Ruwat, and you will give him this letter. He will pay you."

"Well now, Commander, I do like to be paid in advance in matters such as this when I've not dealt with the shipper before."

"Captain Streen, are you doubting my nature? Be

assured that I have no need to stint you for your coin. And besides, this is for the cause."

"Aye, that it is and I honor you for it, but if I trimmed my sails for the cause every time, I turned around, the *Ivory* would not be mine for long. We must make money, and I must get my cargo to Talion as soon as I can."

"Captain, I am shocked at such a lack of patriotism, but I must put it down to the vagabond life lived by those who go to sea. I will give you five silver pieces, and when you see Ruwat, he will give you five more."

Glaves altered the letter to Ruwat and then bade the Captain farewell.

With a sour chuckle, he poured himself more wine. Silently he toasted the future. Just a few more days of this, and he, too, would board a ship for home. Porteous Glaves drank deeply and then emitted another roar of laughter.

At the gate to the arena, Relkin and Miranswa climbed out of the ricksha, and he paid the ricksha men with two copper pennies.

The guards held them while a message was sent at his request to Captain Hollein Kesepton, who served on the staff of General Hektor. A few minutes went by, and then the Captain appeared. He seemed flustered.

"What is it? This is no time for jests."

Quickly Relkin explained. Kesepton ordered that the girl be taken to the quarters of the weather witch. Then he sent Relkin back to his post.

"You and the others will be punished for this you understand. Right now we have more important matters to deal with."

"Others?" said Relkin, trying to keep up the pretense.

"Swane and the rest. They were clever enough to mistake a priest of Auros for a pimp, and he took a dislike to young, arrogant foreigners hunting for whores in his neighborhood. So he arranged for them to get a beating. They were dumped at the gate here from a dung cart."

Relkin gave a low whistle. So he'd been right, after all. In a way.

He noticed men rushing by, there was an air of tension and confusion.

"What has happened?"

Kesepton's brow furrowed. "While you've been out rescuing fair maidens, General Hektor, Major Breez, and the chief surgeons have been poisoned. Their wine at dinner, I believe."

"But how?"

"We've been lax about accepting food and drink from the local people. Something like this was bound to happen sooner or later. The enemy here is well represented throughout the country. Anyone could have slipped them a poisoned bottle."

Kesepton dismissed him, and Relkin returned to the 109th dragons with his thoughts in a whirl. He found the dragons still fast asleep, but the dragonboys were wide-awake. Dragoneer Hatlin sent for Relkin and put him on punishment detail at breakfast.

Swane of Revenant and the others were in a group drinking some hot soup. They had bandages on blackened eyes and bloodied noses.

"You were right, Relkin, we went with the wrong man," said Shim, whose little snub nose had been broken in the beating. "How did you make out?"

Relkin restrained any urge to boast. Mono's eyes were blackened, and his face was rubbed raw where he'd been dragged along a street. Swane of Revenant was huddled over, he didn't look up.

Solly Gotinder, who tended Rold, a big brasshide, was stirring some soup in a pot.

"So our man from Quosh is back. How was it?"

Relkin accepted some soup. It was hot and salty.

"Not what I expected."

Solly chuckled, "At least you didn't get beat to a pulp."

"Well, whatever will be, you know. We all make choices in life."

"That's right. Now you got punishment detail in the morning. You better get your head down for a while."

"What's the rumor mill saying about what happened to General Hektor."

"Well, they're hunting for whoever it was that gave them the wine. But we've all been accepting gifts from the locals, so I don't think they'll have much luck. Anyway, I heard that the general had about half a glass of the wine. He's unconscious, but he's alive. Major Breez is dead and so is one of the surgeons."

"So old Pax is commanding officer then?"

"Right, but there's trouble with the Kadeini. They want General Pekel."

Relkin groaned.

"Pekel thinks that since the First Kadein is the senior unit, he should be in command. Of course, Paxion has been a general for ten years while Pekel was only jumped up from commander at the beginning of this campaign."

"Those damned Kadeini think they should always be the leaders."

Relkin sipped his soup glumly and then turned in and tried to sleep. He didn't even notice that the banner he and Baz had captured had been taken from his tent.

Meanwhile General Paxion was confronting a very unpalatable situation. Sleep was out of the question. Paxion was the obvious choice to replace Hektor, but now Pekel was making absurd claims. Pekel was demanding that the leadership of the expedition devolve on him despite General Paxion's seniority. It was unheard of, a complete departure from the rules of the legion. The insult was insufferable, Paxion had been fighting battles when Pekel was still at school.

To make things worse, there were more problems beyond the matter of Pekel. Pekel was not even the complete master in his own legion. Some of the commanders were real Kadein aristocrats and unwilling to take orders from a career officer like Pekel, whom they considered their social inferior.

These men, like Err Dastior and Vinblat, had been insubordinate even to General Hektor, who had threatened to have Dastior flogged if he disobeyed orders again.

Paxion felt almost overwhelmed by it all. But he knew he could not give up. They were but ten thousand men and a few hundred dragons lost in the vastness of Ourdh. They faced a terrible enemy, who, although defeated in one battle, would surely be able to put another army into the field.

The guard pulled back the flap, and the surviving chief surgeon came in. The man was pale and smelled faintly of vomit.

"You are able to function?" said Paxion.

"Yes." The surgeon sat down. "A little unsteady still, but I've purged and I don't think I took enough of the wine. I had but a sip."

"The major?"

"Dead before the meal was over, sudden, painless. That means a nervebane, these things can be deadly."

"The general?"

"Coma. He drank but half of his glass of the wine. The major drank a whole glass, Surgeon Paris drank two."

"And survived the major I understand. We had a report."

"Aye, he did. Surgeon Paris was a large man and used to wine. Perhaps it took longer to work on him."

"And, you, Surgeon Tubtiel?"

"I was drinking from another bottle of wine, a white

wine that I brought myself. The poisoned wine was red, a famous vineyard here. I was going to drink some. I was very lucky."

"Coma?"

"Peculiarly tricky thing coma, sometimes they never wake up. No pattern to it that I can tell. We will simply have to wait."

"Well, we can't wait here. We must move."

"General Hektor should be moved as little as possible, of course, but if we must move on, then we must."

Paxion sent messages to General Pekel and all the other senior officers. They were to meet him for breakfast. By then he hoped he would have decided what to do next.

CHAPTER TWENTY

Dawn broke grey and murky over the chariot arena. Relkin reported to punishment detail, and was given buckets and sent to fetch water for the legion's breakfast. The pump was located on a subfloor of the stables. There were twelve steps between them. Relkin climbed the steps many times before he was allowed a meager breakfast of his own. At last the punishment detail was dismissed, and he ran to take care of his dragons.

He found them breakfasting cheerily on loaves of fresh baked bread smothered in akh brought them by the other dragonboys. They greeted him with dragonish chuckles. They had obviously heard all about his adventures.

Relkin ignored the lofty reptilian comments about the weaknesses of humanity, in particular of dragonboys, and worked on the Purple Green's sore feet with antiseptic and blister sherbet.

All too soon, the cornets were blowing and orders came down for them to form up and march.

While quickly packing his gear, Relkin discovered that the banner they'd captured from the Sephisti was missing. His heart sank. Worse even than the loss of the banner was the thought that someone in the unit would steal it. He reported the loss to Hatlin, who went pale with anger.

An investigation was begun, and Hatlin searched through the baggage but no trace of the banner was discovered. Solly Gotinder, Rold's dragonboy, reported seeing Dandrax wandering through the 109th tents carrying something.

Relkin was left downcast. If Dandrax had taken it, then he quite probably had the backing of Commander Glaves. Getting it back would be no easy matter.

"I don't know what we can do. I'm under a cloud as it is, and we can't just accuse Commander Glaves of stealing it."

The dragons' long tongues flicked in and out for a while as they thought about this.

"Perhaps we have to persuade him to tell us the truth," said Bazil at last.

Relkin shrugged. Dragons were often impractical when it came to human affairs. Glaves was the commander of the regiment; they could not simply twist his arm behind his back. Naturally, Dragoneer Hatlin agreed on this point. The 109th would have to seek justice from a higher authority, and it would not be easy. They had no proof and no way to order a search of Glaves's belongings. Teeth gritted, Dragoneer Hatlin promised to find some way of recovering the banner.

"You have my word on it, Dragoneer Relkin."

Relkin was not encouraged.

"Maybe we ask questions of the man Dandrax," grumbled the Broketail.

Hatlin pursed his lips.

"I never heard you say that," he said.

Dragon eyes zeroed in on him. Then they looked at each other. Hatlin moved away.

"Time will come for it," said the Purple Green.

They fell in and awaited the order to march.

Drums thundered, the cornet shrilled, and the First Kadein came marching past them with their colors held high. Rank after rank of men in grey and green,

steel helmets polished, shields over their backs, went
by and moved out of the arena.

At the rear came the Kadein dragons, leatherbacks,
brasshides, gristles, and greens, a proud sight in their
polished steel and fine leather joboquins. They went
slouching past, their huge swords bobbing together
above their shoulders. As they went, there were a few
terse remarks in dragon speech, things that sounded
like snarl-hisses and grunts to human ears.

Behind the legion came the wagons and coaches
carrying the surgeons and their equipment. Among
them was a small coach, two women on the driver
board. For a moment, Relkin glimpsed Miranswa
there, behind the weather witch. He raised a hand to
wave to her, but his whistle died on his lips when he
found Hatlin glaring at him the next moment. Miranswa disappeared into the wagon as it reached the
gates.

Gloomily, Relkin wondered if he would ever see
her again. Hatlin stormed by, there was a problem
with Vlok's pack. One of the straps was loose.

"Where are we going, Dragoneer?" called someone.

"Ourdh, damn it, we're going to the city of Ourdh."
Hatlin did not sound happy. He berated Swane for
letting a strap work loose on Vlok's pack.

"I ought to make you carry it," he snapped. "Hurry
up and repair it. We're not going to be the ones that
slow down the entire legion."

Swane worked furiously with thongs and needle
while around him there was a buzz of conversation.

Everyone knew this was a change of plan. They
were supposed to be marching full tilt to Dzu to destroy the heart of the Sephisti menace. Now they were
retiring to Ourdh.

"It'll be the Kadeini, you can bet on that," muttered Dragoneer Hatlin as he went by. There were
many rumbles of agreement. The Kadeini wanted to
go home without finishing the job, everyone knew

this. The Kadein First Legion had been due for two years back in Kadein, and had been none too happy with being sent to Ourdh instead.

They marched, swinging out onto Sokwa Avenue and heading into the center of the city, with the whistle and the drum to lighten their hearts. The crowds stopped to stare, and then to cheer them as they went by and the men stiffened their backs and marched as if on the parade ground. They went through the gates into the crowded heart of the city, and the throngs around them grew even larger.

Then they were on the great bridge of Kwa, marching out of the city and across the mile-wide expanse of brown water that was the Oon. This was the last bridge, actually a series of spans between islands, and from here to the gulf, the Oon broadened considerably and could only be crossed by ferry.

On the far side was an extension of the city, and then some suburbs, before they at length moved on into the province of Norim. Once again they traversed a landscape of villages, fields, and occasional ziggurats towering above the palms.

At night, they camped in the open behind a temporary rampart and parapet. Around dawn, they smelled smoke and Paxion sent scouts northwards. They returned by breakfast to report that a fresh Sephisti army had swarmed into Kwa almost as soon as they had left it, and that the great city was now besieged. The smoke they smelled came from the burning of the suburbs.

Paxion called a meeting. The Kadeini officers were gloomy and downcast. They were against going back. Paxion sighed and decided that keeping the legions together was the most important task. They would go on to Ourdh.

Afterward, Paxion called Pekel aside.

"Damn it, man, we're here to fight aren't we?" Paxion grumbled.

Pekel disagreed. "Use your head, General, we don't have the numbers to hold a place like Kwa. You cannot trust the Ourdhi. Today they love us, but tomorrow they could turn on us. They are like that, fickle and vain, cruel and indulgent."

"They welcome us to their city, they fed us."

"By the gods, they poisoned General Hektor."

"Surely you're not suggesting that Hektor was poisoned by anyone but an agent on the enemy."

Pekel waved a hand. "Whoever did it, it happened in Kwa, and I know that my men will not go back. We must go to Ourdh and take ship for home. We must preserve our victory."

Paxion could muster no argument strong enough to change the Kadeini's mind. Paxion was uncertain of his power to command in this situation. If the legions separated, they might easily be overwhelmed piecemeal and the disaster would be blamed on him.

Paxion was left pondering an uncertain future. He had not asked for this command. They were far from home, and they were surrounded by a deeply alien culture. Pekel could well be right, and if the countryside turned against them, then they might have a devil of a time getting out alive.

Still, he felt guilt at the thought of leaving Kwa to the enemy to be sacked and ruined. That smoke bespoke a host of tragedies. Paxion thought of his wife and children far to the north in Fort Dalhousie. He thanked the Mother that they were far from this and perfectly safe, and he prayed that he would return to them soon.

As General Paxion finished breakfast and resumed the march south, Ribela of Defwode awoke in the city of Ourdh after a short but worthwhile sleep. She had returned late at night from an abortive attempt to reach Dzu. The river swarmed with pirates who, lured by the promise of plunder, had allied themselves to the new power in Dzu.

Ribela prepared magic. The news of the poisoning of General Hektor had been waiting for her, brought by Talion scouts sent ahead by Paxion. It seemed the commanders of the legion were demoralized. Ribela toyed with the thought of returning at once with the scouts and trying to infuse them with General Hektor's combativeness. Then she recalled the emperor's prohibition on interference with the military arm. The damage to morale from witch interference outdid any tactical benefit, in the view of the Imperial Council.

So Ribela prepared herself for another course. They still did not know exactly what they faced in Dzu. It was time for her to find out.

She sent Lagdalen to procure a dozen live mice and some food. Then she prepared passages of the Birrak, and went over the pattern of declension and volumata she would require. It was a spell she had used before, but it was always wise to go over it. There were more than a thousand lines of declension, and human memories were fallible, even those of Great Witches.

Lagdalen went to the Merchant Irhan's stables and offered a Marneri silver piece to the two stables boys in return for mice. The boys, overawed, had difficulty at first in understanding her, a woman not clad in the garub, who inexplicably spoke Uld, albeit with a barbarous accent. Then they focused on the silver piece she held up for them.

In less than twenty minutes, Lagdalen had a bag with twelve mice writhing around inside.

Carrying the squirming sack, she ran to the kitchen and requested a loaf of bread and some oil, and then she headed up the steps once again.

On the third landing, she almost ran into the Lady Inula, who was clad in just a dressing gown and white puff slippers.

"By the goddess, what are you doing up at this hour, child? It's barely dawn."

Inula conveniently ignored her own wakefulness. But her eyes eagerly took in the details of Lagdalen's burden. A loud sqeak came from the sack as one mouse bit another mouse.

"Mice?"

Lagdalen nodded. "I must go, lady." Ribela would not want her to waste a moment.

"Yes, I'm sure you must," said Inula, who watched the girl go with eyes filled with calculations. Lagdalen ran up the stairs to the topmost floor. The small garret room that Ribela had taken was darkened and filled with the sweet smoke of lapsulum incense, burning on a square white altar stone that Ribela had asked the Merchant Irhan to move here.

"Thank you, my dear," said the Great Witch. "Release them on the floor and stand by with the bread and the oil. They will be very hungry after a while."

Lagdalen opened the sack, and the mice tumbled out to the floor and streaked away in all directions.

Ribela blew into a set of silver pipes that made sounds inaudible to human ears. The mice froze in place and stared upward with eyes like little glossy black pearls.

Here was the Queen of Mice! They were enchanted. How she drew them to her with those eyes so large and luminous. She played a little song to them on the pipes, and they came to sit in front of her in two rows as neat as if they were schoolchildren on their best behavior.

It was a touching sight, yet Lagdalen was still awed. Even after all the things she had seen Lessis do, she could be astonished at the sight of the magical powers of the Great Witches.

Ribela scooped up the mice in her hands and placed them on top of the altar stone where they formed a ring, tail to mouth, around the pile of smoldering lapsulum. Now they began to circle at increasing speed until they were a blur of little bodies.

Ribela began a passionate declension from the Birrak. The cadences rose and fell as the spell wove together.

Lagdalen remained by the door, watching spellbound, but ready with the bread and oil for the mice, which circled the incense tirelessly.

CHAPTER TWENTY-ONE

The Lady Inula was ushered into the Princess Zettila's apartments. It was breakfast time, and the princess was not amused at such an interruption in her morning routine. But for Lady Inula, she had made allowances. The woman was a barbarian, but one who sincerely wished to please, to ingratiate, to even be accepted into the Circle of the Daughters of Gingo-La.

This would have been laughable but for the fact that the Lady Inula was a conduit for invaluable information about the Argonath and the Witch Isles. Zettila had no independent sources of information there. Inula could be very valuable to her.

And there was also another matter. They had need of a young barbarian maiden. The princess had given indications that if Inula brought them such a young woman, she would be rewarded, perhaps even welcomed into the Secret Cult, the cult of the goddess of Gingo-La in her secret manifestation as Death-in-Life, the Mother with wire hair and steel hands, the death bringer and goddess of the tornado.

Inula's breathless presence here so early in the morning might well have something to do with this latter concern. That was good, for the ceremony would have to be performed soon. Things were collapsing very quickly. The city of Kwa had fallen. The Sephisti had taken the great bridge and were massing for a gigantic thrust south to the city of Ourdh.

And so Princess Zettila awaited her in the room of

bluebirds in the river wing of the Imperial Palace. Zettila was swathed in a voluminous green robe with a full train that was arrayed out to her left like a fan. She sat on enormous cushions and sipped hot kalut.

Lady Inula bowed, curtsied, and took a seat, too close to the princess, but Zettila allowed it. The Argonathi were crude, what could you expect from a people with hardly any history. "Are we truly alone, Princess?" breathed the woman.

Zettila sniffed.

"My servants are mutes. Cut out the tongue and take off the testicles, and a man becomes a useful thing for once."

"Yes"—Inula thought momentarily of Irhan, and his many infidelities—"of course."

"So you can be assured that nothing will leave this chamber. Have some kalut."

Inula covered her embarrassment by blurting out her prepared speech.

"Thank you, Princess. I have come to see you at this inopportune hour because I believe I have the perfect candidate for you; a young woman for the ceremony."

"Is she a mother of children?"

Inula felt a surge of elation. The princess was obviously very interested.

"Yes. As she must be."

"Is she beautiful?"

"Yes, Princess, the goddess will not be displeased with our offering."

"Good."

"She's a young woman, not of this land."

"A barbarian's blood will not be missed."

Inula nodded.

"That is excellent. And I, too, have the perfect candidate, for the Adonis. We must have a boy to complement the girl, and I happen to know of one who will be here very shortly."

"The need is urgent."

"It is. The Imperial Army has broken like a wet reed full of worms. It is we who must halt this threat of the empire."

"And we must hurry."

"When can we obtain the girl?"

"That is why I came, Princess. We can take her right now while her mistress is occupied."

"Who is this mistress?"

"Ribela of Defwode."

"Ah, the witch. She was here already, demanding to see the emperor. We lead her a merry dance."

"Yes, Princess."

"We will teach the Cunfshon witch about great magic. We will show her who wields real power in the world. It is time the witches of the Isle understood that the daughters of the goddess are their equal."

The princess rose and clapped her hands. Slaves ran to her and knocked their foreheads on the floor with alarming force. Brusquely she signaled for them to take up her train.

"The Adonis comes to the city very soon. He will be taken. Even better, we will take one of the giant worms, a sacrifice of immense proportions. We will bathe the goddess's stones in its blood. We will have two pretty barbarians to set before the goddess. She will smile upon our endeavor, and we shall save the empire."

"May the emperor be forever grateful to the goddess."

Zettila sighed. "We can hope for such a fortunate result. Now, return to your house. I will send three men to fetch the young woman. Give them whatever assistance they require."

Inula bobbed her head, awed by her involvement in great matters. For thirty years she had sought this importance, and now it was come. She might even achieve her most secret desire, adoption into Ourdhi society.

Zettila timed it perfectly. At the last moment, she reached out and squeezed Lady Inula's forearm.

"The Circle will be informed of your excellent service. Our thanks to you, lady."

Inula curtsied, and Zettila swept away.

The Lady Inula rode home in her carriage accompanied by a brutal-looking man in a suit of blue linen. He was a mute, of course, so she was spared from having to speak with him. Two more fellows like the first rode on top of the coach, behind her driver Pegsley. She traveled on a cloud of euphoria, although there was a small trouble, a persistent black dot of unease concerning what Ribela of Defwode might do once she discovered the disappearance of Lagdalen. Lady Inula shrugged it aside. The girl was perfect, the timing was absolutely right, her dreams were surely going to come true.

Not long after the Lady Inula had returned to her house, Relkin Orphanboy of Quosh glimpsed the top of the great ziggurat of the city of Ourdh for the first time. One moment there was nothing visible, and the next time he looked up there it was, a distant glittering peak.

A stir went through the ranks. Already they'd been marching through suburbs for a while, a scene that was very similar to that of the city of Kwa. But within minutes, they could tell that the central ziggurat here was much larger than any they had seen before.

The sun shone, it grew steadily warmer through the day while they drew closer to the great pyramids in the heart of the city. At mid-afternoon, they stood down and began building camp on a piece of open land that seemed to be a park of some kind. The surrounding suburb was a dense region of two-story mud-brick houses packed along narrow lanes.

Paxion took some kalut and called Captain Kesepton, who he sent away with a scroll for the emperor.

In moments, Kesepton's glossy brown steed was trotting citywards, for Paxion had also made a point to give the young captain permission to go to the house of the Merchant Irhan, and see his wife, Lagdalen of the Tarcho.

Paxion had been a commander long enough to know that the captain would go there anyway, even if he forbade it, so he made a virtue of the trip. Kesepton had worked hard for him all the way here from Salpalangum. It had been a long, arduous march, especially since the disaster in Kwa, but Paxion had been able to rely on Captain Kesepton's reports implicitly. And besides, Paxion could only too well imagine the agonies that the younger man was going through. The news of his wife's presence here in Ourdh had come only recently, and there were many unknowns. Paxion himself had a hard time sleeping for thinking of his wife and daughters, and they were in the relative safety of Fort Dalhousie.

Paxion prayed he'd get some kind of prompt response from the emperor. It had been days since they'd had a single message from the emperor or from the Imperial Army. As far as they could tell, the Imperial Army had disintegrated. The legions had finished the temporary rampart, set out stakes, and pitched tents before there finally appeared a group of Ourdhi officers, with some horse troopers in escort. One of them was dispatched to speak with Paxion.

"Welcome to you, barbarian Commander," said the little Ourdhi officer with quite obvious disdain. "I bring orders from the emperor's general."

Orders? Paxion shrugged and sipped kalut. He didn't know about orders from an emperor who ran from the battlefield and abandoned his army. He said nothing.

Emboldened, the Ourdhi officer went on.

"You are to break up the barbarian army into ten units, which shall be dispersed according to emperor's plan. You personally are to attend at the emperor's pleasure at the Imperial Palace. We are here to escort you there at once."

Paxion took a deep breath.

"Now just you hold on a minute. I'm not breaking up my command, that is certain. I have sent a message to the emperor, and I will wait here until I receive a reply."

The Ourdhi cavalry officer's face turned to stone. Incredibly, his hand went to the hilt of his sword. Paxion signaled to Full Captain Tremper and a squad of Argonathi soldiers took up their shields.

"You barbarians are now in the sun-blessed land. You must obey the emperor in all things."

Paxion smiled wearily. "Things are not that simple, my friend. Were you at the Battle of Salpalangum?"

The cavalry officer flushed, his cheeks turning dark.

"I was," said Paxion. "And these barbarians are the ones who stood their ground and smashed the Sephisti army. I have two dozen prisoners of the highest quality, all high-ranking officers of their army. I'm sure the emperor will want to tell me what he would like me to do with them. I'm sure they must be questioned."

The cavalry officer blinked. In truth, he was very confused. The barbarian commander would not obey the orders. The officer did not relish the thought of returning to his own commander without fulfilling his mission.

"So I'll wait here until my messenger returns from the city. He won't be long. Would you care to take some kalut?"

Baffled, the cavalry officer declined. Then he and his party cantered away into the late afternoon haze.

Paxion went back to the maps. His scouts had reported seeing parties of black-clad cavalry since about midday. he knew that Kwa had fallen, and he was sure that the Sephisti army must be marching south as fast as it could drive itself.

This was a fresh army, that was the most unsettling thing about it. A second enormous army had been recruited, armed and equipped and sent to Kwa even while the first one had broken up after Salpalangum.

If they had continued on as Hektor had intended, they would have run into this second, vast Sephisti army within a day. They would have had ten thousand against five times that number at the least. Paxion still thought of Salpalangum as a miracle, and doubted the legions could survive a second such onslaught.

Paxion expected that he and the legions would take refuge in the city, help to defend it, and hold it until resupply and reinforcements could be brought from the Argonath. Paxion sighed wearily; the responsibility was a huge burden and his worries gnawed at him day and night. If he could just get his men safely into some ships and sail them home, he would feel he had accomplished all that he could have. He prayed that he would live to see his homeland once again, and have his wife and children beside him.

CHAPTER TWENTY-TWO

In the night, when the red star Razulgab was high in the northern sky, the nightmarish work began again.

Under a heavy rain, the people were driven out of the pens in the heart of the dead city of Dzu. Driven by the whips cracking over their heads and the spears thrust at them by the soldiers of the god Sephis, they stumbled forward. They had been pulled willy-nilly from the pens, they were of both sexes, all age-groups, all starving. It had been days since they'd eaten anything.

Anxiously they huddled together. It was only a week or so since they had been rudely driven from their homes and villages, and herded into the great city. The land had been left empty of people. But the soldiers were adamant, the god Sephis required the people's service and so they must go to Dzu. That or die where they stood.

In the dead city, which had been barely inhabited in recent years, they were met by a teeming army of black-clad recruits. All were intoxicated with passionate belief in the way of Sephis. They sang constantly of their will to slay all those who stood in the way of the attainment of the return of the serpent god to his ancient rule. The village people were thrust into the pens except for the strongest, fittest young men, who were immediately weeded out and taken away.

Then they had waited, gradually getting weaker from hunger. Great masses of poor wretches were constantly in motion, arriving at the pens or being taken from them.

Now they had been selected, pulled out, and herded beneath an arch into the great Temple courtyard. Then they went up the steps to the Temple itself. They passed the feet of Auros. The statue had been broken off at the ankles. Driven down a broad stair into the interior, they emerged in a vast room. At one end stood a scaffold of immense proportions, raised perhaps fifteen feet above the stone floor.

Underneath this scaffolding was a group of men working knee-deep in mud that they constantly stirred with shovels. They worked the mud until it had the consistency of the clay on a potter's wheel.

And now the people were driven forward and herded up the steps to the platform with spear points in the back. And on the platform, they saw the service demanded of them by the new god.

The killers seized them, bound their ankles, and slipped the hooks into the ropes. With speed and precision, they cut their throats and then swung them out onto the long gibbets to drain onto the men and the mud below.

The people screamed, wept, and tried to turn back, but the spear points were too many and too sharp. The whips lashed their skin. Helplessly they went on into the arms of death.

There was a sudden red flash in the room that flared forth for a moment before it cooled to a single point of brightness. The killers paused in their work. The people edged back from the killing zone in a terrified keening mass.

Below them, a trio of figures strode out from the yellow light of a doorway to inspect the mud. The three figures were cloaked head to toe in black, but there, all resemblance ceased. The tallest was high priest Odirak. Beside him stood the former bishop of

Auros, now nothing but a servant of Odirak's kept alive at the high priest's pleasure.

However, it was the other figure that controlled the orb of light that hovered above and behind them. Under the black hood, there burned yellow eyes, a gleam of horn betrayed the beak that had formed over the face of the Mesomaster Gog Zagozt. Compared to this power, the high priest and the bishop were like moths dancing around a lantern.

A man brought a sample of the mud, and Gog Zagozt dipped in a long finger and tasted. It was ripe.

"Taste, and remember. This is the ripeness that is required."

Odirak tasted. He motioned for the bishop to taste, too. The bishop grimaced but dipped in his finger and trembling, placed it to his lips. Something in his heart rebelled at this horror, he could not lick this stuff.

Gog Zagozt leaned closer. "Taste, fool, I will not be able to come and taste all the time. You will taste and inform me when the mud is ready from now on. You must be able to taste . . . or someone else will taste, and you will join the rest."

The bishop licked the mud. It was vile, the blood was thick. He wanted to retch, but dared not. For a fraction of a second, he exchanged glances with Odirak. Odirak was smiling at him, enjoying his discomfort. The bishop had come to regret the day he had first met Odirak.

The Mesomaster spoke words of power. Two more flashes came, and the men below changed gears and set up the molds. Into the molds, they poured the bloody slurry.

The bishop stood beside the Mesomaster trying desperately not to think "wrong" thoughts. The Mesomaster had an uncanny ability to tell what one was thinking.

The molds were filled. The Mesomaster raised both hands and summoned the energies of death that were available. A great red flash erupted in the air with a clap of small thunder, and then came another and another and with each one, a mold jerked while within flashed a dull red light.

At length, all the molds had received invigoration. The Mesomaster turned and walked away. Odirak followed, as did the bishop, who felt a terrible bleakness descending onto his soul. Now he had seen the process by which the new weapon was being forged. Now he would have to live with his conscience for the rest of his life.

The screams of the people resounded in a constant roaring screech as the killers went back to work. The bishop breathed an audible sigh of relief when the door finally swung shut behind them and cut off the sound.

The dark cowl swung his way, the yellow eyes gleamed in the darkness beneath them.

"You tremble at the sounds of death, Priest?"

The bishop hesitated. "I am not used to it," he stammered.

The thing laughed, a strange creaking sound like horns rubbing together.

"Without trolls, your armies cannot stand against the Argonathi. The Argonathi might attempt a further invasion. We will stop that by destroying their expeditionary force. We cannot get trolls in time, they are in short supply and difficult to breed."

He knew this. Ten cows died in agony for every one that managed to give birth to a troll.

"So we must do this instead," said the bishop.

"Right!" said the Mesomaster striding away.

The bishop felt the hot eyes of Odirak on him.

"You seek to curry favor with the great one?"

"I? No, not at all, master."

"See to it that you keep your mouth shut in the future!" Odirak strode off, and the bishop hurried to keep up.

CHAPTER TWENTY-THREE

As the spell progressed, Ribela fell into the deep-trance state. Her lips and tongue moved, part of her mind continued to recite the words, but her consciousness detached from her body and hovered, momentarily floating in the room in Merchant Irhan's house on the world Ryetelth. Detachment was complete, she completed the declension, her lips crackling under the pressure of key volumes. Abruptly the astral image imploded and vanished into a point. No longer did it hover over the world Ryetelth, but now roved through the sea of chaos, which lay beneath all the bright bubbles of the worlds that gave texture to the Mother's hand.

In the general grey backwash that swirled endlessly here, there were vortexes and waves ripping back and forth through the ether. Where they clashed, dark patterns erupted and sounds of heavy electric static clicked and clattered.

This realm was familiar to the Queen of Mice. This was where she had done much of her life's work.

A Thingweight appeared nearby, drawn toward the presence it sensed. To her astral presence, the monster was a small thing, a cloud of shivering silver particles, tentacles pulsating, about the size of a large dog. Blue energies sparked beneath it.

Its tentacles thrust actively through the ether in her direction. They touched nothing, however, for her presence was purely on the astral plane. She was vast, diffuse, capable of instant motion. No Thingweight could harm her.

The mind of the Thingweight was limited, but it knew there was something here. It retracted many tentacles into itself and damped down its energies and prepared to wait. Like a polar bear at a seal's breathing hole, the Thingweight reasoned that sooner or later whatever it was that lurked within the ether would have to emerge. Then it could be seized and devoured.

Ribela ignored it and turned to set her bearings. Another one was coming. They might fight, perhaps even destroy each other. It happened sometimes.

She drove her astral presence forward, penetrating the ether of chaos like a whale sliding through an ocean of mist. She surfed vast combers of static particles and skipped across the mouths of whirling vortices. Briefly she flung through a belt of masses. Whirling shapes tumbled past her, even through her, but they were physical things and she was not. Among the masses were packs of predator clouds, things the size of tennis balls, riding on flickering yellow energies. These things swarmed about her, thrusting tentacles through her presence, but they found nothing to touch.

She went on, leaving the tumbling masses behind. On this scale, she traversed a vast distance, hundreds of thousands of miles through vast vortices and tumbling chaos.

Far ahead she detected something, a trace of presence, an intimation of gravity around some great dread thing, that lay across chaos like a string pulled from its own dark, energetic world and twisted across chaos to extrude into the world of Ryetelth.

This, then, was the thing that sat in Dzu, the reborn god, dread Sephis.

Ribela swung in toward it, as if she were a moth drawn irresistibly to its flame. She probed carefully.

What was this being that was contorted through the worlds like this? How did it avoid the Thingweights and other predators here?

There were many hellish worlds in the substance of the Mother's hand. Ribela knew that this monster might have come from any one of dozens, but knowing just what it was, was of enormous importance. The magic to destroy it would be impossible without a knowledge of its identity.

Closer now, Ribela caught wisps of the thought of the thing. A powerful mind, preoccupied with feeding, which it did on the death energies offered up from endless sacrifices. It blazed on the chaotic mental plane like a nova in a star field.

Slowly she drew closer and was able to visualize the thing, which stood like a vast column of clouds through the stuttering stuff of chaos.

The energies within it were enormous. The world it came from was one where metals ran like liquid under a searing hot atmosphere so dense it would crush anything not made of metals and crystals.

She had it then, it was a gammadion, a demon from a hot world. Ribela knew enough now to understand the magnitude of the task before them. She was awed at the ability of the Masters to even communicate with one of these terrifying beings. Certainly her own efforts to penetrate to those worlds had met with scant success. The minds there were too hard and harsh for much contact with outsiders. They grew like crystals themselves, along straight lines, resistant to change.

How, by the sweat of the Mother's brow, had they managed to negotiate with this monster?

She whirled past, orbiting the thing like a comet around a star and began to surge away, back toward her entry point in the subworld.

She was preoccupied for a moment. These things, called gammadions were generally proof against any magic known to the Sisterhood of the Isles. For deal-

ing with such things, the sisters had always besought
the higher realms for help. From the Nudar and the
Sinni had come assistance against the Abyssions of the
Masters in the first war. When Mach Ingbok attempted translation of his flesh to steel, the Nudar
interfered and prevented his success.

The memory brought more fond thoughts of the
gentle Sinni. The Sinni had given generously of their
selves for hundreds of years. Truly there was a higher
race!

The thing that had been the god Sephis in its earlier
rule in ancient Ourdh had been of a class of demons
called Malacostraca, a suborder among the Gammadions. With the aid of the Sinni, that thing had been
thrown down, and its hellish rule expunged.

Was this another of the same kind?

This gave Ribela hope, for she could summon the
Sinni to her aid, and she knew much of the lore for
the disintegration of such demons. It had been done
at least once before.

And then she felt the tug upon her. It came as an
exquisite shock. Somehow she had been detected,
even though she was barely an evanescence. Worse,
a contact had been established, which meant that
this was no Thingweight but some higher order of
intelligence.

Quickly she sought to cut the contact. Wire thin, it
broke and was reformed in a moment. Again she cut
it and again it reformed.

She glimpsed a flicker of black flame and knew at
once that there was another enemy present, but undetected by her. It was a great power, a terrible
intelligence.

A projection of some kind, black and octopoid, was
growing in the ether beside her. With sudden desperation, she composed a swift disabling spell and flung it
at the thing.

A red flash exploded across the grey shifting substance of chaos. The thing was forcibly compressed to the size of a bounce ball, but it was not flung away. It held on grimly.

Ribela raced toward her entry point. She could shed the thing by returning to her body.

As she accelerated, she continued to clamp down on the thing, compressing it to a ball, but it was hellishly strong and resistant.

Then she began to weaken. Her psychic strength was ebbing and with it her ability to keep the octopoid compressed. Something was very wrong. The mice were tiring. They had not been fed. Ribela could not imagine that Lagdalen would have failed her willingly.

A sick desperation overcame her. If the mice halted then she would have only her own strength, and she might not be able to keep the black octopoid destroyer compressed. A dismal picture formed in her mind. She would be trapped by this thing and delivered up to the monster itself.

She passed a pair of Thingweights fighting, a writhing mass of tentacles, fragments were floating off the combatants and their energies had shifted down spectrum to a deep orange.

She was there at last. Exhaustion was approaching. She returned to the world Ryetelth and hovered once more above her physical presence in the room at the top of the house of the Merchant Irhan.

Lagdalen was gone. The mice roamed aimlessly around the floor, weak and starving. The bowl of oil-soaked bread was on a table too high for them to reach.

She had to return, the black octopoid was regaining full size. Tentacles were clutching around her. With a final effort, she sank into her body. To her horror, she found the enemy's spell clung to her. Still the tentacles clutched hold. She was undone, the thing had reached through her because the protections of her spell were too weak.

Now it began to strangle her. She fought to breathe, struggling to work her lungs. Where was Lagdalen? What had happened?

Her resources were getting very low. The black octopoid was thick upon her. Her breath was dying in her throat.

CHAPTER TWENTY-FOUR

Captain Hollein Kesepton rode through the streets of Ourdh with his thoughts in a whirl. Impelled by the desperate need to see Lagdalen, he fairly cantered across the Zoda, past the gibbets where hung the rotting remains of petty criminals.

The questions revolved in his brain. Was she well? How was the baby? Why was she here at all? These questions had been going around and around in his head for days, ever since he had heard that she had been sent to Ourdh on a mission for the Office of Insight. It seemed incredible that the Lady Lessis would ask this of her. Hollein knew that duty was taken seriously by the upper classes, but with their baby just a few months old, surely Lagdalen could have been spared. She was barely eighteen and had already seen more than her share of dangers.

But then everything about this situation seemed crazy. The city, the war, the land of Ourdh, it was hard to know what was what. There had been a decidedly chilly reception for him at the palace. The palace officials had kept him waiting for hours before finally informing him that the emperor was as yet unwilling to allow the Argonathi inside the city walls. Kesepton was told to return within three hours for a definitive reply.

Why was the emperor behaving like this to the Argonathi legions who had rescued the day at Salpalangum? What did he expect them to do, fight the Sephisti alone?

He grimaced and spat as the stink of the gibbets wafted to him. There were things about Ourdh that any free man had to hate. The rulers here seemed to care little about earning the love and gratitude of the people. The fedd were beaten down.

And yet those same people had welcomed the Argonathi with open arms as they marched south from Salpalangum. Was it just gratitude for their deliverance from Sephis or was there also perhaps a hint of rebellion toward their own cowardly masters in that welcome?

Kesepton knew too well that in Ourdh they hanged anyone who stole so much as a loaf of bread, unless they were of noble blood. Slaves were common in the towns and cities. All the men he'd dealt with at the palace, after all, were eunuchs belonging to the emperor himself. This was a very different culture from his own.

Up the broad avenue he went, between the great temples, all dominated by the vast pyramid of Auros Colossos. Beyond the temples, the avenue became lined with three-story buildings, most of which had shops on the ground floor. Crowds of men stood on the street corners, clumps of women in the traditional head-to-toe black garub pushed through the men. After a while, he found Tasfaar Street, and he turned right and headed south. Tasfaar was lined with the houses of the moderately wealthy. These were tall white stucco houses, most of them set back from the road behind a walled courtyard. He recognized the Merchant Irhan's house by the sign with the white flower of Marneri.

As he approached, a coach turned out of the gate and rattled away pulled by a team of white pacers. For some reason it stirred a vague memory. He had seen this team before, but he could not recall where. He shrugged and rode on to the gate.

At the front door, he waited briefly while Irhan was summoned. The merchant came from his counting parlor, his mind filled with figures and calculations.

At the sight of a captain of the legions, Irhan understood at once who he was and why he was there. This would have to be young Lagdalen's husband, the heroic grandson of General Kesepton.

"Captain, come into my office. Can I have something brought for you, some water, kalut, beer?"

"A glass of water would do wondrous things for my throat, sir."

Irhan lead the way to his office.

"What has happened?" he said when they were behind a closed door.

Briefly Kesepton explained that the poisoning of General Hektor had changed the situation greatly. General Paxion was in command, but was under pressure from the Kadein commanders to return at once to the Argonath. They hoped to embark from Ourdh within seven days.

Irhan was incredulous.

"But the enemy has rebuilt his strength. There is a new army. They are stripping the countryside on the west bank, whole counties are empty now of people. They may have captured Kwa already. If so, then this new army is marching here now."

Kesepton shifted uneasily, unwilling to comment any further. Irhan gestured wildly. "What will be the point if you go home now and abandon us to the hordes of Sephisti?"

Kesepton shrugged. "Sir, it is not my place to criticize the orders. I simply obey them to the best of my ability."

Irhan paused in mid flight, and dropped his vehemence.

"Yes, Captain, I'm sure you do. But it's a tragedy.

We shall all have to flee. There'll be a panic like nothing you've ever seen in your life."

Kesepton crushed his captain's cap in his hands. The whole situation was becoming disastrous. Old Paxion was not strong enough to overcome the objections of the Kadeini officers who were behaving with so little courage.

"Well, sir, all that I do know is that on the battlefield the enemy could do nothing against us. With dragons as spearheads, we can cut up any enemy formation and take very few casualties."

Irhan chewed his lip.

"Yes, Captain, I have read an account of Salpalangum that lead me to exactly that conclusion. Well, whatever will be will be, as you soldiers say."

Kesepton nodded.

"However, Captain, you will have to inform General Paxion that it will take a lot longer to assemble the necessary shipping than seven days. The river below here is infested with pirates, and there aren't twenty vessels in the port right now. Trade has been terrible since the third month of the rebellion. I'm afraid he's being very unrealistic if he thinks he can get two entire legions aboard those ships. And the emperor will have to order them requisitioned, which I doubt very much that he will do."

Hollein had wondered about the same point, and it was moot besides, since the emperor had refused to even allow them into the city proper, behind the immense walls and fortifications that were famous around the world.

"Yes, sir. I will tell him."

"You have visited the palace I take it."

"I am to return in two hours to receive a message, if there is one."

Irhan nodded with his lips compressed. "I'm afraid the emperor is very unpredictable. He's notoriously disloyal."

Irhan sighed, stood up, and put his hands behind his back as he paced up and down.

"You must tell this to General Paxion in the greatest secrecy, do you understand?"

Hollein nodded.

"The emperor is obsessed right now with his mother's plotting against him. To be fair to the man, it must be admitted that his mother is prone to poisoning her sons. She had three and has killed two of them already. There is a nephew that she prefers. At the same time, the general feeling in the court, is that the call for help to the Argonath was a mistake. There is fear that letting the Argonathi "barbarians" in will add a new powerful player to the struggle for power among the great families. At the same time, the more knowledgeable know that they need us desperately if they are to stave off the Sephisti. There is no agreement therefore, and no consensus on what advice to give the emperor."

Irhan sighed heavily.

"Tell the general that I will attempt to rally our supporters and overcome the emperor's mood. He is unfortunately captive to the views of the Princess Zettila, his cousin. She is an extremist .of the cult of Gingo-La. Who knows what kind of advice she is giving him? It is a very difficult situation."

Kesepton drank a cool glass of water. And then broached the real reason he was there.

"I must ask you, Merchant, about the whereabouts of a certain young woman of Marneri, her name Lagdalen of the Tarcho."

"Indeed, I know her well, Captain. And you are her husband of course. I should say that I feel honored to have met you, the hero of Tummuz Orgmeen." Irhan beamed at him.

"Yes, Captain, even here we get the news of the home city. You married very well there, young man. She is a beauty and of the Tarcho themselves."

"Yes, sir," said Hollein. "Is she here?"

Irhan sighed, enjoying this moment.

"Yes, I believe she is. Upstairs on the top floor attending the, uh, Lady Ribela."

"Ribela?" Hollein was confused. Who was Ribela? Where was Lessis?

"Yes, a Great Witch from the Isles, the veritable Queen of Mice."

Hollein's eyes went wide, that name he had heard. Irhan chuckled. But where was Lessis?

"Please go upstairs, Captain, and see your wife. I'm sure she would never forgive me if I did not urge you to. The room is on the right, at the top."

Hollein bounded up the stairs. At the second landing, he was observed through a screen door by Lady Inula, who then turned away and picked up a pipe in which batshooba smoldered.

He reached the top floor. It was deserted, all the servants being terrified of the witch. He opened the door and peeked inside.

It was dark, and there was the sound of someone choking. He hesitated. What if he interrupted some important spell? But if he did not look, he would not see Lagdalen. He ducked inside. The choking sounded worse.

His eyes adjusted to the gloom and at length he saw a woman of striking appearance, clad in black velvet, who appeared to be in great distress. She was on the floor, her legs sprawled out, back against the wall with both hands to her throat as if she were strangling herself. She was also making the choking sounds.

On a small rectangular altar nearby smoldered some incense. There was a table by the door that held a bowl filled with chunks of bread.

The strangeness of the situation did not hide the fact that something was gravely amiss here. There was no sign of Lagdalen. Cautiously, he approached the woman. Something darted away from his foot. A mouse. There were several of them on the floor.

The woman was choking herself to death. He knelt beside her, took her wrists in his hands, and tried to pull them free. He could not, they were held there by a strength beyond that of any man. He tried again, putting a foot to the wall for leverage.

She was staring up at him, trying to mouth something. Hardly any sound emerged.

"What is it? What can I do?" he shouted at her.

A wild hope lit up in her eyes. She swallowed and choked, and then made a great effort and managed to croak, "Feed the mice! Now!"

"Feed the mice," he whispered uncomprehendingly, and then he connected the bowl of bread on the table and the mice on the floor. He whirled and cast the bread to the floor.

The starving mice converged on the oil-soaked bread like small grey streaks. They devoured it in a matter of moments. Hollein Kesepton felt his eyes bulge in his head as he watched the bread vanish. There'd been enough to feed several men in that bowl, and it was gone inside five seconds. And the dozen or so mice were the same size they had been before.

But now they jumped up to the top of the little altar and began circling tail to mouth at great speed around the smoldering incense.

The woman came to life with a convulsive jerk and emitted a low growl deep in her chest. Kesepton drew back on his haunches. Her hands slowly pulled away from her neck, as if she were overcoming an invisible assailant who sought to hold them in place.

Her eyes flashed momentarily, and she uttered a rapid fire blitz of arcane syllables and shook her body violently. There was an audible snap and then a sharp, chemical odor that faded away.

The woman slowly regained her feet. The color was draining back into her face.

Hollein stared at her, amazed by this turn of events. "Lady, are you alright?" He began.

Her eyes were most luminous, peculiar.

"Thank you, young man. I have had a narrow escape. I thank you wholeheartedly for your part. However, I am troubled by something. Lagdalen, your wife I believe, should be here. But she is not. You, on the other hand, should not be here, but you are. Mysterious."

"Where can she be?" asked Hollein, with sudden fear striking his heart. "I came up the stairs a few moments ago, and there was no sign of her."

The witch studied the room.

"No sign of a struggle. But it is unlike her to shirk an important duty. Something is wrong. I shall have to make inquiries."

Ribela started toward the door, then paused and turned to him.

"I take it that General Paxion has camped outside the walls and awaits the emperor's pleasure."

"Yes, lady."

"Come with me, Captain, we need to find our Lagdalen. And then you shall take me to see General Paxion."

CHAPTER TWENTY-FIVE

General Paxion received the bad news in silence. When the young captain had gone, the general gave a great groan and slumped into his camp chair.

What had he done to deserve this? He had always done his duty, and he had served the legions well. Now his career, perhaps his life, was going to be destroyed.

There was no chance of getting the Kadeini to agree to turn about and fight. They were determined to sail for home at once. Paxion could not rouse them, nor could he make them fear him like they feared Hektor.

And on top of everything else, there was a Great Witch in the city who wanted to see him. That was guaranteed to be a headache! He'd probably get turned into a frog.

"Messenger!" he shouted after a long minute of sullen contemplation.

Quickly he scribbled a note and sent it to General Pekel. Within twenty minutes, all senior officers were assembled in Paxion's headquarters tent.

Quickly he briefed them on the situation, sparing nothing.

"The situation is grim, gentlemen. Our choices are to try and force our way inside the city, seize what ships there are, and try to get our men home that way, or to march south to the coast where we might attempt to embark the men aboard Argonathi ships. We could reach the coast in a week to ten days. How

long it would take the cities to assemble a large
enough fleet to take us home is beyond my competence to calculate. The weather witch thinks it would
be at least three weeks, but it could be months."

Paxion stared at Pekel with clear distaste. "By then
we will be surrounded by vast armies of Sephisti. They
are emptying the land over the river, they are taking
everyone. The word is that the serpent god will inspire
even crones to take up weapons and attack us."

General Pekel flushed angrily. He knew what the
Marneri men thought. The Kadeini commanders were
subdued as well. Commander Porteous Glaves, sitting
at the back of the Marneri contingent, was ashen-
faced.

For Glaves, it was the final straw. There was a giant
army of black-clad fanatics marching toward them,
and they were trapped outside the walls of the city by
a weak-brained emperor. They were going to stay here
and argue among themselves about what to do, the
Sephisti would come down and surround them, and
they would all end up being baked alive over hot
coals.

A safe passage out of this hellish mess, that's what
he required. And once more he considered the strange
offer he'd received from the mysterious priestess of
Gingo-La, who had visited his tent. There was a safe
passage for him there, and he hardly had to do a
thing.

As Paxion brought the briefing to a conclusion and
they rose and filed out, Porteous Glaves decided to
give the priestesses what they wanted. It looked like
his only chance to get out of the gathering doom he
foresaw.

The following morning dawned sunny and bright.
Commander Glaves left his tent and sauntered over
to the dragon section. His nostrils wrinkled at the
odors of the great beasts, it was a little like that of

horses, but sharper. Still, it mattered little, he would soon be far away from it all.

"Dragoneer Hatlin!" He called out as he approached. The dragoneer pulled on his cap and straightened his uniform, clearly flustered a bit at the sight of his regimental commander.

"Good morning, sir." Hatlin gave a crisp enough salute. Glaves replied much less crisply and took the dragoneer by the elbow.

"This morning I have arranged a woodcutting party. The cooks require some logs, and there is a request from the engineers for some eight-foot beams. A woodlot has been purchased about eight miles south of here."

"Right, sir, how many are required?"

"We'll need three dragons, I think, and their boys of course. I want the dragons Vlok, Chektor, and the broketail."

Dragoneer Hatlin raised an eyebrow. This was the first indication he'd ever had that the commander even knew the names of the dragons in the one hundred and ninth.

"Yes, sir, those specific dragons?"

"Yes, Dragoneer."

Hatlin was puzzled. "They done something wrong then, sir? Something I don't know about?"

"No, Dragoneer, nothing like that. Send the dragons as named. They will be back this evening."

"Yes, sir. Though I'd like to send Cham instead of Chektor. Old Chek's feet are still pretty sore, he needs all the rest he can get, in case we got a long march ahead of us."

Commander Glaves considered this and then agreed.

"Good thinking, Dragoneer, good thinking. We'll send Cham with the broketail and Vlok. See to it. They're to report to the quartermaster within half an hour."

Hatlin did as he was bid. The dragons were promised beer and extra rations at dinner that night. They grumbled awhile but eventually rose to their feet and marched out. With them went five men on punishment detail who were to split the logs that the dragons would hew.

They marched eight miles to a woodland set at the edges of the city. Here, an Ourdhi contractor showed them the section that had been purchased by the legion.

Immense axes, troll axes, taken by the legion long ago for a more useful task, were handed out to the three dragons, Bazil of Quosh, Vlok, and Cham.

The dragonboys were there to assist their charges and make themselves useful. For the most part, this meant staying out of the way.

The trees they were cutting for the most part were white ash and little more than a foot in diameter. The dragons cut down trees like these with just a few strokes.

Relkin and Swane had hardly spoken since their night out at Kwa. Swane and Tomas still had large bruises on their faces. Tomas was lacking his two upper front teeth now as well and was too depressed to talk to anyone.

Relkin had finally got the whole story out of Mono, though it hadn't been easy. Mono had huge black eyes, a torn right ear, and a badly bruised self-image.

The man they'd thought was a pimp had made them wait in a courtyard outside the beer hall. They'd assumed that girls would be sent in to them there, and they were standing around joking and laughing while they waited. Suddenly a gang of a dozen men armed with staves burst in and beat them black-and-blue. What with the surprise and being outnumbered so badly, they'd had no chance.

Fortunately for everyone, Relkin's own adventures had been too unsettling for even Relkin to boast about. Sometimes he thought wistfully about Miranswa and wondered where she was. Back inside a palace somewhere, he concluded. It seemed to be his fate to be thrown together with beautiful girls who were outside of his social class. He knew he was just an orphan boy, a starveling from Quosh, not the sort of material from which princes are made. For some reason, he felt no urge to boast to the others about Miranswa.

And so it was a quiet group of dragonboys that morning, a fact much remarked on by the three dragons as they marched. When they reached the woodlot and the dragons got down to work, the boys stood well apart from each other and worked with their dragons with little conversation.

The trees fell steadily, and the men on work detail sawed, split, and stacked the logs. As the sun rose, it became warm work and everyone stripped to their waists. But they did not slacken because they were well aware that they would get no rest until all the selected wood was cut, chopped, and shipped.

They filled one wagon and then another and were halfway into a third when a small cart rolled up with four firkins of beer sent down for the woodcutting party.

With a roar of approval, the men downed their tools and broke open the barrels. The dragons took up theirs and gave a measure to each of the dragonboys.

They drank, and ate some bread and cheese and pickles for their lunch. The dragons had akh on their bread, and they ate a dozen loaves apiece.

They finished the beer and quickly became very sleepy. One by one the men, the boys, and the dragons lay down and went to sleep. Snores resounded under what remained of the stand of white ash and carpenter pine.

No one was awake to see the wagon lurch into the clearing a few minutes later. A dozen men scrambled out and rushed to inspect the dragons and the dragonboys.

Relkin was identified by the lack of bruises on his face. He was seized, bound, and placed in the wagon. Then the men struggled to wrap leather bands around the torso of the dragon with the broken-looking tail. Ropes were attached to the leather and wound around a block and tackle in the wagon. Soon, with ten men hauling on the rope, they winched the dragon up and into the wagon.

With a crack of the whip, the wagon sped away the men pausing only to rob the sleeping Marneri men of their purses and knives.

CHAPTER TWENTY-SIX

Lagdalen of the Tarcho awoke to the sound of creaking ropes and the smell of the river. She was blindfolded, bound hand and foot, and lying on a hard surface with a lot of lumps in it. She could hear the slap of water against the bow, and feel the boat move so she knew it was a small boat.

At first she could not recall how she had come to be here. She had been standing by while the Lady Ribela worked great magic in the room at the top of the house of the Merchant Irhan. The mice had been running, and she was supposed to feed them when they tired.

And then, nothing, her thoughts came up against a blank wall. Try as she might, she remembered nothing that would explain her presence here in the boat.

For a while, she lay there and tried her bonds. They were expertly done, and she could barely move a muscle. The boat continued to slap through small waves, and occasionally she heard other sounds, grunts of effort and the whine of rope running through a block.

And then quite suddenly, it came back to her. There had been a sound at the door. She had turned and there had been men, silent men with dark eyes and terrible strength. They had held her down and one of them had pressed a cloth smelling of ether to her face, and she had lost consciousness at once. And now she was in a boat, bound and blindfolded. She had been abducted; it was the only possible conclusion.

Her heart sank. She presumed she was being taken to the enemy in Dzu. It seemed she would never see baby Laminna again. That thought had always been there since the beginning of this mission to Ourdh, hovering like a faraway dark cloud. Lagdalen had faced death before, and she knew how real it could be. Now the thought that she might die was by no means unimaginable. Poor baby Laminna! Poor Lagdalen.

The boat docked, and someone picked her up and heaved her up to someone else on a dock. Unceremoniously, she was dumped onto another hard surface. A whip cracked and she felt movement. Transferred to a cart.

The cart made a short journey, perhaps a mile, perhaps two. She heard gates open and close behind her. She was lifted onto a stretcher. Women's voices in an Ourdhi tongue that was like Uld, but different enough to be unintelligible to her were chattering all around her. Then she was carried into a place of echoes where it grew noticeably cool and quiet. She was taken off the stretcher and laid on some straw. The smell of the straw and a powerful perfume of jasmine filled her nostrils. A voice sighed, and a hand caressed her face and then her body. There came another sigh, and she heard the sound of a door opening and closing. She was left with the silence, lying on her side, on deep straw inside a massive structure.

She could hear absolutely nothing, so she tried to shift the blindfold and perhaps get a peek. Drawing her knees up to her face, she started to work it up. It was tied very tight and it took a long time, but eventually she was able to see from her left eye if she held her head way back.

The results were disappointing, but there was a very faint illumination. Most of it came from an image of the goddess Gingo-La in her most terrible manifestation. Here she was red like fire and possessed seven arms all holding knives or severed heads. Her face, however, was still pale brown and beautiful, the eyes placid, dreaming only of the higher plane of heaven. The illumination came from phosphorescent paint used for the terrible knives she wielded and for the sun and moon and stars above. Lagdalen had never seen such an image, and she was disturbed. There were no images of the Mother in the Argonath.

By the light of the knives of Gingo-La, she made out a few objects in the room, which was of a good size. There was a table, two chairs, a dark mass that might have been a chest.

Once again she tried her bonds and soon realized she was never going to get free by herself. After a while, she lay back on the bed and tried not to imagine the fate that lay in store. There was nothing she could do but wait until they came for her again.

When the news that the emperor had refused to allow the legions to enter the city reached the Queen of Mice, she surrendered to her temper at last. She rose with an oath and went straight to General Paxion. Shortly afterward she went to the palace again, this time with Hollein Kesepton at her side and six Talion cavalry troopers behind.

At the gate, the guards and troopers bristled at each other, and she beguiled the guards with a charm, and they let the Argonathi pass without more ado.

Distantly, Ribela heard Lessis's voice telling her to be sparing in the use of her strength when working in the field. But Ribela was no longer prepared to tolerate the insolence of the Ourdhi. They were male, they were deceitful, and they were treacherous and ungrateful. She had had her fill of them.

Inside the palace, they were met once again by the wall of silence. A dozen eunuchs in scarlet robes with earplugs jammed in place stood between them and the imperial apartments. They would communicate only by writing on a slate with chalk. They would write only in Uld.

Ribela nodded to Captain Kesepton. He reached out and ripped away the earplugs from the highest-ranked eunuch.

Ribela spoke a few syllables of power and then a declension. A small spell gripped the fellow, and she was able to look into his eyes.

Soon after that, she and the captain were marching through the Imperial apartments lead by the high-ranking eunuch. They reached a set of double doors with a pair of guards outside.

These were deaf mutes, but at the sight of the instructions written for them by the ranking eunuch, they opened the door.

Inside stormed Ribela.

The emperor and his court were stunned at the intrusion. Ribela gave them no chance to recover. She immediately launched into a vehement denunciation of them, their policies, and their general faintheartedness. She compared them to capons, she insulted their courage, and simultaneously worked an enchantment upon them.

Banwi wanted to scream orders for the immediate execution of the woman in her black robes with silver mouse skulls, but he could not once those terrible eyes locked onto his own. He could only sit there and listen to the tirade. After a while, she turned to him personally and bent close to his face to describe in horrifying detail the evil fate that would await him once the enemy triumphed and dragged him back to Dzu as a captive.

He had blotted it all out for a few hours, but she brought it all back. It was just as the rooster's head had foretold. He would be eaten slowly, like a bonbon, by this demon in Dzu. Banwi screamed, fell from the throne, and thrashed on the rug foaming at the mouth.

A portly monstekir, Bornok of the Chaji, inter-posed himself.

"Begone, witch, you have done your damage now. The emperor is having a fit."

It was quite true. The little emperor was roaring in rage and chewing the carpet at the same time. Ribela expressed a rapid fire declension and broke the fit. Banwi went limp.

Another monstekir thrust himself forward. He wore an elaborate costume of yellow and green silks, with white hose and enormous puffed shoulders.

"Lady witch of the Isle, may I recommend that we put the emperor to bed now."

"No!" snapped Ribela. "He must give orders to let the Argonathi into the city at once."

The monstekirs, the stekirs, the grand vizier all jerked back with a hiss. Ribela fought to keep her temper under control.

"You cannot leave them outside. They are your only hope of withstanding the coming siege of this city."

There was a nervous licking of lips. The situation was getting out of control. They had all heard that the Sephisti were halfway to Ourdh. Within hours, their advance scouts would be in the suburbs of the city.

Banwi was whimpering.

"Stop that stupid noise!" Ribela went to Banwi, crouched beside him, and looked into his eyes once more.

Banwi got to his feet. The color had drained from his features. In a voice like a husk of itself, he called for writing materials. Orders were to go out to the gates to allow the Argonathi in.

Paxion immediately began the process of moving his troops into the city.

The great city walls had just five enormous gates. Each was the center of a small fortress. Each was

supposed to be held by two thousand men. There were
seven other bastions, each one half the size of the gate
forts and each meant to have a strength of one thousand men. There were seventeen miles of walls, and
they were forty feet high throughout with fifty-foot
turrets every two hundred yards. A small force, as
little as fifteen thousand strong, could in theory hold
these walls.

Paxion met with the general of the city guard whose
responsibility the walls were. The general was the
monstekir of Bogra, an obese man named Sosinaga
Vokosong. Lord Vokosong was an exception to the
rule among his class. He was a seasoned warrior, and
he welcomed the presence of the Argonathi troops.
Paxion and he agreed that the Argonathi should take
over a section of wall to either side of the Fatan Gate,
on the northeast of the city. They should also take
over the defense of the great Fatan Gate. Only the
regular gate-operating crew and attendant engineer
would be left. This would give Lord Vokosong another two thousand Imperial troops that he could add
to the depleted forces in other gates.

By nightfall, the legions were in place.

Observing these preparations, a group of well-
placed men gathered in a large house in Solusol, the
district just south of the Zoda.

These men were high-placed functionaries in the
civil administration, for the most part, although there
were also a few merchants.

They greeted one another with the raised palm and
the closed eyes of the initiate to Padmasa. All were
self-described "magicians" who thirsted to learn more
of the great knowledge of Padmasa.

A man known to them only as Magician addressed
them. They listened with respectful silence. They were
to immediately begin an agitation against the Argonathi "invaders." The Argonathi were unclean and
would forgo ritual slaughter of animals. They would

bring down plague on the people. They were also
known to be sexually indiscriminate and would rape
everyone, man, woman, and child. Rumors of rapes
and child abductions would at once be started. Obscene barbarian sex orgies were to be described in
horrid detail. Argonathi were also said to be greedy
and eager for coin. Robberies and break-ins were to
be described, the more to whip up the city people.

The agents listened and went forth to begin their
work.

CHAPTER TWENTY-SEVEN

The first sign of the coming of the Sephisti was always the smoke. When the wind blew from the north, the fedd would lift their heads and smell the burning of the lands. Then refugees arrived, and soon they would join them, packing the roads to the south.

They had heard that the Sephisti took everyone, from the children to the oldest crones, and sent them to the dread city of Dzu. They had heard that no one ever returned.

Usually only a few hours behind them would come the first scouts, small men on dark steppe ponies, Baguti cavalry in the service of the Masters. The Baguti fell upon anyone who had not gone down the road ahead of them. Old and sick, infants, they were all seized and driven northwards at once.

Then more cavalry would appear, squads of black-clad men with the fanatical gleam in their eyes of the worship of Sephis. Most of them wore fragments of armor taken from the fallen Imperial army. They would root around in the villages for fugitives and food supplies. Messages would go back to the central horde.

Then they would move on, following the Baguti.

And soon there came the sound of drums, the thundering drums that announced the coming of the army. Hundreds of drums thrummed an endless *boom boom, boomity boom*, that seemed to take over the world and fill it with fear. And finally the very horizon would darken with the first masses of the men in black. Soon the masses would solidify into endless columns, pouring forward on every road.

Tens of thousands of them, organized into huge divisions, would tramp past, in their eyes the fanatic gleam of the hypnotized, nothing else.

For hours it would continue thus, with the thundering drums and the tramping lines of men, and then at last it would be over. Quite abruptly the columns would end and there was only the rear guard, a long line of cavalry troopers ready to kill any stragglers. And when they were gone, the roar of the drums would fade until all that was left was the crackle of the flames burning in the fields.

To the south, in the great city of Ourdh, panic reigned. The upper classes fled in coach and carriage for the southern parts of the empire and jammed the roads leading to the south gates. In the port, vessels willing to risk the river pirates slipped out, laden to the gunwales with more. But for the great mass of the people, there was nowhere safer to go.

Meanwhile, the men of the Imperial Army and the Argonathi legions prepared the defenses. The regiments were allotted sections of wall to hold. The engineers and the dragon squadrons came together to plan counter mine strategies. The dragons were trained in the use of shovel and pick, and usually dug in units of three, one with a pick and two with shovels. When they tired, they would be replaced while they picked up their energies with beer and food. Working this way, they were capable of digging wide tunnels at a tremendous rate.

The soil here on the alluvial plane of the Oon was not perfect for mines because it was so often soggy. However, there had been little rain in Ourdh for weeks, and the ground was dry enough. Paxion expected a significant enemy effort in this area.

The dragons were also trained in the art of toppling siege towers. For this they were equipped with long poles. Working in groups, they could push siege towers over on their sides.

For such work, of course, the dragons had to be protected. A line of wicker shielding was woven and erected down the center of the walls.

There were complaints from Ourdhi officialdom about the enormity of dragon appetites. They ate as much in a day as a dozen men. They drank too much as well. After a day or so of this, General Paxion decided to show the officials exactly why the dragons were so important.

The officials were briefed on the danger of mines being dug under the walls. The walls of Ourdh were massive and well built, but they could be undermined. The only way to prevent mining was to drive counter- ermines into a mine, kill the miners, and collapse their mine.

Three young leatherback dragons carrying picks and shovels stepped forward to a spot on a lawn outside the gate to the Imperial City and began to dig. The pick ripped up six-foot sections of the turf, and the shovels scooped up a cubic yard at a time. In a matter of minutes, the dragons were ten feet down. The Our- dhi officials changed their minds. From then on, the dragons were offered all they could eat and drink.

The demonstration took place on a sunny day with a breeze out of the north that made it worthwhile to wear a light coat. When it was over, Porteous Glaves headed for General Paxion's quarters, on the second floor of the Fatan Gate. He was scheduled to report to the general concerning the disappearance of Drago- neer Relkin and Bazil Broketail.

Glaves fidgeted a while as the general completed a message and sent it off by courier. At last Paxion looked up. His eyes were bloodshot and his face was filled with weariness.

"Ah yes, Commander Glaves." His lips compressed in dislike. Paxion had never gotten over his dislike of the man and his stupid leather collars.

Glaves smiled ingratiatingly.

"Well, Commander, what have you discovered?"

Glaves spread his hands and shrugged expansively.

"Very little, sir. The facts of the case are few. As you know, sir, they were on a woodcutting party for our cooks and engineers. About noon, a cart showed up with four barrels of beer, which apparently were drugged, though we never found the casks or any direct evidence. Everyone slept for hours, dragons included. When they awoke, it was almost dark, and the dragon and Relkin of Quosh were gone."

"Your own inclination then, Commander?"

Glaves feigned discomfort with what he was going to say next.

"Well, we know that the boy had gone over the wall in Kwa and returned with a young woman who was apparently of noble birth. She has since been returned to her family here in the city, I believe. However, we have been unable to interview her. I have a slight suspicion that she has lured the boy, who has taken the dragon with him, to serve as private bodyguards to this noble family. They might do very well in such service, certainly with far less risk to themselves than they would find in the legions."

Glaves paused. "I hesitate to make any firm conclusions, but this suspicion does trouble me."

Paxion tossed the quill down on the table, rose, and paced up and down.

"I find it hard to entertain such suspicions. I've had the occasion to meet that pair, and they seemed most unlikely to desert."

"Indeed, sir, indeed. The boy won the Legion Star, after all. The dragon had been presented with a new sword, forged by eleven smiths. It seems incredible that they would abscond after such generosity from the legion. Still, we cannot ignore this possibility."

"I still do not connect the two matters. If they wished to abscond, they could have done so before this."

"Perhaps they are hiding right now somewhere in the city. These noble families have considerable resources. Perhaps they waited until they were close to the city. Perhaps they were aided and abetted by the family of the girl."

Paxion swallowed heavily. It seemed preposterous. But what other explanation could there be? Unless the enemy had for some reason wanted to take a single dragon and dragonboy prisoner. But the enemy would have slain the others in their sleep. It made no sense.

Eventually Paxion dismissed the commander and sent for Captain Kesepton. When the captain had saluted and sat down, Paxion tried Glaves's theory on the captain.

Kesepton rejected it vehemently. The pair from Quosh were dedicated soldiers, they would never be happy as trained poodles for some family of wealthy foreigners. He suspected it was the work of enemy agents somehow. Perhaps they had contracted with local criminals for this. A dragon and dragonboy to be delivered to them for study and research.

"Then why would they want the boy?"

"Who knows a dragon better than his boy?"

Paxion sighed and asked after Lagdalen, was there any news? Had the witches detected anything? Kesepton shook his head, the worry had put lines on the younger man's face. He had not slept in days.

Paxion dismissed the captain and returned to brooding on his own. He had many problems facing him, but nothing quite so raised his hackles as this disappearance of a dragon and dragonboy team. He could not believe that they had deserted the legion, he simply could not.

Meanwhile Porteous Glaves rode a ricksha through the teeming streets to the rear entrance of the Temple of Gingo-La. There he presented himself and asked for an immediate audience with the priestess "Fulaan."

He was led into a darkened room and told to sit on a low chair.

A dim red light came on, and he saw a figure towering above him on a throne.

"You wished to see me?" said a familiar voice. The same that had offered him his escape in return for a dragon and dragonboy. She spoke Verio with a slight accent.

"I did. You have what you wanted."

There was a long silence.

"Yes."

"And I want to discuss what I want."

A longer silence.

"We have considered this already. It was felt that you are a fool and that we might safely cheat you. After all, you have committed treachery, treason. Your legion would hang you, I believe, should they learn the truth."

Glaves was sweating. The woman continued.

"But we did not decide to cheat. Nor did we accede to the idea of simply killing you. Or of taking you as a slave and castrating you and sending you to an outlying city."

"No!"

"Without your tongue and your testicles, you would soon vanish into anonymity."

Glaves mopped his brow. The nightmare seemed endless. Was there no way out? These cheating, deceitful Ourdhi.

"No," said the woman, "we decided instead to honor our part of the bargain. So you may now tell me what we might do for you."

Glaves swallowed heavily, his mouth had gone dry. Never, never, would he tread beyond the lands of the Argonath again!

"I need a boat, but not yet. I will only make my escape when I am convinced that all is lost and that the enemy will take the walls."

"Oh-ho," the woman gave a ghostly chuckle. "So. You want us to have a boat kept ready for you when the time comes."

"Yes."

Again that awful chuckle. "It will be done."

CHAPTER TWENTY-EIGHT

Relkin's eyes fluttered open. He groaned and tried to turn over but discovered that he was handcuffed and chained to a ring hanging from a stone wall. He observed that he was in a dank dungeon, walled in damp stone. Dim light filtered into his cell from somewhere high above through a shaft in the center of the ceiling. Under him was a layer of fresh straw and then flagstone.

Wearily he pulled himself into a slightly more comfortable position. How in the name of the bad old gods had he ended up here? Was he under arrest? What had he done to merit such treatment?

Try as he might, all he recalled was a woodcutting detail. They'd been working hard under the hot sun, and then a wagon had rolled up with lunch and some beer to wash it down with.

And then he vaguely remembered a feeling of wooziness right after that lunch and a strong urge to take a nap. And that had been strange since he'd had only a single draft of the beer.

After a moment's thought, he came to the conclusion that either the beer or the food had been drugged.

But who would do such a thing, and why?

He'd been drugged and abducted. Which meant that there was no one to look out for his dragon, or for the great Purple Green. His dragonboy's heart started to thump hard at that prospect. Without him to protect them, they would be open to poisoning and who knew what else.

Then he got around to examining the chain and the ring in the wall. The chain was heavy and well made. The ring in the wall looked as if it would have resisted the efforts of the Broketail or even the Purple Green.

He gave a tug on the chain anyway. It was solid. He cast around the place for a tool with which to work on it. Nothing presented itself. His belt, his dirk, even his shoes, were gone, leaving him with just tunic and hose.

Until someone came for him, he was going to stay put. He made an effort to put out of his thoughts any speculation on what his captors might want with him. It was not easy to do. Here in Ourdh, there were vast numbers of slaves and a large percentage of them were muted by having their tongues cut out. All at once his future appeared grim and quite uncertain.

At length, the dim light above waned, and he surmised that the day was coming to an end. Darkness settled in and he strained his ears for sound, any sound.

Nothing disturbed the silence, however, for a long time until quite suddenly he heard a thud nearby, then footsteps, and then the door to his cell was unlocked and opened.

A torch was thrust in and by its light he saw the figures of three women, all wrapped from head to toe in the black garub. Their faces were hidden behind veils. They examined him frankly and discussed him among themselves in one of the tongues of Ourdh, he knew not which.

They laughed together, a discomforting sound, and one of them reached down and pinched his cheek. He snarled at them, and they laughed again. Then they rose, went out of the cell, and left him in the darkness once more.

The questions about his future multiplied feverishly

in his mind. Somehow he had to escape and get back
to the 109th in time to protect his dragons. Somehow
he had to get out of here.

There were no answers. After a while he dozed. In
his dream, he was back in the catacombs beneath the
city of Tummuz Orgmeen. An army of rats bore him
along on their backs through tunnels illuminated by
luminescent slime weed. A voice whispered in his ear,
encouraging him not to give up hope. He turned to
see the speaker and found only a beam of light, like
a bright star seen through a fog. Was it the Lady
Lessis? He reached out a hand into the light, and it
dissolved and with it the dream of Tummuz Orgmeen.
He shifted uneasily on a greasy swell on an ocean of
leaden aspect beneath storm clouds. Birds of war
sailed by.

He was awoken once more by a gentle shove on the
shoulder. Someone leaned close over him, a deeper
patch of darkness than the rest. He caught a scent of
jasmine. There was a flash of light, a match struck.
His eyes adjusted, and he found himself staring into
the face of Miranswa. Her veil was pulled up over her
forehead. She wore garub.

He opened his mouth, but she pressed her hand
across his lips.

"Keep quiet!" she hissed in a whisper. Her eyes
flickered back to the door.

"If they catch me here, they will kill me, understand? And then there will be no one to help you
escape, and you will go under the blade of the goddess, and your blood will spill down the temple on the
night of the full moon."

His eyes widened involuntarily.

"Blade of the goddess?" What in all the hells was
this? Since when did the Mother take life?

"Yes," she said, "you are to be sacrificed. The high
priestesses work a great magic, they will sacrifice to
the goddess to obtain her support."

He struggled to stay calm.

"Well," he whispered, "perhaps you have a key for these manacles?"

She inspected them carefully.

"No. But now I have the number, and I know where the keys are kept, I will see." The match went out. After a moment she struck another.

"In the meantime, keep silent, do not attract attention."

"Hold a moment," he whispered. "Where am I? Why do they want me?"

She leaned forward, looking lovelier than ever he remembered.

"This is the Island of the Goddess, in the center of the river."

"Why me?"

"It is always better in these matters to shed the blood of foreigners. And the girl you will be sacrificed with is also of your kind."

"A girl from Argonath?"

"Yes. I saw her today when she was bathed in the Mother's milk. She is beautiful in a barbaric sort of way. I felt sorry for her. But they will cut her throat and spill her blood down the steps when the moon rises tomorrow. If you are still here, they will mix your blood with hers."

A horrible thought suddenly crossed his mind.

"This girl, where was she taken from?"

Miranswa shrugged, "I do not know exactly . . . the city, I think."

Lagdalen! It could only be she.

"We must rescue her," he whispered with sudden determination.

"Impossible," she said. "I risk everything just to save you. She cannot be rescued. She is held in another dungeon below the great temple."

"Just tell me where she is and leave the rest to me,"

he said, although he felt far less confident then he sounded.

"Fool! I can save you only once, in return for what you did for me. You proved yourself to be an honorable person, but if you are taken again, then you will be beyond my help. As it is, I risk my life for you."

"Yes, of course, I understand." But if the girl from Argonath was Lagdalen of the Tarcho, how could he not make an effort to save her?

She gave him a look of utter disgust and blew out the light. After a while he heard the doors close behind her, first his cell door and then the outer one. Then there was silence.

CHAPTER TWENTY-NINE

The dragon was awoken by hunger. A real genuine famishment that threatened to set flame to his breath. By the old gods of Dragon Home, he swore he hadn't felt such a need for food in months. His stomach seemed to cleave to his backbone.

The next discovery was even more unpleasant. He was tied up with impressively massive ropes. Indeed, they were close to the size of cables. His arms were pinioned to his body, as were his legs and tail. Even his neck was roped and held down to the floor. No matter how he struggled, he could not break his bonds, although he rolled about on the floor and struck wooden pillars on either side.

Cursing in dragon speech, he craned his head about. The light was very dim, but his nostrils told him immediately that he was in a stables and that he was lying on a flagstone floor. Dragon sight is more acute than that of humans, and despite the dimness of the light, he was soon able to make out certain details of the place. There was a wide entrance at the far end, a door of wood. Light came through the door through tiny chinks around its edge. He redoubled his examination of his bonds.

They were disappointingly thorough. He tried to angle his lower jaw to come at one of the ropes with his teeth, but the rope around his throat was particularly tight and his efforts to bend his long neck cut off

his air in no time. He desisted with a gasp and then
more curses.

He bellowed for food a few times on the off chance
that his captors were waiting to hear from him and
would now rush in with some hot bread, some cheese,
perhaps some grilled lamb. By the gods, he thought,
even legion noodles with plenty of akh would be fine.

At the fifth bellow, the doors opened and men with
spears pushed in. Behind them came women clad in
the garub of Ourdh. Cautiously they approached and
examined him. They brought no food, not even the
scent of any food.

Furious, he roared questions at them in Verio.

One of them, the only one who spoke Verio, fainted
when she realized that this huge, muscular animal was
actually talking to her. She hadn't been fully prepared
for that. On an intellectual level perhaps she had
known this, but somehow the legend of the intelligent
wyverns of Argonath was not the same thing as the
reality. The other priestesses shrank back, cringing
away from the sheer size and obvious ferocity of the
monster.

He was obviously not about to break his bonds,
although he heaved about on the floor, he could not
loose his limbs or his tail. Nevertheless the men
jabbed at him with their spears, from a general sense
of wanting to do something to take control of the
situation. As they jabbed, they shouted in loud voices.
Like the priestesses, they were rendered highly nervous by the prospect of intelligent language coming
from an enormous animal of ferocious aspect and
legend.

Bazil cursed them, spat at them, and wished,
longed, for the fiery powers of the ancient drakes.
One roar from old Glabadza and all these impious
humans would be crisped and blackened.

Alas, the modern-day descendants of those mighty

dragons had no fire glands, no oil to flame. Bazil came up with nothing but a mighty belch.

He informed them that if they were going to poke him like that, they might as well go ahead and kill him then and there. He wasn't going to survive much longer without something to eat anyway.

They stood back at a sharp word from one of the women. Bazil craned his head around and did his best to be winning. Perhaps they could see their way to sending him some soup, some broth, even some gruel, if that was all they had.

The women stared at him stony-faced and then turned away. His voice rose. At the very least, they could give him some gruel. Even the miserable oats that they gave the horses, anything would do.

But then his visitors retreated, closing the doors and extinguishing the light without any glimmer of understanding of the hunger of a dragon.

Hopelessly he roared after them in a passionate rage, but to no result. He was left to the darkness and the many questions he could not possibly come up with answers for. Such as where was this place? And who were his captors? and what did they want with him?

By the roar of the old gods, this was a fine situation for a dragon to be in, trussed up like some doomed fowl ready to be roasted on a spit. How in the names of all the clouds had he ended up here?

Sadly, he wondered where the boy Relkin was. After a moment, he concluded that the boy was either dead or taken, too. Although, why they'd want him was a mystery. If they were intent on cooking a dragon for their supper, why would they want to throw in a scrawny boy? They'd probably knocked him on the head and tossed him aside.

While the broketail dragon pondered these things, great events were in motion all around him. On the great ziggurat of the goddess, beneath which he was imprisoned, the preparations were underway for the great magical work that was to be done when the moon rose to the zenith. Thousands of priestesses, artisans, and slaves were at work. Galleys bearing the elite of the cult of Gingo-La as the death goddess had docked in the little port on the northern end of the island. The work of the coming night would see the destruction of the demonic enemy in Dzu and afterward the glory of the goddess would be shown to the land. This was to be the time when the goddess would rise to the ascendant, and the heretics who worshiped Auros would be overthrown.

Secondly, there were the banks of the rivers, where great armies were on the move.

On the eastern bank, a vast horde had now invested the city of Ourdh. More than one hundred thousand Sephisti fanatics were encamped outside the city's walls. In the suburbs, there was mass looting and destruction as the Sephisti soldiers, simple fedd for the most part, discharged their inborn hatred of the well-off townsfolk and their sophisticated way of life.

While the fedd were thus preoccupied, the Sephisti engineers were hard at work. Siege engines were under construction at a dozen sites. To get the necessary timbers, the Sephisti simply pulled down nearby buildings and looted them of their beams.

Watching all this from the walls were the men of Argonath and a remnant of the Imperial Army, which had remained with the emperor in the city. These were the best troops from the Imperial Army, and the only ones with any real stomach for the coming fight.

The emperor would have fled, of course, but Ribela of Defwode was now permanently at his side, and she would not allow it. The emperor and his court were going to stay in the city and provide the citizens with heart for the siege.

Messages had gone back to the Argonath, describing the situation and calling for supply from the sea.

The great ships of Cunfshon, massive three-decker ships of oceanic trade would have to be diverted to assist this effort. The river would have to be cleansed of pirates. A fleet of warships was essential.

Meanwhile, the engineers of both the legion and the Imperial Guards division worked together to repair the walls and prepare their defense.

The dragons were a key resource. Their skills at toppling towers would be invaluable. In addition, stations for boiling oil on the ramparts were set up. When oil ran low, they would switch to water. An army of servant women was conscripted and set to carrying and stacking firewood and laying up jars of oil.

In the legion forts, the archers from Kenor were all at fletcher while the legion smiths were busily transforming scrap metal, ornaments, even kitchen utensils into arrowheads by the thousand. Elsewhere the engineers constructed catapults and trebuchets, and gathered rocks for them to hurl over the walls at the enemy.

General Paxion had risen to the challenge. This was the kind of battle he could really comprehend, a battle of supply. He drove himself and he drove everyone else to a maximum effort. Some of the Kadeini, and to his shame some of the Marneri officers, were still promoting the dream of escaping by ship. There were not enough ships to lift off one legion, let alone two. Paxion drove the Kadeini to make greater efforts. He ordered Pekel to set aside all illusions of immediate escape. Long before a fleet big enough to do that could be assembled, they were going to be fighting for their lives here. The Kadeini were vital to the defense of the walls; without them the defense would be impossible. There were upwards of twelve miles of wall, thirteen major forts including the massive Barracks on the north end and the Port Tower at the southernmost extremity. The two legions between them were now responsible for four forts and the Fatan gate. There were more than three miles of walls on their front, and there were many weaknesses along the walls, particularly to the south of the Fatan Gate where the ground was friable and the walls had cracked. The engineers were busy all along this stretch rigging weapons to defend the places where the walls were dilapidated.

With the Queen of Mice solidly ensconced at the emperor's elbow, Paxion had little trouble in satisfying the most outrageous demands from the engineers. He worked until he dropped, and he slept a few hours and rose and worked on. Paxion was no general for the open field, where dash and aggression often meant everything, but in this kind of contest he felt he could compete with the best of them.

So far there had been little contact with the enemy and not a single casualty. In fact, the Sephisti had hardly done more than fire a few arrows for ranging purposes, and close off the roads outside the big gates. There was a nasty methodicalness to it all. The great army of Sephis would take the city when it was ready and not before.

While the east bank of the great river saw the preparations for war mounting steadily, the west bank was not quiet by any means. Closer to the Island of the Goddess than the east bank, the west bank was also only twenty miles south of the city of Dzu. During the afternoon, a large body of Sephisti soldiers approached the river there.

From the shore, they could easily see the great ziggurat of the goddess. The commanders surveyed the situation briefly and then ordered work crews to tear apart the nearest villages, pulling the houses down and separating out all the usable timber. On the riverbank, other crews prepared to build rafts.

CHAPTER THIRTY

In the dungeon, the hours slid by slowly and the night gave way at last to another dawn. Relkin was grimly aware that if he didn't escape soon, it would be the last dawn he would ever see. He grew increasingly nervous as the daylight hours went by. Where was Miranswa? If she didn't hurry up, it would be too late. He would end up on the altar stone high above his dungeon.

At length, he sensed the waning of the daylight. His heart began to sink. Miranswa had failed. Perhaps she had been caught in the act of taking the keys. Perhaps she had simply decided that it was too risky. Perhaps she would be there watching, among the throng of junior priestesses, when they cut his throat with the obsidian blade and then dug his heart out of his chest and offered it to the moon.

He felt his throat constrict at that thought and again when he considered the next. For as soon as they had finished with him, they would place Lagdalen on the same stone, repeat the sacrifice, and blend their blood on the thousand steps that descended from the altar.

Relkin hunched down by the wall and tried to blank out all thoughts. It was too painful otherwise. But the day was gone, and it was definitely turning dark now. The moon would rise shortly, and then they would come for him.

At that very moment, he heard the outer door opening. Then the inner door swung open. He steeled himself. He would not show the fear he felt, he would hold his head up. He would die like a soldier of Argonath.

But instead of the guards, it was Miranswa, at last, panting from her efforts and carrying the precious key.

"I have it," she whispered. She struck a light.

The key went into the cuffs, but there it stuck. Miranswa found it hard to turn. Her fingers did not have the strength. She struggled with it while Relkin tried not to panic. Again and again she worked at it while Relkin advised her to shift the key around in the lock, sometimes a certain set was required, a certain position, especially if the lock was old and perhaps a little loose.

But nothing seemed to work and now Relkin began to pray that it was the right key. Had she made a mistake? If so, then he was doomed.

And then there came a click, and she gave a grunt of triumph and made one more effort. A gasp escaped her lips and then with a rusty *ka-chunk*, the lock turned and the cuffs fell open. A moment later, Relkin was out of the cell and at the outer door peering out poised to run.

"Wait," hissed Miranswa, thrusting a bundle of clothing at him. "Put these on. You must pass as a temple slave."

Quickly, he stripped off his Marneri wool breeches and his good cotton shirt. He noticed that Miranswa did not turn away, but watched him closely. He felt a sudden embarrassment and quickly donned the white tunic and breechclout, each of which carried a wide, vertical red stripe.

"Now you are safe unless someone asks you a direct question. In the unlikely event that someone does, pretend to be mute. Nod as if you understand, bow from the waist, and then go away quickly as if you are obeying a command. When you leave here, turn right and you will soon find a main passage that passes beneath the temple from north to south. Go north, and once you're outside the temple go on down the avenue. You will see lights ahead. That is the port. There is a barracks there for slaves, so it will be quite normal for you to be walking in that direction. When you get there, you must find a way to get aboard a boat heading to the city. Several leave every night."

"I must thank you, Miranswa."

"You will thank me best if you hurry away now. Very soon they will come, and once you are missed there will be a hue and cry raised. You don't want them to recapture you, do you?" But he did not leave as bidden.

"Where is the girl you spoke of?"

Miranswa frowned. "Do not speak of her; you cannot save her. Go now!"

"Where is she?"

"Go, you fool." Miranswa pushed at him.

Relkin seized her by the shoulders and looked into her eyes.

"You are a friend, Miranswa, and I would never wish to harm you, and I am in your debt, but you must tell me where the Lady Lagdalen lies. If I am to be taken again, I will make sure they kill me, I will not betray you."

She could see that he was immovable. Nothing she could say would change his mind.

"Ah, what is the use?" she said to herself in Uld. "You are barbarian anyway, and everyone knows they are all mad."

Still her heart felt heavy, and she had to fight back tears.

Well anyway, she herself was quite safe. There was no need to worry. If they recaptured him, which they would surely do, they would just sacrifice him, and there would hardly be time for them to question him and force him to give up her name. So she would just blink back her tears and return the stolen key before priestess Guda ever woke up from her nap.

Miranswa sighed. Her efforts had been wasted. Perhaps here the goddess was giving her a lesson. Those that the goddess had selected for sacrifice would die for her, and there was no way to change their fate.

In a broken whisper, she told him where to find the Argonathi girl. "On the upper tier of the ziggurat, in a room close to the high altar. They washed her in the milk of the Mother this afternoon. Since then, she has been wrapped in swaddling and awaits the knife."

He relaxed his grip, but did not move away.

"Thank you, Miranswa, for everything." He bent forward suddenly and kissed her on the lips. There was an electric tingle in that kiss. He hadn't expected her to return it as she had. Could it mean that she cared for him as he did for her? And how would he ever see her again? It was as if they lived on different worlds.

"Wish me luck," he said.

"Go," she said still stony-faced, but then she softened. He was a mad barbarian, yes, but such a nice young barbarian. Really it was a terrible pity that he was going to waste his life in this way. And he had saved her life, she would always be in his debt on that score. She would infinitely prefer sacrifice to the goddess on her altar to the living death of enforced prostitution, and he had rescued her from that. She had had to try and save him, if only because she had a conscience that wouldn't let her sleep once she knew of his imprisonment. He was a barbarian, but he had behaved with such decency that he had captured her heart.

"Go then, and may the goddess forgive me and let you live. Good-bye."

Still he hovered there peering into her eyes, entranced, smitten.

"Miranswa."

"Go." She pushed him away. He took a few steps. "Good luck," she whispered after him.

Relkin slipped away and hurried through the outer passage to a wide oval door guarded by two massive men with turbans and scimitars. The guards barely glanced at him. The servitor's garb hid him perfectly.

On the main passage he was even safer, temporarily. This passage was thirty feet wide and crowded with considerable numbers of temple servants who looked much like himself.

He returned to the task ahead. Somehow he would have to obtain some weapons. Then he had to climb the ziggurat, find the room in which Lagdalen was imprisoned, and somehow rescue her.

There was very little time. The moon was rising.

He came to a crossing. To the right was a broad staircase that ascended to the ground floor. He was now on the grand passage, some sixty feet wide with horse-drawn traffic in the center lanes.

The crowds here were largely composed of women, and he noticed with a shock that here, at last, the women of Ourdh went without the all-covering garub and veil. Here, within the temple of the goddess, they wore their hair openly and dressed in gowns of silk and satin with exquisite coloring and designs. Their walk here was different, free of constant deference to men. There was an independence, a strut that he hadn't seen in Ourdh before.

He hurried along, looking for a stair to ascend. There were side passages here, lined with shops and temple offices. There were also fanes to the goddess in her many incarnations. Some were empty and shuttered up, while others were filled with worshipers in the midst of their ceremonies. Hymns were sung while the priestesses performed the arcane gestures and lit the candles of significance.

He dodged out of the way of an elegant brougham pulled by a pair of beautiful black geldings. There was quite a lot of horse-drawn traffic all of a sudden, and the air had changed, there was a breeze.

He'd reached the end of the great passage. It seemed that there were no accessible internal staircases. He would have to climb the great tower by the open public ramps. The crowds there would be thick, his progress would inevitably be slow. At the top, there would be a throng and some kind of barrier between the public space atop the pyramid and the altar. It seemed a hopeless task. He needed a more private space.

He decided to try to find an inner stair once more. Perhaps the side passages lead to such stairs. At random he turned and plunged down the first side street. He found himself on a narrow pavement perhaps nine feet across. On either side were rows of small doorways fronting tiny shops where skilled seamstresses plied their trade. In their windows were displayed the lavish gowns that were worn within the temple bounds, beautiful concoctions of turquoise silk, white satin, lace, and ribbons. Caught up with amazement at the beauty of these fabrics and the artistry of the styling, Relkin failed to notice quickly enough that he was the only male in sight, apart from a couple of guards who were leaning over a stall that sold hot tea.

The tea woman saw him first and pointed him out with a sharp word. The guards lurched up with oaths and gesticulations. Relkin realized his mistake at once. He bowed and then started back. In his haste, alas, he walked right into a portly woman swathed in a vast gown of purple silks with puff sleeves and lace collar. She stumbled backward with a shriek of dismay, and Relkin fell on top of her. Her outcries redoubled in volume.

He was back on his feet in an instant, but the damage was done. The woman in purple continued to voice her complaints and the guards dropped their tea and leapt toward him.

Relkin ran back up to the main passage. At the corner, he ran into another woman, a lemon seller, and sent her plate of cut lemons flying. More loud complaints went up.

A hue and cry was building up behind him.

A white carriage blocked his way for a moment. Something about it was familiar and then he glimpsed Aimlor, the surly coachman of the Princess Zettila. At the back of the carriage was a running board where footmen could ride during a processional.

The carriage suddenly picked up speed, traveling in the opposite direction from which he was coming. For a moment, he was obscured from his pursuers, they were scattering to avoid Aimlor's blundering horsemanship. Relkin sprang up onto the running board and was carried back through the pursuit. No one noticed him, they were all intent on the hurrying fugitive somewhere ahead in the throng.

Nor did Aimlor look back, Aimlor's attention was fixed on the horses as he guided them out of the passage into the open air. Outside, under the night sky, a vast crowd was moving up the outer stairs to the first tier of the ziggurat. Lamps were lit at every corner of the stair, thousands of women devotees carried candles. Relkin's eye flicked up and caught the mass of the pyramid at last. Tier after tier rose above him, each aglitter with thousands of candles and lanterns. Relkin felt a naked awe; there was no structure on this scale in the Argonath. It was a mountain built by men.

The carriage rolled on, picking up speed slightly as the passage broadened into a wide avenue that continued on to some smaller buildings about a mile away. Relkin hung on as Aimlor suddenly turned and took a side road that ran down a short gulley and then hooked back to the base of the pyramid on the eastern side.

Relkin had been preparing to jump off, but now

kept his place as they jounced along a much rougher
road to a set of stables tucked under the eave of the
temple mass.

They came to a halt at last, and Relkin slipped off
the running board and skipped into the nearest stable
door.

From the sheltering darkness, he watched Aimlor
open the carriage door and assist the Princess Zettila
as she stepped out. She hurried into the stables and
was met just within the far door by a man whom Relkin could not see very well.

Aimlor resumed his seat on the carriage. Relkin
listened carefully. There were many open stable doors
here and dozens of horses. Many wealthy devotees of
the goddess kept a coach and pair here solely to bear
them up and down the avenue from the docks to the
temple. However, most of the coaches and horses
were out on this evening, promenading on the avenue.

Stable workers were gathered together somewhere,
he could hear their cheery conversation and exclamations. There was a certain excitement due to the festi-
val atmosphere.

Relkin slipped back into the darkness. Perhaps he
might find a weapon back there.

He avoided the stable workers and kept to the shadows as much as possible. There were occasional lanterns hanging from the pillars supporting the ceiling.
He took one to examine a room filled with equipment,
but found no weapons. It was all horse and carriage
equipment.

Some stable workers came by laughing together. He
extinguished the lamp and dodged back in the dark
and fell over something. One boy laughed, and they
all made loud meowing sounds and went on their way.

Relkin's back hurt where he'd landed on a wheel.
With a groan, he staggered out and continued the
search.

He kept to the shadows until he found a rear area

that was relatively quiet. The light here was very dim, since the stable lamps were all in the front. He dodged around a corner into a side passage with storerooms filled with hay.

Behind him somewhere in the dark, a cat yowled and several horses snorted in their stalls. In the storage space, he hid himself behind some straw and tried to think of a way to get a sword.

The task ahead of him seemed insuperable. It was agonizing to think that Lagdalen would die up there on that altar when he was down here simply unable to come up with a plan. He had to have a plan!

He had been there a few minutes, long enough to get seriously depressed about his chances when he heard a familiar voice demanding food, any food at all, for a starving dragon. He stood up, his heart beating wildly, and knocked his head on the crossbeam. With stars in his eyes, he headed toward the source of that voice.

Ahead he glimpsed more lanterns, and he ducked aside as a pair of guards emerged from a large darkened doorway. The Princess Zettila emerged behind them, and they closed the door and barred it.

The dragon continued to demand food, listing all of its favorite things starting with whole roast chickens and going on to venison pie and noodles lathered in akh.

The princess disappeared, accompanied by one of the guards. With a grunt, the other man pulled out a bale of hay and sat down and leaned back. He set his spear against the wall beside him and placed a hand on the hilt of the sword he wore. Relkin's eyes glittered in the dark.

CHAPTER THIRTY-ONE

The guard, Yoka, leaned back against the rough wood of the stable door and sighed with boredom. The great monster tied up on the other side of the door continued to snort and mutter to itself. Yoka wondered idly what it was saying. It was amazing to think that an animal like that could actually talk. But that's what the priestesses had said, quite distinctly, the damn monster was trying to talk to them in the barbarian tongue of the north.

For the umpteenth time, Yoka spat and prayed that those ropes were strong enough. If that dragon got loose, the goddess alone knew what it would take to recapture it. Yoka hoped they were going to hurry up and kill the damn thing. Weren't they planning to sacrifice it at the end of the ceremony and spill its blood down the stairs? Something like that. It couldn't come too soon for Yoka.

By the breath of the goddess, he hated this duty. He wished he was back with Tofor and the others on his regular detail on the third tier. You got a good view of things from there.

He yawned. At least there were compensations on this job. You could sit down, and you could even take naps when both guards were present. From this vantage point, you could see right through the stables to the front entrance. You could see someone coming long before they could see you, so there was plenty of time to get back on your feet and look watchful.

Still, he knew he was missing the fun on the third tier. There was sure to have been a round of beer sent up by the priestess of Tork, who always stood on the third tier during sacrifice ceremonies, surrounded by her assistants. She was the wife of a wealthy land-owner in Bogra, and she was always generous with the beer and the food. All the guards would be in a good mood, looking forward to the sacrifice and the singing afterward. The goddess would be called on to protect her servants from the demon in Dzu. Afterward there would be a carnival on the main avenue, all the way to the port. But unless they sacrificed the dragon, too, Yoka would miss everything.

He kept his eyes on the front entrance. The other guard, Rozaw, would be awhile yet. Once he'd seen their visitor into her carriage, Roz would try and get some beer for the two of them. The beer stall was just fifty yards away, but Yoka was sure that old Roz would put one or two down his gullet before he headed back with a job. So he didn't expect him anytime too soon. He cursed and then he chuckled. He'd have done the same thing, of course.

Yoka was so absorbed in these thoughts, that he failed to see the slim, determined-looking youth creeping up on him along the wall. Nor did he see the leg of a wooden stool that the youth had in hand. In fact, Yoka failed to react until the very last moment, when something made him look up, and he saw a blur flash down and felt it club him along the side of the head.

The next he knew, he was kneeling on the floor and his helmet was rolling away in front of him. Something struck him hard on the back of the head, and he went out like a light.

Dragoneer First Class Relkin of Quosh bent over the man and checked for a pulse. Relkin prayed he hadn't killed the fellow. It had not been his intention. After a moment of panic, he detected a steady throb.

Relieved, he took Yoka's sword, then levered up the bar across the door, and slipped inside.

A vast bulk lay there groaning to itself. In the light that flooded in behind him, Relkin could see his dragon encircled a dozen times in cables as thick as a man's wrist.

"It's alright, it's me," he said in a whisper, aware that the dragon was watching him approach with drawn sword and that the dragon was in a wild mood.

There was a long silence.

"Boy Relkin?"

"In the flesh."

"Boy Relkin?" roared the dragon astonished. "That is good, I not believe it possible."

"Thanks for having faith in me."

"You are welcome. Please now, use blade and free this dragon. I have terrible itch."

"Well, I suppose I should."

"Hurry."

Relkin started hacking at the rope that bound the dragon's forearms together at the wrist. Yoka's sword was not the sharpest, and it took several blows to even cut into the heavy rope. While he sawed away, the dragon interrogated him.

"Where is this? And why are we here? Who are these people? And why have they been starving me?"

"Some island in the river, there's a big pyramid, temple to their goddess. They were going to sacrifice me."

"Sacrifice dragonboy?"

"Yeah."

"Then they want to sacrifice dragon, too, eh?"

Relkin paused for a moment. He hadn't thought about it, but now that Bazil had mentioned it, that did seem the most likely reason they would have brought a two-ton dragon to the island. "Well, I guess so, I can't think why else they'd have gone to the trouble to bring you here."

"They make big mistake."

"They still have Lagdalen."

"What?"

"For this sacrifice of theirs."

"I see. Dragonboy and girl for appetizer, and dragon for main course."

"I don't think they eat their sacrifices, Baz. It's not like when we sacrifice some grain to the goddess or slaughter a steer for her. They were going to slit our throats and pour our blood down the big staircase. That's the way they measure these things here."

"Damn wasteful, if you ask this dragon."

Relkin heard the tone in the dragon's voice and whistled to himself. Somebody was going to catch it, and soon. This dragon was angry.

"And they have Lagdalen, dragon friend?"

"She's up on the top of the pyramid. We have to try and rescue her."

"Of course." Bazil's eyes glowed. He was ready to take on his captors no matter how many of them there were. Then he caught a movement down by the front of the stables.

"You better hurry up, someone is coming." Relkin looked over his shoulder. It was true, the other guard, jug in hand, was coming through the stables.

Relkin renewed his assault on the ropes, sawing back and forth with the blade. The ropes were resistant. He was still only half through the first.

Rozaw saw the prone body of Yoka. He set down the jug with an oath and stumbled forward while drawing his sword.

"Hurry, boy, or all for waste, and we both end up as sacrifice," growled the dragon.

Relkin made another effort, but the rope continued to resist. The guard burst into the room with sword in hand, and shouting for help he ran to attack.

Relkin dodged aside and parried the first sweep.

Then he counterattacked with his speed against the bigger man's strength.

He beat the man inside, lunged, and old Roz felt the sword cut through his jerkin to his belly as he flinched from the blow. He put a hand down there and found that he had barely been cut, but it had been close.

Relkin circled. Old Roz realized how out of condition he really was. This boy had almost gutted him. Old Roz was starting to wish he hadn't jumped in here quite so fast. Not only was this boy a good swordsman, but the damned dragon was writhing madly and looked as if it might break its bounds.

It was time to reach into the old bag of tricks. Roz had learned a few in his days as a beer house brawler.

He regained the initiative with a short swing, and mixed in a sucker punch that caught the boy on the shoulder and spun him around. Roz chuckled, the old tricks they always worked best on the young, but Relkin came back with his foot up and planted it solidly in Roz's paunch. Old Roz doubled up and went down gasping. Relkin went back to a furious assault on the rope. It was giving, but oh so slowly. He sawed on it again, cursing the while.

Old Roz recovered his breath and, flushing with fury, lurched to his feet and took another wild swing at the youth. He missed and traveled around off balance. As he spun by, the flailing sword just nicked the tip of Bazil's nose. Hot blood spurted while the dragon convulsed with a tremendous hiss. The huge muscles in his body stood out in stark relief. The cable that was partway cut broke with a loud snap.

Roz stood there irresolute for a fatal second. The monster's ropes had broken! How could this have happened to him? It had ruined a perfectly wonderful day.

Then he realized that the dragon was still hampered, bound at the legs and roped to the wall. Disas-

ter could still be averted. Roz plunged in with a
scream of desperation, and Relkin met him blade to
blade. Roz took a hack, and Relkin slid away behind
a stable post. Wood chips whined through the air.

Bazil roared with frustration as he unwound the
ropes from his arms and shoulders. He took hold of
the steel ring in the wall and gave a mighty heave.
Nothing happened for a moment and then with a sudden loud crack the metal in the pin broke, and the
dragon fell backward with a crash and rolled between
the two combatants.

Stable boys were coming, drawn to the uproar. Relkin dodged Rozaw again and tried a sweep of his own.
Rozaw beat that aside and lunged. Relkin sidestepped
the blade, but ran into that sucker punch again. He
staggered and ducked just as Roz punched again. This
time old Roz's fist caught Relkin on the forehead with
a solid crack that spoke of broken knuckles. Relkin
went down on hands and knees, momentarily stunned.
He heard the guard howling with pain, but it seemed
as if he were a long way away.

With an effort, Relkin staggered to his feet, stumbled forward, and shoved at the guard. Rozaw was off
balance, and he stepped back a pace or two while his
face contorted with rage.

"Why, you little whelp," he began.

And then huge dragon paws closed around him and
lifted him off the ground. Rozaw gave a scream of
raw terror and fainted. The dragon dropped him in a
heap on the floor and took his sword.

The stable boys bounded into the room. Relkin was
still dazed, and his sword arm felt about as useful as
a piece of wet wood.

With a cry that sounded a little wild and weak, he
challenged them. They came on with looks of determination. A brown-skinned boy about his own age
swiped at him with a broom, and he barely warded it
off with the sword. He and the boy tried to kick each

other and missed. The other boys closed in with knife and cudgel. Relkin couldn't face all three of them. He felt as if he could barely lift the sword.

The broom cracked off his shoulders. He ducked away and swung weakly at the one with the knife. The broom hit him on the back of the legs. He was getting real tired of the one with the broom, who was both active and most aggressive.

The one with the knife darted at him, the one with the cudgel was waiting for him to break to the right, and the broom waited on the left. Relkin had a bad feeling.

Then the stable boys suddenly turned on their heels and fled.

"What?" said Relkin stupidly. "Hey come on back here, you cowards!" he shouted.

A big hand landed on his shoulder and he was facing a freed dragon, who roared with joy and gave him a hug that drove the breath out of his body and rattled his bones.

Boy and dragon faced each other.

"Boy, you do hell of a job there. You almost free me."

"Well, I wanted to keep it interesting," said Relkin when he got a breath back into his lungs. "I thought you were having such a good time here, as a sacrificial guest."

"You succeed. Now we have to get out of here."

"Well, we don't want to go out that way," said Relkin, pointing after the stable boys. They could hear their shouts from the front.

"Is there another way out of here?"

"This way," said Relkin, and he lead the dragon away down a passage lined with empty stalls. Eventually they came up against a wooden door.

Bazil sank his claws into the rim of this door and broke it in half. It had not been designed with such usage in mind.

On the other side, they found themselves in a hay-loft with an opening directly above through which the hay was delivered.

Relkin swarmed up the side of a stack of baled hay and swung open the door. He found himself looking down a short access passage used primarily by hay wagons.

"Climb the straw."

"Oh, good idea. You think straw hold up weight of dragon?"

"Try it. C'mon."

The dragon stepped up on the hay. It held him momentarily, but then it collapsed and he slid back to the floor.

"Dragonboy wrong once again."

Relkin dropped back to the floor. He pointed to a stoutly built hay wagon standing in the corner.

"Now that looks more like it."

Bazil put his shoulder to the bales of hay beneath the door and shoved them aside. In less than half a minute, he had positioned the big cart right under the open doors.

"Better hurry, they're getting excited back there," said Relkin.

Behind them now, they could the hear the sounds of pursuit. Suddenly there was an intense outcry.

"They found the guards," said Relkin. "They'll be here soon."

But getting a two-ton dragon onto the old hay cart wasn't the easiest thing in the world. The cart tended to tip over when he put his weight on it. Finally on the fourth try, he got both feet aboard and raised his head through the trap door to the outside. Now came the really hard part. He got his shoulders up and began to slowly heave himself through.

It was slow work. Strong as he was, it was hard to lift his own bulk through the door.

"Come on, Baz, hurry, they're coming."

Relkin jumped onto the wagon, pushed, and almost got flattened when the dragon lashed his tail in frustration.

Three guards were at the door. Relkin drew the sword and jumped back onto the cart.

"Forgive me," he whispered.

He jabbed the dragon sharply in the glivvers with the tip of his sword.

With a scream of outrage, Bazil exploded through the door into the street.

Relkin swung himself up right behind him, and the guardsmen missed him by a hairsbreadth.

Relkin slammed the hatch shut on them in the next moment.

The dragon had a very dangerous look on his face.

"Dragon not like dragonboy very much."

Relkin knew denials were pointless.

"We're outside, right? We're alive. Ease up a little."

The dragon hissed.

"Look, I'm sorry, but aren't you glad we got out of there?"

The dragon hissed quietly for a second or two.

"By the roar," he said. The big jaws clacked together in anger. "Someday," he growled and then, with an effort he stopped himself. "Alright, where by roar of old gods are we?"

Relkin had already crept down the narrow hay passage to its mouth.

"Look at this!"

Bazil joined him.

They looked out on a scene of ceremonial splendor.

The hay passage exited on the south face of the temple. To their right, the surface dipped down to the base of a huge staircase that swept straight up the face of the temple in three long flights.

Around this stair was grouped a crowd of highborns and on the stair itself was the procession of high priestesses, already more than two thirds of the way to the top.

The scene was lit up by hundreds of great lamps posted on ornate, brass lamp stands set at regular intervals beside the great staircase.

Both the boy and the dragon could clearly see the finery of the ceremonial gowns. The priestesses wore vast trailing affairs of lace, satin, and chiffon in pink, pale green, and yellow.

The orchestra, arrayed on a parade ground in front of the pyramid, began a loud, urgent piece of music. Drums rumbled thunderously. Her worshipers called the goddess to take note of their magnificent ceremony in her honor.

"When they reach the top, they kill Lagdalen dragon friend, correct?"

"Yes."

"We have a long way to climb."

"Afraid so."

"By the roar, but I am famished."

"When this is over, we'll eat well, I promise."

"You have promised before, what did that ever mean?"

"I would like to point out that I have achieved a pretty good record when it comes to fulfilling promises."

"So you say, but then you have human memory."

"I'm not sure I accept all the claims made for other kinds of memories," said Relkin quietly.

"Hmmmph. Let's go."

"Right."

CHAPTER THIRTY-TWO

The moon was high in the sky, and the ceremony was now entering the climax. The musicians played the anthem of the goddess, an andante, the viols soaring high while the drums began their thunder.

The priestesses had almost reached the top. Now was the time for everyone else to get to their places. The highborn women, clad in elaborate costumes, began to move onto the great stair. The trumpets were raised. The drumming grew steadily louder as the climax approached.

One group of women was heading for their place on the stairs when they noticed something move in the ornamental shrubbery that lined the lower part of the great stair. To their astonishment, a ten-foot-tall dragon lurched out of concealment. A lithe youth darted out behind the dragon. Swords glittered in their hands.

The women opened their mouths to scream just as the trumpets blew, and for the moment they went unnoticed. The dragon and the boy shouldered through the startled crowd of highborn women and marched up the steps of the first flight. As they went, the panic grew until it infected the entire lower tier. Suddenly the ceremony was forgotten, and, scattering their pride to the winds, the aristocratic ladies of Ourdh trampled one another on the stairs in their attempts to escape.

The guards, massed on the first tier, drew their

swords and stepped out to do their duty. They were hesitant to a degree. Word of what these dragons could do on a battlefield had spread since Salpalangum. Their commanders bellowed and laid about them with their staffs, and slowly the guards moved down the great stair.

The dragon came straight up toward them. On the way it tested the brass lamp stands, tugging at each one as he passed. Quite soon he found one that moved a little on its foundation. The dragon tossed the sword back over its shoulders and caught it with the broken-looking tip of his tail. Then he grabbed the lamp stand and heaved on it. With a whine of tortured metal, the bolts eased out of their marble sockets and then the lamp stand came free.

It weighed perhaps two hundred pounds, and Bazil Broketail wielded it like a club.

The guards extended their spears in a mass of points. Their commanders were bellowing for reinforcements. Archers had been sent for but had yet to make their way up the staircases through the mobs that jammed them.

The crowds on all sides were now torn between panic-stricken flight and the urge to see the spectacle. The monster was about to be slain by the temple guards. Who would not want to see this? The mobs stopped running and gazed upward to the top of the first flight of steps on the great stair.

Meanwhile, Relkin ran lightly back and forth behind the dragon, as he would in any battle, except that this time he had no bow. Still, he whipped Yoka's sword about him. His arm had recovered some of its strength, and he felt ready to try anything. After all, he'd come a long way since he'd woken up in the darkness.

Bazil reached the hedge of spear points. He hefted the lamp stand and swung it in front of him in a great sweep, snapping spearheads from their shafts and driving the men back.

Some of the men drew their swords and darted at the dragon with suicidal bravery. The crowd cheered. But Bazil hefted the lamp stand as if it were a two-handed sword and swung it through the men at waist height. Men were knocked flying like balls from a bat. Still, one determined fellow ducked the lamp stand, then bounced back to his feet, and slashed at the dragon's knee.

Baz pulled back sharply and almost lost his balance. While he struggled to stay upright, the man slashed his flank. Relkin hurled himself headlong into the guard's side and knocked him backward. The fellow gave an oath, but held onto his sword. Now he steadied himself and lunged at Relkin, who parried, ducked, and barely parried again. The guard was a good swordsman, and Relkin's arm was growing tired. The blade was coming. Relkin met it, but felt his own sword struck from his nerveless hand. He was defenseless at last. The death stroke rose, and the man gave a scream of triumph and brought it down. But instead of sundering Relkin in two, it rang off the end of the heavy brass lamp stand, suddenly interposed.

The guard looked up at the dragon, stupefied, caught in dragon-freeze.

Bazil wasted no time on ceremony. He kicked the man, knocking him fifteen feet through the air. The body rolled down the stair to the bottom. The watching crowd gave a groan.

The other swordsmen hesitated once more. They hadn't expected the monster to lash out with its feet like that. Indeed, they had expected to see the huge thing carried up the stair at the end of the ceremony to have its blood poured down the steps in glory of the goddess. A couple of the more dumbfounded forgot to move back in time, and the lamp stand caught them on the next sweep and connected hard. Their bodies flew over the heads of the others and landed with dull thuds on the tier above. The rest of the guards wavered, a few started running.

A couple of brave civilians with small ceremonial swords ran up from the bottom of the stair. Relkin met one with a slash and a parry, and shouted a warning to the dragon.

Baz saw the man coming and met him with the tail sword. The man flailed valiantly, but his ceremonial sword was knocked out of his hands the next moment.

Weaponless, he fell back. His fellow continued to duel with Relkin in a halfhearted way, but he too desisted when the tail sword swished through the air above his head. No one else followed their example.

They mounted the next tier and met no opposition until they reached the top. A single guard remained, to bar their way.

Relkin whistled to the man, caught his eye, and indicated with his thumb that the man should retreat. The guard hesitated, and Bazil made play with the lamp stand. The man backed away and ran for the exit, where he joined the mob of elaborately dressed women.

Relkin noticed that his dragon was breathing hard and that there was considerable evaporation from the open mouth. In such conditions, dragons could overheat and suffer dehydration. He cast around and gave a whoop as his eye lit on a keg of beer, abandoned by the guards. It was nicely set up on a crosstrees, with a couple of mugs hanging below.

"Just a moment, Baz. Are you as thirsty as I am?"

The dragon didn't hesitate. He scooped up the keg, which was still a third full, and punched a hole through its end with a massive thumb claw. He took a long swig, then poured some into a cup proferred by the dragonboy.

They drank deeply and then went on, toward the

top tier, with fire in their eyes. Baz tossed away the empty barrel behind him. It clattered down the stairs.

By this point, the astonishment among the high priestesses had given way to horror. They stampeded for the exits from the top tier, but this level of the ziggurat was much restricted and thus there were few ways down. A mob of aristocrats bunched at the exits. Elaborate robes and lavish gowns were torn and ripped. Silks were crushed underfoot, chiffon and puff shredded by the nails of the desperate.

The dragon and his boy reached the top tier a half minute later, and found it almost completely deserted. In the center was an altar raised up to the goddess. Seven copper mirrors concentrated the moon's light on the altar stone where Relkin and Bazil were to have been sacrificed.

A small cluster of high priestesses stood there utterly aghast as Relkin and Bazil advanced on them, weapons at the ready.

"Where is the Lady Lagdalen of Marneri?" he shouted at them.

"Fool boy," snapped the dragon. "They speak their own tongue, they not understand you."

But at that moment Relkin recognized one of the priestesses.

"That one there, wearing the black. She's the one I spoke to at Salpalangum."

It was true, there was the princess, she of the white coach and the big blond coachman. He placed himself in front of her.

"You are the princess who spoke to me at Salpalangum."

The Princess Zettila stared at him with an expression of acute perplexity. Her world was coming down around her ears. This boy was like some manifestation of the worst devils of hell.

He pointed at her.

"I know you speak the tongue of Argonath, I know you can understand me."

Zettila's lips moved, but no words came.

Already the enemy fleet was landing on the shores of the isle. The sacrifices could not be made. The ceremony was in shreds and all was lost. The enemy's armies would swarm over them and destroy everything. The great temple of the goddess would be profaned.

"Where is Lagdalen of the Tarcho?" said Relkin leaning in closer. It was as if she were in a trance or something. A priestess to his left produced a small silver knife in her hand.

The motion was not missed. The dragon raised the lamp stand. The priestesses cowered back with little shrieks.

Zettila stared at him, the destroyer.

"What do you want?" she said at last. He was holding a sword to her throat. She had decided that she didn't want to die.

"Princess or not, I will kill you if you do not answer me. Where is the girl from Marneri?"

Zettila's rage got the better of her.

"You must not do this. You destroy the world. Look!" Zettila pointed to the western shore of the island. There, illuminated by hundreds of torches, they saw a flotilla of rafts and boats from which an army was disembarking.

"Who are they?" said Relkin, alarmed at the sight.

"You little fool! Those are the servants of Sephis. If we do not complete the ceremony to summon the power of the goddess, they will overrun the temple and bring an end to everything."

"Ceremony? You mean sacrificing me and Baz here?"

She turned eyes filled with tragedy upon him. "It is vital, I implore you to accept this honor. You will be remembered for all time. Place yourself on the altar and convince your monstrous beast to do the same. You must. The goddess demands it." As she said this, Zettila attempted to cast a spell, but Relkin was wise to it and backed away with a curse.

"Sacrifice yourself, lady. We ain't interested. Besides, I don't think your magic's going to do much to that army. You don't have time. So just tell me where Lagdalen of the Tarcho is."

He seized her by the wrist. Her mouth froze in shock. Never in her life had she been manhandled by someone of the servant class. This was appalling, the end of civilization.

"Where is Lagdalen?"

Still she would not speak, and Relkin was loathe to strike her, but time was short.

Bazil lurched forward a stride and thrust his head close to her face. "Answer the boy!" he said quietly.

Zettila heard the monster speak to her, albeit in the barbarian tongue, and felt her heart stop. The eyes were so huge! Yellow with black pupils that had such an unholy luster. Zettila was frozen. Relkin pinched her arm to break her out of dragon-freeze.

"Where is the girl?"

It was hopeless. Relkin was about to resort to desperate measures, when another priestess spoke up.

"The girl is in the room beneath the altar."

Relkin stepped back.

"Well, better late than never. My thanks to you, madam."

"Go away," hissed the woman.

Relkin investigated and located the door. It was bolted on the outside. He released the bolts and found Lagdalen of the Tarcho, bound and gagged, lying on a narrow bed.

It was a moment's work to tear away the gag and cut her free. She was staring at him with astonished eyes.

"Relkin? It *is* you. I thought I heard your voice. Thought I was dreaming."

Relkin hugged her hard.

"How in the name of the Mother did you find me?"

"Now that is a long story. Maybe we should talk about it while we move."

"Has the enemy army landed yet?" said Lagdalen.

"You knew about that?"

"I heard them talking about it this afternoon when they were making me take a bath in milk. They didn't realize that I understand their language."

"Hey, me and Baz were going to be sacrificed, too."

She stared at him in shock.

"I have a friend on the inside, you might say. She helped me get free. I found Baz, and we busted out, climbed up here, and got you out."

"Sounds like the Relkin of old. Getting someone into trouble."

"I earned her favor honestly enough, Lagdalen of the Tarcho."

The dragon leaned close. "What did they do to Lagdalen, dragon friend?"

"Well, actually nothing much, except for not giving me anything to eat."

"They do that to dragon, too. Terrible thing."

Now they could hear screams resounding from the woods on the western side of the ziggurat.

"It sounds like we should get out of here."

They went down the main stair on the south face of the ziggurat as quickly as they could. Ahead of them were the high priestesses, with Zettila in their midst, scampering down a walk to a dock. They followed them, moving along quickly, keeping to the shadows.

CHAPTER THIRTY-THREE

The moon rode high above a ghastly scene. The isle of Gingo-La was overrun by an army of men with dead eyes, whose will was not their own. Among these men strode giants with blank faces, whose flesh was mere mud, but mud instilled with terrible strength.

Together they crushed and dispersed the small force of guards who tried to block their way near the ziggurat of the goddess. The giants moved like bizarre automatons, with the knees rising high, prancing in unison. Spears sank into them, but did no lasting damage. Swords cut deep, but could not stop them. They wielded heavy clubs and axes with which they dashed out the brains of men who stood against them.

Through the gardens, they moved in a swift rapacious horde. Crowds of women thronging the docks were suddenly assaulted by men swarming out of the trees. A sudden eruption of screaming cut the night.

Now a scene of cruel pandemonium broke out. The men forced the women into a tight group. Then they were pulled out in ones and twos, and formed into a line while the collars of slavery were clasped around their necks. Finally they were urged westwards under the crack of the lash in the hands of gangs of imps, the dwarfish minions produced by the Dark Masters of Padmasa in their places in the High Hazog. These particular imps were heavily built and very pale of hue. They wore the black uniform of Sephis, and they cracked their whips with absurd gusto. The ships at dockside hurriedly cut their ropes, and the oarsmen pulled away with frantic haste. Perhaps two-thirds of the women on the island were aboard the barks and galleys, but hundreds had been left behind.

Only now did the highborn captives comprehend what was happening to them. They had been captured and given over to the control of imps. It could only mean that they were to be transported to the White Bones Mountains, to the city of Axoxo. There they would be imp mothers until they died, their bodies worn out by constant impregnation.

Their piteous wails rang off the ziggurat of the goddess, who, alas, was unable to stretch forth her hand to save them. Fervent prayers went unanswered, and they were marched away to the waiting rafts where they would begin the nightmarish voyage to their terrible destination.

Forewarned, Bazil, Relkin, and Lagdalen avoided the port, and instead made straight for the riverside through an extensive garden with raised beds of flowers, immaculate lawns, and lush orchards.

Through the gardens were scattered fragments of the gorgeous clothing of the priestesses, a sleeve hanging from a rosebush there, a train sparkling with points of brilliance there.

At one point, they heard screams and looked back to see a group of men running from a squad of giants who moved with a strange high-stepping unity, as if they were enormous puppets. They virtually danced as they went with a ponderous kind of grace. Over their shoulders they carried heavy clubs. The men and the giants disappeared into an orchard where only the giants' heads could be seen above the trees, bouncing up and down in the bright moonlight.

Bazil wondered if he was hallucinating.

"They look like men, not troll," he said slowly.

Relkin too was baffled. "No troll I've ever seen before."

"Not troll, look like men, almost walk like men. Troll walk like bear."

"I don't know what they are, but there's an awful lot of them. I counted twelve, how about you?"

Sudden screams came from the orchard where the prancing giants had begun to catch up on the fleeing guards. The huge clubs rose and fell.

Bazil remembered that he had no real sword, only the slender blade taken from Rozaw, the guard.

"Too many for us I think. Better we leave."

"But there are no boats," said Lagdalen pointing to the empty shoreline. The gardens gave way to a sandy beach and then the river, gleaming under the moon's light.

"We swim," said Bazil.

"But it's miles, and there could be crocodiles."

"Crocodile tastes good I am told, even raw. Like chicken."

The dragon held up the guardsman's sword, as if it were a kitchen knife. Lagdalen hesitated briefly and then recalled what these dragons were like when aroused to combat. This confidence was perhaps well-founded. She shrugged. "I suppose there isn't any other way."

The bouncing heads were turning in their direction now. Relkin urged them to hurry. The giants were prancing toward them through the small trees.

They ran down the beach and into the waters of the great river, which was cold with the spring flood. Relkin and Lagdalen hesitated when they ran in it up to their knees.

"It's so cold," said Lagdalen.

The dragon, of course, found it delightful and had already splashed in and floated away, powering itself with sweeps of the great tail.

Relkin looked back. The giants, which he saw now were at least ten foot tall, were prancing through the gardens toward them.

The water was cold and there was a current, but Relkin was a good swimmer and he knew that Baz, like most wyverns, was a real aquanaut. Lagdalen, too, was quite capable in the water.

They paused to tread water and look back. The giants strode the beach but did not enter the water. They turned and pranced along the water's edge, heading north. The noise from the northern end of the island was beginning to taper off as most of the captured women were marched away across the island by the imps.

The remaining captives, mostly servants and guards, were stripped, bound, and prepared for their own, shorter journey to hell. In groups of fifty, they were driven in the path of the women to the transports waiting to take them to Dzu.

Bazil floated easily in the water, cool with the spring torrents from the north. Like most wyverns, he was well at home in the aquatic environment. Perhaps some strain from the sea monsters of old had found its way into the wyvern line, but they were powerful swimmers and could cover long distances with little difficulty. Nor did cold water trouble them. In fact, they relished it.

When they tired, Lagdalen and Relkin rode on the dragon's back. Although they were wet and cold, they still found it possible to marvel at the wonder of this journey, riding across a vast river in the dark, with the full moon illuminating everything with a silvery powder. The dragon drove on through the water like some unusually energetic and enormous crocodile.

The Oon was so enormous that out on its breadth they lost sight of any land, except islets that marked the many shoals. Eventually, even the leatherback dragon tired. They paused for a while at one of the more accessible islets.

While they first were in the water, they had seen a number of sails, both those of the small barks of the priestesses of Gingo-La and others, more rakish, usually dark, on narrow boats crammed with men, that pursued the barks. After a while, these craft drew away and they swam on alone.

The islet was very modest, perhaps forty feet in length. There were a handful of skeleton trees, none taller than ten foot, and a beacon, a polished brass globe atop a twenty-foot pole that was visible on moonlit nights and warned of the shoals around the islet.

They had not been there long before they spied a sail and watched its rapid approach. It was a two-masted Ourdhi bark, and it was running in front of the breeze and aiming very close to the shoals. Behind it they saw a long black galley that, when it drew closer, they could see was crammed with men. The oars were rising and falling at a tremendous rate. The galley was gaining on the small ship.

It seemed they were fated to witness the ship's capture and the apprehension of more of Ourdh's highborn women by the agents of the Masters, but then with shocking suddenness, the speeding galley struck the shoal and rocked to a halt. Oars and spars flew up with the impact, the bow broke asunder, and the ship sank quickly in about ten feet of water.

Bazil sighed. "We going to have company here pretty soon," he said wearily.

"I think we'd better swim," said Lagdalen.

They returned to the water and resumed their progress eastwards. Out on the river, ahead of them, sped the bark, saved by its risky passage of the shoals. The passengers, fortunate indeed not to have been taken by the pirates, who would have sold them to Sephis, would be in the great city before dawn.

The swimmers would take longer, but they would get to the eastern shore. When Bazil tired again, they allowed themselves to float downstream for a while before resuming the thrust to the east.

As they went, Relkin tried to place the events he had witnessed on the island into the situation in Ourdh as he understood it.

"This may seem like a strange question to you, but nobody has ever told me what it is exactly that we're fighting here. What is this thing they call Sephis? Is it really the god brought back to life?"

Lagdalen hesitated. "The Lady Ribela told me that she thought it was a demon. It might have been trapped here by the enemy's magic and forced to do their will."

Relkin shivered. As always, the doings of the dark power made him profoundly uneasy, but this was peculiarly terrifying. The Masters had power even over great demons. The idea made the hair on his neck stand up. His mind flashed back to the strange human-like giants, with their high-stepping jerky movements. What were they?

They went on without speaking while the moon sank to the horizon and the stars were left to shine with merciless brilliance. Relkin fell to thinking of the future. He had survived the servants of an alien goddess, and the thought had occurred to him that the Great Mother must have some special interest in him because she put him in great danger time after time and always got him out of it. But why would she pick on him, an orphan child of an obscure village on the Argonath coast? He had not been born high enough to be worthy of her favor. Worse, he was not devout, not in the least. He'd barely gone to the Temple once he was old enough to know he didn't have to. He invoked the old gods, the donoi gods, whenever he required the assistance of the heavens, and you weren't supposed to do that, they always told you in the Temple School.

But perhaps what some scholars said was true, and the old donoi gods were actually aspects of the Mother, misperceived by men. This idea had been used to keep alive their names even to the day of the Empire of the Rose and the rule of the witches.

His favorite was Caymo, the god of wine and of song and good times in general. Caymo was a brown-skinned god with a white beard and a bald head and a prodigious belly in which he could put away enormous quantities of wine. Then there was Vok, the god of the ocean and shipping. And then there were harsher gods, like Asgah of war and Gongo of the death ride. Relkin really thought of them collectively, as just "the old gods" or sometimes as the "donoi gods."

Whether they existed or not, some deity seemed still to have some purpose for him. Why else would Miranswa have been sent to free him? Why else would he have have survived at Tummuz Orgmeen when they faced insurmountable odds? There had to be some purpose. But what it might be, he could not say, and he wondered if he ever would.

His thoughts of eventual retirement and of life as a farmer on the frontier seemed now perhaps too conventional. Possibly he should aim higher. Perhaps he should seek advancement beyond serving as a dragoneer. He could apply to the schools of wizardry. He would go to the eastern isle then and learn the great arts.

Then he remembered his dragon still cheerfully thrusting forward through the cool waters right beneath him, and he felt ashamed. How could he even dream of abandoning the broketail dragon? They were bonded together until the death of one or the other. Even in retirement they would stay together, forming an economic unit on the frontier.

Besides that, they were still hundreds of miles from home and caught up in a huge war with unknown consequences. It was possible he'd never live to see Kenor again, let alone retire there.

The sky brightened in the east, and dawn broke over the world of water and sky. Bazil rested on another islet, and soon after that they glimpsed the eastern shore of the great river.

They waded ashore, exhausted and cold, on a muddy flat bordered by a forest of palms and skeleton trees. They were hungry and worn. Relkin scouted the forest to discover a muddy track that wound away northwards.

The countryside here was the usual mix of small fields and mud-brick villages, plus a number of villas of all sizes up to places that were virtually palaces.

One thing was common to all, however, they were empty. The land was denuded of its people.

Relkin and Bazil knew what that must mean. The siege of the great city had begun, and they were outside the walls, alone, behind enemy lines.

"We are south of the city," said Relkin.

"Then we can swim again."

"Upstream?"

"We have no choice."

CHAPTER THIRTY-FOUR

The news went out at the beginning of the evening watch. The broketail dragon and his boy had come back safe and sound. Naturally, they had a wild tale to tell of some harrowing adventures involving the beautiful priestesses of the goddess Gingo-La. Everyone wanted to hear the details of that one!

Celebrations began at once. The legions were in need of something to celebrate, since they were now under siege and it looked like the siege would soon become a trial of strength.

Beer was released from the Imperial cellars, fires were lit by each regiment, and the songs of the Argonath were sung with gusto by men, women, and dragons alike.

The 109th dragons were especially jubilant. The loss of the broketail had been a serious blow to morale. To the younger wyverns, the broketail was a living legend and a source of inspiration. They were intensely proud to be serving alongside him, and had been much downcast when it appeared that he was gone forever.

As for the Purple Green, he had been hell on an eggshell ever since they'd learned of Bazil's disappearance. Everyone, dragoneers and dragons alike, had tiptoed around him. No dragonboy had dared go near him, although he had broken scales and a split talon. The news of their return was almost enough to make him fly again. His great wings unfurled and flapped

mightily while he roared his challenge call. People
dived for cover and several complained of ringing in
the ears for hours after.

But that evening the wild one timed his arrival perfectly. Even as he finally took his place in the welcome
line, the Broketail appeared with Relkin riding on his
shoulders.

Cheers rang off the walls. The wyverns roared their
welcome, and the Purple Green stepped out to clasp
forepaws with Bazil.

"Welcome back, broken-tailed friend."

"You thought you'd seen the last of this dragon."

"They say you swam across river."

"Of course, it is not hard to swim."

The Purple Green roared at this thought.

"You wyverns are a weird lot. Dragons don't swim,
they fly."

"Men say that sea monsters were the mothers of
wyvern kind. Of course, men say many things."

"Men say too many things, by the roar of the old
gods it is true."

But Baz had something else on his mind right then.
"Is that beer I smell?"

"Plenty of beer. Delivered in time to honor your
return." Dragoneer Hatlin spoke up from among a
mob of dragons. "And we're ready to broach it, too."

Bazil gave a ponderous salute. Relkin dismounted.

"Dragoneer Relkin and the broketail dragon reporting, sir!"

"At ease, Dragoneer, and welcome back. You seem
to have gotten into the thick of it again without any
help from us."

"Well, there were these beautiful priestesses, and
they were going to sacrifice us, but I persuaded one
of them to unlock my irons, and, then, well . . ."

Hatlin held up a hand. 'Uh oh, I don't think I want
to hear the rest of this."

"Oh wonderful," sneered Swane of Revenant. "While

we've been sitting here getting by on semolina and water, you've been wining and dining with a bunch of priestesses."

"Cut it Swane," said Tomas Black Eye.

Bazil leaned over toward Hatlin. "This dragon has had nothing to eat for days. What have we got?"

"I think the cooks anticipated your arrival. They had a boil, there's hot semolina and some roasted roots. We're under siege now. Supply is getting more difficult. But we do have beer, plenty of it. The emperor opened his cellars for us. He didn't want to, but I guess he had no choice."

"Lead the way, this is one thirsty dragon."

A cheer went up as the young dragons hoisted him to shoulder height and bore him in to the fireside. A roar came from the rest of the Eighth Regiment, and somebody gave him a pail of the emperor's best lager. He toasted them, and they saluted him back.

And thus it went, and something of a wild party took place behind the walls of the besieged city of Ourdh, causing confusion in the ranks of the vast army that surrounded the walls. The sounds of merriment, and of singing and drumming echoed off the walls and the towers along the Argonath sector by the Fatan Gate.

But after eating as much semolina and akh as he could stand, the dragon grew weary. After downing a keg of beer, he fell asleep, suddenly and irrevocably.

Vlok took his arms, the Purple Green took his legs, and they carried him back to the 109th's lines, which were set up just inside the Fatan Gate. Relkin saw his charge laid out and made a swift inspection. He winced at the sight of all the bruises, and most seriously there was the cut where the guard's sword had slashed Bazil's flank. Relkin took up swab and disinfectant, scaling knife and probe.

As for Lagdalen of the Tarcho, she was not present at the celebrations. As an officer of the Insight, she had duties to attend to. She went directly from the riverside, to the house of the Merchant Irhan. There she found Irhan in mourning. The Lady Inula had not returned from the Isle of Gingo-La.

Fending off the merchant's queries as to where she had been and what had happened, Lagdalen inquired after the Lady Ribela. Irhan sent her to the Imperial Palace at once in his carriage.

At the Imperial Palace, she was conducted to the quarters occupied by the Great Witch Ribela, a suite right beside the emperor's own personal apartment in the Grand Palace.

Ribela welcomed her back with little emotion. She waved away Lagdalen's apologies concerning her disappearance during the spell saying.

"That was not your fault, child. That was treachery at work in the house of the merchant."

Carefully, omitting nothing of importance, Lagdalen recounted the events of the past few days. Ribela listened closely, and when Lagdalen had finished drew her hands together.

"Excellent, my dear. I am greatly relieved to see you alive and well. You have brought back some important information. And now I suggest that you go down the passage to your bedroom. You have now suffered direct experience of alien fanaticism in the matter of religion. You need to rest."

Surprised, but grateful, Lagdalen made her way to the room down a corridor tiled in marvelous blue and white patterns and entered the designated room. There, to her incredulous delight, she found her husband waiting for her.

"A miracle," she said. "The lady?"

"And General Paxion. They said it would be alright for us to be together, at least for one night."

"Oh, my husband," she relaxed in the strength of his arms.

It was a miracle. Together, they did their best to

make up for all the time they had been apart. He was radiant, she ecstatic. There was even news from Marneri, including a note from Wessary, baby Laminna's wet nurse. The babe was well and had hardly even been sick a day since her mother had sailed away.

And now the darkness that had engulfed her for so long was suddenly broken. Lagdalen could almost allow herself to relax into a perfect spell of happiness. But the pain of her absence from her baby broke through the spell. Every so often it would grow to be too much, and she would weep softly.

For his part, Hollein held his young wife close through the precious night hours. He did his best to comfort her. He himself was too overjoyed to sleep. These past few days had been a nightmare as he waited to hear some word, some fragment of news concerning Lagdalen's whereabouts. And now he had her back, and she was well and sound. It really did seem like a miracle. He promised to contribute to the Temple as soon as he was back in Marneri. The Great Mother had been looking after him and his.

And he had to hope that she would continue to do so. Truth to tell, he was getting just a little anxious himself. The enemy had been building dozens of siege towers and was readying for a massive attack. From what he'd heard General Paxion say, he knew that there would be no reinforcement for weeks. Nor would there be much resupply. The river pirates had cut off grain shipments, and the people left in the city were fast using up the available supplies. All in all they were going to be pressed to hold out for more than ten days let alone two or three weeks. A month would have them eating the city's rats and rationing the dragons to bare subsistence.

And by the way the enemy was preparing, it was possible they wouldn't even last that long. The walls were miles long, and they were too few to man them

in strength. The citizenry showed a surprising lack of
interest in this problem. The enemy knew this and
planned to build so many siege towers that they would
overwhelm the defenders by dozens of simultaneous
attacks. It was going to be hard to deny them success.

And while the young captain mulled these concerns,
reunited in tender matrimony by special dispensation
from a Great Witch and a general, that same general
and great Witch were engaged in earnest conversation
about much the same topics just a few rooms away.

"The emperor?" asked Paxion.

"Under sedation again. Since the disappearance of
the Princess Zettila, he has become depressive and
prone to fits of nervous anxiety."

"I must impress on him once again that we have to
have better supplies of food and water for the men.
He keeps entrusting this to his grain factors, and they
steal us blind. About one third of the flour ration is
being stolen. This has to stop."

Ribela nodded gravely. "Of course. But remember
that this man is weak, long governed by eunuchs.
Without the Princess Zettila to share his plotting, he
is listless, devoid of energy. It is hard to move him to
do anything."

"But he is protected against the charms and snares
of the enemy, is he not?"

"With the aid of your weather witch, I have constructed some defenses." Ribela sounded slightly
annoyed.

"So it cannot be some subtle attack on the emperor
then?"

"I have kept watch over him for several days now.
There was a small spell. He had been infected with
irrational fear of the enemy, a terror of Sephis. So
strong was the fear that he could not face it to even
protect himself from the threat. We have lifted that
spell."

Paxion grimaced at the thought, Ribela continued,

"However he is still dazed from the aftereffects, and it is hard to get through to him."

"Astonishing that the enemy could have gotten so close to the emperor."

"Not so surprising I am afraid, given the emperor's sexual proclivities. However, we have discovered the eunuch that had taken the emperor's blood and hair. We questioned him closely. The man swears he was alone. I do not yet know whether to believe him. We will continue to question him until we are satisfied."

Paxion whistled at the thought of that questioning.

"I am glad that you are here to guide the emperor, lady. I hate to think what our situation would be without you."

Ribela allowed a faint smile to show.

"And yet our situation is none too good even with me here, now is it?"

"Alas, no it is not. The loss of General Hektor has gravely weakened us."

Hektor's comatose body remained in the surgeon's tent. Ribela had visited the poisoned general and had done her best to alleviate the condition, but still the coma could not be broken. Coma was notoriously tricky.

"You are in command now, General."

Paxion smiled grimly. "Unfortunately, as you know, my right to command is challenged by General Pekel. I have not been a field commander for many years. Pekel thinks I should not be here. Sometimes I think I agree with him."

"Excuses, General?"

"If you like, but the Kadeini would not continue with Hektor's plan without Hektor to make them. They would not follow me to Dzu."

"A great pity. It would have been relatively easy then to destroy the thing. Now I fear it will be far more difficult. The enemy has vast numbers and considerable energy, and is about to test our defenses."

"They are building thirty-six siege towers, lady. Many of them by the East Gate. The wall north of the gate is weak, and they have a ram there that is making progress. I expect a breach within a day or so."

"What pattern of attack do you expect?"

"Simultaneous, wherever they can wheel one of those towers up to the walls. They have tremendous numbers, and all they need to do is to overwhelm us. We will be running from place to place to counter them.

"The Imperial Guards? Will they fight well?"

"Yes, I think so. Their morale seems very high right now. They tell me that it is because the emperor cannot desert them this time."

Ribela's stern face broke into a faint, wintry smile.

"Well, they are right about that. Banwi Shogemessar has nowhere to go. And for us, there will be reinforcements. But it will take time. As for the grain factors, I wonder if it is not time for us to move against them and take control of the grain supply ourselves?"

"Attack the Ourdhi guards?"

"We will approach General Knazud. I think he will prove cooperative."

"Well, that would be a step in the right direction. If we can get grain enough, then we can feed the men properly."

"Well, it can be done. After all, we opened the emperor's cellars did we not?"

Paxion chuckled. "This night will be good for morale. Especially with a hard fight coming up."

"And, General, there will be reinforcement and resupply. I had word in the past hour from Cunfshon."

"What can we expect? This will really lift the men's hearts."

"Well, it will not be immediate. It will take two weeks, perhaps three."

Paxion's face fell.

"A legion from Cunfshon is coming and a fleet with enough supplies to last us for months."

"This is good news, indeed. If we can survive the coming test of strength, then perhaps we will have a chance in the long haul. But for that, we must have better rations for the dragons. Their metabolisms are so intense that they must eat to keep up their strength."

"We will seize the granaries, and the dragons will be fed. I expect that once we get rid of the factors, there will be an adequate supply. We will talk to General Knazud today."

Paxion's eyes widened at this summary assumption of power. The Great Witch had decreed that they drop the diplomatic niceties to ensure the survival of the legions. He wondered why he himself had not asked for this. Too long as a fort general he concluded.

"And the broketail dragon's return will be good for morale I think."

"Indeed it will, lady."

"Well, at least we can say that we will have reinforcements and, in time, enough strength to take the field against the enemy. There will be a second legion from Cunfshon and then a legion from the cities, regiments from here and there, stripping the garrisons. That will give us five legions."

"Twenty-five thousand men and eight hundred dragons, lady. Such a force would be match for any army on this Earth."

"Yes, General, I think you may be correct on that score."

"Meanwhile, we must hold the walls with ten thousand."

"We must. But within two months, we will take the field and break through to Dzu and cut out the source of this dreadful power."

"What about this report of giants in the enemy's ranks? What is to be made of this?"

Ribela tightened her lips. "Yes, the blood myrmidons. They are another horror of the Dark Arts of the Masters. It takes the blood of many people to bring one of these things to life, and they can only keep their strength for a single month, from the moment of their creation."

Paxion was ashen-faced. "They are slaughtering the people to make these things then?"

"Did you not hear that the land is empty of people on the western side of the river? Even as we speak, huge columns of fresh victims are being marched to Dzu from Kwa and the country around here."

"That many?"

"We will see the myrmidons soon. They are a terrible foe."

CHAPTER THIRTY-FIVE

The siege of Ourdh was now into its tenth day and already supplies of food were very tight. Outside the walls, the enemy displayed a powerful appetite for activity. Wooden towers set on massive wheels rose up from the ruins of the suburbs amidst an infernal clatter of hammers that went on day and night. Catapults had been completed on the sixth day and ever since had been lobbing great chunks of the walls of fine houses from the suburbs over the city walls, where they crashed in the streets and smashed into houses.

Beneath the walls, a deadly war of mine and countermine had been going for several days. And here a new enemy weapon had appeared, the giant men made of mud. These creatures were of human shape, but almost ten feet tall and weighed half a ton. Only the fact that little intelligence resided behind their utterly blank faces gave the dragons an edge. It was like fighting a herd of almost unkillable imbeciles armed with hammers. In the darkness beneath the walls, there was usually little room for maneuver. It was a contest of grappling and rending with teeth and talon. It brought to the surface the primeval dragon. And yet the mud men kept coming in a seemingly endless supply. The dragons were getting tired. It was a worrying addition to the struggle.

As the siege wore on and the supply situation in the city deteriorated, Commander Porteous Glaves felt the jaws of a gigantic trap shutting around him. Darkness and doom rode through his dreams. He drank whatever wine or whiskey he could obtain, but it was getting harder by the hour as supplies in the city ran low.

With the lack of supplies had come a marked increase in the city's meanness. Corruption was mounting. Everyone stole from the supplies meant for the legions. This had meant starvation rations for the men and officers for the past couple of days; a bowl of porridge and a handful of dried fruit. There had been no meat of any kind for days, and there had been hardly any of the famed Ourdhi beer. The men were unhappy as hell.

The whole thing was getting very trying.

Glaves had not exactly enjoyed the long march from Salpalangum, or even the trip down the Oon, but arduous as they had been, the rations had been adequate. In Ourdh, at least, one could buy some excellent wines. In fact, in retrospect, it had all been rather jolly, in a way, sitting around camp fires while the men sang the songs of the Argonath. The food had been, well, basic, and Glaves's traveling cot was narrow and hard, but with Dandrax to serve and the interesting wines of Ourdh to explore, it had not been without its rewards. He had thought of many colorful images to use in later life when he addressed the political clubs of Marneri. Indeed, even the Battle of Salpalangum was taking on a rosy glow now, in the light of what they had come to.

Glaves never visited the regiment's section of wall. The sight of the siege towers was too depressing. Glaves left the inspections up to the captains. Glaves knew that the men hated him. To tell the truth, he hated them, too. And he loathed the dragons now, damnably inconvenient beasts. They had quite ruined his hopes of an early exit from the siege.

Glaves had taken over the house of the Merchant

Saubraj on Fatan Street. There wasn't much to drink there and it had soon run out, but Glaves had remained, holed up in a salon on the first floor while Dandrax was sent to scour the city for decent wine or some Argonathi whiskey.

Occasionally he would be forced to come out, to attend General Paxion's pep meetings for the regimental commanders. He hated these events with a passion and could barely restrain himself from denouncing General Paxion out loud for incompetence.

After all, Paxion had willingly led them to this doomed position. General Hektor had been mad enough, but Paxion had decided that they had to defend the city of Ourdh. This had sealed their doom. Instead of escaping on whatever shipping was available, Paxion was staying put.

Even Hektor's body, in a state of coma, had been kept in Ourdh where the damned surgeons poked and pulled at it in a vain attempt to reawake intelligence within the hulk. Glaves had seen it, he knew that Hektor would never awake. It was just as well. Hektor probably would have ordered them to attack the enemy or something equally insane.

But the loss of Hektor had not prevented the very worst thing from happening. They were trapped here, and soon they would be fighting for their lives on those walls.

Porteous Glaves knew now that it was every man for himself in getting out of this. He told himself that he really had no choice. The damned priestesses had broken their word, and so there was no chance of getting a boat now. They acted as if it was his fault that the dragon had broken loose and escaped!

That damned dragon! What did it take to get a little cooperation out of the world? It was all so frustrating.

And so he had convened the first of his secret meetings with the Kadeini regimental commanders. They were quite receptive to his idea. Some kind of peace had to be negotiated. It was utter folly to just let two legions be destroyed in a hopeless siege. They were all going to starve to death in a week or two more. There were just no supplies.

Eventually a "Committee of Emergency Action" was set up, consisting of Commanders Hayl and Vinblat of the Kadein First, Commander Glaves of the Marneri Second Legion, Captains Sikker and Rokensak of Kadein, and Captain Ferahr of the Kenor Archer detachment.

Glaves had received no encouragement from any of the other officers in the Marneri Second. They seemed blind to their doom and were determined to stand behind Paxion until they were overwhelmed by the seething hordes of Sephis. Well then, let them have their wish. It would make it easier for Glaves anyway, when he got back to the Argonath.

Now he had brought the committee together to meet with the very useful Euxus of Fozad, who was their link to the enemy beyond the walls. Euxus had business dealings with Dzu, from before the resurrection of the serpent god. He knew the priests of Sephis, he'd sold them oil and wine for years. Naturally, he also had extensive business in the city of Ourdh. He thought he could bridge the gap between the armies and help begin the negotiations.

Euxus was a narrow-faced fellow with a black mustache and a direct, stern gaze from dark eyes. His black hair was severely cut, and he dressed in a suit of dark brown silk and expensive shoes. He was clearly prosperous, although somewhat forbidding of countenance. However, he possessed a golden tongue and could be perfectly charming. The men from Kadein were ready to believe him. He seemed eminently trustworthy. They were eager, even desperate for the chance to escape the trap.

The Kadeini entered Glaves's quarters looking expectant and watchful. Introductions were made, the conversation begun, and quickly an atmosphere of general agreement arose. Euxus would be the perfect emissary for them.

"There remains a single major difficulty," said Euxus. Eyebrows shot up.

"The good General Paxion, I mean. He will not agree with our position."

The men from Kadein shrugged. "Something's gotten into the old fellow."

"It's that damned witch they sent from Cunfshon, that's what," snarled Commander Glaves.

"Is he then the final arbiter?" purred Euxus.

"I say drop Paxion and promote General Pekel. Old Pekel could be brought round to it," said Commander Vinblat.

Glaves bit his tongue. Excellent, they were making progress. He looked at Euxus and saw the man's eyes gleaming as he stared at Vinblat. Something about those eyes made Glaves suddenly uncomfortable.

"Then I should continue my efforts to begin negotiations?" Euxus inquired.

"Go ahead," said Commander Vinblat.

"What about General Paxion?" said Captain Ferahr, the Kenor bowman. "Are we not even going to give old Pax a chance? He might see it our way."

"Look! We're going to be eating the Talion horses in the next few days. After that we'll be eating the leather on our belts. Old Pax just has to understand that staying here is a recipe for complete disaster," said Captain Rokensak.

"But how are we going to do it?"

There was a silence.

"He has to stand down and hand over authority to Pekel."

"What if he won't?"

"In that case," murmured Glaves, "he will have to be restrained. If he wants to die that badly, then we'll leave him here for the Sephisti to find when they take the place. We'll leave him here with the emperor."

There were grins around the table. The Emperor Banwi was not popular with the legions.

"We won't see a whit of resupply for at least two weeks. White ships or no white ships, we won't make it that long."

"It's all wrong. We won a great victory, and now the general's gone and bungled it."

"The Ourdhi have no provision at all for a siege. Their granaries, pathetic!"

Euxus provided them with the final shape of their offer. "We should propose that the legions agree to abandon the city and head either south to meet the white ships, or east to the mountains and the long march home."

Everyone was agreed, though the bowman Ferahr was still unhappy at the thought of laying hands on General Paxion and "restraining" him. Glaves assured him that it would all be taken care of and Ferarh need not be involved in the slightest. Ferahr seemed to accept this.

The Kadeini left, and shortly afterward, so did Euxus of Fozad, a charming, but somehow chilling presence. Glaves was left with the dregs of a bottle of whiskey that Dandrax had purloined. He stared out the window and across the small garden to the wall and the houses on the far side. It was set then, his course. They would remove Paxion, negotiate a way out of this, and then get out of this death trap city and march south.

Although, in fact, Glaves had already decided that it would be better if the legions marched east and went back home over the mountains. That would take them months. Glaves himself would be going home with the first white ship to leave for the Argonath.

Once he was back in Marneri, he would resign his commission and start his campaign to win election in

Aubinas. His position was already strong there. With a military reputation, from the great victory at Salpa-langum and surviving the disaster in the city of Ourdh, he would be able to mount an overwhelming challenge to old Klosper, who held the seat. At last, he would be on his way to real power in the white city.

CHAPTER THIRTY-SIX

Thunder and lightning rocked the skies over the great city that night. On the walls, men and dragons tucked their heads into their freecoats or took shelter under the wicker withe fascia that had been erected down the center of the wall to provide protection from enemy arrows. In the flashes of lightning, the men could see the siege towers only a few hundred feet distant. Even in these conditions the work did not pause in the enemy camp. Thousands of slave workers were being driven to complete the towers.

Beneath the walls, the deadly game of mine and countermine continued. Only the skill of the weather witches and the efficacy of their ground-sensing spells had protected the besieged so far. Digging a mine to bring down the walls caused vibrations that could not be hidden. To the sensitive weather witches, the vibrations could be calibrated to betray the location of the mine.

With the power of the dragons to call on for speed in digging, the defense had stopped the enemy time after time. So far not a single section of the walls had been breached. That night it was the turn of the 109th Marneri to be working in the hastily sunk countermine just west of the Fatan Gate.

The countermine had to be narrow so as not to sap the walls above, but it had also to be wide enough for a dragon to work in. These constraints produced the typical tunnel, cut through the riverine rocks beneath

the walls, only eight feet across at the narrowest point
and a mere ten or twelve farther out past the walls.

In these confines, a gang of mud-covered dragons
took turns working the tunnel face with huge shovels
and digging bars. Well-fed dragons were capable of
driving such a tunnel at a prodigious rate. They had
tunneled forty feet since taking over from the 86th
Marneri Dragons a few hours before. Despite the pre-
cautions of a tent at the entrance, the floor of the
countermine had become slick and muddy with rain
that had seeped down from the surface. The air
reeked of dragon exhalations and warm, wet mud.

While the dragons dug out the face and shoveled
the dirt back behind them, a huge gang of equally
muddy men worked at removing it on wheelbarrows,
trundled in an endless line back up the countermine
to the surface.

A second line of men brought the timbers used to
prop the tunnel back down the passage around the
line of barrows. As fast as the dragons cut the ground,
the engineers worked to set in the props and beams.

The scene at the tunnel face was lit by a pair of
lamps toted by dragonboys who squeaked past the
great wyverns and did their best not to get crushed to
death. Thus illuminated, it was a scene from some
strange anteroom to hell. The floor even angled downward, as if the intention were to deliver them to some
classic hell of ancient myth.

Every ten feet they paused and the engineers and
the weather witch came down to listen at the forward
wall. The weather witch had been working on this
tunnel for days now without sleep, but she showed no
signs of the exhaustion she felt. She pressed her head
to the earthen wall, her eyes shut. The dragons all
around her were silent while they watched her intently.

She held up her hand and clenched her fist, the
signal!

They were very close now.

Ahead, only a few feet away, lay the enemy mine. Every so often a heavy cart was rolled back from its front wall laden with dirt and rocks. The faint rumble of the cart was detectable by those with keen senses.

The assault party prepared itself, and the digging dragons were replaced. Old Chektor put down the shovel and squeezed his way back to the surface while the Purple Green and the broketail pushed their way to the front. To help them dig, they had Vlok already in place with a digging bar. They were all equipped with the new kit devised by the dragonboys to help in this strange and dismal combat. There being no room to wield great swords, they carried massive knives made hurriedly from iron stripped out of the city by the legion smiths. The knives were crude, almost triangular, but heavy and sharp enough to cut apart the mud men. The dragons wore gorget, breastplate, helmet, and vambraces for the heavy forearms and thus were well protected on the upper part of the body. The hind legs were left unencumbered.

Behind them was a force of fifty swordsmen and an equal number of spearmen.

Tensely they awaited the final moment. The weather witch conferred with Dragoneer Hatlin. A message was sent back to the gate to confirm and call for reinforcements, and the order was given.

The dragons took up the massive shovels and began digging fast and furious, doing nothing to minimize the noise. All caution was abandoned now.

The ground here was relatively soft, river plain with mud stones and gravel. The shovels sank in, scooped it out quickly, and tossed it back to the mud-soaked men of the digging detail.

They in turn hastened back through the crowd of armed men waiting for the break-in. The tension was already high, and now it rose to breaking point.

The Purple Green had not taken to the art of shovel wielding and now mostly just got in the way as Bazil and Vlok dug into the tunnel face with a furious energy. The shovels went faster and faster, and the muddy earth was thrown back too quickly for the men to carry it away. The Purple Green complained in loud hisses about the dirt getting on him, but it was impossible to avoid his active bulk in the narrow space.

For a minute, then two, they dug like this, and then Vlok's shovel broke through to empty air and he gave a hiss of excitement. Then Bazil cut through and cleared a big hole. Below them was spread the enemy mine, a scene out of real hell.

Thousands of slave workers, roped at the neck, struggled to push heavy carts filled with dirt. Filling the carts was a mass of the giants, the mud men, working with shovels at the cutting face of the mine, which was very large, much larger than any that had been seen before. The face was forty feet across and if allowed to continue to the wall, would have brought down a deep section. The countermine had broken through into the upper part of the sidewall. There was a five- to six-foot drop to the floor.

Bazil and Vlok jumped down into the mine tunnel. The slave workers scattered with a chorus of shrieks. The overseers drew their swords, then thought better of it, and retired up the mine as well. Chaos broke out in that direction.

Then the Purple Green dropped through, and the ground shook briefly under his weight. The great wild one seemed to fill the whole tunnel. He tipped over a cart and then hurled it down the tunnel straight into the ranks of a squad of onrushing mud men.

More dragons came tumbling in along with men and boys with lanterns. The dragons recovered themselves quickly and flung themselves at the mud men. The giants deployed hammers and picks and struck at the dragons with their mechanical rhythm. The dragons had learned to seize the giants by the arm and to stab again and again with their heavy knives. The big triangular knives did horrible work on the creatures, but they were still hard to kill. Hammers and picks bounced off dragon helm and plate. The hellish scene became the site of a grim battle. The sounds were those of dragons cursing, knives and hammers striking, and men shouting the war cries of Argonath as they joined the struggle.

Relkin dropped in behind the first dragons and almost got crushed by the next dragon down, big Cham. Cham's backside caught him on the shoulder, and he was flung to his knees. He jumped to his feet, dodged out of the way of any more wyverns from above, and looked up in time to see Bazil crash headlong into the ranks of mud men at the face of the tunnel. Behind the broketail came the Purple Green. The dragons and the giants tumbled together in a thrashing pile of gigantic bodies. The mud men were not as effective at this kind of wrestling combat. The dragons wielded their stabbing knives and worked to dismember the stupid, but horribly active monsters of blood-soaked mud.

More giants lurched forward and began smashing their shovels down upon the dragons and giants indiscriminately. Vlok and Cham cannoned into this second line and bowled them over. With much sibilant cursing, they got back on their feet and began the grim work of chopping the mud men to death.

Relkin had been dodging closer to the conflict, with his dirk at the ready. Suddenly he found himself confronting a squat, heavyset figure no taller than himself. The face was a mask of hate, a contortion of the human norm with a splayed nose almost flattened against the skull and a wide gash of a mouth in which were gathered a crowd of peglike teeth. It was unquestionably an imp, and Relkin was astounded to see it there. Imps belonged in the North, on the traditional battle field with the enemy.

The imp ended all speculations by slashing at Relkin with a short sword. He dodged back, bounced off the wall, and sagged against the imp. The imp grasped Relkin by the neck with a strong hand, got the sword up, and was about to run him through when somebody hammered it over the helmet and distracted it long enough for Relkin to twist out of its grip and knee it in the guts. It dropped back with a gasp of pain.

He caught sight of Swane of Revenant's face for a moment, lit up by a lantern in Mono's hand. Swane winked at him, counting coup for saving Relkin's hide. Then the imp recovered and swung at him. Relkin got his dirk up just in time to parry a chopping blow aimed at his face.

He shifted to his left and the imp tried an overhand, which he parried but with a grunt of effort. In truth, the imp's sword was too heavy for the dirk, Relkin's whole arm was already numb. Desperately he swung the lantern in his other hand and smashed it atop the imp's helmet. Oil and flame blazed down the imp's back, and it emitted a howl of woe. Relkin drove in, got his dirk into it, and then pushed it off its feet.

On the ground now, it thrashed helplessly, and he stepped over it and went on. Men in the black robes and iron armor of the Sephisti shock troopers were trying to get to the dragons from behind, and only the dragonboys stood in their way. Swords were matched against dirks and bows. The boys could not stand for long against such might, and in the nick of time a few Marneri swordsmen joined them and engaged the Sephisti.

Now the fighting became generally fierce and confused. The light from the lanterns was lost in the sea of surging fighters, and it was hard to make out friend from foe. Relkin found himself jammed up against two men in the black cloth of Sephis. He tried to free his dirk, but his arm was wedged too tightly. Behind him were a row of Marneri swordsmen, their shields

pressing him up against the Sephisti. The eyes of the
Sephisti blazed with a crazed rage. Relkin saw no intelligence there at all. But since no one could move
except to sway back and forth as the pressure ebbed
and flowed, he was safe from them for the moment.

Then suddenly, one of the giants pushed in, peeled
away the Sephisti, and struck down with his hammer
at the men of Marneri. These hammers weighed thirty
pounds, and to be struck by one meant death. Relkin
barely ducked the hammer that swished down and
crashed into the shield behind him. The hammer rose
and fell, men struck at the mud man, their swords
biting deep into the wet flesh, but not deep enough
to sunder the thing.

The hammer slammed down again and crushed another man of Marneri. Relkin stabbed his dirk into
the thing's thigh. In a moment, it was jerked from his
hand as the giant moved. It took no notice of the
knife in its leg, or of any other wounds. The hammer
swept down and a man's shield flew through the air
with the man's arm attached.

Relkin was fond of that dirk; he'd had it a long time
now. He dove in close and tried to pull it free.

The giant struck him on the side of the head with
its elbow as it drew its arm back to aim another hammer blow. Relkin was bowled over and found himself
on his knees, seeing stars.

He started to his feet and a swordsman behind him
struck him down by accident, the blade glancing off
Relkin's helmet. Relkin fell facedown in the mud and
lost consciousness.

Of the rest of the hard, muddy battle in the enemy
mine, he knew nothing.

He awoke quite some time later, lying on a stretcher
in a dark place. His head hurt, his helmet was gone,
and there was a bandage around his forehead. When
he probed at it with his fingers, he felt dried blood,
thick and crusty in his hair and down his neck.

A big hiss from behind him turned his head. A massive shape stirred in the darkness and a familiar reptilian visage slid into view.

"Ah, that is good, boy awakes at last. I have waited long time."

"What happened?"

"Long messy fight, but we destroyed tunnel."

"Where am I?"

"Hospital tent. They brought you back here without telling me. But I search whole damn tunnel and I find no sign of worthless boy, so I know that boy still live."

"A good thing, yes?"

"By the roar of the ancients, a good thing yes. Worthless boy may be, but much worse to have to start all over with new one."

Relkin moved and his head throbbed. He gave a groan and lay back. All he remembered was the dark, the Sephisti, the mud, and the giant. He'd been getting to his feet and then wham, something had struck him down. He was lucky to still be alive. He thanked the good Mother for her blessing. At the same time, and guiltily, he thanked the old gods, too. You never knew who was really looking out for you, after all.

The dragon finished his inspection and leaned back.

"Yes, worthless boy lie still and rest head. Dragon take care of him."

Relkin sighed at the thought of such tender care, but kept his mouth shut and after a while drifted off to sleep.

CHAPTER THIRTY-SEVEN

The Imperial Granaries were a trio of huge, windowless buildings of plain ocher mud brick dominating Fatan Street in the city's Tapazit district. Here, where Fatan Street curved westwards, the temples loomed in the mid distance, but the great six-story-tall granaries were the ruling presence. Normally they were the scene of intense activity, a chaos of dealers and workers, merchants and haulers.

Since the seizure of the granaries by the Argonath legions, however, a strange calm had descended on the place. Silence reigned through the halls of commerce. A hundred swordsmen occupied the place, and no native merchants were allowed in. The black market was snuffed out at a stroke.

The Argonathi rationed everything very closely. No longer was it possible for the wealthy to pay for extra supplies of grain or beer. The city rocked with the anger of the upper classes. Pressure was brought to bear on the emperor, who called the witch Ribela into his presence and ordered her to release the granaries back to the control of the Imperial bureaucracy. Ribela refused and after swallowing hard a few times, Banwi Shogemessar was forced to pass that reply back to those who pestered him about the new, austere rationing.

The stern-faced young legionaries at the granary had executed the first couple of thieves and threatened to do the same to anyone who proffered a bribe. The Ourdhi withdrew in genuine puzzlement.

But human nature being what it is, a few bribes were soon being offered anyway. The legionaries would not take them. Not only were they under the eyes of a weather witch much of the time, but their own sense of honor was involved. The bribe offerers were placed under legion discipline and, in front of the ranks on parade, they were stripped, pulled over the sawhorses, and given twenty strokes.

The city reacted with horror and outrage. Hostile crowds hissed at the marching soldiers. From the back of the mobs came missiles, usually stones or lumps of horse dung.

General Paxion called a meeting of the leaders of Ourdhi society and warned them that if the people of the city continued to behave thus, he would take the legions, break out, and leave the city of Ourdh to the Sephisti.

This intelligence was reported to wider circles and then spread into the general populace. Quickly, the open hatred of the legionaries subsided. But the people of the great city were unused to privation and their grumbling grew into a steady, sour murmur that left things very tense between themselves and the foreign legions that defended them. If they were hungry, it was all the fault of the foreigners.

Assured of control over what resources they had, General Paxion was able to give enough grain to feed the dragons and keep up their strength. The men understood how important this was. By now they had all seen the giant mud men.

The dragonboys of the 109th went down Fatan Street every day to collect the evening ration. For this purpose, they used the cook's cart, which was pulled by a pair of steady mules named Darcy and Sorrow.

The third day after their fight in the mine was like any other. The boys, although sore and weary, roused themselves and took the cart to the granary. There they loaded sacks of barley and oats. A few withered turnips and some onions from the emperor's vegetable garden were all they had to liven up the resulting grain mush. But at least everyone's belly would be full at supper time.

Relkin still had a field dressing on his head, but he'd been back on his feet for a day and a half and returned to duty.

Despite a vigorous scrubbing, his jacket was still heavily stained with blood, however, and his breeches were torn at the knees. Even his bandage was grubby. But when he looked around himself at the others, he saw that he was not alone in his scruffiness. They were all looking battered. Swane of Revenant had a head bandage, too, and his shirt was open revealing another bandage wrapped around his chest. Tomas Black Eye had cuts and abrasions all over his face where he'd slammed into a shield. Shim had a broken nose, and Mono was limping. Everyone's clothes reflected the wear and tear of the battle underground.

Still, when they reached the granary, each one of them took his place in the line, moving the sacks of oatmeal and barley to the loading dock. After a check by the guards on the dock, they loaded the grain onto the cook's wagon.

While they were staggering about with the sixty-pound sacks of barley, some officers on horseback rode in and dismounted. Relkin hardly looked up since he was bent under another sixty-pound sack at the time. He dropped it into the cart and turned around to find Captain Kesepton standing there. After a salute and an embrace, Kesepton held him at arm's length.

"Thanks to the Mother, you survived." He frowned. "But only just. Lagdalen told me you'd been in the infirmary. You were asleep while she visited you, but the broketail dragon was there, and he told her all about your condition."

"Lagdalen came? He didn't tell me. I am sorry that I could not have been awake for her visit."

Kesepton gripped the youth's shoulder hard for a moment.

"We will never forget what you did, the two of you. I feel as if I owe you for my own life. I know that the Tarcho will want to reward you somehow. In fact, I think you're going to find yourselves quite legendary by the time we get home again."

Relkin looked down, suddenly embarrassed. The others were sneaking looks at him from the corners of their eyes. And just when he'd been beating down his old reputation as a braggart.

"The dragon would not leave the island without Lagdalen dragon friend," he said. "She is very special to us."

"I believe it," said Hollein. "And we were grieved by the news of that fight in the mine. Especially when we heard that you had fallen."

"It was hot work," said Relkin. The other boys murmured in agreement. "Worse than Salpalangum anyway."

"But the fighting 109th got the job done once again," said Kesepton in a slightly louder voice to include all the dragonboys.

The boys looked proudly at one another.

"The dragons fought like demons, sir. You should have seen it," said someone.

"So I heard, and I heard that the dragonboys fought hard, too, and took plenty of knocks."

"Everyone's still at their posts, sir," said Relkin.

"A tough bunch, that's what I hear." Kesepton took Relkin aside for a moment.

"Dragoneer, I want you to report to the infirmary once you've taken that lot back to the gate. That dressing needs changing."

"Sir?"

"And Lagdalen is there today, and she would love to see you."

Relkin's face brightened at once. "Yes, sir, Captain."

The sound of horses' hooves interrupted them. A group of officers rode into the loading dock. In their midst was General Paxion himself. The general made frequent, unexpected visits to the granary. He was determined to ensure a disciplined control over the city's food supply during the crisis. There would be no corruption on Paxion's watch, ever.

He dismounted and personally checked the logbook. Carrying it in his hands, he came to the edge of the dock and saluted the dragonboys.

"Well-done, you lot. The 109th are living up to their reputation as the best damned squadron we have!"

The boys visibly swelled and returned the general's salute with unusual crispness. Then Paxion spotted Relkin, and Kesepton and strode toward them.

"And may I add how glad I was to hear of your survival, young Dragoneer. Heard you'd taken a knock."

"Thank you, sir, but I'm alright, sir."

"Good, though you need to do something about that jacket, Dragoneer, it's a disgrace."

"Yes, sir."

Paxion softened and smiled. "And tell me, young man, how is our friend the wild Purple Green doing?"

"He's adjusting still, I'm afraid. He finds the food very boring."

"I expect he does. But at least it's regular, eh?"

"Yes, sir."

"How about his feet? I was worried about his feet. His kind are more used to flying than to marching."

"We solved his foot problem. I had him wear some sandals. Got them made back in Fort Dalhousie."

"Sandals, eh? Ingenious. Well, carry on, Dragoneer." Paxion turned to Kesepton.

"Captain, a word with you, I have a message for the Lady Ribela."

Kesepton and General Paxion strode away. Relkin rejoined the others and the cook's wagon trundled off with Darcy and Sorrow at the head. As they went, Relkin found all the other soldiers staring at him with considerable interest. It was not every day that they saw the general chat with a dragonboy.

Relkin's thoughts were whirling with strange ambitions. So, Relkin Orphanboy and the broketail dragon were going to be legends by the time they got home. And General Paxion was interested in the wild dragon and even spoke to a mere dragonboy about him. It seemed that great things lay in their future.

Then he remembered where he was and what lay outside the city walls. The future might just as likely include death in the coming struggle.

Relkin said little as they walked back up Fatan Street and ignored the few digs that Swane of Revenant tossed his way. The native Ourdhi stared at them with hatred and suspicion. Oaths and loud spitting followed their passage. Women made the sign of the evil eye. Relkin ignored it all.

At last they reached the end of their route. The bulk of the city walls and the massive gate towers loomed over them. They unloaded the grain at the cook's station and then went to fetch water.

When the water was set to boil, the boys went back to their dragons and passed around the happy news that food was being prepared.

After eating his bowl of oatmeal and onions, Relkin quickly climbed the tower and examined the scene outside the walls.

"It is finished," said Mono, who was already there.

"Yes, I can see that," said Relkin.

The last siege tower on their front was completed. The hammering had ceased. It was sixty feet tall and stood upon four huge wheels at the base. Its front and sides were clad in hides that were constantly wetted, and it was roofed stoutly with beams covered in copper. At the top it was thirty feet wide, and there were stairs all the way down the back for the enemy hordes to climb.

"Won't be long then," said Relkin, feeling a pang of dread. Four towers at once. Mud men coming over the assault bridges in a constant stream. Behind them a swarm of mad-eyed Sephisti.

"The dragons will be hard-pressed. They're tired already."

An enemy catapult let go out beyond the towers and a heavy stone was launched, arching over the walls and falling with a crash into the gate courtyard.

"I don't think we're going to get much time to rest."

With whistles blasting, a new group appeared on the scene. A labor battalion, men yoked at the neck like animals and driven by the whip. They were marched at the double up to the rear of the siege tower and chained to the great shaft that drove it.

Standing over them were imps, clad in the black tunic of Padmasa. Relkin shivered. The great enemy put forth its strength here. These mud men were not the work of the Ourdhi, their magic was of an order of magnitude more terrible than anything the Ourdhi were capable of. If the dragons failed, then the walls would fail, too, and then there might be no future at all for a renowned orphan boy from the obscure village of Quosh.

Within five minutes, the slave laborers were chained in place. The whips cracked loudly, the imps bawled, and the great siege tower wobbled in place and then, slowly, began to move, rolling forward one revolution of the giant wheels. The pace picked up as the sweating slaves overcame inertia and the tower rolled forward toward the walls.

There were curses from up and down the walls, and

a few arrows whickered out and stuck in the shields at the rear, which protected the slaves.

Then the imps roared fresh orders, and the tower wobbled to a halt. The men shifted position, the whips cracked, and now the tower rolled back, away from the wall.

Relkin stared after it in a very somber frame of mind.

On the other side of the city, amid lush gardens and the cooling breeze from the great river stood the Imperial City behind its own fifty-foot high walls, the fortress within the fortress. Here Captain Hollein sought out the Great Witch.

First he tried the Imperial reception hall and learned that the witch was most definitely not in attendance that day. So he went on to her own, private quarters, which were adjacent to the throne room. From there she could be close to the emperor throughout the day. Due to her presence, a vast change had come over the day-to-day business of the Empire of Ourdh. The emperor was now accessible throughout the day. There were no more afternoon sessions in the harem, no more drinking bouts lasting for days. Instead, Banwi Shogemessar, for the first time in his life was behaving as a true monarch.

She was not there either, however, according to the po-faced eunuchs guarding the door. When he showed them the general's seal on the message, they told him to go to the roof of the palace. It was six stories up and he arrived slightly breathless, but found the witch, standing alone on a section of the roof that faced northwest, toward the distant city of Dzu. Around her feet surged a small crowd of mice.

Should he disturb her? What if she was in the midst of some strange magic? He hesitated a moment and she turned around and he felt the pressure of those dark eyes once again. There was no masquerade with Ribela, the aura of power was plain to see.

"Lady Ribela, I have a message from General Paxion for you."

"Speak, Captain Kesepton."

"It is written here," he handed her the general's letter. She glanced at it and then returned her gaze to him.

"You are here to tell me that General Hektor has been transferred to the cutter *Gastes*. The ship leaves soon."

"Ah," he said, unsure.

Ribela caught the question in his eye. "You want me to free your wife and send her back to Marneri."

He could not speak.

"I am afraid I cannot let Lagdalen of the Tarcho leave just yet. We need her here."

Lagdalen had given enough for a girl her age. She was a mother now, her babe in the arms of someone else. Had the witch no humanity? Indeed, she seemed quite chilly and distant.

"I know that you have strong emotions on this matter. But at this moment, you must consider your duty to our cause. My mission continues, and for the success of that mission I need someone with the experience of Lagdalen."

"She is too young to give so much," he protested.

"Hush, Captain, she is older than most dragonboys. She serves, and she has indeed given much for our cause. Do not dishonor her service now because of your patriarchal concerns."

His eyes blazed. Then she offered him an olive branch.

"Captain, within eight days I shall be able to replace her. There is a fleet now rounding Cape Hazard. Six white ships, an armada virtually, carrying supplies and a full legion from Cunfshon. Lagdalen's replacement is aboard the leading ship, the *Spruce*."

Kesepton took a deep breath. So, one more week of danger for both of them. A week in which Laminna might be made an orphan. The witch expected him to be pleased with this. It was better to humor her.

"Thank you, Lady Ribela."

"Lagdalen will one day be a credit to the Office of Insight. She has a natural talent for the work, I think."

"Lady, she has resigned the Office."

"A temporary matter, Captain, I am sure. One like your Lagdalen will find many roles in life. For now she is your young mother goddess, your wife, and the mother of your child. But in time she will find herself new duties, I am confident of it. Lessis was right to choose her."

To Hollein Kesepton, it sounded more like a sentence to an early death.

"Next week we will be solidly resupplied. Behind the *Spruce* are *Oat* and *Rye*, the largest ships we have."

"Well, lady, that is good news, indeed. I only hope that we will still be alive to greet them when they come. The enemy will attack very soon. We will be hard-pressed to stop them."

"We must stop them, so we will."

There was no mistaking the Lady Ribela's titanic strength of will. As he rode back to the lines by the East Gate, Kesepton wondered if willpower on its own would be enough to sustain them when the mud men came across the walls.

Relkin reached the infirmary in time to catch Lagdalen still at work there, sorting freshly washed bandages. They embraced, she looked exhausted, her young face lined and streaked, but still she found the energy to hug the dragonboy and to ask him a dozen questions in less than a minute.

Briefly, he described the fight in the mine and the aftermath.

"But the young hero of Quosh has survived yet another bout with death," she said lightly.

Her eyes lit on the bandage again.

"That needs to be changed," she said firmly.

"Well, I have orders from Captain Kesepton to get it changed."

"Ah, of course, I should have known. And you seem no worse the wear for it all, I do so hope that that is true."

"I will fight again, we will stop them."

She felt again the cold shiver of fear. Relkin sounded uncertain despite his brave words. The enemy would keep on attacking until it won its way in.

"I have heard that we will be reinforced within a week."

"Six white ships, and a legion from Cunfshon."

They would hold them. They had to hold them.

"We will all be on the wall there if we are called," she said.

"And Lagdalen of the Tarcho can wield a sword, I have seen her."

Lagdalen smiled. She had learned many things in the past year, things that would have been unimaginable before.

"If I have to, I will."

"You have been working here a long time, I think," he said. "You should sleep, Lagdalen dragon friend."

"Ah, sleep, I remember it well. Actually I'm going to my bed as soon as they come and collect General Hektor. He's being sent home on the cutter that put in yesterday."

Relkin had seen the ship, with her white hull and beautiful lines, a three-masted brig built for speed and maneuverability in shallow waters, ideal for getting through the river pirates of the lower Oon.

"I have heard that the general will never awake."

"I don't know Relkin, he may. If his condition can be changed anywhere, it is in Cunfshon."

Lagdalen removed Relkin's bandage and changed the dressing. The wound was healing well. While she worked, he told her about the walls and the spirit of the 109th. The dragons were tired but their morale was still high, in part because they'd won such a victory in the mine the other night. The dragonboys were battered, but game, and they were ready for whatever might come.

And there was a lot to come.

When she'd finished, he stayed to help sort the bandages, long ones for bindings and short ones for dressings. They finished just before the men from the cutter arrived. The surgeons came out of their operating room to give the general a final examination.

Relkin saw that the great Hektor was now the color of wax and his face was sunken. It was hard to reconcile the man on the stretcher with the great general he had seen riding before the legions only a few weeks before.

Then Hektor was gone, borne swiftly through the streets to the white cutter and the voyage to Cunfshon.

CHAPTER THIRTY-EIGHT

The man known as Euxus of Fozad slipped quickly along the secret passage beneath the walls of Ourdh. The passage exited in the cellar of a suburban villa that had once been owned by the real Euxus of Fozad, an unfortunate who had already made the grim pilgrimage to Dzu.

The villa had been largely demolished, and its beams removed for the giant siege tower that had been built nearby. The man, who was actually the Magician Thrembode the New, stepped out of the ruins and headed for the headquarters of the Sephisti army on the East Gate road. As he went, he smiled, noting that the siege towers were completed. The new generals were keeping their men up to a very exacting pace. But it was all quite unnecessary. He, Thrembode, had the key to a far easier victory.

He hurried to his meeting.

In the operations tent of General Klend, he found the high priest Odirak and two other priests that he had not met before, tall, pale men of dour expression who barely returned his greeting.

Abruptly he became aware of another being. The tent flap opened and a man-size entity strode in and positioned itself in front of him. It wore a floor-length black cloak with a heavy hood, and the hood covered its face with darkness, but he saw the glint of horn reflected from that dark. And suddenly he saw the eyes, as if small fires had been ignited in nothingness, they flickered like little flames.

A Master? He shuddered inwardly. One of the high and mighty themselves had come all this way? It seemed incredible.

Then the hood fell back, and he saw revealed a Mesomaster. The metamorphosis had taken place on the lower part of the face. There were no lips, no teeth, only the gleaming beak and the frills of horn around it. The eyes, too, were inhuman, but the upperpart of the head remained recognizably human still, there was even a patch of lank grey hair, pulled back and tied in a knot.

So, a Mesomaster, halfway to the strange physiology of the Masters themselves. The power radiating from the figure was overwhelming to those who could sense it. Thrembode felt it clearly on many planes and knew that he was being examined by a mighty intelligence. Not since he had last faced the Blunt Doom of Tummuz Orgmeen had he felt such a gaze.

He darted a glance to Odirak. The high priest had hinted of this, that there was a greater power than even that of the demon in Dzu at work here. A Mesomaster, by the old gods this was a turn of the black pages!

"And so our Magician Thrembode returns from enemy territory," said the thing suddenly in its weird rasping voice. "What news does the magician bring me of his band of traitors?"

"They are still debating our terms, master."

"Still? Do they not realize their position? We attack in a matter of hours. If your plan is to work, it must work now. Or else we attack and to hell with them."

"Ah, well, I hesitate to thrust myself into situations beyond my competence, but surely we can hold up the attack for a day or so. The Argonathi are weakening. Soon I believe they will give in to the logic of the situation, and then they will march out and the city will be ours without loss."

"We cannot wait long. We must have the population of the city to renew the myrmidon force."

Thrembode felt his hair rising. The stories he'd heard about what was going on in Dzu were utterly bizarre.

Odirak leaned forward to interject.

"And if the Argonathi do accept our terms, they will be taken in the open field. None may be allowed to return home alive. The god demands this."

Thrembode was appalled, this would he a terrible waste.

"Surely not the officers, wouldn't we want to reward our traitors and to send them home where they could work for us?"

The Mesomaster made a strange sound, like the buzzing of several bees.

"Heh, heh, our magician is a sly fellow with a cunning wit. But he forgets our purpose. We fight to instill terror in our enemies. Only an enemy that is utterly terrified of us can be crushed quickly enough for the schedule that has been decided on by the High Command. We must adhere to the schedule."

Ah, the schedule! Thrembode gave a mental shrug and abandoned the traitors he'd summoned up from the enemy camp. The schedule of the High Command was vastly more important. How foolish of him to even question it.

"And so if no one lives to tell the tale, the terror will be the greater," he said.

The Mesomaster buzzed again briefly.

"Exactly. Two entire legions shall vanish. The Argonathi will never know what happened. They will lose all contact with Ourdh, and we shall be able to produce the largest army the world has ever known. With that we shall crush the Argonath and go on and finally destroy the isles themselves and end the foul perpetrations of the witch cult."

Thrembode rocked on his heels and kept his mouth shut. So did Odirak. No other response was wise or even permissible. This was high policy. The Mesomaster turned to General Klend, who had so far remained completely silent.

"Klend, we attack at noon."

Thrembode saw it looking at him next.

"Magician, go back and tell your traitors they have only a few hours in which to make themselves useful to us. After that, their moment will be gone and they will die with the rest."

"At once, master." Thrembode bowed and saluted with the clenched fist to his chest.

Thrembode the New was not the only person caught up in the gathering storm who felt disappointment with the direction things were heading.

Away across the city, in the Imperial Palace the Emperor Banwi himself wept on his pillow. It was a very fine pillow, with a silken casing from the Quuf dynasty, and this was not the first time Banwi Shogemessar had wept into it. It was a good pillow for weeping into, quite absorbent, in fact.

The little emperor wept because he had never felt so alone and so bereft in his entire life. How had he ended up in this terrible position? He could still only barely believe it possible.

All day he sat the uncomfortable throne and dealt with the business of the empire. Out in the vastness of Bogra, a fresh Imperial Army was being raised. Almost fifty thousand strong now, this force would join the army of the southern monstekirs, the dukes of Canfalon and the stekirs of Ralezwar. Together they would have more than one hundred thousand men, enough to attempt to raise the siege and drive off the Sephisti horde. But all this seemed to require a thousand political decisions every day. Banwi hated making these decisions, but they had to be made and he had to make them.

Worst of all, the damned witch watched him the entire time like a hawk. Banwi had almost forgotten what it was to enjoy the pleasures of the flesh. It had been weeks since he had drunk more than a single mug of ale. If it wasn't the constant audiences with generals and monstekirs and representatives of other monstekirs, it was the special meetings with the witch herself and the Argonathi generals. There wasn't an hour of leisure in his entire day. The woman was inhuman in her demands.

Banwi pined for the Princess Zettila. But she had been lost in the wreck of the cult of Gingo-La. No longer could she advise him on the struggle with his mother and her favorites. Instead, he spent every waking minute on the business of the empire. Had she been able to witness this change in her cousin, Zettila would have marveled.

However, Banwi Shogemessar did not love the witch for achieving this transformation. He hated her, and he also feared her. And worst of all, he could feel a slow-growing nugget of respect for the witch in his heart. Even his hate would be tinged with respect! It was absolutely too horrible to be borne!.

But he had to admit to himself that his mother's machinations had abruptly come to an end after Ribela had done something unguessable in the dark on a moonless night. His mother was reported to have fled far up-country, to the Patwa valley estates.

Instead of having his mother to terrify him, he had the ugly old witch with her demands and haughty eyes and her ghastly descriptions of what was happening in Dzu, and what would happen to him and all his subjects if he did not obey her and fight to save the empire.

And when he slept, there would be the dreams. Terrible dreams in which a voice told him over and over again that he would be taken by the monster and slowly devoured.

He heard a swish, and the curtain was drawn back.

"Go away, I want to be alone," he said.

But the intruder did not go away.

"I said I wanted to be alone." Surely the witch would not dare to bother him again that day. He'd done enough by the holy breath of Auros. His ass was aching from sitting on that throne for nine hours straight.

But it was not the witch; instead his aunt Haruma stood there like a dumpy pudding clothed in black silk.

Haruma!

"How dare you come to me like this," he began.

It was all Haruma's fault. Haruma had told him to trust the Argonathi. Haruma had told him to offer battle to the enemy. Haruma had opened the door to all this horror.

"Go away. It is all your fault."

Harum came forward, knelt, and pressed her forehead to the floor. It was as she'd feared. The Fedafer had gone to pieces in the last few days. His face was red from weeping.

"My lord, my Fedafer, your humble servant begs you not to say such things. Your humble servant seeks only to assist you in overcoming the evils that threaten the ancient well-watered land."

"You advised me to accept the Argonathi offer of help. I did this and what happened? The foreign devils occupy the city and have seized control of the granaries. I am eating porridge, three meals a day of porridge! It is abominable."

"My lord, my Fedafer, your humble servant begs forgiveness, but would point out that the Argonathi are also holding the walls of the city against the enemy."

"But porridge? I hate porridge, I want duck and

roasted kid and some wine and some time in the harem. I have tasted no honeyed lips in ten days!"

"My lord, my Fedafer, your humble servant begs to remind you that this is a time of war; all your subjects are subject to privations and discomfort. They are united in their love for you, and their morale is the greater in knowing that you share in their privations because you must direct the defense of the city and of their lives."

"Oh, bah! I am not directing the defense of the city. I do not care about the defense of the city. That is something for generals to do. I want roast duck with crackly skin and sweet-sour coconut dressing, do you hear?"

Banwi turned his back on her and sulked on his pillow.

Aunt Haruma came close and knelt beside him.

"My lord and master, darling Banwi, allow me to help you. I know you are exhausted by your labors. I know that the foreign witch is not easy to deal with."

"Easy? She is a torment. A slave driver, a monster in human form. She has forbidden me the use of my own harem."

"My poor nephew, my Fedafer, my master."

"It is absolutely terrible, Aunt. I'm living like some damned military officer or something. And the witch wants me to constantly think about the enemy, and I cannot bear to think of the enemy. They are waiting for me. I see them in Dzu waiting for me with smiles of malice. I cannot sleep, the dreams are too terrible."

He broke down into sobs, and plump, comfortable Haruma did as she had done many times and took the little emperor to her bosom, comforted him, and rocked him gradually to sleep. She reflected that poor Banwi had never been suited to becoming an emperor in the first place. It was just his bad luck that in his time as Fedafer, this terrible rebellion would burst forth from ancient Dzu.

"Go to sleep, my Fedafer," she sang softly to him.

Outside the nightingales were singing and the moon was rising, now a thick crescent, sharp and bright in the east.

CHAPTER THIRTY-NINE

The Committee of Emergency Action met once more in Commander Glaves's quarters on Fatan Street amid an atmosphere of anxiety and gloom.

The committee had swollen in numbers in the past couple of hours. Surgeon Tubtiel of the Kadein First Regiment, First Legion, the fabled "One and Ones" had appeared and then Commander Uzpy, also of the One and Ones, showed up. The sight of the row of completed siege towers, dozens of them, had concentrated people's minds quite wonderfully. General Pekel himself had finally sent a representative, a young half-captain named Dashute.

Through these hours, Glaves reveled in the thrill as his salon became the center of a whirl of intrigues, with news, rumors, and scraps of rumor, being borne in by the Kadeini officers, who hung around the fringes of the action.

But all such excitements come to an end, and this one ended dismally with the return of Euxus of Fozad. After Euxus had spoken, Porteous Glaves felt as if all the color of the world had been drained away, all that was left was clay.

Euxus of Fozad had given them the bad news. The enemy would attack the next day at noon. If they were going to offer anything to the enemy, they would have to offer it now. They would have to do it that very night.

Essentially it meant that they would have to mu-

tiny. They would have to seize General Paxion and
put him under guard. Just possibly they might have
to kill him.

It was too much to ask.

"Old Pax is always accompanied by a security guard
now, at least twenty men from the Marneri legion,"
said Commander Vinblat sadly.

"I can't expect my men to follow me in an open
mutiny," muttered Commander Uzpy. "They're not
ready for that. It's too soon."

"Why must we act so soon? Why don't we wait?"

Glaves, too, wondered why they might not wait.
What difference would a few hours make? But Euxus
of Fozad was adamant. His contacts with the enemy
said that the attack would go on immediately unless
the city was surrendered.

"Perhaps you might seize a gate and open it tonight.
That would be accepted favorably by the leaders of
the Sephisti."

The Kadeini were aghast.

"Open treachery! Is that what you want? Replacing
old Pax with General Pekel is one thing, but opening
the gates to the enemy is another," boomed the archer
from Kenor, Captain Ferahr.

"I will never betray my men," snapped Commander Vinblat. "I am a man of honor first and
foremost."

Euxus snorted nervously. Fools! "What ailed you?
Can you not see that this is your only hope. Your only
chance of escape?"

"Count me out!" barked another commander.

"Nor will I stoop to common treachery," said Surgeon Tubtiel with a hiss of indignation.

Glaves's jaw had dropped open. This was unimaginable. He'd got them this far, and now that they had
a possible way out and they wouldn't take it. Euxus
of Fozad's face, normally so smoothly impassive, now
betrayed a degree of irritability.

Desperately Glaves threw himself into the fray.
Something could be worked out. Surely another day
or two would make no difference.

Euxus of Fozad could not agree. It was not up to
him; it was what he had been told. The enemy believed that it would take the walls. It had overwhelming force. A vast army, stiffened with the
terrible blood myrmidons, was waiting for the signal
to begin the assault. The enemy felt that the committee had not done enough to earn serious consideration. They must open a gate or prepare to die with
the rest.

Alas, the Kadeini could not agree to that, and they
departed in an angry mood. In the salon they left a
wide-eyed Glaves, who dug around desperately in a
cupboard for the remnants of a bottle of whiskey.
Empties, they were all empties! There was nothing to
be found.

However, Euxus of Fozad had not given up completely. He nodded at Glaves and produced a slim
silver flask.

"Perhaps you would care for some of my own personal distillate?"

Glaves snatched at it and swallowed three gulps of
the black drink. It was like nothing he'd ever tasted
before, spicy, alcoholic, and fiery indeed.

In a few moments, his eyes bulged in his head as
the black drink took effect. Euxus smiled benignly and
then suggested that Glaves could save the situation
himself. All he had to do was order his own troops to
open the Fatan Gate.

Porteous Glaves lurched up and was about to shout
his agreement, but the black drink checked his tongue.
One of the disarming capacities of the black drink was
that it would spur the tongue of the uninitiated to
unusually scrupulous truthfulness.

For a moment, Porteous Glaves struggled. He had
a vision of himself leading his men to open the gates,

but he knew that it was a fraud and within seconds it
dissolved to ashes. He could not lie.

"My men would not obey such a command. I cannot
do it."

"Surely you are too modest? You are the commander, after all."

"My officers would not relay such orders."

"Are you not a popular commander, much loved
by his troops?"

Glaves gave a big sigh and seemed to collapse back
into his seat.

"My troops hate me, they're ugly and ungrateful . . ."

"Ah, so." Euxus of Fozad had feared as much.
"Well, in that case, my poor fellow, it's up to you.
Perhaps you can figure out some way to open the
Fatan Gate tonight. If the army of Sephis held even
one gate, then the entire defense would be utterly
compromised. The loss of life would be far less than
it will be if the attack is launched. And, of course, if
you opened the gate and lead your men out to surrender, then you would be well rewarded."

For a second, Porteous Glaves stared up at the man
and then he began to giggle. The giggles rose in tiers
to violent laughter and continued into a near-hysteric
fit. He was red-faced, manic, when Euxus left the
house and scurried away into the shadows.

Eventually the laughter descended into sobs and
shuddering deep breaths. With tears rolling down his
cheeks, Porteous Glaves stood in the window and
looked out across the doomed city. It was very dark,
hardly any lamp oil remained. The temple pyramids
were picked out by the moon's light. He had no hope
left at all. Alone he could do nothing. Even Dandrax
was of limited utility and would refuse suicidal orders.
The gate was heavily guarded, the men would not be
taken unawares. It was impossible, it seemed that he
was going to die here in this wretched foreign hellhole
and that he would never get back to punish Ruwat for

suggesting this mad scheme of joining the army to gain political preferment. Tears of rage formed in his eyes, and slowly trickled down his cheeks and dripped off his chin.

CHAPTER FORTY

The day dawned bright and clear, a few fluffy white clouds scudded across the sky in the early morning and a cool breeze blew down from the north.

At the Fatan Gate, the cooks boiled up a mash of porridge and everyone ate well; men and boys from their bowls, dragons from their tubs. There were the usual complaints about the lack of flavor, of akh, of variety in general, but at least everyone's stomach was filled. When they finished, they took up their positions and waited.

On the wall, they watched impassively. Everyone knew what was coming this day. Relkin worked on his dragons, with assistance from Hatlin, who had formed a certain bond with the great Purple Green.

Hatlin worked on the Purple Green's blisters and bruises leaving Relkin free to deal with Bazil. Bazil had a sore spot, on his right shoulder, where he'd been struck by a mud man's hammer in the fight in the mine. From Relkin's knapwood box had come the old standby, Sugustus's Liniment and Scale Tonic for the adult dragon.

The leatherback had been moving his arms around, stretching his muscles, but he paused for the liniment to be applied.

"That shoulder still sore," he grunted.

"Should have rested it more."

"How to rest it when we train all day with the poles?"

A good question and one for which Relkin had no
answer. The poles in question were laid out on the
wall, ready for the dragons to wield. The engineers
had calculated that four dragons, pushing on one side
of a siege tower could topple it with poles at least
forty feet in length. A row of tall conifers in the Imperial City had at once been selected, trimmed, and removed by the Argonathi engineers much to the horror
of the gardeners. Dragons had trained with the poles
ever since.

"All day yesterday, they ask dragons to pretend to
push with those poles. We hate the poles."

"Hold still, I want to get this well under the scales."

The dragon grumbled but stilled its vast bulk. Relkin spread the liniment across the massive shoulder
region with the palm of his hand. The muscles underneath the thick leatherback-skin scales felt tight, hardened by the constant work and exercise of the siege.
With so little beer in the diet and so much exercise,
the dragons had all lost a little weight and were, in
fact, reaching peak form and strength, although Relkin was worried about the lack of fresh foods and
akh. Dragons needed the good things in akh to remain
healthy.

Of course, all this hardening of muscle and increased fitness had come at the expense of their good
humor and even of their morale. With the food as
boring as it was, the great beasts had to have something to look forward to in each day, and in Ourdh
that had become the excellent beer.

The Purple Green was the last to get up onto the
walls. Because the Ourdhi had built their walls to
human scales there was no room for dragons in the
interior spaces, not even on the staircases. So the
dragons got up and down on huge wooden steps built
by the legion engineers.

"By the roar of the ancients, it is a strange thing
for a dragon to be doing," said the Purple Green as

he sat beside them and curled his long tail around himself. "Climbing up onto a wall so we can fight with sword." He carried the dragon sword and was wearing more armor than he had ever agreed to wear before, including the huge new helmet that the regimental smiths had made for him. Relkin knew that the Purple Green had come to understand the dangers of the life he'd taken up. But for the wild one to have to ask Relkin for help with extra armor would have been too much, a loss of dragon face. It was good that Hatlin was filling in.

"Strange?" said Bazil, who had taken Ecator from its long scabbard and was working the beautiful blade with a whetstone. "How is it strange? We always fight, that is what we do."

"No, my wyvern friend, I mean the climbing is the strange thing to do. We are dragons, we should fly down and seize the prey, that is what we do!"

Bazil chortled. "I would like to fly, just once, to see what it is like."

"Bah, wingless wyvern, you are crawling things!"

"Yes," said the leatherback, calmly, refusing to allow the wild one to ruffle his scales, "but crawling things that fight!"

The Purple Green grunted with sour amusement. "As for that I am a crawling thing, too, now." He took up a whetstone and began to work on his own blade. It passed the time to work the stone back and forth over the long, gleaming steel, honing the edge. A sharp edge was more important than ever because it was hard to cut the mud men apart without one.

The sun slowly rose in the sky. As it approached the zenith, the scene outside the walls began to change very swiftly. Quite suddenly great gangs of men, chained at the neck and urged on by imps with whips, flooded forward to the rear of the siege towers. Other men, in the black of the Sephisti army, ran forward in streams and climbed into the towers.

Whips cracked, imps bawled encouragement, and the towers came to life, shaking and rattling as they jerked forward and began to roll. And now began a thunder of drums as the drummers of Sephis began a constantly repeated *boom, boom, boom-it-ti-boom*, that went on and on until it seemed to pound in one's blood.

Some ranging arrows streaked out of the towers as they rolled forward. No reply came from the walls, discipline held firm, and nobody wasted their arrows.

Thousands more men were swarming out of the suburbs and forming around the base of the siege towers. Among them were teams pulling forward catapults and trebuchets that had been assembled nearby. As soon as these siege engines were in place, they began hurling a flurry of great rocks soaring over the walls and crashing into the city behind.

Among the great stones, there were bottles of blazing oil and some of these began fires inside the walls. But most of the buildings close to the walls had already long been abandoned and pulled down to give the legion engineers more room to work, so there was little to damage. Now the legion's own trebuchets, built with masts from the shipyards, started to return the enemy's fire. Ranging slowly on the siege towers as they came onward. Soon rocks were striking the towers, and the hides began to break apart here and there.

The Argonathi archers had more targets now, and the first shots from the wall arched out at the towers. The flight of arrows began to thicken. Onward came the towers, the drums boomed louder and louder. The screams of men and the oaths of imp overseers mingled with the rumble of the huge wheels. And over everything thundered the drums.

On the walls, the weight of the defense huddled down and waited. The dragons and most of the men were actually back behind the withe and wicker shields

that were set up down the middle of the wall. Along
the battlements, only the dragonboys and the archers
from Kenor waited with their bows at the ready. The
boys used Cunfshon crossbows, beautiful little weapons that could be fired again and again, quickly and
efficiently by a well-trained operator. Their range was
not that great, however. The Kenor men employed
the long bow, which took great strength to pull but
which could fire a great distance and could be fired
quickly, up to the limits of the bowman's strength.

Now the bowmen began long-ranging shots on the
upper decks of the approaching siege towers. And
more shots were returned, the arrows whistling overhead and sticking in the withes.

Approaching head-on to Relkin's section of the wall
came the closest siege tower. The sides were covered
in wet hides except for the drawbridge. There was
little to shoot at, except the enemy archers on the
upper fighting deck.

Relkin loaded his bow with a quarrel bearing an
armor-piercing point and waited. Beside him, he
found Swane of Revenant.

"Using a steel point on your first shot?" said Swane.

"Not going to get too many shots before they lower
that drawbridge."

Swane had an expensive broad head on his bow, as
if he was expecting a clean shot at someone's flesh.
Relkin stopped himself from commenting. The enemy
on the towers wasn't exposing any flesh.

Swane was unable to stand still, however. He kept
aiming and then giving up in disgust. He cursed under
his breath, but he didn't change his arrow and kept
looking for some target.

An arrow from the tower shot by. Swane snarled
something unintelligible, released his catch, and his
shaft shot out from the walls and stuck into the base
of the drawbridge.

"No more firing there," snapped Hatlin. "We will

keep our discipline, or I'll take names. No firing until the order."

Swane grumbled under his breath and shifted away a few paces. Relkin looked away. It was always Swane's way, to overreach and embarrass himself.

It was a beautiful day. The sun beamed down through occasional white fluffy clouds, the breeze was cool, and there was fragrance from fruit trees on the wind. For a moment, he could almost imagine that he was far away from the walls of ancient Ourdh.

But the drums never stopped their booming thunder, and so the illusion could not hold. And then the first great stone fell out of the sky, slammed into the top of the battlement, bounced, and smashed a hole through the wicker shield and shot over the inside of the wall.

"Dragons deploy shields," ordered Hatlin at once. They'd been lucky, that first rock hadn't struck a dragon unprepared.

Arrows started whistling over the battlement and sticking in the withe barrier. More rocks were coming. Relkin watched one climb high above him and tumble over and over, then crash into the battlement about a hundred feet up the wall from the gate tower.

Another rock, smaller, whipped across the battlement just above him and Swane, then bounced and skipped over the dragons and fell inside the city.

They stayed behind the battlements and watched as the tower wobbled, shook, and rolled toward them. Suddenly a rock hurled from inside the walls bounced off the tower's upper right side. The huge structure shook, and a section of hides was torn open. A gap had opened up.

A Kenor bowman ran up and loosed an arrow from his longbow into the gap and followed it with three more. Arms came out of the hole and frantically pulled at the hides to close it.

Arrows whistled around the Kenor man, and Hatlin

ordered the dragonboys to open fire on the upper
fighting deck, which was now at the extreme edge of
their range.

On came the tower. More arrows flashed from the
uppermost deck and showered down around them.
The Kenor bowman gave a sudden grunt as an enemy
shaft sprouted from his shoulder behind his steel
epaulet.

He sank to one knee with a groan. Relkin scrambled over beside him and took a look. The arrow had
a broad head, it would have to be cut out by the
surgeon. Relkin gave the man the bad news and
turned his attention back to the oncoming monster.
An arrow bounced off his helmet with what sounded
like a very loud clang. He got down behind the battlement again, reloaded his bow, took careful aim, and
then fired at the upper deck. His arrow shot over the
hide barrier and disappeared. He reloaded again and
again, using simple points that had been mass-produced
in recent days. Between them, the dragonboys were
now keeping a constant flow of arrows, nicely spaced,
over the rail. As soon as a Sephisti archer showed
himself, he was fired on.

The tower was close now. The drawbridge would
soon be able to drop down and lodge on the battlements, and then the enemy would pour across.

Gathering from both sides came the men of Marneri.
First were a dozen more bowmen who joined the dragonboys and added a lethal punch with their heavier
shafts. Now the wall had fire superiority, and the archers on the tower could only get off the occasional
arrow.

Swane yelled something and pointed. Relkin glanced
up and saw another big stone reaching the top of its
trajectory. He dodged backward and then dove to his
left as the stone smashed down on top of the wall and
shattered into a hundred flying shards.

There were screams and groans all around him, but

miraculously he was not hurt. He got to his hands and feet, scrambled back, and slipped through the gap to the relative safety on the other side of the wicker wall.

The dragons were cursing and rubbing sore spots. A few fragments of rock had burst right through the withe, but neither Bazil nor the Purple Green had been struck. There was a touch on his shoulder; Relkin spun around to face Hatlin.

"They're both alright," he said.

Hatlin frowned. "Leave them, get back to your position, Dragoneer!"

Relkin hurried off, arriving in time for another rock to explode on the parapet about a hundred feet to his right. This time everyone was already crouched down, and there were fewer cries of pain.

Relkin peeked over the battlement. The sky had suddenly darkened with arrows, and now they came down by the thousands all around him as massed archers let loose below the walls.

He, Swane, and the others pressed themselves close to the battlements and prayed that no rocks or arrows would find them. Meanwhile the withe-and-wicker wall was studded so thickly with arrows, it looked as if it had grown fur.

The siege towers were now accelerating toward the wall on their final surge.

"Prepare to receive the enemy," called Hatlin. A similar cry was going up and down the walls as all the towers closed in.

And then the tower was above them, and still Relkin had found no real target to shoot at. He saw a man, quite clearly, on a crowded stair, exposed by a torn-away hide. There were hundreds of men in there. Relkin rose and fired smoothly, and saw his shaft sprout from the man's side and heard his scream, just forty feet away.

Another point bounced off the battlement beside his head, and he ducked.

"Here they come," snarled Swane of Revenant standing and firing at the enemy bowmen above them.

"Dragons take up the poles!" yelled Hatlin, and the dragonboys danced backward, firing as they went. The withe barricades came down. The dragons surged forward and thrust their poles out through the battlements.

The siege tower rolled forward, the poles slammed against it and held it steady. Now more poles reached out to the right side of the tower. Bazil, the Purple Green, and Vlok were all leaning into it, and the tower began to rock and tilt, with one huge wheel coming up off the ground. At once the whole tower slewed around as the slaves continued to thrust on the shaft and did not halt until the rear was exposed.

With whips flailing, the imps sought to get the men to reverse and pull the tower back from danger.

A storm of arrows flew up from the archers below and began to sprout all over the dragons, sticking out of the leather of their joboquins and from their hide in between armor plates.

The Kenor bowmen stepped to the wall and laid a suppressing fire down into the mob below, but the numbers were against them, and barely a diminution in the enemy fire was achieved.

Now Chektor came up and so did Cham, and they laid their poles against the tower on the same side. The dragons pushed with all their might and slowly the huge tower wobbled up, tilted again, and stuck there, raised off one wheel but no further.

Enemy arrows were hissing around the dragons and sticking in joboquin and dragon hide alike, but the wyverns would not give up. An arrow sank into the Purple Green's cheek, and he began a ferocious growling. He then reached down and made an enormous final effort, heaving his pole against the side of the tower so hard that the pole splintered and the tower wobbled over, gave a great groan from its timbers, sagged, cracked, and fell over into ruin on the ground below.

All the men on that section of the wall gave a great cheer, and the cornets played the charge over and over. The dragons emitted long, exultant roars and pressed their huge forehands together.

Then they turned and went to assist elsewhere, for only a few towers had been toppled successfully while a few more had been broken or had their drawbridges jammed. Others had reached the walls and lowered their drawbridges. Now the battle would be fought in earnest.

CHAPTER FORTY-ONE

And now the battle of the walls rose to a crescendo as the two sides came to grips and the dark shadow of the enemy was cast across the future of all. For defeat meant annihilation for the men of Argonath and, indeed, for all the cities of the fair land of the eastern coast. Men and dragons alike were united in their stand, they would not retreat, and only death would take them from their places.

Above the constant clash and clamor of the combat boomed the drums of Sephis to be answered by the silver cornets of the legions blowing for the charge, the wheel, the retreat, and the quick response.

And through all the roaring chaos of war, the bellowing of the dragons came triumphant and loud, like echoes from the ancient swamps of reptilian struggle, erupting through the chaos of mere Mammalia.

On their left, the 109th discovered a siege tower had slipped through the dragon poles of the Marneri 66th and discharged a squad of the giant mud men onto the wall. The dragons of the 66th were forced back a few steps and kept busy holding off the mud men. A horde of Sephisti soldiery poured across the drawbridge behind the giants and fell upon the defenders. Soon a chaotic fight occupied a good one hundred yards of the wall. Through the battle loomed the giants. Men drove their spears into the soggy stuff of these monsters only to have them wrenched from their hands as the giants moved on with hardly any reaction. The mud men merely reached down and smashed at the men with heavy hammers and huge clubs. Men could not hold up under these impacts, and shields and helmets were crushed again and again until the legionaries scrambled back to evade them. The enemy held a section of the wall. The men of the Argonath could not stand against them. Doom rose like a dark cloud above them.

Then the dragons of the 109th arrived, with a front four dragons deep and the rest behind to lend their muscle to the effort. The four dragons at the front lined their shields up to make a wall of metal and hide, and then they pushed forward in step and drove into the mass of the enemy like a steel plow carving through clay.

The mud men struck at them furiously, but dragons had felt harder blows from trolls, and they struck back with gleaming dragon sword and soon had the advantage.

Bazil Broketail hewed the first giant he ran into, and Ecator clove the thing from neck to crotch, then it fell apart in disorder.

"Disgusting," Bazil said, his eyes gone wide.

The great Purple Green had lofted a giant over his head and now hurled it right off the wall like a missile.

"Score one for me, too," he replied.

Vlok had turned aside a hammer blow and then cut off the head of a mud man. The thing returned to the struggle undaunted.

"What does it take to kill these things?" he snarled.

"Is like fighting vegetables," said the Purple Green.

Bazil put a foot up on another mud man's chest while he extracted Ecator, which had sunk deep into the thing and stuck.

A space was opened for a moment. A brave Sephisti lunged at the dragon's side with a spear. The movement was detected, however, and Relkin spun on the spot and snapped an arrow into the man. It jolted him, but stuck on his mail coat and failed to penetrate.

The fellow was game still, thrust again with his spear, and managed to get it into a gap between the cuisses on the dragon's leg and the mail apron hanging below the joboquin. He tried to thrust it in deep, but Relkin was on him in the next moment with a scream of battle rage, and landed with both feet up, driving into the man's side. The Sephisti was bowled over, his spear came loose at once, and the dragon carried on with no sign of a wound in the leg. The mud man was downed, and Ecator swung over in a gleaming arc of white steel and clove it in two.

Relkin scrambled to his feet before the Sephisti, but already several others were there and he ducked back from their spear points.

" 'Ware this side," he yelled up to Bazil, and reloaded his bow. Out of the corner of his right eye, he saw something huge loom over him, and by instinct alone he evaded the huge hammer that swept down and powdered the brick where he'd been standing.

Relkin fell back and was almost brained by the leatherback's tail, which rocketed past as Bazil braced and swung a backhand into the mud man. Relkin ducked another tail as big Vlok shoved in with his shield, dug it under the arm of the mud man, and toppled it.

Relkin glimpsed Ecator whirling down through the sunlight, reloaded again, and ducked another tail—this time Cham, who was pushing in behind the broketail and Vlok. Relkin scuttled forward, but there was little room now. A press was building up as the dragons drove back the mud men and confined them, so they squeezed the huge army of Sephisti behind them.

"Kill!" roared the Purple Green as he lofted another mud man above the fray and hurled it bodily off the wall, its legs kicking frantically.

"Kill!" The Purple Green was in his element, finally getting his own back for the mistreatment he'd re-

ceived from the enemy. They had doomed him to foot
soldiery. They would pay, by the roar of the ancients
they would pay!

And all the time, completely without thought, the
dragonboys reloaded, took careful aim, and fired
again and again. They sent their shafts into the men
behind the giants, knowing too well that no arrow
could so much as disturb one of the huge beings of
mud, but taking a toll on the Sephisti soldiery, which
was now losing the ability to fight back due to the
tightness of the press.

Still the enemy mass continued to fall back under
the impetus of the fighting 109th. The second line replaced the first, and fresh dragon arms and swords
took up the work while Bazil, Vlok, and the Purple
Green, plus old Chektor, sidled back to the rear for
a breather. Dragonboys rushed up and began checking
them for wounds, for damage to their equipment, for
breaks in the straps holding the armor, for bruising
and swelling, for a hundred things that might affect
their great charges.

The cornets were blowing wildly. Spearmen were
ordered forward into a line behind the dragons and
let loose to spear the mud men and try to pin them
together, helping to immobilize them and make it easier for the dragons to dismember them.

The spearmen, however, were not as adept as dragonboys in avoiding dragon tails, and several times men
were knocked flying as one of the great beasts lashed
its tail for balance while wielding dragon sword. Indeed, it was the hardest art for a dragoneer to learn,
sensing the lash of tails. Getting clipped by a dragon's
tail could knock a strong man senseless.

The spears went home, the dragon swords rose and
fell, and the two dragon squadrons worked their way
toward each other, compressing and squeezing the in-
vading force back against the battlements. Many mud
men had been cut to pieces and thrown over the walls.

Others had been chopped in half and left on the walls. The Sephisti soldiers were scrambling back onto the siege tower, but there was a jam of traffic from both directions inside the tower and the crush on the wall was getting unbearable. Once again, the Argonathi technique of war had immobilized an enemy.

Still it was arduous work, and the dragons switched lines again and again before it was over.

And even as the siege tower rolled back, defeated, and the last mud man was toppled from the wall, the enemy's trebuchets renewed the bombardment and rocks began slamming down onto the brickwork again.

There were screams of pain and bellows from dragons, too. Big Guttupeg, a yellow brasshide from Aubinas in the 109th was killed outright by a boulder that fell directly on his head.

The cornets blew frantically, and officers moved up and down bellowing orders, thinning the position out, removing the tempting target of a great gang of dragons and men clustered together.

Orders came for the 109th and the 66th to rest. The sectors on either side of theirs were also freed from the invader. In fact, the enemy had been forced out of all but a couple of sections by the river gate where the Imperial Guard held the line. Dragons had been sent to help, and the situation was under control.

Exhaustion set in, dragons slumped down, men collapsed where they stood. Only the archers and dragonboys remained active. Relkin peered over the wall. A vast heap of dead, mostly Sephisti soldiers, had piled up there like scree at the side of a mountain slope. Among the corpses were chunks of the mud men, already decomposing into sluglike masses of a dark slime. He shivered, the magic of the enemy was truly terrible. It was as the witches said, there was no choice but to fight.

The quiet was eery after the roar of battle, Relkin noted no targets in sight, and the enemy had pulled

back out of range. Even the trebuchets had fallen silent, having run out of rocks to hurl.

Relkin asked Hatlin for permission to leave his post.
It was granted, and he hurried back to examine his
dragons.

The dragons were huddled over in a morose group,
cleaning and sharpening their swords. Plate armor had
been pulled loose, helmets tossed down.

Relkin caught a look from Swane and knew at once.
The great beasts were upset by the death of Guttupeg,
the brasshide from Aubinas. His dragonboy had been
Jiro Belx, who was sitting red-faced, holding back the
tears, on the inner battlement. Relkin didn't need to
know that the body of the brasshide was on a cart
down below. The dragons would mourn the young
brasshide. They had come together as a unit during
the long trip south, and they had fought together at
Salpalangum and on the walls of Ourdh. Guttupeg
had impressed all with his quiet, respectful manner.

But Guttupeg was not their only casualty. Mooz, a
hard green from Seinster had a broken rib and a suspected broken shoulder. He had been helped down
the engineer's steps and was being treated back in the
dragon tent. Big Cham had a spear wound, and both
Vlok and Swane had arrowheads in their flesh.

Swane gritted his teeth and made no sound as the
surgeons took the barb out of his buttock, and Relkin
found a degree of respect grow for the boy from
Revenant.

Relkin had found that Bazil had taken a shallow cut
from that spear thrust between the cuisse and the
apron. It was impossible to bandage, so he used disinfectant on a clean cloth, then packed it with boiled
mud, the old Sugustus brand, of course. He would
have to hope it would hold and that they would see
no action for a while.

The Purple Green had a few long scratches and
some bruises from hammer blows. Relkin prepared

poultices and found Dragoneer Hatlin there to help
bind them in place.

"Good poultices, Dragoneer Relkin," said Hatlin.

"Thank you, sir."

"You fought well, and so did this pair."

"They did, sir, thank you, Dragoneer."

The dragons did not look up; they were oblivious
to human concerns. They muttered together in dragon
speech and worked the whetstones on their blades.

CHAPTER FORTY-TWO

The walls had held. The Argonathi had not given way, the great enemy was denied its prey.

In fact, that enemy had been savagely dealt with. A third of the siege towers had fallen. Hundreds of mud men had been lost. Even the catapults and trebuchets had fallen silent having run out of ammunition.

The mighty military machine that had been concentrated around Ourdh to destroy the legions had ground to a halt. An eery quiet persisted, split only by the screams of wounded men as they were taken to the surgeons' stations and dealt with.

Treading through the tent city outside the walls, the Magician Thrembode observed the signs of defeat. A lethargy hung over the troops, who sat around small fires, eating and drinking with little conversation. Few men even looked up as he passed.

Once again he reached the conference tent of General Klend. Klend was not looking very well, in fact, he seemed a little green in the face. High priest Odirak was also looking withdrawn. The other priests were absent. The reason was obvious enough in the hunched shape that stood alone on the far side of the space. Thrembode could feel the Mesomaster's anger quite clearly. It blazed like a hot star on the astral plane. Still Odirak was moved to say to him, "The Master is displeased by General Klend's failure."

Klend shot the high priest a vicious look. Thrembode nodded, the dolt Odirak could not sense beyond

the normal plane of gross materiality any more than
poor Klend. But at least Klend knew better than to
say anything to his betters.

The Mesomaster had not yet so much as acknowl-
edged Thrembode's appearance. The figure in the
black cloak was intent on a small message scroll.

Thrembode looked at Klend. Klend looked away
unwilling to meet his eye. Thrembode surmised that
Klend might not be long for the world.

Abruptly the Mesomaster finished reading. With a
contemptuous gesture, it tossed the scroll to Klend.

"See to the repositioning of our remaining siege
force. Resupply will be achieved within two days. You
will have everything ready to renew the assault within
four days. Understood?"

Klend grasped at the scroll as a drowning man
grasps at a line.

"Yes, master, of course."

"The enemy will be resupplied after that. Their fleet
has been delayed by our pirate allies, but it cannot be
stopped nor can it be defeated. The witches remain
the rulers of the oceans for good reason. So we must
be ready on the fourth day, when they will be at their
weakest. They are hungry now, but they will be starving by then."

"They must be defeated!" said Odirak fervently.
"The god demands their sacrifice!"

The Mesomaster was tired of Odirak's witless piety
in this bogus religion. The thing in Dzu was no god,
it was but a malacostracan demon, chained here in the
world Ryetelth and made to do the bidding of the
High Ones. Odirak had been the priest of a dying cult
and had found himself suddenly elevated to un-
dreamed-of heights. The Mesomaster found Odirak
irritating. He forebore from disposing of the high
priest because he understood that the cult's hierarchy
was vitally important to organizing the war effort. If

not for that need, Odirak would long ago have gone into the blood pool.

"Clear the tent," hissed the Mesomaster. "I must talk with the magician alone."

Klend and Odirak left hastily. The bizarre horned face turned to him.

"Magician, you have now the opportunity to serve yourself well. In fact, you will even be forgiven by the High Ones. You will be allowed to live."

"Surely that was not in question."

"Hah! That is so like the surly young magician, who lacks humility before his betters. Nay, protest not, I know everything, Magician. I know what took place at Tummuz Orgmeen."

Thrembode did his utmost to betray no emotion, but his pulse raced. How much did they know? In the fall of the city, he had escaped and gone south. He'd spent the winter in the spice islands.

"Yes, Magician. You served the Blunt Doom, but you did not love it. They are hard to love are they not? In fact, the Doom had found your services lacking in quality and zest. You were about to suffer the consequences of the displeasure of the great Doom."

"Now, I . . . "

"Nay, do not attempt to dissemble, nor to weave some skein of cunning before my eyes. You know you cannot hide the truth from me!"

"Believe me, master, when I say I have no such intention."

"Believe you? Believe a magician of your rank? Hah, that will be the day. I will not believe you, but I will command you and you will serve me well, or else."

The flames in those eyes danced brightly.

"Yes, master." Thrembode knew when it was time to be submissive.

"You have bungled many operations in the past

year or so, Magician. This bungling has not gone
unnoticed."

"Bungling, I protest!"

"You lost an entire network of agents in Kadein.
Then in Marneri, a perfectly planned assassination was
missed because of your clumsiness. You were then
forced to flee, and you were chased across the Gan
to Tummuz Orgmeen by the witch Lessis."

"Chased is too strong a word."

"In Tummuz Orgmeen, you lost the Princess Besita
and brought on the destruction of the Doom itself."

"I, no, I did not. I must protest!"

"Your protestations are meaningless. This is what I
was told in Padmasa."

"Urgh." Thrembode's throat constricted. If this was
what they believed in Padmasa, then he was done for.

"Anyway, the fact is that we have received a sharp
check in our progress, and this is not acceptable. We
shall have to try your traitors once more. You will
contact them and see if we can get them to give up a
gate."

The Mesomaster held up a gloved hand. Thrembode
imagined the horn talons inside the black glove. Was
it really worth it, he wondered, to achieve all those
powers and end up looking like that, a demon of dark
green horn and yellow flame?

"If you can deliver up a gate to us, then I shall
intercede for you with the High."

"Yes, master," Thrembode reflected that the Mesomaster Gog Zagozt would be a powerful ally. A magician needed such friends if he was to survive long in
his current line of work.

"Good. Can it be done, Magician?"

"Yes, master, we have several possibilities to
consider."

"Good, spare me the details. Get me a gate."

"Yes, master."

I'll get you a gate, I'll get you the entire wall, you'll

see, Thrembode thought to himself and prepared to leave.

The Mesomaster wanted to talk, however. Thrembode smiled attentively; such opportunities to ingratiate oneself with the powerful came but rarely.

"It is a troubling situation, Magician. You see, we must take the city and soon. There are many reasons. You are privy to stage-three secrets, so you may understand the weakness of our myrmidons. They must be replaced shortly. We require the population of the city for that task."

Thrembode envisaged the slaughter that would involve. The screaming, the horror on the psychic plane.

Mesomaster Gog Zagozt continued. "But even more important is the fact that we have trapped a great hag here."

Thrembode looked up with a slight tremor of alarm. A hag? Here?

"Yes, Magician"—there was a gloat to the Mesomaster's tone—"I, myself, detected her. She is very sly, very insubstantial on the astral plane. But I sensed her. She is one of their greatest, perhaps the greatest of all. If we can make sure of her, especially if we can capture her, then, well, need I say more than that the future would be filled with boundless opportunities."

Thrembode was riven by extreme emotions. On one hand, he saw the great opportunity offered by the Mesomaster and on the other hand he shivered with odd fears. Thrembode had had a number of close calls in dealing with one of those hags.

"Is it the Grey Hag, Lessis?"

"No, no," the Mesomaster grunted evilly. "No it is not that one, she lies on her death bed in Marneri. An assassination in which no magicians were involved."

Thrembode exulted. "That is wonderful news, Master. I congratulate whoever was responsible."

"So you should, Magician, so you should. So! Now

you see what is at stake here, go back and win us a gate."

Thrembode left the general's tent and returned at once to the ruined villa. Once more he became Euxus of Fozad and made his way back into the city.

Within the walls, he found an air of disorder. Mobs of starving men and women were gathered on street corners. In some places they were quiet, simply staring at the desultory street traffic. At other places they were boisterous, and there were shouts of rage and sudden chanting of slogans in the native tongue.

Thrembode noted these signs of discontent with satisfaction as he hurried down Fatan Street and turned in at the house taken over by Commander Glaves of the Marneri Second Legion.

Glaves was drunk. Dandrax had successfully robbed a merchant's house and come away with some powerful Ourdhi distillate, called yaak. Glaves had been drinking it steadily all day.

Porteous Glaves had decided he couldn't take any more of this. To avoid a court-martial and execution, he had been forced to join his command and actually witness the fighting on the walls. He'd lost control of his bladder when a boulder fell out of the sky and crushed a man just five feet away. The shame and mortification were mingled in his memory with the terror he had felt all that day.

He'd been trying to forget ever since. The sight of Euxus irritated him immensely.

"Begone! We have nothing to discuss!"

But Euxus did not go. "To the contrary," he said sternly, "we have a great deal to talk about. But first you must become sober."

"What? How dare you? You Ourdhi popinjay. Get out!" Glaves flung an arm menacingly toward Euxus.

Euxus seized his hand and squeezed it in a certain way that caused excrutiating pain. Glaves tried to cry out for help, to summon Dandrax, but no words came to his lips. Instead, he found himself staring into Euxus's dark eyes while words of power throbbed around him.

Glaves clutched at his head with his free hand, everything seemed to be spinning. A strange, draining sensation took over, as if something were being wrung out of his body, organ by organ, and deposited in his stomach.

Then with no warning, there came a nausea so intense that his innards jumped like springs. He staggered to a window, leaned out, and vomited a reeking spew of alcohol and bile. The convulsions went on and on with terrible intensity. At one point, it seemed as if he might throw up his own organs, even his eyeballs threatened to pop out of his skull. And then at last it was done with, and an exhausted, limp Porteous Glaves sagged onto a chair and sat there gasping for breath. The strange man he knew as Euxus of Fozad leaned over him and fixed him with an unwavering eye. Porteous was no longer drunk.

Thrembode worked on the Argonathi commander for a long time, but eventually gave up in disgust. The man was in a deep funk, his mind was like jelly, and there was hardly a fiber in his entire being. He wept constantly and bemoaned his lot.

The situation was clear, the Argonathi would not betray a gate, especially not after the battle on the walls. The men of Kadein might have been persuaded to march out of the city and go south, before the battle, but now that they had withstood the attack and taken casualties, they would stand fast until death or starvation took them.

"They will starve then, or they will be destroyed. It will not matter in the long run. You will starve with them. You have been quite useless."

Glaves turned a sullen, vomit-stained face up to him.

"Who are you really?"

Thrembode smiled. "An observer, my dear fool, just an observer."

"You know the enemy, what will happen when they take the city?"

Thrembode's smile became ugly. The fool deserved a little truth in his life.

"They will slaughter most of the population and drain their blood for the life stuff of fresh giants."

Glaves's eyes grew round. His face, already pale, went white.

"No one will escape, will they?"

"No they will not. Good-bye, Commander, try to die bravely."

Thrembode swept out of the commander's quarters and melted swiftly into the crowds.

At the sign of the Blue Pelican, he turned into a tavern's door and made his way to the back room. His agents were there, summoned for a rare meeting. It was a great risk, but he needed a swift response and so it had to be taken.

"The groundwork has been laid. Now we must have action. The Argonathi will be resupplied in a few days. We must take advantage of the hunger. We must set a match to this pile of kindling."

CHAPTER FORTY-THREE

Day by day, the food supply dwindled to virtually nothing. Two days after the victory on the walls, the legion commissary cut off all further rations for the population of the city. What was left would keep the legions alive for a few more days. The populace would have to tighten its belt and get by on scraps for a while. At least there was water and as yet, little disease.

There were ugly scenes outside the granaries when the doors were barred to the people. A mob built up until at length Paxion ordered a detachment to clear the street. At the same time, he increased the size of the force holding the granary and organized mounted patrols up and down the street between the granary and the walls. This gave the Talion troopers something to do and ensured a constant flow of intelligence about conditions at the granary and in the districts between the granary and the walls.

The mobs reacted with mounting fury, but after discovering the mettle of the legionaries in a few serious clashes, the crowds faded. Paxion put a team of archers to work ferreting out snipers, and the arrows out of the alleys ceased as well. Hour by hour, the city's stomach tightened and the grumbling grew louder and louder.

Paxion toyed with the idea of removing the remaining food supply and parceling it out to the legions, but finally decided that for the amount of time involved, just a few days now until the arrival of the white ships, it was not worth the risk of starting riots by moving food supplies around. They would hold the granary and they would hold the walls, that was all that was really essential.

Ribela suggested that the emperor be protected as well, but Paxion swore he would have nothing to do with the treacherous little Fedafer.

"I doubt that the men would lift a finger to save him from the hanging he so justly deserves."

Ribela gave up. Lessis's words rang clearly in her mind. The military had to control its own destiny. The Fedafer would remain protected solely by his eunuchs.

Meanwhile General Paxion had noted that the enemy had nearly completed repairs to the remaining siege towers and was at work rebuilding several others. He pondered the possibility of a sortie, a sudden night assault to burn the towers.

However, his idea was not received enthusiastically, particularly by the Kadeini commanders. They talked of nothing but the casualties that could be incurred. Paxion told them he would let the men of Marneri take the risk and earn the glory. The Kadeini grew even more upset and fretful, and charged that he was splitting the command and ruining morale.

Paxion held off but did not let go completely of the idea. The fleet would soon arrive, and they would then be solidly reinforced. If they could hold the walls as they were, then they could hold them far more easily once they were reinforced and re-supplied.

The dinner bells rang from the cook fires and the legions took their evening meal. The sound of the bells and the smell of the huge caldrons of cornmeal stirabout attracted crowds of Ourdhi who stood there at the edge of the various regimental camps, kept back by the line of men with shields and spears.

The legions ate. The Marneri Second was centered on the Fatan Gate, inside which was a cleared space where the cooks had set up their station among the tents of the engineers, the junior officers, the duty administrative office, and a dozen others. Relkin took back two buckets of the porridge for his dragons and then collected a bowl of the stirabout for himself. It wasn't much, but at least it filled his belly for a little while.

The crowd outside the lines was restless. There was a lot of shouting going on, and an occasional brick was thrown from the rear.

A coronet blew and within a few seconds, a pair of Kenor bowmen took up positions on the roof of a nearby building that overlooked the scene. Another brick was lobbed high toward the soldiers. Before it landed, a shaft had streaked past in reply. There was a sudden shriek. The brick throwing ceased.

Relkin got up to the roof of a three-story tenement, the tallest building on that section of the street. He watched the crowd for a while as a sensation of food-induced lassitude seeped through him. He was tired through and through. Tired of Ourdh, tired of being hungry, tired of the siege. He was also tired of grouchy dragons, and the great beasts were getting exceedingly grumpy of late. Dragons hated to be hungry. Dragon discipline, the only thing that kept these huge carnivores in check, enabling the mingling of dragons and men in the legions, had always depended on feeding the dragons adequately. Right now they were not getting enough to calm the fire in their bellies, and they were becoming intractable.

They were all on edge. It had reached the point where just thinking about food was getting painful. And if the rumors were true, then it was only going to get worse.

Still, the sun was setting in a sky striped with long clouds and the breeze was from the south, warm and soft. It was good to relax for a moment and just watch the crowd slowly mill around and then disperse.

Eventually the sun was gone, and Relkin left his spot and went across the regiment's camp area to the blacksmithing operation. A fighting legion had a strong demand for smithing and so a large blacksmith shop on Fatan Street had been taken over by the legion. The local proprietor had been paid in good silver coin, of course—Paxion was a stickler for the proprieties.

Relkin had several pieces of equipment at the smiths. The Purple Green's helmet had been struck a couple of times by hammers and had some dents. Bazil's left cuisse was dented, almost pierced, and a piece of chain mail had been torn away, just ripped out somehow in the fury of that fight on the wall. Then there was a notched tail sword and an order for arrow points. Like the rest of the dragonboys, he was having to fletch a new supply of arrows. Most of the shafts they'd recovered from the enemy's fire had to be cut down to fit their Cunfshon bows.

Relkin was tired but he was still glad for a good reason to stay away from the dragons. The Purple Green had hissed at him that morning and bared its formidable teeth when he nipped some skin while trying to cut a broken talon. That whole finger was painful now because of that split talon, and the wild one was in a foul mood. For a second, he'd come close to lashing out at the boy.

It was the closest Relkin had come to getting struck by a dragon since he'd been young enough and stupid enough to play a painful trick on his own involving a tack. If they didn't get resupplied soon, it might be too dangerous to go near the wyverns.

Inside the smithy, there was a crowd of men and dragonboys surrounding the fire pits. Hammering filled the air along with the stench of hot metal and smoke. Neither the helmet nor the cuisse were ready. The apprentice smith who gave him the news was exhausted, with gaunt eyes peering out of a face blackened by smoke. Relkin collected a dozen arrow points, and returned to the warm, spicy air outside.

He set off for a walk along the road outside the lines. There were just a few people on the street. With starvation ahead, the populace had largely retired to their beds.

Here and there on the corners were beggars. Mostly men but with a few women sprinkled among them, clad from head to toe in the black garub to indicate that they were not prostitutes.

As he went past, these people called out in broken Verio for food. Relkin had nothing to give them. Up ahead there was an argument among some of them, angry voices were raised. A woman was shoved out into the street by two men.

Relkin halted in front of her, she turned, and he saw her face and recognized her instantly.

"Lady Miranswa?" he said.

"You?" she said quite astonished.

"The Mother must have willed it," he said.

"Your goddess of the north, a cold sort of goddess, I think."

In truth Relkin put as much faith in the old gods as he did in the Great Mother, and he would not argue about religion with anyone, especially not with Miranswa. The memory of that kiss, just before they parted in the Temple of Gingo-La was strong. There had been feeling on both sides, he knew that.

"You who rescued me from slavery and then shattered the power of the goddess, you are here now to taunt me in my misery."

"I would not taunt you for anything, Miranswa Zudeina. I remember what you did for me and what happened."

She became irritated.

"I swear I had no idea, I thought you might perhaps

escape, no more than that. I did not foresee that you
would destroy everything."

"I did not destroy anything. I rescued my best
friend in the world, and I rescued my dragon. I would
die for either of them. They have long since earned
that of me."

She saw something in his face that frightened her.

"What did I do? Oh goddess protect me!"

"Miranswa, what are you doing here?"

Her eyes dulled at variance with the bitterness in
her voice.

"Food," she whispered.

He nodded.

"Have you any food that you could give me?" she
said with a sudden eagerness.

"No, but I will get you some."

"I have not eaten for days. There is no food in
the city for one such as I, discarded by family and
friends."

"Your family has done this to you?"

"Hah! They would kill me if they could find me.
My Aunt Elekwa has taken control of everything.
She has my inheritance and will not give it up
easily."

He leaned closer to her.

"I have not forgotten what happened."

"Oh the Island of the Goddess? Forget it, it meant
nothing."

But in truth, it had not been so meaningless. Relkin
found her a place to rest, a cleared space in the back
of one of the cargo wagons. The wagons were parked
in lines inside the wall near the Fatan Gate, a stone's
throw from the cook fires for the Eighth Regiment
and the 109th dragons.

He went to the cook, called in a favor, and received
a small bowl of barley mush that had been held over.
He gave this to Miranswa, who ate it with the fevered
passion of the starving.

Then she slept while he watched over her. She was very thin and completely exhausted. He covered her with his own blanket and then went back to check on his grouchy dragons.

CHAPTER FORTY-FOUR

The mood in the starving city had risen to a fever of rumor and hate. At night, there were attacks on the granary, by bands of two or three hundred men, driven to desperation by their hunger and that of their families.

The Argonathi soldiers and Kenor bowmen were too much for these attempts. But they were a mark of the passions rising in the city.

The white ships alas were still days away. There was a sense that anything might happen in the time before they arrived. Officers were enjoined to prevent any incident that might provoke the crowds, it it was at all possible. If attacked, however, they were to fight back at once and subdue their attackers. Killing them if necessary. "Be fair but be firm," that was Paxion's order.

And those great, fat vessels of oceanic trade were still many miles to the south, threading the channels of the great river and maneuvering against the pirates that infested the lower reaches.

In the morning, Relkin rose early and begged for a small bowl of food that he took to Miranswa where she slept in the back of the wagon. She said little and took the food. Then before he left, she kissed him on the cheek. He felt his heart leap, and despite his own fatigue, his step grew lighter and his vision more clear. But she did not look up when he attempted conversation, and a little confused by it all, he backed out of

the wagon, returned to the cook fires, and collected
the ration for the dragons, a bare half a pail apiece
of corn mush.

When he set it before them, they did not respond
to the usual greetings. The evil mood was intensifying.
They took the food with barely a grunt and long hard
stares from huge, predatory eyes.

It was horrible. Relkin's dragon, the only family he
had ever known, was turning on him slowly, degree
by degree. In truth, the great beast he called "Baz"
was a predatory animal that ate men and anything else
it could catch. Now it was starting to look at him as
if he were food.

The dragon was fighting it, but despite his intelligence and indisputed civilized veneer, the dragon
mind was losing control of the situation to the raw
instincts of his terrifying ancestors.

With the Purple Green, they were close to having
a really dreadful crisis. The Purple Green was close
to breaking point. The wild one felt none of the moral
compunctions against eating human flesh that were
bred into Argonathi wyverns. His conscious mind and
his instincts were one, in this he was more of a natural
beast than the wyverns. Thus he had more control in
the end over his instincts. It was just a question of
whether he had the will. He did not share the respect
for humankind that the wyverns did. If he snapped,
he would wreak terrible damage, and it would be the
wyverns who would be called on to subdue him.

There had never been a wyvern mutiny. The Argonathi
generals had always treated the dragon units as the
battle-winning formations they were. But conditions
of starvation could erode dragon discipline. There had
been solitary incidents.

Relkin, of course, suffered particular discomfort.
His relationship with his dragon was the most central
thing in his existence. Never before had there been a
taint of mistrust between them. Now he had seen that

dragon's hunt stare. A sudden hard glitter of interest that struck a chill through him and almost gave him dragon-freeze.

As for the great wild one, he stayed in the dragon tent and Relkin put his food by the flap and barely peeked in. The Purple Green was just frankly dangerous to be around. Unfortunately, there was a problem. Relkin had had to abandon some of the grooming tasks, and Dragoneer Hatlin was too clumsy by everyone's admission for the one job that really had to be attended to.

The broken talon. There was an infection growing at the base of that talon, and it needed to be burst and cleaned with disinfectant. That, of course, was going to sting, and Relkin doubted he could get away with it.

He broached the subject to Bazil. The leatherback from Quosh was unhappy with the idea.

"You want this dragon to come between you and the wild one? You ask me to fight my brother dragon?"

"Fight? No, just back me up so he doesn't kill me."

"Bah, useless dragonboy, why should I care?"

"He has an infection there, it's going to get very painful soon if we don't do something about it."

"Purple Green of Hook mountain will make his own decision."

"He is unapproachable, you know that. You are almost unapproachable."

"Damn fool dragonboy, I am starving. Battledragon must eat. There are things happening in my mind. I do not always know what I am doing. It is as if I lose control of myself."

"Well, eat the damned Ourdhi then, but don't eat the dragonboy, all right?"

"You think this is funny. You don't understand. It is not something that dragon controls, it controls dragon. I starve and I see everything as food."

"The ships are coming. They'll be here in a couple of days."

"Hard to wait that long."

"I know, old friend, I know. But in the meantime, the Purple Green's hand will swell and get really painful. He might lose his hand, or even die."

"Bah, humans think they know everything about dragons. Purple Green is a wild dragon, what do you know about him?"

Relkin swallowed.

"Not enough, but if you'll help me just a little, we can save him a lot of pain and trouble. Isn't that worth it?"

It took time and persuasion, but at length the leatherback was worn down. Of course, the great Purple Green would not hear of it at first.

"Tell them to stay away from me," he growled. "They are starving me, and I cannot be near them. They are food."

Bazil patiently pointed out that the talon injury would get significantly worse and very painful if left unattended. Much against his will, the Purple Green had to agree. He had been in the legion long enough now to see the point of this. Such wounds as he had suffered had all been healed quickly and relatively painlessly. In the past, wounds had often been a hideous business of rot, suppuration, and considerable agony. The Purple Green had experienced firsthand the value of a dragonboy's care. And thus eventually he agreed to try.

After the evening meal was over, far too soon for everyone concerned, the Purple Green sat still by the camp fire. Relkin approached cautiously and examined the split talon.

There was a swelling, tending to yellow in color around the base of the talon. There was no time to lose. Slowly, carefully, he explained what he was going to do.

Bazil and Vlok now took up stations near the wild one, ready to intervene in case he lost control and attacked the boy.

Relkin gingerly pressed the area at the base of the talon. The Purple Green hissed a little but remained still.

Relkin pulled out a sharp pick from his box and with a quick jab burst the painful swelling. Pus oozed up, and the great dragon hissed again, much more loudly.

Relkin looked over to Baz and Vlok. They seemed quite unconcerned. Relkin took a deep breath, applied pressure, and slowly, carefully forced out the rot until it ran clear.

The wild dragon emitted a number of growls during this procedure, and Relkin was sweating profusely when it was done. Now came the real test. He looked up at the Purple Green. The monster was lost in some reptile haze beyond human imagining.

Relkin took up a swab, soaked it in disinfectant, then began to clean the wound and the whole area around the base of the talon.

The wild dragon shuddered and shook as the sting began, and the hissing became loud and continuous.

Bazil and Vlok got to their feet nervously.

Relkin now poured a small amount of disinfectant onto the area. Now the Purple Green's tail began to lash around wildly. A stack of logs by the fire was knocked over with a crash. The noise coming from the great carnivorous jaws was close to a huge whistle. Relkin backed away slowly.

They all stood there waiting while the Purple Green hissed and slowly subsided.

They were still standing there when a couple of dragonboys ran up and yelled something as they went past, heading into the tents. At the same time, Relkin became aware of a gathering clamor somewhere in the distance, down the Fatan Street.

The dragons too were standing tall and looking off into the distance. The Purple Green was shaking the hand with the newly disinfected wound, but otherwise seemed unconcerned.

Swane of Revenant came running up from the smithy carrying Vlok's forearm-armor vambraces.

"What's going on?" asked Relkin.

"A riot in the city. Down at the granary. Ol' Pax will be sending the cavalry."

There was already a rumble of horse hooves coming from somewhere not too far away.

Relkin looked back to the dragons. They were sniffing the air.

"The city burns," said Bazil.

CHAPTER FORTY-FIVE

All across the city, the cry of rage resounded and the poor swarmed out of their quarters and headed down the roads to ring the granaries and bellow for food. When none was forthcoming, they began looting in the surrounding district and setting fire to the houses of the wealthy. Soon smoke was billowing up in a dozen places.

The Ourdhi authorities soon gave up any attempt at imposing order; complete chaos loomed. However, General Paxion did not hesitate and sent the Talion horse crashing through the mobs to reinforce the garrison in the granaries. But as the mobs grew larger, it became impossible to maintain steady communications with the granaries. Sections of Fatan Street were burning out of control, and the city fire teams had been unable to get through.

It was madness, the suicidal rage of a scorpion in a fire. Nobody even knew exactly what had inspired the riot, although a lot could be laid to the barrel of the black drink that had been given to a street gang on Canary Street. They had lead the mobs marching on the granary.

Here and there around the city the mobs caught individual legionaries who had been away from their posts for one reason or another. Their heads went to adorn pikes, and their bodies were torn to pieces and even eaten by some.

In vain did the leaders try to contain the rage. The

mobs were completely out of control, and a xenophobic lust for blood had taken over.

A hostile crowd had even gathered in the Zoda and had called on the Fedafer to show himself to his people, in order to reassure them that he was alive and not under the control of an alien witch as the rumors had claimed.

The emperor refused and since the witch was, in fact, the only person strong enough to make him, it seemed pointless to do so. The sight of the witch herself would have excited the mobs to even greater outrages. So the emperor cowered in his palace and the witch stayed with him, to keep him under control as much as anything. The mob grew even more enraged when the emperor did not appear and several fires were set in the buildings around the Zoda. The gates of the Imperial City remained shut, however, and the mobs were unable to gain entry.

A somewhat confused sea gull kept General Paxion informed of developments. The bird flew back and forth between the palace and his personal tent carrying a small scroll attached to its leg. The scroll was imbued with magic, being seemingly of a thick paper. However, messages written on it disappeared shortly after being written, and only reappeared when opened by the person they were addressed to.

Paxion held the walls, the gates, and the granary. His cavalry was keeping sections of the Fatan Street and the East Gate Road open. The Great Witch held the emperor and seemed physically safe for the moment. Paxion assured Ribela that he was confident that he could break through to the Imperial City at will and escort her to his positions on the wall if necessary.

The gull vented an odd squawk now and then as it flapped its wings on takeoff, and then soared back across the city and was lost in the haze of smoke covering the Bogra quarter. The haze was getting so thick, you could no longer make out the ziggurats in the distance.

General Paxion was fighting against a slow-rising sense of panic. He knew they just had to last a few more days before they were resupplied, but the combined pressures of the siege and now the riots, were becoming overwhelming. Furthermore, General Pekel did not inspire confidence in Paxion. The Kadein legion was undoubtedly exhibiting morale problems. This legion had been due for a rest period in the home city. They had served five years on the frontier. They had been packed and ready to leave Fort Redor when suddenly they had been told they were not going home to Kadein, but instead were being sent south to the empire of Ourdh for an unknown length of time. The legion had not taken the news well, and although the men had served well enough, the officers were a malcontent lot.

Paxion frequently heaved a sigh. The riots seemed like a sign of doom. Just a few more days and they'd have been resupplied and able to feed the people again. Now who could say what might happen, the whole city might burn to the ground. He wondered if he'd ever see his wife and children again, ever have the chance to walk down Tower Street in Marneri or visit the opera in Kadein.

Captain Kesepton came to the command tent around an hour after the first fire. He remained, working over the big map they'd spread out of the city, charting the areas of riot and fire. Kesepton plotted out routes around the riot-torn areas for cavalry patrols.

Paxion took him aside to tell him that Lagdalen was safe and with the Great Witch.

"No one is probably safer in this entire city," said the general. With a rueful nod, Kesepton had to agree. Paxion examined the map that Kesepton had been working on. The Saubraj area around the granary was in flames and the mobs were very thick on the Fatan Street north of the fires.

Along the road to Gunj from the East Gate, there were more fires and very heavy mobs who had attacked a small settlement of foreigners, darker-skinned people from the continent Eigo. They were busy hanging these poor folk from lamp poles, a release of long simmering racial hatreds.

"We still have adequate communications along the walls to all the gates, and our camps have been left alone," said Kesepton.

"The rioting remains localized then."

"It's concentrated in two areas really. There's the mob at the granary and the mob on the East Gate Road. There are also small crowds in the inner city plus a big one on the Zoda."

Paxion smiled grimly. "I hear that the Fedafer's not too popular with his people today."

"I honestly think they'd like to kill him, sir."

"Yes, no doubt."

Suddenly Paxion became aware of a familiar vibration, a steady thrum that shook and shuddered through everything.

"What's that?" he asked. The officers went outside. Immediately it became clear. The drums of Sephis were beating again. The enemy was attacking the walls!

Rocks came hurtling over the wall to smash down in the tents and campsites. The cornets blew high and shrill summoning the legions to battle.

Paxion ran to his tent, pulled on his sword and coat, and hurried outside. A moment later, a massive rock landed on the tent and smashed it to the ground. Paxion was left staring, gulping for air. The rock was as big as he was. If he'd stayed in the tent another second, he would have been mashed to a pulp. He felt a cold sickness in the pit of his stomach.

All around him the legions were in motion, men,

boys, and dragons thundering up the steps and ladders to their places on the walls.

The command tent was coming down, the staff were hurrying toward the Fatan Gate. They would reestablish the command post in the courtyard there.

Another great rock hurtled over and landed in a muddy slough on a vacant lot. Men nearby were galvanized to swifter movements.

Paxion hurried toward the gate tower.

CHAPTER FORTY-SIX

Officers came flying down the lines, yelling into the tents.

"To the walls!

The legions convulsed.

"The siege towers are rolling."

In frantic haste, dragons were strapped into armor and joboquin, and ordered up the steps to the walls. In truth, they needed no orders. They were in a fighting mood, eager to take out on some unfortunate their rage over the short rations of the past week. Someone would discover that it was a serious mistake to starve a dragon!

Relkin had had to tighten the straps on the dragons' joboquins, they'd lost considerable weight. They were slim, hard-fleshed, and they seemed battle ready, but he wondered if they'd also lost endurance.

On the wall, the scene was familiar enough. Arrows sleeted overhead, and the rising arms of the trebuchets below launched rocks by the dozen high into the air.

Relkin found his place. Swane slid in beside him.

"How's the broketail dragon today then?"

"Hungry and ready to kill someone. How's Vlok."

"The same. They scare me when they're like this."

"Yeah, they scare me, too. I'm glad I don't have to fight 'em."

"Hah! You're dead right about that."

There was something different in Swane's voice, a

tone was missing. The bigger youth wanted to say something.

"Look, uh, Relkin, I got to get something off my chest. If we don't make it out of here, I just want you to know that I was wrong about you. Thought you were a bag of wind, all boasts and no muscle, I was wrong."

Relkin stared at Swane for a long moment. So now the boy from Revenant wanted to bury the battle ax. "Well, Swane, I hope you're right about that, I think this fight's going to test us all." Relkin proferred his hand, and they shook on it.

A huge rock bounced off the parapet five feet away from them and caromed high over the wicker and disappeared, heading into the city. Powdered brick dust blew over them. Swane coughed and spat.

"Yeah, I know what you mean."

The bombardment was intensifying, and all they could do was huddle close to the lee of the parapet and pray that they didn't get hit by one of these whirling boulders. In a zone about one hundred yards distant from the walls, there was a solid line of trebuchets and catapults, their arms rising and falling steadily as they hurled their missiles at the wall.

A rock crashed down and demolished a section of the wicker barricade. A dragon bellowed with pain, and Relkin looked back with a tremor of sudden fear, but his dragons were alright. In fact, the wounded beast was Kasaset, a freemartin in the 66th dragons. Her leg was smashed, and she was down rolling in agony.

Another rock bounced off the bricks, powdering them as it did so. They ducked and crouched and prayed that they wouldn't get hit while dragonboys in the 66th did what they could to aid poor Kasaset.

The siege towers were already very close to the walls, and now Hatlin ordered the dragons to take up the poles. Arrows came over thickly and began to stud the dragons like feathers, mostly sticking in the leather of the joboquin, but here and there getting through to dragon hide. The dragons hissed with barely suppressed rage during this.

The siege tower accelerated. The dragons rammed their poles against it and heaved. For a moment it stopped dead, but then the imps below put on fresh teams of slaves and drove them on with their whips. The siege tower shuddered and shivered as the two forces strove, and then with a groan of tortured timbers, it forced its way past the dragon poles.

With oaths and hissing rage, the dragons scrambled back and reorganized themselves. Once more they set their poles against the side of the tower. They planted their massive feet and heaved hard. The tower shuddered and began to tilt, the dragons thrust again, but the towers had been weighted down with ballast in the bottom level. They did not tilt as easily as before.

Far below the wall, the imps screamed in rage and lashed the slaves beneath them. Once again the tower shuddered, fell back on both wheels, and rolled forward past the dragon poles.

The siege tower was in range of the wall. With a screech of chains, the drawbridge came slamming down on the parapet and across it stormed a line of the giant mud men. They pranced in unison and raised their hammers in a line. Then the dragons struck them and all unity vanished in a melee of shield and sword and clamoring steel.

In the thick of it was Relkin of Quosh, firing as fast as he could load his bow, trying to keep the enemy archers on the tower above under cover.

The dragons hewed through the mud men and kept them off the walls. Sephisti soldiery got through, however, and kept the dragonboys and the legionaries busy preventing any attacks on the dragons' backs.

The fighting went on and on, and then came terrible news from the wall above the East Gate. A Kadeini unit there had broken and fled. The dragons were

overwhelmed, three slain and the rest driven from the
wall. An army of Sephisti soldiers had begun entering
the city and attacking the East Gate from the rear.

The 109th fought on, there was no choice, because
more giants were tramping forward across the ruined
mess of their forerunners. The great swords rose and
fell, tired dragons reached within themselves for re-
serves of strength, but now the poor diet of the pre-
ceding days began to tell.

The dragonboys ran out of arrows and frantically
searched around them for usable ones from the
enemy. Their rate of fire slowed drastically, however,
and now the surviving enemy archers atop the tower
began to assert themselves. This descending fire soon
took an effect. Shim of Seant went down with an
arrow through the throat, and he was dead before
they turned him over. Big Likim, the brasshide, would
need a new dragonboy when this was over, and little
Shim would never see his beloved hills of Seant again.
Krusp of Aubinas was next, an arrow in the chest and
another beside it in the next second. Once down, he
lay still. Now Berholt, the youngest leatherback,
would need a new dragonboy. The dragons, too, were
taking their share of this deadly rain of arrows. The
Purple Green had a dozen shafts sticking out of the
neck protector that Relkin had insisted he wear. It
was only leather, but it provided a thick collar beneath
the rim of the helmet and above the joboquin. Dragons disliked wearing them because they restricted
movement, but they did stop arrows. All the dragons
were studded with arrows now, but their swords continued rising and falling as they fought on.

Still, the situation was dire and growing worse with
every moment. And now came the final torment. The
trebuchets opened fire again, dropping their rocks on
the struggling host, not caring whether they struck
their own forces or not, as long as they might strike
down dragons.

Big Kibol of Blue Hills was killed outright by a rock that shattered his skull. Rupp, a green from Montok Hills, was struck on the shoulder and lost the use of his arm. Then Berholt, the young leatherback who had already lost his dragonboy Krusp, was struck in the middle of the back as he bent over a mud man to pull out his sword. Berholt went down with a fractured spine. He could not move. The mud men beat him to death with their terrible hammers.

A man in black Sephisti garb dodged through a gap and into Relkin's zone. Relkin met him with an arrow that stuck on the fellow's shield, and a furious attack with sword, knee, and fist. The man was too big for Relkin and absorbed his blows and shoved him back to arm's length to gain a little room to wield his own sword. It would have been the end of the orphan from Quosh, but Swane struck in from the side and distracted him, and Relkin got clear of the sword stroke in time. Relkin notched his last arrow, aimed, and fired. The shaft sprouted from the man's face, just below the eye. He did not fall, however. Instead he gave a scream of rage and pain, and charged at Relkin, his sword ready. Relkin threw himself forward, rolling into the man's legs trying to knock him off his feet but came up short when the Sephisti stopped him with a heavy sandal in the chest, knocking the wind out of him. The man was standing on him, and the sword was rising. And then the Sephisti was suddenly gone, crushed by another great boulder dropping out of the sky, which landed so close to Relkin that he bounced several inches into the air.

Swane helped Relkin to his feet. Both were splattered with the crushed man's blood.

"That was too damned close."

Relkin nodded and struggled for his breath. He saw Ecator rising and falling in the dragon's hand. The dragons were undoubtedly tiring. There seemed an endless supply of the mud men. They were still pour-

ing across the drawbridge in line after line, waving
those hammers. It seemed the very crack of doom had
opened beneath the fighting 109th.

Unfortunately it seemed that way to others, including General Paxion. The situation had reached a crescendo of events and now there was too much to
absorb, too many orders to be given, and Paxion
couldn't concentrate, the panic was taking over.

He had not become ineffective, however, he was
still trying to keep control.

To deal with the break-in north of the East Gate,
he'd sent messages around through the city to the
units on the far side ordering them to press hard on
the flank of the break-in. Meanwhile he'd sent orders
to another Kadeini unit, posted just to the south of
the East Gate where there was little pressure, to leave
the wall and clear the enemy away from the rear of the
East Gate.

Then came the news that a battering ram had been
brought up and set to work against the East Gate
itself. A moment later it began pounding, a persistent
vibration that shook the whole gate structure.

Another siege tower had been wheeled up beside
the first on the breach, and now the flow of the enemy
across the walls was doubled.

Paxion was in an agony of suspense. What was happening to the north of the break-in? He'd lost communications, but clearly the efforts to compress the
enemy and stem the breach had not succeeded yet.
He sent Captain Kesepton to try and restore contact
with the forces in the north, and Kesepton rode away
at a gallop and disappeared.

And then came the dire announcement that the mob
had set the granaries on fire. Frustrated by the stout
defense of the gates, the rioters had thrown torches
through the windows and ignited the grain dust inside.
Some of the chambers had exploded, and a conflagra-
tion was consuming all the remaining grain.

A tired, disheveled officer from the Kadeini appeared to announce that the effort to clear the rear of the gate was going very slowly. There were simply too many Sephisti, and they had been reinforced with mud men who were now getting down from the wall itself. With mud men in the fray, the troops could only stop them if the dragons could hold them, and the dragons were tiring.

Another man popped up to announce that columns of the enemy were marching away into the city; they were deep into the Norit Quarter and were starting to attack the support stations behind the wall farther north.

Paxion clutched at his head. They were lost. They could not close the breach, and they could not stem the enemy now pouring through it. They would be surrounded on the walls, doomed to be eventually pulled down and slaughtered.

"Withdraw," he mumbled. "Withdraw to the Imperial City, at once. That's our only hope."

CHAPTER FORTY-SEVEN

The order to abandon the wall came down to the 109th during a short lull. The dragons had pushed the mud men back onto the drawbridge and a brave engineer had died setting the drawbridge timbers alight with oil. While they blazed, the mud men were reluctant to step forward, the first indication Relkin had seen that they were anything more than automatons.

There was a moment's indecision. They were supposed to retreat? To where? How could they just let the enemy take the walls? But the cornets were blowing insistently and ingrained habits of discipline set their feet in motion and thus they left the wall, climbing down the dragon stairs and destroying them behind them to keep the mud men at bay.

On the ground, a general retreat was in progress; men, wagons, horses, dragons all caught up in a confused tangle were heading down the Fatan Street, straight into the rising murk from the inferno at the granaries.

The 109th formed up and marched. Dragoneer Hatlin sent Relkin running ahead down the column to scout out conditions.

After getting through a mass of men from the Eighth Regiment, Relkin came upon some wagons. Among them he found the one he'd hidden Miranswa in.

He ran up and jumped onto the back. Inside were wounded men, a dozen or more. He ran along the running board and found Miranswa herself holding the reins. Her jaws were clenched tight with concentration, and she barely glanced sideways at him.

She let out a whistle.

"You? By the breath of the goddess, I should have known it. I should have known you'd survive." She gave a bitter laugh.

"You don't seem to have needed any help."

"Of course not." She pulled hard on the reins. "Mind you, I haven't done this kind of thing since I lived on my family's summer farm. I'm a little out of practice."

Relkin marveled. Miranswa did seem to know what she was doing. He was impressed.

"What happened on the wall?" she said.

"I don't know. We heard that they got in down by the East Gate. We had pushed them right back onto the siege tower when they told us to retreat. It seems crazy."

"So now we're all going to the Imperial City, and there we'll starve to death."

"No, I told you, the white ships are coming."

"That I will believe when I see them."

"They're coming. There's another legion with them. We'll be able to hold out indefinitely after that."

Miranswa shrugged. "So you say. You said I would be safe in the wagon."

"Yeah, well, I didn't think we could lose the wall."

"Let us hope you are right about your white ships."

He tried to kiss her, but she turned her face away from him. He slid off the wagon and ducked back to report to Hatlin.

However, Relkin instead joined the dragons, who were tramping along in a tight group, despondent and dour. Dragons hated to march in armor; it always pinched their thick skin and rubbed and caused sores. In this situation, there was no time to take the armor off. They had to make their way right across the burning city to the last refuge available to them, the Imperial City.

Ahead of the dragons there were detachments of cavalry, the Talion horse, who were earning their keep this day by keeping the roads clear of the mobs. On the flanks there were Kenor bowmen scuttling through the side streets to take down snipers and rock throwers.

But there was nothing they could do about the fires except detour around the worst ones and step gingerly through the hot rubble left by others.

Behind them a rear guard of sorts was set up by skirmishing groups from the Eighth Regiment who, with the aid of a few bowmen, kept the Sephisti troops from harrying too hard upon their heels.

The march was long, and they passed many harrowing sights. They detoured widely around the blazing hulk of the granaries. The thick smoke seared their lungs and throats. What little water they had was soon gone.

On they marched, slowly sorting out into recognizable units, with the wagons bunched together between them. Once they were into the marching rhythm, it took over and each was left to his own thoughts.

Relkin felt a strange numbness overcoming his mind. They had been driven from the walls of the city. The granaries had been burned out. Was it possible that they would go down to defeat here? Relkin had fought in a number of battles, large and small, but he had never tasted bitter defeat like this. It was inconceivable, but it was happening. Miranswa might be right. They would starve to the point where they would be too weak to stop the enemy breaking into the Imperial City.

He shrugged. Death had always been a companion in his service in the legion, and he had been in tighter spots than this. He set himself to think about the weapons, moved up closer behind his two dragons, and began surreptitiously examining their equipment. The Purple Green's helmet had more dents. Bazil's tail sword was notched. As soon as the smiths got a fire going, he resolved to get these items seen to.

On they went, down Fatan Street and through the temple district. On the great ziggurat of Auros, there was a vast crowd of worshipers, imploring the god of rational belief to come down and save them from the demon at the gates. The crowd hardly even glanced at the legions as they tramped by. Relkin tossed in a prayer of his own. He didn't know much about the rational god. They called him the "sea bull," and he was said to possess the largest penis in the universe— that much he'd heard—but of the cult of rational deity, he knew nothing. Relkin wasn't sure if there were really any gods or goddesses at all, but he figured if there was one, then there might as well be dozens, so there was no harm in praying to all of them. He tossed off a prayer to the old gods, especially Asgah, the god of war. If Asgah remembered the fighting 109th, would he please take a hand in helping the white ships get up the river? It didn't seem that much to ask.

They crossed the Zoda with indignant mobs on either side who hurled insults and even the occasional brick. The bowmen roved up and down, however, and kept the brick throwing to a minimum.

There had been a skirmish at the gates of the Imperial City where some of the court eunuchs had tried to prevent the Argonathi from entering the hallowed ground of the Imperial City. But the men of the legions dispersed the guards and the eunuchs, and moved in to occupy the walls.

A second, sterner fight broke out in the Fortress of Zadul, which formed the buttress of the southern half of the Imperial City. Assisting the eunuchs here were some men from the Imperial Guard. The legionaries attempted to negotiate but were rebuffed, and in the end they were forced to slay a number of the Imperial Guard to clear the fortress. At the end, some men broke discipline and tossed quite a few palace eunuchs off the upper towers after rousting them from their hiding places.

Meanwhile poor General Paxion was struggling to hold onto his sanity. Everything that could have gone wrong had done so, it seemed, and now he was boxed into an impossible position. The pressures of the catastrophe were crushing. But the commanders rallied around him, even General Pekel was cooperative for once. The Kadein regiments occupied the North Tower and the Water Tower complex along with all the northern stretch of the wall. The Marneri regiments filled up the south side and the Fortress of Zadul, which had seven towers and an extensive system of dungeons and subterranean chambers. Captain Kesepton worked incredibly hard at keeping the general staff operating, and with everyone's cooperation, they managed to slowly bring some order to the chaos and settle the two legions, the Talion cavalry, and all their wagons into the Imperial City, which already teemed with an army of eunuchs, another army of sexed slaves, and a considerable force of guards.

While all this went on, the engineers inspected the walls and began feverish repairs to the weakest places. In general, the condition of these walls was not good. They had not been rebuilt in centuries, and the mud brick of their construction was crumbling. The walls of the Fortress of Zadul, on the southeast corner were, however, in excellent repair.

Work began at once, repairing walls, building trebuchets and catapults, and settling in the dragons, horses, and legionaries in quarters that were cleared of the eunuchs and slaves.

Paxion refused to have the eunuchs simply pushed out the front gate as the other officers wished. Instead, they were penned up with the slave population in the walled city of slaves, an enclave several acres in extent near the north wall not far from the North

Tower. Inside was a teeming population, all in an advanced state of hunger. However harsh their fate among the slaves they had formerly ruled, the palace eunuchs were saved from that which now befell the inhabitants of the great city.

It began almost as soon as the Sephisti had occupied the entire city. The black-clad soldiery moved efficiently through the various quarters, pulled out the entire population, and sent them stumbling up the roads in dense, terrorized groups.

At the city gates, the people were met by a great gang of imps who took control with a cracking of whips and the thudding of clubs. They were roped together at the neck, fed a meal of grain mush from troughs, and then driven to their feet and shoved northwards on the long march to Dzu.

By mid-afternoon, the enemy was assembling trebuchets, catapults, and siege towers on the Zoda. From the walls of the Imperial City, the legionaries could look out at the war machines and feel their hopes sink, hour by hour. It seemed that all was lost. The enemy was determined to overwhelm them in their weakened state. Dark clouds of smoke drifted north from the burning going on in the palace district, to the south of the Imperial City and the Fortress of Zadul. The men were silent, each turned in on himself, making inward farewells to loved ones and the world, preparing for death.

And then at nightfall, like a winged miracle, there came a glimpse of a tall-masted ship to the south, and a breeze brought her canvas crackling out in the unmistakable pattern of a great white ship from Cunfshon. A cheer went up, and the word ran around the walls in seconds. Someone began singing the song of Argonath, and everyone on the walls took it up and bellowed out the words. For a while, work stopped on the siege engines, and the enemy looked up with wonder on their faces.

On the shore by the palace jetty, a crowd accumulated that kept watch for other sails to the south. However, it became clear that this ship was alone, as slowly but steadily, it beat upstream and then glided in to drop anchor about a quarter mile offshore of the city.

The Imperial barge put out at once with Captain Kesepton aboard with a message from Paxion. It returned soon afterward with Captain Peek of the ship, the *Nutbrown*, a cruiser from Cunfshon, detached from her usual trade run across the Bright Sea and sent to Ourdh with a cargo of wheat in her holds for the legions. *Nutbrown* was not one of the largest white ships. Indeed at eight hundred tons, she was less than half the size of such giants as the *Oat* and the *Rye*. Still, she carried enough grain to feed the legions for weeks. If they were able to hold out that long.

CHAPTER FORTY-EIGHT

The siege continued, and though the city had been lost along with its population, the legions themselves were arguably in a stronger position now, walled up in the Imperial City, than they had been while stretched out around the city's walls. The capstone to their position was provided by the arrival of the *Nutbrown*, which had given everyone full bellies and a renewed sense of hope. For many, it was as if a bright light had suddenly been lit across a plain of unremitting dark. And with the food came the knowledge that soon, within a day or two, a fleet of white ships, including the giants *Spruce* and *Rye* would arrive, bringing reinforcements and supplies for months.

They just had to hold out until then, if they could. The enemy gave every indication that he would attempt to storm the walls before that moment came. The siege towers were rising quickly in a thunder of hammering.

At a weak spot on the walls near the North Tower, the enemy had set a ram to work, and the walls had begun to collapse quite quickly. General Paxion, by now a gaunt-faced man with haunted eyes, hesitated for a while, agonizing over the risks, and then agreed to the proposal from Captain Kesepton and others that a sortie be mounted before the wall collapsed.

There was a postern gate near the ram, and at dusk it opened. A sortie party of volunteers from the Kadein regiment that had broken and run on the wall, the

third, rushed out and fell upon the ram and its opera-
tors. Barely a handful escaped, and the ram was torn
apart, its major members hewed through by the
dragons.

The enemy immediately began rebuilding the ram
and posted a large guard force beside it. But the sortie
had done its job and bought them a few more hours.

Meanwhile a constant barrage of missiles fell from
the sky, crashing here and there into the Imperial
City. Here a great stone fell through the roof of an
apartment structure crushing dozens of eunuchs, there
a slab from a wall of some city building came down
and exploded on the flat ground outside the Grand
Palace sending loose bricks flying through the guard
and passersby.

Of course, the Argonathi engineers had worked to
reduce the enemy's advantage. Sections of stables and
eunuch housing had been torn apart, and trebuchets
and catapults had been constructed that were busy
hurling back many of the missiles that had been tossed
into the Imperial City. The Argonathi trained their
own weapons on those of the enemy, causing the
Sephisti rate of fire to fall drastically after a while.

And yet every few minutes there would be a cry of
"beware above," and everyone would look up at another great chunk of mud-brick wall, ripped from
some building, whirling through the air and falling
with a great crash somewhere among the palaces and
temples of the Imperial City.

The small palaces, the Blue Porcelain, the Green
Jade, and the Yellow Lacquer, were all looking badly
battered. They were not designed to withstand an assault of this kind. The Grand Palace itself, though
more solidly built from the same mud brick as everything else in the city, was looking much the worse for
wear, too. But here it was a cosmetic effect; the stucco
exterior had been shattered and knocked away in
places, revealing the brown and brick beneath. But

the walls of the Grand Palace were massive and would withstand considerable bombardment.

The same was true of the small ziggurats for Auros and Gingo-La that occupied the center of the Imperial City. The white stucco that made them shine so brightly in the sunlight was breaking away, but the structures themselves were so massive that the damage was really very slight.

The legions had been quarters in protected places, in the guard quarters along the inner base of the wall and in the towers, especially in the Fortress of Zadul. Some units were in the basements of the palaces, including the Grand Palace.

On Paxion's orders, the Imperial City's normal population, the army of priests and slaves who kept the empire's machineries running, were confined to their quarters except for the eunuchs, who were forced out and pressed into the walled slave compound.

Paxion had set up his headquarters in the Fortress of Zadul and the Marneri men were billeted in the fortress and the gate house. They also held a major weak point, the narrow-sided tower that anchored the southern wall of the Imperial City at the water's edge. That tower was small and poorly constructed. Its foundations were weak, and it was actually pulling away from the wall itself. It would take little to bring it down in ruin.

The enemy was fashioning a ram just beyond the range of the Argonathi trebuchets. It would be at work within a few hours. Within a day or so at the most, the tower would fall and the enemy would mount an assault.

Still the mood in the Eighth Regiment and the 109th dragons was virtually cheerful. They had been billeted in a basement of the Grand Palace itself. It was a big roomy space, dry and warm. Dusty furniture and enormous rugs had been stored there from previous dynasties. The dragons pushed the stuff up against the walls except for the rugs, which they spread out three deep and lay down on.

Dragonboys brought them another prodigious meal of bread, akh, and a stew of beans and vegetables. There was even some beer, a dark Cunfshon ale, with which to wash it down. The dragons had grown used to Ourdhi styles of beer, which were usually sweet and sometimes pale. The Cunfshon ale took some adjusting to, but dragons would adjust to any kind of beer as long as it was well made.

Of course, they mourned their dead, but the wyvern spirit was hard to extinguish, and after a ritual toast to the departed, their mood lightened. They even sang a few songs. All agreed that the new 109th had welded together into a seasoned fighting unit. They pitied any enemy that had to face them.

Soon they all slept soundly and the space reverberated with dragon snores. When they awoke, there was another large meal of hot wheat cakes and a heavy dose of akh. There was a dash of hot kalut, too, and everyone took some.

The rhythmic thudding of the ram working on the tower continued. It had gone on and off through the night as the engineers came up with new ways to tear the roof off with the ram or to tip the whole construction over, which they managed to do on one occasion. Now the ram was back, however.

In a space surrounded by piled furniture from an ancient dynasty, Bazil of Quosh worked on his sword's edge with a whetstone. Nearby was the great wild one who was being refitted for both joboquin and breastplate. Relkin was tightening the straps of the joboquin, pulling the big harness together after repairing a ripped section. Both dragons had awoken after about six hours of straight sleep. They were in a quiet, reflective mood.

It was not fated to last long. Vlok, who had

attached himself to the Broketail and the Purple Green in recent days, approached with a heavy tread.

"I have had a dream," he announced.

It was rare for wyvern dragons to have dreams. The others looked up with interest.

"That is unusual," said Bazil.

"I am troubled, I thought I would tell you about it."

"Why choose me to tell your troubles to?" asked Bazil.

"You will understand when I tell you."

"Ah. Go ahead then."

"The dream began with a view of the world of the ancients, when dragons ruled alone."

"Before the humans came?"

"Correct. There was a world for dragons and they were of many kinds and they lived in many different ways. Until one day the sun was blotted out of the sky and the waters were darkened and nothing grew."

Bazil's whetstone had stopped.

"And through the darkness came a line of fire which burned the land. And we were there, all of us, dragons of the legions, standing on a shore."

"Ocean shore?" said the wild one.

"Yes. And on the land, there was the fire and the fire was burning the land itself and it burnt it right up to the shore and it was burning right between our feet. The whole world was on fire and this was why the sun was blotted out of the sky."

Vlok paused, the others were silent.

"We could not fight this fire, we had nothing that would put it out and we could only retreat into the water. The waves broke over us and we went further into the water. We threw away our weapons and dropped our armor and our helmets and swam out into the water and away from the burning land. We could not go back."

Vlok fell silent.

"That was it?" said the Purple Green.

"Yes. I do not understand it."

The Purple Green gave a heavy hiss and turned huge eyes on Vlok.

"Wyvern does not see the meaning in this dream?"

"I don't think so."

"Well, this dragon does. It is clear enough. We all die here, and our spirits fly away to join the ancestors in the shades."

This last was said in dragon speech, but from the way the others reacted, Relkin understood.

Relkin let out a whistle. Dragon heads swiveled to pin him with large black pupils.

"Boy know nothing about this," said Bazil.

"I didn't say anything."

"Good. That is best."

"Wait, I think the dream is clear."

"It is clear."

"But it doesn't mean we all die here. Maybe it refers to the past, to the time before men came to the world."

"It is clear, we all die here. Vlok has seen the future in his dream." The Purple Green said this with a dismissive finality.

They fell silent, bemused by this idea.

Bazil's whetstone continued to work along the edge of Ecator, giving the shimmering blade a sharpness that would drive it through anything short of steel or rock.

"This dragon not die easy" was all he would say.

Not far away, another small group contemplated the immediate future with concern. In a cellar of the Blue Porcelain, a surreptitious meeting was taking place of the Committee for Emergency Action. Porteous Glaves, General Pekel, and several Kadeini commanders were there.

They were not happy.

"This is a death trap," said Glaves.

"You've said that several times," said Pekel.

"Well, nobody seems to see that there is only one solution."

"You want us to run like cowards and leave our men to die here?"

"Without officers, our men will all die anyway. We must be preserved to the end."

"An admirable thought," said Captain Rokensak.

"Bah, nonsense, we'd be branded cowards by the world. I could never hold my head up in public again." General Pekel would not go along with it.

"Well, it's too late to negotiate with the enemy. They're going to bring down the wall before long anyway."

"We'll be fighting in the breaches before nightfall."

"They'll keep coming now until we fall, they have such enormous numbers."

"More mud men."

"Thousands of them. They will overwhelm the dragons in the end, and then we will all die."

"Die in this stinking pit of a foreign place. I would rather die in Kadein."

"He has a point . . ."

"It is so simple. The *Nutbrown* can take off a thousand or more. We should put the wounded aboard and then move the officers across depending on seniority. We must first persuade Paxion to shift his command post to the ship."

They stared at Porteous Glaves.

"Ha-ha, that will be a fine day," said someone.

"I doubt we'll live to see it," said Captain Rokensak.

"Ol' Pax would rather fall on his sword than do something like that."

Pekel arose and gathered himself. "Excuse me gentlemen, but I have pressing business to attend to." The general was leaving.

Glaves had failed. Once again he had been able to

achieve nothing in his efforts at treachery. He chewed his thumbnail and watched helplessly as the others slipped away. He desperately wanted a drink, but not even Dandrax could find anything now.

They were all gone, except for Captain Rokensak.

"Look, Commander Glaves, I'll be honest with you. I'm more interested in saving my own skin than I am of keeping up my military reputation. I'm with you."

Glaves turned on him with the desperation of a drowning man. "Then we must find a way of recruiting enough men to be able to seize the *Nutbrown* and secure her and keep control of her."

Rokensak sucked in a breath. "By the tits of the Great Mother, won't that be piracy?"

"What does it matter what they call it if we're alive. Everyone else here is going to die. We'll tell them that we were the only survivors."

"We'll have to kill the *Nutbrown* crew."

"Yes. A tricky point, that. We'll have to think of something but if we don't do it, then we won't be thinking about anything."

Rokensak thought it over.

"What about your contact, Euxus of Fozad?"

"I have no more contact with him. When last I saw him, he told me that they will kill all of us. They will drain our blood into mud and create more of their mud men."

"They will kill all of us?"

"Not one will live."

Rokensak exhaled noisily.

"So, we have no choice. We will put your plan to the test. I will get the men, you will provide us with the officer rank we need to get aboard the ship."

They shook on it and departed.

CHAPTER FORTY-NINE

When he'd finally pulled the Purple Green's joboquin into shape and replaced all the leather lacing inside the breastplate, Relkin found himself with a rare moment with nothing pressing to do. Both dragons were asleep and really he should have slept, too, but the rhythmic thud of the ram at work had left him too tense to sleep.

He reported to Hatlin, and then went down to the riverside and sat on a low wall by the jetty. From there he could see the *Nutbrown* riding at her anchor, half a mile out. The smell of the river was briny and rich, a smell of life. It helped clear the stench of smoke and burning from his nostrils. The great clouds of smoke had dissipated as the city burnt itself out, but the smell lingered.

The ground trembled every half minute as the great ram struck the south waterside tower. Relkin sighed. It was only a matter of hours before they'd be up there on the breach, forming a line and fighting off the enemy's assault force. How long they would hold out was unknowable, though Relkin knew that his dragons would fight as long there was a breath left in them.

As for himself, well, he had but a handful of arrows and then his sword. Not much perhaps to lay in the balance, but he was feeling a lot stronger than he had in days. A few good meals and some rest had put the fire back in him. He would fight until his last breath; he would never give up.

And then? Then he guessed he'd find out whether there was a Great Goddess, or a God, or no gods at all, or maybe even a whole lot of them. Whatever there was, he thought he had to have a reasonable chance of getting into Heaven, if they had a heaven. There were certain larcenous events in his life to overlook he knew, but he was a soldier so what could you expect? Plus he had two huge war beasts under his care, and he had to do questionable things now and then just to make sure he did his job well. Surely the Great Mother could understand that? Better at least than certain quartermasters and dragoneers he'd known.

Suddenly, with a cold shock, Relkin realized he would miss the world. He didn't want to die. It seemed a pity to have lost the future he had dreamed of and discussed endlessly with the dragon. It seemed terribly wrong somehow.

He scanned the softening horizon. Could the fleet arrive in time? Would the enemy attack the breach continuously without letup? How far away were the great ships? How long could the legions stand the pressure?

He shrugged and shook his head to get rid of the bitter taste in his mouth. Too many questions for which there were no immediate answers.

His eyes caught a movement. The *Nutbrown* had lowered a boat. He saw it move smoothly away from the side of the ship and watched as it approached the jetty. There were six men rowing, and the boat moved quickly over the water. Within a few minutes, he watched two figures hurry down the jetty, approaching his position on the wall.

He recognized one of them at once; it was Lagdalen of the Tarcho. The other was a tall angular figure, clad in a black cloak who walked with a most regal stride. Ribela, the Queen of Mice, he assumed.

The ground trembled again as the ram struck home.

The two women had drawn close. He could see the witch's long, narrow face and even the glint of those forbidding eyes. Relkin knew at once that this was not the Great Witch he had known on the mission to Tummuz Orgmeen. Lessis of Valmes had a very different manner.

Relkin wondered if he dared even wave hello to Lagdalen, or whether he would get her in trouble if he did. He caught her eyes, though, and she let out a shriek of delight, ran to him, hugged him, and then turned to the witch.

"My lady, this is my friend, the dragoneer I told you about. May I introduce you?"

The witch directed a penetrating gaze at him, and Relkin felt immediately uncomfortable, as if many past sins were now being exposed to the light of day.

"You may."

"Then, lady, I will introduce Relkin of Quosh, dragoneer of the 109th Marneri, serving in the Second Legion."

"Ah yes." The black eyes sparkled with interest. "You are dragonboy to the famous dragon with the broken tail."

"I have that honor, lady. That is the greatest dragon alive."

"Of course, I am sure of that. You are also caring for the most unusual dragon in the legions as well, a wild drake, with wings, who volunteered for the legions. Is this not so?"

"Yes, lady."

"Most unusual, you must be worked to the bone. I understand that the work of a dragonboy is virtually constant."

"Worked to the bone, yes, my lady. But the Dragoneer Hatlin, he helps me with the Purple Green."

"And the dragoneer knows that you are sitting here, idling at the harborside as well?"

"Yes, lady, both dragons are asleep."

"A rare moment then. Well, tell me something, boy, your wild dragon, has he recovered any of the strength in his wings?"

"No, my lady."

"My esteemed colleague Lessis attempted to cure the condition."

"Yes, my lady."

"But the wounds were too deep and they had healed, and thus there was nothing that our magic could do."

Relkin just stared at her. This witch seemed to know everything; it was just a little frightening.

"I remember that we discussed it," she went on. "Lessis and I. Alas, I know little about the dragons and their comrades in arms. Lessis is far more skilled with these things than I."

Relkin kept silent, awed by the thought of these mighty ones conversing about his dragons.

"And you, my young friend, for someone with the reputation of a complete rascal, you have done well. You redeemed yourself and more when you restored young Lagdalen to us. I had almost given up hope."

Relkin was tongue-tied. The woman smiled.

"Lagdalen may stay here with you for a few minutes. I know that you are good friends and have much to say to each other. I am glad to have met you. I hope you will be my friend."

The ground shuddered. "The ram," said Lagdalen.

"Yes," the witch looked up and bit her lips. "It will be a close-run thing, will it not?"

Relkin looked her in the eyes. "Yes, my lady, it will be very close."

Ribela left them, and Lagdalen sat beside Relkin on the wall. She laid her head briefly on his shoulder.

"I am so glad to be able to see you for a few moments. There is so much to tell."

"The Great Mother must have willed it."

She looked at him, "You, of all people, who always invokes the old gods."

"I would not use her name in vain, not with you at least."

"You better not." Lagdalen had broken all the rules and had been thrown out of the Novitiate, but her faith in the Great Mother was strong.

"And maybe we will be relieved in time. Another legion would be a help."

"Captain Peek assured the Lady Ribela that the fleet will be here on the morrow."

"I hope so. The tower won't last much longer, they say. We'll be fighting there by nightfall."

"That soon?"

"Yes. They rebuilt the ram, the roof rides right down on the ground. We can't get a hook under it anymore."

A shout on the distant wall made them turn their heads.

" 'Ware above" came the cry repeated across the Imperial City, until a voice finally shouted it out to the people at the jetty.

Relkin looked up and pointed. A huge block of mud-brick masonry tumbled in the air overhead for a moment, and then it landed with a terrific crash on the southern side of the little ziggurat to Auros, Emperor of the Universe. Brick and plaster broke up in a great cloud and pieces ricocheted out across the area below the temple.

Cornets suddenly pealed, and men broke out from the guard barracks along the base of the walls and began moving the trebuchets around to face the south. Men with signal flags communicated with the spotters on the wall.

Within a few minutes, the legion trebuchets were replying, their beams thudding against the uprights in a hurried rhythm as they hurled rocks at the enemy's great trebuchet.

"It is hard to talk of pleasant things with all this going on."

"It is never hard to talk of anything with Lagdalen of the Tarcho."

"It is wearing on the spirit, though. I pray that the ships will get here in time."

"So do we all. Of course, our troubles won't be over. We'll still be fighting them over these poor walls and they won't stand up to much and the enemy will be able to bring their numbers to bear. We'd be better in the open field where the dragons can maneuver."

"But if we have to, we can board the great ships. Have you ever seen the *Spruce*?"

"No, but I have seen *Wheat* and *Barley* at harbor in Marneri, they're just as big."

"Then we will be saved, for the ships will come tomorrow."

Relkin smiled and hugged her.

"Then our hearts will be strong with that knowledge, and I thank you for it Lagdalen of the Tarcho."

They talked for a while of other places and other times, far from the besieged Imperial City of Ourdh, but at length Lagdalen rose to her feet.

"You must feed two great dragons, Relkin. I have to feed two dozen hungry little mice."

"Mice?"

"You remember the rats in Tummuz Orgmeen and the magic they worked?"

"How could I ever forget?"

"It is something like that." She smiled at his incomprehension. "Good-bye for now, my friend, may the Mother watch over you and keep your arm strong, and may she also watch over my friend the broketail dragon."

Relkin waved good-bye to her and heaved a sigh. He was too young for her, and that was the sad, ineluctable truth.

He sat there and took one last look at the *Nutbrown*

riding at her anchor. Vlok's dream came back to him, and he shivered, feeling faintly uneasy.

"The ground was burning, right under our feet . . ."

Suddenly he was aware of another presence beside him. He turned his head and gave a start. It was Miranswa, wearing a cotton shift and sandals.

"Hello, Relkin," she said.

"Where have you been?" he asked. "I looked everywhere."

Miranswa smiled enigmatically.

"I saw you talking with the girl."

"Yes, well, that was Lagdalen of the Tarcho, my best friend in this world."

"She could have received the honor of sacrifice, of having her blood spilled down the side of the ziggurat."

Relkin's mouth tightened into a line.

"No one will kill her while I can prevent it. We are like brother and sister."

Miranswa sat beside him, and moved close.

"You stare at the ship. We could be safe if we could be on the ship."

"Not me, you're talking desertion. They'd hang me and they'd be right to."

"But what will you do when they break over the walls this time?"

"We will stand and die where we stand. It is simple."

"It is terrible to think of death. I do not want to die."

"Nor I, Miranswa."

Suddenly she pressed herself against him, he held her and their lips met.

"Have you ever lain with a woman, Relkin?"

"In actual fact, no, though not from want of trying."

She smiled. "I thought so."

"Where have you been sleeping?" he asked.

"I could not remain in the wagon. They were

searching them, and I did not want to be thrust into the slave city. I hid myself. Come with me, it is a safe place, we can go there now."

"My dragons," he began, suddenly uncomfortable.

"They can wait for an hour. They are asleep, I know, I checked there for you. Come, I offer you that which you have never had and which you may never have again." She took his hand.

He accompanied her through the fruit orchard of the Imperial Gardens and beyond the gardens to the small Temple of Gingo-La set in the northeastern corner of the Imperial City.

Beneath a staircase, Miranswa pulled back a narrow door. Within was a small room. Relkin pointed up at an inscription on the wall in the Uldi script of Ourdh.

"What does that say?"

She glanced at it.

"This is the house of the goddess of love."

"This?"

"This is her temple."

"I have not had the best experiences in the temples of your goddess."

"This is the house of the goddess of love. What we do here is sacred, Relkin. Come, lie with me and learn about the art of love."

Relkin did not argue any further.

Inside the Grand Palace, Lagdalen and Ribela prepared for another great spell saying. Ribela wound strips of black cloth around her wrists and prepared some lissim twigs for burning.

As she did so, she half turned to Lagdalen.

"I was glad to meet your benefactor at last. I have heard much concerning this young Relkin of Quosh. He seemed an honorable sort, not at all the sort of scamp that I had imagined."

Lagdalen cast her eyes down to the bowl in which she broke fresh bread into small chunks.

"He has grown up a lot since last year. He is now a soldier."

"Yes, I saw that in his face. He has seen much of the harsher side of life. And, of course, I know what he and you achieved together. Your courage in that terrible place has already earned you both a place in the history of heroes."

Lagdalen blushed. The Lady Ribela had never spoken to her about what had happened at Tummuz Orgmeen.

"It was the Grey Lady, my part was really quite small."

"That is a very long spell my dear and not an easy one. I think the Mother was guiding you that day, and she does not guide those who do not deserve her favor. Your heart is brave and true Lagdalen of the Tarcho. One reason why I insisted that you accompany me and leave your baby behind. You have the strength to become a Great Witch, my dear, if you develop the patience and the desire."

Lagdalen was shocked. She had never thought of herself as a witch at all. She had been thrown out of the Novitiate. Her academic career was a complete failure. And here was the Queen of Mice telling her that she could be a Great Witch, not just a Witch of Standing.

"It is time," said Ribela. "You will bolt the door, my dear, and do not leave the room unless you absolutely have to. I shall not be more than an hour or two in the trance state. Keep the mice well fed, they will come to you as they usually do. They will be very hungry."

The Queen of Mice unlocked the mouse cage that they kept in this room. The mice, dozens of them now, tumbled out and eagerly explored the bowl of bread soaked in oil and sprinkled with salt. Ribela hummed something under her breath, reached down, and ran her hands through the mice, holding them and squeezing them gently.

Then she began to keen on a higher note, and the spell saying began.

CHAPTER FIFTY

In a locked and barricaded chamber, Lagdalen watched the lady work up the great magic. At times the air seemed to swirl and sparkle, and she thought she heard distant music playing. At other times there was a sudden waft of ocean scent. Sensory misperceptions caused by the magical power.

Throughout the spell casting, however, Lagdalen's part was simple. After a few declensions to put herself in a wakeful state, she fed the mice and broke bread into the bowl.

Ribela pronounced a swift stream of charged syllables, and the mice whirled around her feet and became a blur. From her lips, there burst the volumes of power and the declensions that shaped them, and quickly she sank into the state of deep trance.

Once more her consciousness detached from her body and hovered, ready to go a wandering. However, for this mission she was not employing the pure astral projection. She would need to do, as well as to observe. This would vastly reduce the size of her "node" in the dark sea of chaos and would also give her a slight degree of physical presence there. That, of course, meant that she would be vulnerable to the predators of that world.

The final volumes came with a burst of energy. She felt the implosive effect and her mind view sank down into the subworld hallucination of chaos.

Long practice had given her the ability to read the

patterns of the swirling, formless backwash of grey static. Likewise she heard the true sounds of this world, high wispy notes like the playing of pipes tuned above the reach of the human ear. But it was hard to detect these faint sounds above the heavy rasp and wheeze of electrical sparking that raged through the chaotic realm.

Carefully she concentrated her mind to the sensory task and scanned about herself in all directions. The characteristic piping tones of a Thingweight did not present themselves in any direction. She searched for the other, lesser predators. To have to fight off one of them would create such a noise here that a Thingweight would be bound to come.

She detected several within her range, but there were none lying along her projected course.

The distance was not far and thus there was no need for the energies of a Black Mirror, another signal that could easily draw the great predators. She could move through the ether, not with the speed of her astral self but more swiftly than during a physical translation through the Black Mirror.

Forward she sped toward the sector of her interest. As she approached she scanned carefully, unsure as to what she should expect. There was something new in this evil worked here by the Dark Masters—something she had never encountered before.

And then she saw a strange fountain of dark energies ahead, a sudden blaze of black fire across the nether realms. It was repeated, again and again and again.

She moved toward the source. Another pulse came. The energies were strong, but they were in the class she had expected. This was magic from the Masters, from the higher levels of their dread codes.

She made transition, rising out of the subworld of chaos and rematerializing as a blue wisp of fire about six inches tall. Her node floated through the darkness above a scene from hell.

Thick smoke arose from a fire at one side of a large warehouse space. Lines of imps, armed with swords and whips, compressed a great mass of humanity between them and forced them up a set of stairs.

At one end of the room, a raised floor had been set up with rows of gibbets. Beneath the raised floor, naked men stirred a great pool of mud.

On the platform the people were slaughtered, their throats cut and their bodies swung out, heads down to drain over the precious mud below.

As if from far away, she heard the clamor of those about to die. As a wisp of fire, she lacked acuity on the auditory range in the higher world. To one side the mud was poured into big molds, it ran with a soupy texture that was chilling to see.

She felt a presence, a sudden power on the higher planes. A dark, hunched figure had entered the warehouse. This was the source of the black fire, this was the entity she had sensed near the demon in Dzu during her near-disastrous astral reconnaisance.

She was curious. A Master? Come here to Ourdh to fight this petty struggle? Why would they not send a magician, or even a Doom? But she could tell at once that this being was far beyond any Doom in its strength.

The figure gestured and a great flash of dark energy suffused one of the molds. Ribela sensed the sudden invigoration of the mud. The spell was harsh, based on death energies, but it was also quite simple in a sense, and very vulnerable to her countermeasures.

Another flash came, and another and another, and it was as if red lightning was crackling through the room. On it went until all the ready molds had been invigorated. Ribela marveled at the power of it. Truly the Dark Arts of the Masters had elevated them to a level of strength beyond anything known on a world like Ryetelth. They had earned a move to a higher board, a place where gammadion and hawkbishop dueled.

Below, on the floor, sweating teams of slaves hauled the molds aside and brought in empty ones to be filled. The freshly invigorated molds were stacked along the wall, where a great pile of them was already waiting. The dark being turned and left the place of death. A heavy door shut behind it.

At once the killing resumed on the raised floor. The slaves stirred the mud below. And down from the ceiling dropped the wisp of blue fire that then scuttled across the molds, pausing at each one to insert a positor and press home a zest of corruption, a tiny spell to undo the invigoration. There were a great number of molds to visit, thousands in fact, for the enemy had been hard at work creating a new host of the giant warriors of mud since the fall of the city. Soon they would be hardened and ready, in time for the follow-up to the grand assault on the breach.

Through the stacked molds flitted the wisp of fire, injecting each and moving on like some busy parasitic wasp in a forest filled with prey.

The mud men would harden, and they would even awake. But as soon as they awoke, the corrupting spell would begin its work. In time, they would soften again and dissolve.

At last she finished, arose, and surveyed the scene. The job was done. She composed herself and made the transition to the subworld of chaos once more. She floated there for a moment, clearing her thoughts. This was a drastic mistake, for hovering nearby was a great Thingweight, a towering mass of shifting shapes set atop glittering energies. Tentacles flashed forth from the base of the thing and speared through her position. In a trice, she was held and tugged toward the monster's underside where the receptor surfaces would already be warming in anticipation of the feast.

There could be no escape, not in this astral form, except to retranslate to the world Ryetelth again, immediately. It was hard to concentrate, but Ribela steeled herself and after a moment achieved her aim and slipped the grip of the Thingweight and reappeared as a wisp of fire, floating just outside the dread warehouse where they made the men of mud.

Beneath her was a great jostling mass of humanity, slowly being pushed into the warehouse doors by armed men and imps.

She was in a terrible quandary. As the wisp, she could fly back to the Imperial City and complete a double translation. It was a physically taxing process to travel in this form, but it could be done. Or she could wait here and try the route through chaos once more. The problem was that as a wisp she could not pass through solid walls or doors. She would be forced to wait outside and dart in when doors were opened. On the other hand, Thingweights could be incredibly stubborn. The one that sat over her position in the subworld would stay there for hours in the hope that she would show herself again.

With a mental sigh, she made her choice. The wisp turned and fluttered toward the distant river and the Imperial City. Darkness had fallen. The enemy ram worked on. The defenders awaited their doom.

The southwest waterside tower fell near midnight. It went quite suddenly. There was a crack in the lower course of the outer wall that had grown progressively wider as the ram pulverized the outer layers. Suddenly it gave, and the front section of the tower sheared off and collapsed, spilling out over the ram in front.

For a moment, the rest of the tower stood there. Then slowly, gracefully, it collapsed, falling in on itself and sliding down into the waters on the river in ruin.

From the enemy lines came a harsh cheer and the drumming began, the terrible drumming of Sephis.

Catapults and trebuchets were at work at once, hurling missiles across the ruins of the tower.

In the rubble, men worked to free a few survivors. Dozens had been caught in the collapse, including several engineers. Others hurried to set up a barricade along the top of the pile of brick rubble that now constituted the wall. Archers from both sides were at work, but in the moonlight the task was easier for the enemy archers, since on the pale mud-brick rubble, the defenders stood out quite clearly, while in the dark outside the walls, the Sephisti were hard to see.

With the drums booming, a force of mud men began to form up in front of the breach. Around the giants grew a swelling mob of Sephisti soldiers, augmented here and there with foul imps, creatures hatched in the dungeons of Axoxo in the White Bones Mountains. These imps were trained to fight dragons, to cut hamstrings, to hack between the legs, to stab into feet.

The 109th dragons, along with the 66th and the 25th were set to hold the breach. They waited far back, however, as the storm of missiles fell on the men erecting the barricades, but at length the cornets shrilled and they moved forward, dragonboys behind each dragon, with swordsmen and spearmen from the Eighth Regiment behind them. Dragonboys picked up arrows as they went along, adding to the thick quivers each had now amassed.

Up the steep pile of rubble they went. Engineers had already set up prefabricated dragon steps. One set of these had been smashed by a rock and so the 66th and 109th had to share another. It was crowded, and it slowed their arrival on the top of the breach.

Rocks continued to fall from the sky, although by now the Argonathi trebuchets inside the Imperial City were zeroing in on the enemy's machines. One by one, they were either struck and damaged or pulled back to a new, safer position.

But the end of the rock fall was only the signal of

the beginning of the real test. Now, coming up the slope, straight at them, was a solid regiment of the mud men. Behind them boomed the drums.

Dragons sucked in their breath and drew their great swords. The giants raised their hammers and began swinging them in that mad, automatic rhythm. They came together with a crash of steel, shield to shield, swords rising and falling, hammers striking sparks off dragon helm and dragon shield.

The moon rose high above the scene and cast its pitiless light across the ruined tower and the struggling mass atop the breach. The fight was stern and virtually endless. The giants of mud came in a constant stream and soon even the stoutest hearts were tiring in the line of great dragons of war.

As for the dragonboys, they had a desperate time of it. The new style of imp was very troublesome, indeed they had suffered casualties and even lost a dragon, Kreuzun, a leatherback from Lake Gana in the Blue Hills. Two dragonboys were down, Geff, who fought with Kafskella the freemartin from Aubinas, was dying from a sword through the guts, and big Solly who fought with Rold had lost a leg, crushed by a mud man's hammer. Kreuzen had died under those terrible hammers, after he was hamstrung by a plucky imp.

Mono had a scrape on his thigh and another on the side of his head, but he was still on his feet. Swane had caught a sword slash over his helmet that had stunned him for a while. He was also limping from a blow to his ankle, but he, too, was still in the fight. Tomas Black Eye had been struck a glancing blow with a mud-man hammer and was incredibly lucky to have no broken bones. His shield was dented and useless, however, and he could hardly stop the trembling in his arms. Relkin had scrapes on his ribs from an imp's shield and a rake down his left arm where another dying imp had dug in its talons.

These imps were great fighters and had been well trained. Dragonboys alone could not cope with them, and it was fortunate that they had the men of the Eighth Regiment to sustain them, for the imps would otherwise have soon killed all of them and started it on the dragons.

But the breach in front of them was strewn with dead men and the ruins of dozens of the mud giants. And at last there came a respite. The mud men stopped coming, the fire from the Argonathi trebuchets had become too intense for the moment. The space in front of the breach was cleared, but further back a great new mass of mud men was deploying. The assault would be renewed.

However, the 109th and 66th would not have to face it. Cornets shrilled and the battered dragon squadrons were pulled back and replaced with fresh units.

Wearily the dragons trod back to their billets where they lay down with groans. Exhausted dragonboys picked up their boxes and went to work at once on their dragons, cleaning and stitching wounds, checking for broken bones, examining sword and helm for needed repairs.

Beyond the walls the drumming began again, and with harsh cries the enemy resumed the assault. Once more the din of war erupted across the breach. The moon continued to glare down with baleful light upon the struggle.

CHAPTER FIFTY-ONE

"It's a simple plan, Commander, and your participation is vital for its success." So said Captain Rokensak trying to bolster Porteous Glaves's confidence. They were all worried that Glaves might fail the test.

"I only hope it works," Glaves said irritably. He was wearing his summer cloak and full uniform. Behind him lurked Dandrax.

"Would you listen to that?" said one of Rokensak's men, a crew of Kadeini soldiers from various regiments.

He was referring to the battle in progress at the top of the breach. The distinctive sound of dragon sword cutting through armor and helmet rang out again and again, pealing like the bells of death over the harsh uproar of men's voices lifted in the chorus of war.

Glaves shuddered.

"It's only a question of time. We can hold them off for a few hours, but when all the dragons lose their puff, then what?" said a surly fellow with a black eye patch and a scruffy uniform with the double trefoil badge. The badge said he belonged to the Kadeini Second Regiment of the First Legion, a famous unit with a long history of valor.

"Only a matter of time." The words went around and around in Porteous's brain.

"This is the best thing to do Rokensak. Somebody has to get back to tell the story."

The black eye patch nudged him with a hideous

familiarity that would have earned him twenty lashes at any other time.

"And it might as well be us, eh, Commander?"

He heard Dandrax chuckle. Dandrax had become increasingly unsympathetic lately. Once they returned to Marneri, Glaves thought that Master Dandrax would have to be dispensed with. The man knew too much.

He looked up, straightened his shoulders, told himself that this was the only way out.

Sergeant Villers of the Kadein Ninth Regiment, First Legion, was whining to someone. "We didn't sign on for this mass suicide. We were due to go home. It ain't fair."

"Shut it, Villers," snapped Rokensak. "Move."

They filed down onto the quay, thirty desperate men, half on a cart, covered in bandages, the other half looking almost as damaged.

At the end of the quay were the *Nutbrown*'s boats, watched over by her boatmen. Glaves flourished a parchment scroll.

"Take me and these wounded men to the ship. I have orders from General Paxion to the captain."

This was the vital moment. If the boatmen rumbled him now, they were done for. But messengers, even parties of a dozen or so, had been going out to the ship ever since she'd docked. And so the men and Captain Rokensak took places in the boats, and the boatmen pushed out and began rowing for the ship.

The sound of the fighting on the wall continued to ring out through the darkness of the night.

Glaves was aware that keen eyes with telescopes would be giving them all a scrutiny, but at night, and with the disguise of wounded men, they would be fooled.

At the ship's side they maneuvered while the hooks were lowered and the stretcher cases were raised smoothly to the decks. Porteous Glaves rode up in the sea chair. Some of the others scrambled up the netting over the side, others rode up on sea chairs.

Glaves found a stout woman in brown uniform with a leather hat standing in front of him.

"Captain Peek?"

"No, sir, I am Shipmate Doon. Captain Peek is asleep."

"Ah, be so good as to lead me to him right away. I have important orders for him."

"And who would we be telling the captain is calling on him while he is asleep?"

Porteous drew himself up and loaded his voice with every ounce of authority he could manage.

"I am Commander Glaves of the Marneri Second Legion. I am a personal emissary from General Paxion himself, who is in command here."

There was a twinkle in the woman's eye. She had seen her share of puffed-up army toads, and this one was a prime sample. Captain Peek would have this one for breakfast.

"You wish to disturb Captain Peek, Commander? Are you sure about that. Could you not just pass me the orders."

"My good woman, there's a battle to the death going on. Can't you see that? There is a need for greater coordination of the forces here. General Paxion has sent me to work with Captain Peek. That much you may know, but the orders I have here are from General Paxion for Captain Peek's eyes only."

"Well, in that case," said Shipmate Doon, "you'd better come this way. But don't say I didn't warn you. Captain Peek, he don't like to be woken up unless it's real important.

Glaves nodded to Dandrax and Rokensak to accompany him. The rest of their party would soon be on board. Now for Captain Peek. They moved through the ship to the captain's cabin.

Doon indicated a door, and Glaves pushed past her

and rapped heavily on the wood. Then without more ado, he burst it open and surged inside.

Captain Peek's quarters were modestly appointed. There were some chairs, a table, a rack of scrolls, and another for equipment. The captain himself was already dropping out of his hammock.

"What the hell is this?" he roared.

Glaves was startled. Captain Peek was a huge man, tattooed on the face and arms, long grey hair, and heavy arms. There was a distinctly wild look in his eyes.

Glaves hesitated, looked back, and saw Rokensak closing the door.

"Captain Peek, I have been sent by General Paxion to take control of this ship. We have to ship all of our wounded out, right away."

"You'll take my ship over my dead body!" roared Peek. "You have no rights here, I have my ship's commission from Cunfshon, no Argonathi has powers above that."

"Captain, it is only a temporary thing. The battle is lost. The legions are doomed. It is only a matter of an hour or so. The wounded must be brought off."

"Damn you, I'm the captain of this ship, and no one, not even General Paxion, can tell me otherwise. And we will stay here on our anchor until I decide we leave. If the situation's as dire as you say, then I agree that we'll have to try and take off as many men as we possibly can. We'll put every boat in the water, we'll build rafts, we'll find a way to take everyone."

Glaves saw that there was absolutely no possibility of co-opting Captain Peek.

He motioned to Dandrax.

Peek saw the motion and from somewhere drew a cutlass in the next moment. Dandrax drew his sword. With a banshee shriek, the captain attacked. The two big men grappled and shoved back and forth. In the melee, Glaves was bowled over and crawled for safety beneath the table.

Peek was getting the upper hand, Dandrax was bent back over the table, and Peek was close to freeing his cutlass arm for the death stroke.

Rokensak sidled over and stabbed Peek in the back and repeated the blow twice more before the captain succumbed and fell to the floor.

"Alright, draw your weapons, we go out fighting," muttered Rokensak, who had gone quite pale.

They pulled open the door and lunged out. Shipmate Doon had no time to react before they were on her. Rokensak's sword cut her down. Next they ran lightly across the steps to the steering deck where they killed the steersman and took the second mate hostage.

In the waist of the ship, the "wounded" men now rose up as one and attacked the sailors. Surprise worked to their advantage. This sort of treachery the hard-bitten sailing crew of the *Nutbrown* had never imagined.

The fight raged for a few minutes until those on deck had been killed, disabled, or forced to dive overboard. The wounded men had slammed tight the hatches, locking the rest of the crew inside the ship. Then they raised the mainsail, loosed the anchor, turned the *Nutbrown*, and sailed her away from the doomed city of Ourdh.

CHAPTER FIFTY-TWO

They found the emperor red-eyed, too worn to weep anymore. He was disheveled and his bed was a mess. There were pillows and blankets scattered all around, where they'd been thrown in fits of rage.

Poor emperor, he was weak and the dreams were more than he could stand. The thing spoke to him. It was as if it were in the same room with him, it was so real, so horrifyingly real. It wanted him. It wanted his love. It wanted his soul. It was so confident that it was going to win. Poor little emperor, he was dying and no one would help him. The priests were useless, they said, "Be rational unto thy situation, Auros commands thee."

"Be rational?" he screamed at them. "How can I be rational? There is a god of death alive in a pit beneath the city of Dzu, and it intends to have me as its servant. How can I be rational about that, especially since it has now destroyed my armies and conquered my walls."

The priests of Auros looked back at him with sad cowlike eyes. In truth, they too were lost. They had no answers and all had come to doubt even the existence of Auros.

The monstekirs of the court were even less useful. They had all fled the city long ago. That was why there wasn't a boat to be had now. They had all gone south to the delta and Canfalon.

Princess Zettila was gone, lost to the enemy in the

debacle on the Isle of Gingo-La. Her addiction to the cult of the goddess had finally done her in. Banwi sobbed. He missed her the most, it seemed.

And finally Aunt Haruma was gone, too. She'd announced that she was tired of his "sniveling" and that he was a disgrace to the name of Shogemessar, and she had left, and gone to her own apartment and shut the door.

There were just the guards at the door and a few slave eunuchs to bring him his meals. He was alone.

Except for the witch. She came to see him frequently, altogether too often.

Now she was there again, with that young beauty at her side to whom he was not allowed to say more than two words at a time without the witch cutting him off. They had come in through the side door again, a door to which only they had access through the next door chamber. She came unannounced, unsmiling, terrifying him with those dark eyes that seemed to bore into one, peering into one's innermost secrets.

He pulled himself to a half-sitting position.

"As you can see, I am quite desolate. I want to go on the ship. You must make it possible for me to go aboard the ship, before it is too late!" His voice rose in a little shriek.

Ribela did not smile, did not betray her emotion.

"You were troubled again in your dreams, sire. Will you accept my help at last? I am skilled in dream soothing."

"Hah, and let you completely take over my mind? Never, damn you. Just get me onto that ship. That's all I want now. I will board the ship and sail away and never see my home again."

"Sire, Your Majesty, you must pull yourself together. You must stop this sniveling! You are a man and the Fedafer of the well-watered land. You must not disgrace your ancestors."

"My ancestors are dead. They had their turn. I am alive, and I want to stay that way."

"You must remain in the Imperial City along with your troops. Other armies are gathering, aid is coming. By tomorrow night, there will be another legion here and enough food and equipment for us to withstand an indefinite siege. We might even be able to take the offensive."

Banwi Shogemessar, Fedafer of Fedafers of the well-watered land stared at her. She was mad.

"Don't you understand, you crazy woman. They brought down the tower. They are attacking now and will continue until they break through. Don't you understand? I know what it wants! It wants me, it tells me so in the dreams."

"Your person is very valuable, Your Majesty. You are the Fedafer of the well-watered land."

"Exactly, and at any moment now they are going to break through, and then we will all be captured and dragged to see Sephis the Terrible."

"Say not that name in this place, sire. It defiles the very air. That is not a god! There are no gods like that. All these idols you worship in this old land are not gods, there is no divinity in them. The thing we face is but a demon, an unwilling servant of the enemy. And it is not alone. The great enemy put forth its hand here. Use not the names of your old gods. They are gone now, sent to the shades to rest. It is not a god that we face in the pit below Dzu, it is but a demon."

Banwi was aroused now. The damned witch dared to dismiss the gods of Ourdh as being dead and gone. There was no end to the effrontery, it was too much. Banwi exploded.

"So you say, but what you say is mostly worthless. Damn you women, you've destroyed our noble realm. I should have known this would happen from the first moment they suggested the alliance. You have been conniving and conspiring from the start. This is what you wanted, this is what you have desired. To throw down our throne and let the dark serpent rule the land."

Ribela's eyes snapped.

"Sire, I will not accept or listen to such words. The Empire of the Rose has put its strength behind you, and thus far you are still Fedafer in Ourdh."

"The city has fallen. Lest you forget, woman, we have already been defeated. It is just a matter of time now."

"There have been mistakes made, I admit that. But the situation will change very shortly for the better believe me."

"Hah! You live in a fantasy world, all you witches. I will have nothing more to do with you."

The emperor reached for the bell to summon his guards.

Ribela curtsied. "I am sorry to be unable to assist you, Your Majesty," she said in a formal tone. "I will leave you now. Be of good heart, do not fear. We will survive this time of darkness."

Ribela swept out with Lagdalen behind her. The guards watched them go with frank suspicion and dislike.

The door slammed closed behind them, and they started down the corridor. But before they'd gone ten feet, there was a sudden, piercing scream from within the Imperial bedchamber. They turned back. The guards were already opening the door.

The guards went through and there came terrible sounds of desperate, brief combat. One of the men was hurled directly out again, his chest stove in by a hammer blow. There was a brief shriek of agony. Steel rang on steel.

Ribela did not hesitate. Lagdalen followed, wishing she had more than just a long knife to hand. The guards were dead. Standing over them were giant forms, menlike things ten feet high that held huge hammers in their hands.

The Emperor Banwi Shogemessar, Fedafer of Fedafers, Emperor of emperors, etc. etc., was being unceremoniously stuffed into a sack by a trio of burly imps. His screams made them laugh ferociously.

The giants turned toward them. Lagdalen screamed. They had no faces, no features whatsoever. They were like unfinished statues. The nearest one swung a hammer with a head the size of a watermelon, and both women dived and rolled. The hammer whooshed past above them.

Lagdalen was at the door. Ribela stopped and spat a stream of fiery words. A bolt of blue fire burst from her fingertips and struck full on against the thing. It rocked back on its heels and blue energies traveled across its surface. Then the energies changed color, and red sparks sizzled instead. The thing rocked forward and started moving again.

Ribela shrilled another set of syllables and set them spinning, a disassociation spell for vortid integuments. The mud man's hammer rose. It seemed immune to such quickly spoken spells.

Ribela went for the door, but the other one was already there.

She glimpsed the sack containing the emperor being carried away by the imps down a set of stairs exposed beneath the floor of the chamber.

The hammer swung, another hammer was speeding her way, and she jumped back and felt the thing slice the air just in front of her face.

She could die here in an instant.

Another hammer bounced off the wall just above her head. She slid away from the giants and at the same time away from the door. They turned, in unison, an eery sight. They moved together and their hammers went up and down, they were like enormous mechanisms.

Ribela was trapped. She looked back to the hidden hatchway in the floor. It had been under a carpet. The room was in tumbled disarray, the bed overturned. These giants had lifted the door with such violence, they had overthrown the carpet and all the furniture piled on top of it.

The hammers swished by again. She tried to dart through between them, but a huge leg swung out to block her, and she bounced off and landed on the marble floor. She turned. The things were standing over her.

But they were not quite what they had been. Their movements had slowed and as she watched, the breath frozen in her throat, they slowed further, and the hammers dropped from their hands and bounced on the marble floor. The giants began to liquefy and soften. She stared, sobbing for breath, and in thirty seconds the huge things had slumped to rude piles of mud that continued to collapse, eventually spreading out into a treacly brown mess all over the floor of the chamber.

The Mother be thanked!

Ribela scrambled to her feet, breathing hard, shaking.

"My lady, are you alright?" Lagdalen was there, her dirk gleaming in her hand.

"Oh, my dear, that was a close call, too close indeed!" She steadied herself.

"The spell we forged was slow to work. I think because it had to be so small, so lacking in volume, which made it immune to the defensive systems." Ribela sighed. "But it grew, and at the end it grew very quickly." Ribela gestured to the slime. "The fighting will be over for a while now."

And indeed they could hear the shrill bark of the cornets from the walls, something was happening there.

"But the emperor?"

"Taken by imps, down those steps. Poor man, he

was right. We failed to protect him adequately. Shall we investigate?"

Lagdalen swallowed. Accompany a Great Witch and this was what was likely to happen to you. But what happened next was more than Lagdalen had even expected.

Ribela put a foot on the steps to descend and froze in place. Something was coming, something terrible, something that could make even the Queen of Mice pause.

Up from the darkness below came a figure, man-size, hidden beneath a heavy black cloak, surrounded by an aura of power. Ribela took one step back and steadied herself. The other figure halted halfway up. Lagdalen saw flames where there should have been eyes, Instinctively, she crouched beside a pillar seeking to make herself invisible.

Ribela spoke words in a tongue unknown to Lagdalen, harsh emphatic phrases. The other being laughed, a weird buzzing chuckle. In the dark beneath the hood, Lagdalen saw a glint and sparkle, as if of glossy horn. The eyes were like windows onto hell.

It spoke, a voice of rasps and inhuman grating, in the same tongue. Ribela shouted something and raised a hand, but the dark figure gave a sudden hiss and a bolt of red fire leapt out from its hand, striking Ribela in the chest. The witch gave a strange, inarticulate cry and was flung backward to the floor. The smell of burned cloth and singed flesh rose into the air. The tall figure in the cloak rose up from the darkness and stood over the fallen witch. After a moment, it kicked her prone body.

Lagdalen crouched behind the pillar, too afraid to move a muscle.

Imps appeared around the tall form in black. It gestured to the witch, and they bound her with chains and then bore her away on their shoulders.

At the sight of the imps, Lagdalen felt a familiar,

red anger explode in her, and she went forward silently and hurled herself at the figure in the cloak.

It saw her only at the last minute and a hand whipped around to bat her away. But even as she was knocked down, her dirk sank into the figure's chest.

Lagdalen was on all fours, staring up into the face of a man that had become a thing, a monster, all horn and dead white skin. It emitted a weird croak of dismay and pulled forth the Marneri knife. Red blood glinted in the lamplight. The thing snarled and gestured to her.

Imps ran to seize her. She punched one in the face, but it kicked her and knocked the breath out of her. Strong hands grasped her arms and bound her. She was lifted up and carried away down into darkness.

CHAPTER FIFTY-THREE

General Paxion would not come out of his room in the Fortress of Zadul. He had retreated into a shell and would not respond to his staff. Over and over he mumbled a prayer for forgiveness to the wall while nodding his head.

Paxion no longer understood the world. It was as if he had been accursed. He was a simple man, brave enough, a soldier for his entire adult life. Perhaps he was not the best battlefield commander, he could accept that. He'd worked hard, though, at the job of running a fort in Kenor, and he'd done well enough at that. He had a good, solid reputation.

It seemed unjust that all that should be destroyed by this wild, terrible campaign in the heat and dust of Ourdh. But if that was the fate chosen for Paxion by the Great Goddess, then he accepted it.

He had been prepared for death just hours before. He had taken up the sword and was ready to go out and die fighting the enemy when the end came and the mud men came pouring over the breach. But death was not to be his fate. Eternal ignominy had been selected for him instead.

Something unknowable had intervened. Everyone was calling it a miracle, and those men who disdained the Temple and any religious belief were seriously re-thinking. Those who knew the powers of the Queen of Mice understood that some tremendous sorcery had been achieved. Paxion understood that.

But before he might enjoy the feeling of being saved from imminent death, his heart had been brought low by the news of the attack on the *Nutbrown* and the apparent desertion of a commander, a captain, and thirty-five men from the Kadein legion. Shame had overwhelmed him.

And then came the news of ultimate catastrophe. The emperor had been abducted during the battle. Even worse, incredibly so, was the fact that the Lady Ribela, the very Queen of Mice was missing, along with her assistant. The only possibility seemed to be that they had been taken along with the emperor.

The entire expedition had crashed in disaster: they had lost the city of Ourdh, they had lost the emperor, and now they had lost the Great Witch Ribela. Paxion knew his name would go down in history as one of the great military blunderers of all time.

He turned his face to the wall and began to recite his prayer. He would not speak to anyone. It was as if he were no longer there.

His staff, dismayed, left him alone. They informed General Pekel, who now took over the command. Unfortunately, General Pekel was in a strange mood as well and spent much of the time pacing up and down rubbing his hands together and talking to himself.

When Kesepton approached him and requested permission to pursue the enemy down the tunnel that had been found in the emperor's bedchamber, Pekel barely seemed to listen before agreeing. Kesepton wanted to go alone. He did not expect to return.

In fact, General Pekel was secretly obsessing about that damned coward Glaves and Captain Rokensak. They had been there for the meetings with the sly Euxus of Fozad. They knew that Pekel had been ready to treat with the enemy. If they were recaptured by anyone but Pekel, they would be sure to sing a lengthy song and implicate as many others as they could.

Pekel sweated at the thought of it.

Here they were, saved by a miracle, with the white ships only hours away now, and he, Horatius Pekel, was undone. If those cowards were recaptured, his career would be over.

Pekel hardly heard the earnest young captain, but he knew what the fellow wanted. If he wanted to commit suicide trying to get his wife back, then that was alright with Pekel.

As for the witch and the emperor, Pekel really didn't care that much. Like everyone else, he despised the Ourdhi ruling elite and, in particular, the emperor. And like many men of Kadein now, he distrusted the witches and disliked their interference in the affairs of men.

Thus he bade Kesepton go to his death and resumed pacing. The white ships were coming. Pursuit of the *Nutbrown* would soon be organized. Pekel gazed into a distinctly unnerving future.

In the emperor's bedchamber, Kesepton found a group of grim-faced young men and dragons waiting for him. They looked as if they'd seen some hard fighting. There were head bandages among them, and scrapes and scratches aplenty.

At their front was Relkin of Quosh with his two mighty dragons behind him. Relkin was dirty and worn except for a fresh bandage on his head.

"I've scouted down the tunnel for half a mile, sir," said Relkin. "It turns slightly to the right there."

"Thank you, Dragoneer," said Kesepton with a tight smile.

"Captain Kesepton?"

"Yes, what is it?"

"We're coming with you. We can't leave her in the enemy's hands."

"I can't allow it, you will be needed here."

The broketail dragon leaned forward and rumbled. "Lagdalen dragon friend will not die alone."

Kesepton swallowed and saluted the dragon. "My

friend you do us great honor, but I cannot allow you to do this."

The other great beast leaned forward. Kesepton almost went into dragon-freeze, he'd forgotten how huge the wild dragon was.

"You cannot stop us, Captain. I go with the broketail dragon, we die together. Perhaps it is a good time to die."

Kesepton could not answer for a moment. That these huge monsters of war would be willing to throw away their lives by following him was a tribute to his wife and to himself, that brought a lump to his throat.

Two more wyverns stood forward. Kesepton did not recognize them at once, then saw the brasshide, Chektor.

"Captain, I fought at Ossur Galan and Mount Red Oak. I will come, too."

"Thank you, Chektor."

The dragonboy Mono was beside his dragon. Kesepton recalled that Mono and Relkin were the sole survivors of the original 109th Marneri dragon squadron.

The other wyvern was a leatherback.

"Vlok come, too. Where the broketail and the wild one go, goes Vlok."

"Swane of Revenant, sir!" snapped the dragonboy.

"Sir?" said Relkin.

"What is it, Dragoneer?"

"The legions will be resupplied today, will they not?"

"They will."

"And the enemy will not be able to attack again for hours."

"So we believe."

"Then we must go. We were privileged to fight alongside the Lady Lessis. We know how important the Great Witches are. We have to do this, we have to recover the witch. Even beyond our duty to find our friend is the need to rescue the witch. It must be done or our whole campaign here is nothing but a disaster."

Kesepton nodded. The lad was correct, and he reminded himself that while Relkin was but a youth, only the Great Mother herself knew what terrors he had already dealt with in his time in the catacombs of Tummuz Orgmeen.

"So be it, perhaps this is what Heaven wants from us. Perhaps the Mother has selected us all for this service."

"Perhaps," said Bazil. "But dragon heart say that there is no fate, the future is made by the present."

Kesepton moved down the stairs, and looked off down the tunnel with the aid of a torch.

It was wide and roomy, cobbled.

"Big enough for a coach and horses," said Relkin, easing down beside the captain.

"Exactly what I was thinking."

"We questioned some of the eunuchs," said Swane. They said the passage was once used by the empresses to ride to an island in the river where they used to meet their lovers."

Kesepton whistled. "The empresses of old must have had a pretty passionate nature."

"They also said that the slaves who dug this tunnel were all slain when it was completed to keep it a secret."

"But the secret was not kept."

"It was discovered by the first emperor of the Shogemessar dynasty and walled up. The eunuchs forgot to warn us about it."

"The enemy found it without difficulty, I take it." Kesepton was bitter. The Imperial Court had been nothing but difficult, haughty, impossibly demanding, reactionary, and xenophobic. Kesepton had formed a poor impression of the great civilization of Ourdh.

"I wanted to kill the damn eunuchs, but Dragoneer Hatlin stopped me."

"As he should have. We do not kill our allies without good cause."

"Sir, we hate the damned eunuchs here. Fact is, we pretty much hate all the people in this city."

Kesepton nodded. "Understood. But our principle remains the same. We do not kill anyone except the professed servants of the great enemy."

"Yes, sir," said Swane.

Kesepton set off down the tunnel. "Come, there is no time to waste if we hope to find them."

They stepped down into the tunnel, three boys, three wyverns, and a massive, wild drake.

"It must have been a small coach."

"Small horse, too," growled Bazil.

"Afterward I will eat a horse," said the Purple Green. "By the roar of the old gods, it is close in here, in this human hole."

They set off at a brisk pace, using the light of a single torch, although they carried several more in case the first burned out.

CHAPTER FIFTY-FOUR

The tunnel extended for miles beneath the waters of the river. At first, this occasioned some jokes about the empresses of Ourdh and the lengths they would go to in order to see their lovers in peace and quiet. But the experience palled swiftly. They tunnel was damp and cool. Ahead stretched the slow-curving walls and the endless cobblestones. Hundreds, perhaps thousands of men had dug this tunnel. A colossal effort that must have cost a fortune.

Then, at last, the walls ended. A set of steps rose up in the dark to a massive door. They put their ears to this door, but heard nothing.

Kesepton gave the order, and Chektor hewed into the door and broke it through. It was large and imposing, but not designed to be dragon proof. They stepped out into the night. It was nearly dawn, and they were standing in the ruins of what had once been a large house. The roof and upper floors had long since vanished, and the remains were little more than decayed ruins.

Beyond the house was a tangled forest of palms and pines. They pressed through them for a quarter of a mile and found themselves upon a beach fronting onto the dark river. Startled monkeys scampered away through the forest with shrieks of alarm. The river stretched away to the lightening horizon where dawn was beginning to show its first glimmerings. There was no sign of land.

"This is the eastern bank," said Kesepton. "Let us see what lies on the other shore."

The island was a mile long and a third of a mile wide at its widest, a sliver formed atop a sandbar. When they reached the southernmost tip, they immediately noticed a light out upon the river. It moved slightly and was doused. Then there was another in almost the same place. It remained alight and in one place.

"A ship," said Kesepton after studying it with his field telescope.

Indeed, it was a large vessel, square-rigged, and standing fast about a mile farther west, in the lee of the island. There was something strange about the ship, however. She carried no sail and seemed not to move. In the current there should have been some movement.

Kesepton understood at once.

"She's caught on a bar, my friends. It's low tide, and she came in too close to the island on this side."

Kesepton continued to study the ship, which was barely visible in the very early light of dawn. Suddenly he let out a low whistle.

"As I hoped, it's the *Nutbrown*."

They all stared into the murk.

"How deep is the water there?" said Mono.

"On the lee side of the island, the water will be shallow, the sandbars extensive."

"Hard to swim if we're carrying armor and shields," said Bazil Broketail.

"We'll leave those behind. If we're successful, we can retrieve them later," said Kesepton.

Relkin pointed to the east. "Dawn soon."

"We should hurry then, before the sun rises. We'll be easily seen in an hour."

Without further ado, they marched out into the shallow waters toward the ship.

After going half a mile, the water was waist high

on a dragonboy, and the dawn light was strengthening, though it was still semidarkness.

They began to hear distant shouting from the ship, angry voices railing at one another. A chorus of boos and roars, more snarling and yelling, then a scream and several more screams.

"Sounds like they may have fallen out with each other," said Swane with considerable satisfaction.

"If we hurry, we may arrive unannounced," said Kesepton.

At length, they had to swim the last few hundred yards, which they did holding onto the backs of the dragons, since the dragons could swim far faster in the current than any man.

They reached the side of the ship, which was stuck fast at the bow. The argument continued. There appeared to be two factions exchanging insults and curses. Intermingled with these came occasional clashes of metal and sometimes a thrown object would hurtle off the ship and splash into the river.

Then a boat splashed into the water on the far side, and men plunged down around it. Other things were thrown after them, but they made themselves lively and within a few minutes had rowed out of range, although they continued to yell insults.

By then the dragonboys were already up the side and were releasing the landing netting stowed along the gunwales. It clattered down to the dragons below.

At last somebody saw them and let out a scream of alarm.

"Pirates!"

The men came running, swords out.

"Not pirates," snarled a voice, "dragonboys!"

"What the hell?"

Captain Kesepton came over the side, and the men pulled to a stop.

"That fornicating staff captain," said someone at

the rear. Kesepton strode toward them with no sign of fear.

"You are deserters, and you'll hang unless you surrender at this very instant and help me on my mission."

"It's the damned whelp of old Kesepton's."

"Paxion's pet staff officer, he's very well connected."

"What says you we take him for a hostage, lads," said a man with an officer's uniform.

Kesepton turned to this man.

"Captain Rokensak, why are you not with your men at your post?"

Rokensak's lips twisted into a snarl. "Because I'm here, you stupid Marneri eunuch. Because it's death to stay back there. I mean, why the hell are you here then?"

Rokensak's sword was up between them, Kesepton stepped back lightly.

"You will end in complete disgrace, Rokensak. I don't understand it."

"Stupid whoreson of Marneri, let my steel explain it." Rokensak flung himself on Kesepton, and their swords rang off each other.

The other men, Kadeini troopers, also came forward, and the dragonboys were forced to engage them with their light swords. The legionairies were seasoned veterans, and the boys were pressed hard and slowly driven back to the ship's side.

And then with an immense effort a dragon arm came over the side, and with a huge grunt a two-ton leatherback rolled onto the deck and hauled itself to its feet. In its hand gleamed the dragon sword.

Another dragon was coming. The first reached down and helped haul up the second one.

The Kadeini men looked at each other, turned, and ran. Kesepton and the boys pursued them, but with Rokensak in the lead, they dove into the river and swam for it.

The dragonboys knocked open the hatches and were rewarded with a sudden eruption of angry, confused sailors who'd been locked up below for hours.

"What happened?" said Kesepton.

"How should we know? The hatches were suddenly locked hours ago, and we've never gotten an answer since. Was it mutiny?"

"Deserters from the Kadein legion, I'm afraid."

"Where's Captain Peek."

A search of the Captain's quarters, however, revealed no sign of the *Nutbrown*'s master but did disgorge Commander Glaves and his manservant, Dandrax, holed up behind the door where they'd been confined since the beginning of the fight.

They pulled him out. He was bellowing threats and curses the entire time. Then when Glaves found himself in front of Kesepton, with dragons standing on the ship's deck, he fainted dead away.

Dandrax came peacefully once they'd poked him out of the cupboard where he'd taken refuge. They were bound at the wrists and set side by side on a bench.

Glaves seemed shocked into complete silence. Dandrax shrugged when questioned. "I work for the man, what am I supposed to do?"

"Where is Captain Peek? And Shipmate Doon?"

"You've got no evidence that was anything to do with me. Ask the Kadeini."

"The Kadeini are not here, you are," replied Kesepton. Dandrax spat.

"There will be a trial, that's all I can say."

"What happened back there then?" asked Dandrax. "How did you escape?"

"The battle is over, for now. The mud men stopped coming. Something went wrong with them. They addled and dissolved into mud."

Dandrax whistled. "Great sorcery then."

Kesepton nodded, he knew it had to be the work

of the Great Witch. He'd seen things the previous year that he would never forget.

"Yes."

Dandrax gave a big sigh. "Then my master's scuppered and so am I."

Glaves stared ahead of himself in complete apathy. He made no response to questions put to him.

"You did not have to obey him when he told you to murder. Or to steal this ship."

"What?" Dandrax was indignant. "And not be paid for all I've done on this expedition? He owes me good gold coin, and plenty of it."

"And so your motives are frankly mercenary. If you killed Captain Peek for money, you will hang."

Dandrax looked down. "So that's it, right? You're going to pin it all on me. They'll let this fat bastard go, right? They'll give him a reprimand while they hang me! That's how they do their justice in the cities. The rich men get away with it, the poor man hangs."

Kesepton turned away from the fellow.

"You'll get justice. And if you killed Captain Peek or Shipmate Doon, then you'll hang for it, off the yardarm of this ship most likely. And if you didn't, then you'll live, though you may serve time in prison. But you'll get justice, and so will your master."

Kesepton stormed back to the deck, boiling with anger at Glaves and his treachery.

"Where do you wish to go, Captain?" It was the mate.

"Can you take us to the city of Dzu? We need to get as close as we can today."

"Dzu, the city of Dzu?"

"Yes."

"Well, yes, of course there may be pirates."

"We have to reach Dzu. With the dragons aboard, we can defeat any pirates that might dare to board."

"We'll be there by noon."

"Then we must go slowly, for we should enter the city under cover of darkness."

"So it will be, Captain."

CHAPTER FIFTY-FIVE

The door to the cell opened after several hours, and a party of imps brought the Lady Ribela in on a stretcher and laid her on the floor beside Lagdalen.

A slave, his face terribly cut and broken, brought her some hot water and some clean rags. Then he produced a small oil lamp, lit it, and set it beside the stretcher. The slave tried to whisper something through his broken teeth, but he was interrupted by a blow.

"Alright, enough, get out of here," boomed a harsh voice. The slave cringed and crept away. A brutal-looking man in black stood over her. A large whip was coiled at his hip.

"This hag has been bruised a little. You are to tend her and make sure that she's fit for travel. She's going on a little ride to the mountains."

"What do you mean?" Lagdalen was carefully examining the lady. She had been terribly ill-used. The fingernails from her hands were gone, and there was dried blood everywhere. The flesh of her upper arms and belly showed the marks of hot irons and pincers, too. Lagdalen felt a great anger rise inside her. The man suddenly leaned down, grabbed her by the hair, and pulled her head back.

"She's going to fly. A rukhbat has been sent for. It will take her to Axoxo. You have heard that name, I am sure."

Axoxo, it was a name of death, a name that ranked with Tummuz Orgmeen. A fortress for a Doom. But the rest of his words left her puzzled. To fly? A rukh-bat? What did he mean?

"She may not be well enough to, ah, fly after what you've done to her."

"If she isn't, then your head will be the first to be taken. The master will demand it. Though I think it would be a terrible waste of one so pretty. It is not often that we gets to sample the pleasures of the females of the witch isles. I had not realized how comely they might be." The man stroked his crotch and leered at her, then released her and stood back. A moment later the door closed behind him, and she was alone.

The water was hot and it would not stay that way so Lagdalen went to work at once, cleaning and bandaging where possible. It was heartbreaking work, but eventually she was done and sat there staring at the witch, willing her to live. Lagdalen grew drowsy and dozed. She awoke with a start. The witch was awake and peering into her face.

"Girl" she whispered, "are you well?"

"Yes, my lady?"

"Is it safe to talk?" Ribela's voice was scratched and throaty.

"I think so. We are alone. This is a dungeon, two floors above ground I think. They brought me here after they separated us."

"Have they harmed you?"

"No, my lady."

"Thanks be to the Mother of us all. And my thanks to you dear Lagdalen for your aid." Ribela held up her bandaged fingers. "You learned a lot in your work with the Grey Lady I think."

"Yes, my lady, I did."

"Good, that is why I chose you to accompany me. Listen to me now, we have much to do if we are to avert disaster."

"Yes, my Lady."

"While I have been sitting here, I have concocted

a plan." Lagdalen leaned closer, and Ribela whispered in her ear.

And while the Queen of Mice whispered thus, her enemy convened another small conference in a cell not above one hundred feet away.

The Emperor Banwi Shogmessar had been confined here since they had brought him in. He had wept and begged at the door, but there had been no response. He dozed on the narrow mat, lost in mourning for his former life.

Suddenly the door opened, and in strode a tall figure hidden beneath a black cloak. The air went cold, the room trembled with power. Banwi felt his mouth go dry and his throat constrict. An inhuman face, surmounted by eyes that flickered like yellow flames, bore down on him. A weird, rasping voice spoke.

"Welcome, precious Emperor, welcome to the Temple of Sephis."

"Don't hurt me, please don't hurt me."

"You fear mere physical torment?"

"I fear everything, master." Banwi got to his knees.

"Do you know who I am?" said the voice.

"No, not at all, I would never tell. Just let me go, please. I am sorry, I never meant to—"

"Shut up!" snapped the harsh voice. "I am the Mesomaster Gog Zagozt."

Banwi shuddered. That such things actually existed. It was just as Aunt Haruma had told him. She had been right, the priests had been wrong and so had Zettilla. But it was all too late now. Much too late.

"What do you want with me?" Banwi managed to say at length.

"You are about to enter a new phase of your existence. Up to now you have been useless, a burden to the very people you were supposed to tend. Fedafer of the well-watered land! Hah! A pitiful joke."

The figure leaned down and took Banwi's face in a

powerful grip. The eyes flickered close to his own.
Banwi came close to screaming.

"Now you will become useful at last. You will live
out your days as a faithful servant of Sephis."

The Mesomaster gave a great laugh, released Banwi,
and pushed away.

A snarled command brought a pack of imps into
the cell who seized Banwi, bound him, and drove him
ahead of themselves down a stone-flagged passage.
There was a guarded doorway, two huge men armed
with sword and shield stood there. They looked down
as the emperor was pushed through by the imps, with
the figure in the black cloak coming up behind.

They emerged in a large space, lit only by a flame
burning atop a large stone altar. Past the altar was a
deeper dark than the rest of the place, as if it were a
great pit. Banwi sensed something in that dark. His
hair stood on end, and he tried to back away.

The imps laughed and shoved him forward. A whip
cracked against his shoulder, another slashed him
across the buttocks, and he jumped with a little shriek.

"Silence," roared the voice. "You are in the holy
presence of Sephis himself."

"Two tall men in the robes of priests had appeared.
They came forward and took the emperor by the
arms. They began pulling him toward the altar stone.

"No," wailed Banwi Shogemessar, and he dug in
his heels. The two tall men jerked him off his feet and
carried him the rest of the way before dumping him
on a stone platform that projected out over the dark.
Banwi realized he was indeed standing over a great
pit. A strong fishy odor was rising from below.

The Mesomaster mounted the stone altar. He uttered a brief incantation. Something stirred below in
the dark depths.

Banwi felt his bowels turn to ice. A mass was shifting around in the pit, rising toward him through the
dark. An enormous mass, larger than a whale, a great

serpentine body ten feet thick equipped with a strange set of four long arms tipped with pincers and claws. The body was covered not in scales but in plates of chitinous armor.

Two vast black eyes, the size of dinner plates, bore down on him from above. Banwi stared into those eyes and felt his will drain away like blood from a mortal wound. What was left of him was ready to serve the serpent god.

CHAPTER FIFTY-SIX

The land on the west side of the great river was silent and dark. There were no lights, no friendly yellow lamps across the flatland.

Above the city of Ourdh, the river split in two. The main stream headed due south and swept past the headland on which the city of Ourdh had been built. The second stream broke westwards for thirty miles and then trailed away southwesterly before splitting again. On the northern bank of this stream stood the even more ancient city of Dzu.

They passed a line of enormous ziggurats, "Pachipandi," said the mate, "the temples of the old god, the serpent god."

"They like to build temples here don't they," said the helmswoman, old Tarano. "Everywheres you look, they got another one. Must give the Mother the giggles every time she looks at it." The mate chuckled.

"It must be something to do with living in such a flatland," said Kesepton, who was marveling at the effort that had gone into these huge, now rotting, pyramids. "These people need some real mountains to inspire them. They ought to come up and see our mountains in Kenor."

"I think you be thankful in the end that Ourdhi peoples not ever come to Kenor," said old Tarano.

"Why so?"

"There are a hell of a lot of them. Could fill Kenor right up."

The *Nutbrown* nosed into a creek mouth about half the distance to the city.

"Any closer and they'll see our sail."

Kesepton agreed. "Many thanks to all of you. We will leave you here."

Kesepton and the dragonboys went over the side and reconnoitered the area around the west bank of the creek. They saw no sign of human activity and signaled the dragons. The great breasts climbed down thick netting to the water. Then their armor and shields were lowered to them, and they formed a chain and passed it to the shore. Dragonboys sweated to haul the metal up onto the beach while Kesepton kept watch.

Soon the dragons came ashore. The *Nutbrown* slipped her moorings, pulled back out into the broad channel, and turned to leave. They were on their own.

From Kesepton's understanding of the map, they were just a few miles from the city, across the base of a peninsula. Dragons put on armor and slung their shields and swords across their backs.

Dragonboys worked carefully on the cords and retainers, making sure that everything was a perfect fit. They worked in the darkness, by feel rather than by sight, but they were so familiar with the joboquins and the fastenings that it was actually better that way.

When all was ready, they set off and marched westwards in a short column, with the dragonboys ahead as scouts and Kesepton behind them, with the dragons behind him.

The first thing they discovered was that the countryside truly was empty of people. The rumors had been true. They passed a village where doors sagged open and debris littered the streets. A skeleton lay in the crossroads. A skull still rocked atop an assegai thrust into the ground.

The skeletons of cattle and donkeys were seen alongside the roads. They passed through another

empty village, and then another. It was as if some
terrible pestilence had swept through the place and
annihilated the population.

"Where is everybody?" said Mono after a while.

"Gone to the new god in Dzu, I'm afraid," said
Kesepton.

"What's he do with them?"

"The witch told me they make the giants from
human blood."

"Mother protect us!"

"So that rumor was correct," said Swane. "We
heard about that before. I just couldn't believe it.
Something so evil."

"The enemy always uses life for its magic," said
Kesepton. "It destroys life to obtain power. That's
what they taught me, and I have seen that it is true."

Hollein Kesepton did his utmost not to think about
Lagdalen, about she who he cared more for than for
his own life. He did not think in terms of revenge, he
simply prayed that she was still alive and that they
had not hurt her. Revenge would come later.

They went on and crossed over a wide bridge, massively built, and found themselves in the outskirts of
what had once been a huge city . Once it had been a
mighty place, now it was a virtual ruin.

The walls had long since vanished, torn down and
taken away to build other things in the surrounding
region. Buildings had decayed and fallen in. Other
places had burned down. Bushes and small trees grew
throughout this section, even in the center of what
had once been streets.

This part of the ancient city was empty of people
and had been for a long time. They went on through
long dead streets and then quite suddenly they heard
the sound of metal-shod horses riding through the
streets somewhere not too far ahead.

With remarkable speed, the dragons slid into the
ruined houses and hid themselves. Kesepton watched

them and felt a shiver run down his spine at the sight of such predatory skill. He remembered that in the wild, dragons ate whatever they might catch, including men.

Along what had once been a main avenue passed a troop of cavalry in the black uniform of Sephis. Some of the horses reacted to the faint smell of dragon with whinnies and nervous movements. The cavalrymen took no notice, however, and trotted on without investigation.

Now they emerged from their hiding places. The dragons moved with a stealth that continued to surprise Kesepton.

At one point they waited behind a long ruined wall while Relkin went forward to scout alone.

"What happened here?" whispered Swane, gesturing to the ruins. "This looks like it's been this way for a long time."

"When they threw down the old Sephis, they threw down the city as well. That was long ago."

"A dead city, dedicated to more death, may the Mother preserve us!" muttered Mono.

Relkin returned and described the next stretch of their journey. Kesepton went over it carefully and then sent them forward. They went on, moving quietly through the ruins.

Eventually they began to see more activity. In the central regions of the city, some of the buildings had been repaired. The great Temple to Sephis was a circular block seven stories tall that still dominated the city, although much of it was in ruins, too. It had been converted to a temple of Auros and so had received a certain minimum of care over the decades.

Close to the center, the streets bore a traffic of carts and wagons. Groups of soldiers in the black uniform of Sephis were also visible. Then they saw a party of imps, a dozen strong. They wore a costume that was new to Bazil and Relkin, with black leggings, knee-high boots, and a leather cape fringed in white around the neck and shoulders.

"Imps of the Doom in Axoxo, ruler of the White Bones Mountains," said Kesepton.

"We saw imps driving the slaves on the enemy's war machines. But they did not have that white neck on their capes," said Relkin.

"They came from the deep Hazog, with the enemy engineers. This war was something the enemy had planned for a long time."

They slid closer to the heart of the city.

"The dragons will hide here while we scout forward," said Kesepton.

Kesepton and the dragonboys pushed on, and the dragons withdrew into the ruins of what once had been a large brewery. The great vats had been torn down, but there were still fermentation pits half full of rubble from the roof. The dragons hid in these pits.

"We sit, they go, what happens if they don't come back?" said the Purple Green.

"There is a saying, 'When we come to that horse, we will eat it,' " said Bazil.

"You have a saying for everything, leatherback dragon."

"Bazil is smart," said Vlok.

"Smarter than Vlok, that's for sure," said old Chektor. Vlok growled but did not challenge big Chektor.

"What is this thing we go to kill?" said the Purple Green. I have heard things but I do not understand."

Chektor looked at Bazil.

"Why do you look at me?"

"Are you not friends with the Great Witch Lessis? So you know these things."

"Boy told me things; that is all I know."

"So?"

"So it is a demon, something not from this world."

"What does this mean?" said the Purple Green.

"There are many worlds, this is all I know, and this thing comes from one far from ours."

"Are there dragons in the world from which this thing comes?"

"By the roar, how should I know?"

"Well, you know a lot about these things."

"I am not a witch! I am a fighting dragon." Bazil's voice had gotten loud.

"Shh," said Chektor. "Someone comes."

They hushed. Tails flexed with small swords and maces, just in case.

But it was only Relkin.

"Dragonboy!" hissed Chektor.

"They always take their time."

"What is situation?" said Baz.

"I think we have a route, follow me."

"Wait," said Bazil. "You either have a route or you do not. What do you mean 'think' you have route?"

"We have a route. You'll just have to jump a little to get started."

They moved through empty streets to a ruined aqueduct that had once conducted fresh water from upstream of the city to the homes of the wealthy.

Through this structure they were able to cross a wide avenue, right in front of a constant enemy presence with many guards, and not be seen.

They clambered down from the aqueduct in a neighborhood of long-since-ruined mansions. Palm trees towered above them. They tiptoed through gardens that had long since become small forests and at length emerged outside a huge building, seven stories tall and one hundred meters long completely surrounded now by scaffolding. Repairs were underway at the Temple of Sephis.

Kesepton appeared out of the shadows.

"We've found a door that's big enough for dragons. It's guarded, but lightly. The enemy does not expect an attack. This is the center of its power."

"We give them a surprise,"said Bazil.

"By the roar, we'll do that and more," growled the Purple Green.

"Once we go beyond that door, then we will be in unknown territory," continued Kesepton, "but you understand that. We will have to strike at once, as swiftly and as terribly as we can. We can only rescue Lagdalen and the witch if we destroy the dark power here. Surprise is our only tactic. Beyond that, it will be up to us."

"If it can be killed," muttered the Purple Green, "we will kill it."

"It will be no easy task, my great friend. This is not a being from our world. It comes from a hotter, heavier place. The witch told me. 'Gammadion' she called it, 'Malacostraca,' she said it was."

"Can steel cut this thing?" said Bazil.

"Yes, I think so."

Baz held up Ecator's gleaming blade. "Then we will kill it."

They were all agreed. In the dark, Captain Kesepton slid across the street and hugged the wall of the Temple. The dragonboys followed. They moved quickly along the wall toward the door where a pair of guards kept a desultory watch. They expected no trouble. Who in his right mind would wish to enter the house of Sephis? They had long since been dulled by the effect of the controlling spell on their brains.

When they were still twenty feet away, Swane and Mono knelt and fired their bows. They could not miss. Both guards suddenly coughed and staggered as arrows struck them in the throat and face.

Kesepton was upon them in the next moment. He finished the first with a downstroke and then thrust home into the second's heart.

They pushed open the door, peered inside, and then signaled to the dragons, who crossed the street one at a time, and slid through the portal.

They were inside the great Temple of Sephis and still undetected.

It was dark just inside the door, but light came from the end of a long corridor just ahead.

They found that the passage opened onto a large hallway, lit by lamps along the walls. A dozen or more guards stood in front of a great set of double doors.

Kesepton turned and clasped hands with each of them, even the great Purple Green.

From here on, they would go forward only by right of the sword.

CHAPTER FIFTY-SEVEN

The Queen of Mice relaxed her muscles and slowed her breathing. She murmured a series of subtle declensions and formed a powerful volume that she released like a long drawn-out sigh.

Slowly the wheels of consciousness spun to a halt in her mind, and she transcended to an astral plane. This was not the subworld of chaos, and it required no power to stay or to travel here, it was a subtle realm, a refraction of the higher worlds such as Ryetelth.

To her mind's eye, she appeared to float through a field of semitransparent blue bubbles, billions on billions of them, each surface reflecting a billion others. She concentrated. The bubbles came to an end, cut off in a cliff wall of phase perception, and now she seemed to float through a clear ether, uniformly lit by the mental energies of living beings all around her. In some ways it was as if she floated in a field of stars, a great galaxy perhaps.

Nearby she sensed an enormous presence, a darkness that was devouring the lights. The thing in its dark pit. Nearby was another powerful presence, a light so bright and hard it was violet in hue, tinged with black. The horned master that had surprised her in Ourdh.

And all around her were human minds, white and yellow points in great numbers. But none of these were what she sought. That lay closer in more humble circumstances. She focused on the most immediate surroundings, on a smaller scale. And here there was a great number of tiny lights, small golden glimmers in the darkness, the minds of mice and insects.

And among these tiny minds, she found a nest of paper wasps built in a crack in the wall of the temple. It was close by, and thus useful for her purpose.

Ribela focused on the queen of the nest, a small ferocious personality. The paper wasp queen was much concerned with food, egg laying, and the numbers of her daughters that were functional at that moment. Some were missing. There were birds nesting elsewhere on the wall. It was interfering with the food supply, and there were many hungry grubs to feed. The wasp queen became agitated as Ribela made contact. The wasp bit her daughters and sisters and buzzed her wings angrily. She could not understand what was happening nor control her reaction. She buzzed madly, abdomen twitching, jaws working, for several seconds, and then quite suddenly all this activity ceased as Ribela set in place a calming spell.

It was not the easiest spell to cast. The insect mind is a terrifying place of absolutes. But at length, Ribela was done and she withdrew. The wasp queen went about her business, but now prepared for what was coming.

Ribela rested, falling back into her body, collapsed into a deep sleep. When she awoke, an hour later, Lagdalen was already awake.

"I have spoken to the guards, my lady. I pleaded with them to release me."

"Good, then we can proceed."

Ribela set herself to rise into the astral mode once more. It was more difficult than before, an hour to sleep was insufficient at her age for this trick. In fact, she was approaching exhaustion. But there were no mice on hand to provide energy for the mightier magic involving the astral plane on the subworld of chaos. She found it hard to simply relax and not drift back into sleep. It was a difficult trick, but at length her tired old head achieved the necessary state.

Close by, outside the door, stood two guards. They knew that Lagdalen was within and they had heard her soft voice, pleading with them. Ribela now had to raise a killing lust within one of them.

Ribela had done without lust on her own part for centuries. It took a great effort for her to recall the mechanisms, the impulses of human nature. Slowly she formed the spell and wove into it the picture of the beautiful young woman in the cell with her glossy hair and firm body.

The guard she had chosen quickly became aroused. The other was virtually asleep, leaning on his spear. The enemy did not expect any trouble from a couple of women locked up in a cell.

The guard fidgeted for a few minutes, but the thoughts of the lush body of the young maiden in the cell would not leave him. Suddenly he broke. He drew his sword and slew his colleague with a thrust from the side. The man died without a sound.

The guard lowered him to the ground and opened the door with the big key from his belt.

Lagdalen put her hand over her mouth and cowered back against the wall. She had removed her leggings.

The man looked down at the witch, who feigned unconsciousness, then he strode across the cell, grasped the girl, and began to pull apart her clothing. Lagdalen went limp, Ribela had told her not to move at this point.

The man was on top of her, clumsily trying to rape her. Lagdalen resisted him but only passively, without striking a blow, gritting her teeth against his hot breath and his beard where it scratched against her while his hands invaded her.

There was a sudden loud buzzing in the ceiling of the cell. An angry horde of black and yellow wasps had flown in through the narrow ventilation slit set high on the wall. The queen had sensed the attack and had considered it a direct threat to her nest. The wasps dropped on the guard and began to sting him wherever they could reach. With loud oaths and cries, the man pushed himself to his feet and slapped vigorously at the swarm that swung angrily around him.

He didn't notice Lagdalen getting to her feet. She struck with her right foot, and he doubled over with a gasp, clutching his abdomen. A wasp stung her, but she remembered Ribela's warnings and did her utmost not to move. Several wasps landed briefly on her arms and face, but they did not sting. They returned to stinging the poor guard, who had gone down on his knees, still groaning from her kick to the belly.

Like lightning, Lagdalen took up the guard's spear and prepared to thrust it home. Ribela spoke sharply, "Be merciful, Sister Lagdalen, this poor man is a slave to the demon that rules here. He knows not what he does."

Lagdalen swallowed and gripped the spear tightly, but she did not plunge it home. The wasps hovered around her for a few more seconds and then returned to attacking the poor guard, who rolled on the floor, groaning.

Then she reversed the spear and rapped the fellow hard on the back of the head with the butt. She was not gentle. He went limp. After a second or so, the wasps stopped stinging him, however, and unconscious, he felt no pain.

The wasps circled up to the vent at the top of the cell and returned to their own affairs.

The door swung open. They locked it behind themselves after dragging the other guard inside and wiping away the blood. They took the men's swords and then slid away down a marble passage. There were guards at one end, so they doubled back and went down another long passage with many doors.

At length, they found themselves in a partly ruined

section. There were guards here, but not on this floor. They came to a broken stair. The steps down were gone, but the flight going up remained. Looking down through the stairs, they glimpsed more ruins and eventually a pile of rubble.

They climbed the stair, which accepted their weight, and reached a higher floor. They could see at once that it was in some disrepair. There were empty rooms and rooms with fallen ceilings and no doors. They concealed themselves behind some rubble mounded up in the center of a large room. Lagdalen went in search of some wood for a small fire. Ribela became very still and set to summoning some of the wild mice that lived on this floor in considerable numbers.

She had already made up her mind as to what she must do. She had to call upon the Sinni. No human witch had the strength to battle such a thing as that which lay in the pit: Gammadion, being of a heavier world.

CHAPTER FIFTY-EIGHT

The dragonboys went first, skipping quietly forward through the hall toward the guards, their bows at the ready. They were not seen immediately. Quickly they closed the range. At fifty feet, they rarely missed a target. When they were a third of the way across the hall, the guards finally looked up, a shout went up. Swords were drawn. A few steps later, the boys fired and arrows sprouted from the eyes of three guards, who dropped like stones.

The rest charged them with sword and spear.

But now the dragons had emerged from hiding and lumbered forward with Captain Kesepton in the lead. The guards saw these great bulks loom up behind the dragonboys, and their mouths dropped open. They turned tail and ran back to the doors to call for help.

More arrows flicked among them, and they tried to make a stand by the doors, but then the dragons were upon them. Men went down where they stood or else they fled inside.

The doors were torn asunder, and lead by the Purple Green, the dragons surged within. They found themselves standing above a vast space, overhung with shadows. They heard the surviving guards calling alarm as they ran down the stairs to the main floor.

In the center of the great flagstone floor was a wide circular hole, a pit of nothingness that appeared to go straight down for an unknown distance.

Surrounding one half of the pit was a raised gallery with seats for several dozen.

Standing near the pit were gathered some fifty men, all in black garb, with subtle differentiations of white bands, red arrow markings, and the like. At the base of the stair from the doorway were another dozen guards, plus the three survivors, who were in little condition to continue with the dragons.

The dragons started down the stairs. Dragonboys put arrows into the guards faces.

The men standing by the pit were the elite of the power groups around the reborn god and his Temple. There were magicians and military officers from Padmasa, agents of the Doom in Axoxo, local commanders and the priests of Sephis, distinguished by their shaved heads and the gold edging to their robes.

All of them were staring openmouthed at the huge intruders now coming down the stairs from the entrance. Great swords gleamed in dragon hands. A guard staggered and fell with an arrow in his skull. The power elite of Dzu emitted a collective scream of fright.

A couple of priests even toppled off the edge and fell into the pit with shrieks of woe. The men drew their swords and fell back in a crouch toward the walls.

The dragons reached the floor of the chamber, dragonboys bounced down among them. Kesepton stood in front of them and raised his sword.

They charged.

The guards were all fighters and they were hypnotized, with a fanatical belief in the reborn god. They put up a fight, but were swept aside in half a minute by arrows and dragon sword.

The power elites had scattered to the walls where they crouched, swords drawn, eyes widened in shock. The remaining priests had scrambled up into the gallery and run to the rear.

Relkin kept them under guard with his bow.

The men around the walls were not eager to attack. They looked for ways to get past Chektor and Mono, who guarded the stair to the doors and gradually they slid down the wall to that end.

Kesepton looked into the pit. What they had come to destroy was down there somewhere. The question was how were they going to summon it to battle?

He vaulted up beside Relkin and called to the priests.

"Does any of you speak Verio?"

Several nodded.

"Then tell me how to summon the thing in the pit."

They cringed and hid their faces from him.

"The god Sephis will rise soon, and he will take you all," said one who wore a gold filet over the black and gold robes.

"The god will take them," said the others in a monotone response.

"Tell me how to summon your god, or I will have to throw you down to him."

But they would not look up.

Kesepton was about to step forward and threaten them more directly when he felt a presence. Something had changed in the room, and he turned his head. A single figure in a black cloak stood on the landing by the doors.

It turned, came swiftly down the stairs, and strode toward them. Eyes glowed like red glimmers of Hell beneath the hood. A great shadow was growing up around it, so that it seemed as tall as the Purple Green.

It stopped in front of them. They saw the horned face and the human skull within the shadow, and it laughed at their expressions of shock.

"So," it snarled, "the armies of Argonath come down to this little ragtag band! A small pack of reptiles, a man and three boys. This is the best they could manage. This is their great blow to destroy us?"

The hands came out of the robe, they too were tipped in green-black horn.

"Hah!" It raised the hands high above its head. "You dare to tread here on this hallowed ground?" They felt a tension rising in the space around them.

"The great one will take you. He will enjoy you. He will feed on you for days."

Relkin shuddered. The thing spoke Verio with a chilling precision. He started. Swane was nudging him with an elbow. "What the hell is that thing?"

"How should I know?"

"Well, you're supposed to be the one who knows all about these things."

"I never made such claims."

"I see a man to kill," said the Purple Green.

"Wizard of the enemy," spat Kesepton.

"What is it, Captain?" said Swane.

" 'Tis something from the Masters of the Dark, that is all I know."

"We kill it then," rumbled Bazil.

But the Mesomaster uttered a series of loud, harsh phrases. There was a flash of light, and a red orb of energy grew between his hands while sparks sizzled in the air around it.

He raised this orb toward the dragons, and from it came a beam of reddish light that struck at the nearest dragon, Vlok, and caused him to bellow from the surprise. He put his shield up against any further flashes and cursed loudly in dragon speech.

The other dragons raised their shields and peered around them. Vlok had taken no hurt. They took a long step toward the being. Dragons were notoriously immune to the magical arts of humans.

The light flashed at them again and again as Gog Zagozt drove home his most potent mental blasts. The boys and Kesepton were down on their knees, grasping their hands as they caught ricochets of these mental blasts. The men back against the wall were similarly occupied. Humans were all too sensitive to such things.

But the dragons took another long step. Gog Zagozt realized that what he been told about dragonish imperviousness to magical effect was actually true. He took a step back.

The swords were longer than a man and could cut through a tree with a single blow. Dragons weighed two tons, and the giant in the middle of the group obviously weighed a lot more than that.

The Mesomaster had not known the feeling of fear in a long time. He found it unnerving. With a shriek, he summoned the great one in the pit.

Let these resistant dragons face their own nemesis! The dragon swords swung, and the Mesomaster darted back with more hastily screamed commands.

The darkness in the pit roiled. Gog Zagozt flung himself back up the stairs, dragons at his heels.

And a silence fell. The dragons were suddenly aware of another force in the room.

The reborn god was rising from the pit—an immense serpent, clad in golden plates of malacostracan armor. It soon towered above them on a body as thick as the Purple Green's, but many times longer. Eyes the size of dinner plates, with peculiarly dull charcoal surfaces, stared down at them. An enormous mouth, lined with sharp teeth, opened and let out a great hiss. A sulfurous odor filled the air.

Below the head, there were four grasping arms, each tipped with three talons. These clutched angrily in the air and the thing flowed forward, over the lip of the pit and straight toward them. It tried to hold their gaze, to hypnotize them as it had enslaved so many men, but the dragons were immune to its power.

The dragons fanned out to form a *V* to receive it. Chektor and Vlok on the flanks, while Bazil and the

Purple Green waited for it face on in the center. Kesepton prowled behind the dragonboys to keep away
any interference from the dozens of armed men
crouched along the walls.

Arrows flashed in to bounce off the armor plate.
Others stuck around the rim of the eyes or inside the
mouth, the only apparent soft spots. The great monster hissed again even more loudly.

Dragons rushed forward and struck down with their
swords. The blades rang off the golden plate armor,
and the dragons fell back slightly bemused. It was rare
that such blows did not penetrate.

A red light glowed momentarily in the center of the
great, dead-looking eyes, and then with the speed of
a striking snake, the long body lashed sideways, hammered into Vlok, and sent him rolling. Swane jumped
backward just in time as that body whipped around,
and the big jaws snapped shut on the spot where he'd
been standing.

Vlok was just pulling himself back on his feet when
the head swung down on him and the jaws closed.
Vlok gave a scream of agony and desperately worked
his sword into the side of the monster's mouth.

The thing gave a convulsive shake, and Vlok flew
fifteen feet through the air and landed with a heavy
thud that shook the whole place. Vlok did not move.

Swane ran forward with an inarticulate scream of
rage and flung himself up onto the monster, stabbing
futilely at its armor plate with his short sword. The
thing plucked him away with one of its forearms and
would have bitten him but for the arrival of the Purple
Green, who shoved forward, rammed his shield into
the demon's face, and hewed down with his sword so
powerfully that it sank an inch into the neck armor.
There was a spray of yellow ichor that covered the
Purple Green from head to toe. The monster dropped
Swane, who scuttled away bruised but not broken,
and turned its full attention on the Purple Green.

The Purple Green had never faced anything larger than himself since he'd been a bantling and challenged the previous dragon lord of Hook Mountain. This creature was larger than anything that had walked on Earth since the days of the ancient reptile lords.

Still the wild one's heart did not quail. Fury too great for any thought of self-preservation had overridden the dragon mind. Nothing but death could end it now.

The battle cry of all Hook Mountain dragon lords rang again and again from the walls and ceiling of the chamber of the pit. The sword came down and bit deeply into the monster's side.

At the same time, old Chektor swung in and slammed his shield into the demon's serpent face. Teeth splintered and the head was forced back, but the huge body lashed out again and struck Chektor away, as if he was some four-ton game ball, and sent the Purple Green rolling backward, too. Relkin dodged out of the way of the wild dragon, fired on the hop, and saw his arrow bounce off the monster's unblinking eye. The great head darted down at him, but the intended strike caromed off a dragon shield and went wide.

A long white-steel sword gleamed as it rose and fell, Bazil hewed down with Ecator, and the blade sundered the gammadion's armor and went deep.

The monster's neck arched, and it snapped down at Bazil going for a grip across the back of the neck, but Baz spun quickly enough to get his shield up between the giant jaws before they could close. The thing took a grip on the shield with its teeth, shook its head, and lifted the leatherback off his feet for a moment before Bazil thrust Ecator into the monster's throat. Well made was the blade Ecator, a bane to all things of the enemy, and it sliced through the armor plate cleanly.

The monster released his shield and pulled back. The great head circled, the eyes coldly examining the dragon still standing. The others were starting to get to their feet.

It struck again, the jaws snapping shut just in front of the dragon to distract him while the body lashed around, sweeping at him with twenty tons behind it. Bazil could not evade it, but he could spring up to meet it, get his feet on it, drive the sword home, and hold on to the hilt. He lost his shield in the process, but Ecator sank in as Baz clung there and was borne upward as the monster turned to bring its jaws to bear. Frantically Baz jerked the sword out of the monster's flesh and slid back. The sword came up between them. The great jaws slammed shut just out of reach. The monster coiled itself.

The Purple Green was back on its feet, but moving slowly, still groggy. Chektor was struggling to get up. Vlok did not move.

It was one leatherback dragon against the gammadion beast. It attacked, the body looping out to his left while the head struck directly at him. He stepped quickly back to his right, while keeping the sword ready with both hands. Still the demon's tail caught him across the legs, and he lost his footing and fell.

The jaws darted in but found the Purple Green in their way, shield and sword ready. The sword lashed down and struck across the monster's head, but did not penetrate the armor plate. Still the great skull rang like a bell, and it pulled back for a moment and regarded the Purple Green with a baleful glare.

Old Chektor lurched forward. The great serpent body contracted and swung itself toward the brasshide, who went down beneath it.

Mono was knocked flying, the monster rode over Chektor crushing him with its weight.

Relkin ran at it, leaping up onto its back and climbing toward the head. It felt him, the head turned, and the jaws raced down and snapped shut just a foot from him as he abandoned his hold and jumped for his life.

Bazil hauled himself back on his feet. Damned boy was going to get killed. Bazil took a huge breath. Damn dragonboys were always getting into trouble. He lurched forward to engage once more.

Relkin tried to roll when he landed, but only half managed it and found himself flat on his back, breathless, unable to move, staring up at the great bulk that was going to crush him to death. Inexorably it slid forward while he started to wriggle, but he was too late and his death loomed over him.

CHAPTER FIFTY-NINE

Relkin's eyes were shut so he never saw his salvation, but before the monster could crush him, a leatherback dragon crashed into its side and stabbed home with the long steel.

It spun around to grapple with Baz and missed Relkin by a handbreadth. The sword sang, and the monster lost one of its four arms. Yellow blood fountained briefly from the stump. Bazil retreated slowly, keeping the sword in its face. The great serpent pursued him, now cautious of that terrible blade but driven on by colossal rage.

Slowly, very slowly, Relkin crawled away. His breath was hard in his throat, his whole body ached as it had never ached before.

The men along the walls were moving in now, made confident by the success of the gammadion serpent. They came on with their swords out, ready to hew down Kesepton and the boys, and take the dragons in the rear.

The Mesomaster urged them on with harsh words. Kesepton did not wait for them, however, but gave a shout and charged, isolating the nearest and driving him back with a flash of swordplay. The others halted. The Mesomaster buzzed with rage, raised his hands, and unleashed a bolt of red fire that struck Kesepton full on. He dropped to his knees, clutching his skull.

Relkin's outstretched hand brushed against his bow.

He pulled himself up to a sitting position, notched an arrow, and wound the bow.

The men were coming forward again, their confidence greatly increased. Meanwhile Baz retreated from the monster while the other dragons were either dead, unconscious, or slowly dragging themselves back to their feet.

The men in back had cruel smiles on their faces, ready for the kill. Relkin, too, aimed.

And then the great chamber of the pit was abruptly illuminated by a great light up above. Hanging in the air above them for a second was an amazing apparition. Golden things like attenuated insects, six feet long, floated within a greenish glow.

Then they were gone again.

The Mesomaster urged the men on with a shriek of command. Relkin shook the spots out of his eyes and fired. His arrow sank into the throat of one of the nearest men who sagged to his knees. Then Relkin saw two slender figures enter the chamber and sweep down the steps toward the Mesomaster. Steel glittered in their hands.

At the last moment, Gog Zagozt sensed them and whirled around. Ribela's knife was knocked aside. The Mesomaster drew his own sword and drove Lagdalen back.

"How did you escape?" he snarled, and whipped around to confront Ribela once more.

She made no response but continued to approach, her great eyes locked onto his.

"So," snarled the Mesomaster, "you have come back for more punishment! You shall have it, hag!"

He spat words of power and raised his hand. Great arms of shadow reached out to the witch and seized her. Ribela shouted something. There was a flash of the white light, and the dark grip was broken. The arms vanished.

"Begone, foul thing," she said. "Too long have you accursed the world."

She raised her hands and released another bolt of white energy. It struck the Mesomaster square on the chest and sent him reeling a step backward. He recovered and buzzed loudly with amusement.

"Feeble!" he said grimly. "I am stronger than you in every way!"

He noticed the girl was creeping up on him with sword in hand. He remembered that knife thrust. He was still healing from it, in fact.

"Aha! The pretty one is here, too. Listen to me, hag. I shall take the pretty one for my own when this is done. I shall think of you often as I use her. She shall be my slave."

Ribela raised her hand once more, and again there came a flash of energies. This time Gog Zagozt was not even shaken.

"Bah! You waste your strength, witch. Your death approaches."

There came another brilliant green-white flash high up in the chamber. He gestured.

"You have called the Sinni to help you?"

"I have."

"They cannot enter here, we have a way of keeping them out."

Ribela felt a new terror at this revelation. The Sinni came from a higher order of existence. They possessed vast energy. Had the Masters truly grown so powerful? This was dread news, indeed.

Once more she tried to blast the Mesomaster to submission, but saw her weapon fail. She was too weak, without the aid of mice.

"Enough of this play!" The Mesomaster clapped his hands, barked a word of power, and brought down a crushing force upon Ribela. Slowly she crumpled beneath it and was ground down to the floor of the chamber. Gog Zagozt threw back his head and buzzed furiously as the force continued to crush the witch, snubbing her like an insect beneath some giant's finger.

Lagdalen threw herself forward at the Mesomaster, but she was caught by an upraised hand. She swung the sword, but it was parried. The horned mouth rasped a phrase, and she could no longer breathe. Her hands went to her throat, and she dropped to her knees. She could not suck air into her lungs.

The Mesomaster laughed once more.

He was interrupted by a sudden shriek behind him.

He turned to see the reborn god trashing from a terrible wound slashed across its throat. Yellow ichor sprayed forth, evaporating into a cloud of sulfurous gas. It sank back into its pit, vanquished by the sword Ecator. A dragon stood there hunched in fury, great sword shedding yellow blood to the stone floor.

Bazil turned and headed for the steps. The Purple Green was back on his feet. With his great sword at the ready again, the men of Dzu fell back, none daring to challenge a battledragon.

The Mesomaster retreated a step. This was an awkward situation all of a sudden. The crushing force had to be lifted from the witch, who gasped and struggled to breathe. These accursed hags were hard to kill!

He looked up, the damned dragon was getting too close. He turned and ran for the stairs. He would fetch some mud men. A dozen or so would suffice to bring down these dragons and beat them to death. He would enjoy that.

He sensed a figure running on his right and glimpsed a dragonboy momentarily. Then he felt something wrap around his ankles, and he toppled and fell just short of the stairs.

The damned boy had brought him down! With a scream of rage, he lashed at the boy and caught him a glancing blow with his horned fist, knocking him away.

A great shadow fell over him. The dragon was there.

"You die now," said the beast. It was incomprehensible. How could it have come to this when victory was within his grasp?

The great slab of white steel came down. The Mesomaster was no more.

Abruptly the air was filled with the sound of distant music, an immense choir of voices singing in eery harmonies. Golden attenuated insects floated twenty feet above the floor.

The men along the wall cowered down with cries of horror. Lagdalen was sitting up, sucking in long breaths of air.

The Lady Ribela staggered across to Relkin's prone figure. The boy was unconscious. She looked up into two pairs of dragon eyes.

"How is boy?"

Her fingers were on his pulse. "He lives, he will recover."

The dragons sniffed. "Good," said one of them.

Ribela stood up. One of the dragons picked Relkin up gently and held him with both hands.

Lagdalen had regained her feet. Ribela suddenly embraced her. Lagdalen was never more surprised by anything than this.

"My lady," she began.

"Thank you, Lagdalen of the Tarcho, by the Mother beside me, Lessis chose well!"

She hugged the girl again.

"The Sinni came. The gammadion has been sent back to its own world."

"Oh, my lady, I thought you were dead."

"I think I may have been. The Sinni revived me. They need me yet, it seems."

Her eyes lit on the men cowering along the wall and the great dragons, the Broketail and the Purple Green, who were standing over another dragon's body.

"Begone!" she commanded the evil men of the power, "and tell all the world that the god Sephis is destroyed. Your Masters have been defeated once more."

CHAPTER SIXTY

With the aid of the surviving priests of Sephis, they hauled the wounded dragons out of the Temple and laid them out on the pavement. It was in the middle of the night, red Rasulgab, the dragon star, gleamed high above.

Vlok was conscious now but in great pain from broken bones in his tail and legs. Relkin helped Swane to fasten splints made from the beams of a wagon and tie them around the leatherback's legs and the broken section of the tail. Vlok hissed the while, but said nothing. Swane had tears in his eyes.

Bazil came over at one point and clasped hands with Vlok.

"Look like you become a broketail, too, Vlok."

Vlok tired to laugh, but it hurt too much.

Poor Chektor was in a worse state. Bazil sat by his old comrade in arms and murmured encouragement in dragon speech. Old Chek was barely conscious, however, his ribs were crushed and he was struggling just to breathe.

Mono sat by his dragon and scratched his ears, fighting back tears. His right arm was broken, and he could do little else. Lagdalen cleaned the various scratches and scrapes with water she brought from the Sephisti cooking fires. The enemy soldiers had dispersed, abandoning everything and fleeing the ancient city of Dzu.

Kesepton and Ribela returned from their interrogation of Odirak. The death of the Mesomaster had broken the enemy's power in Dzu, and the intervention of the Sinni had returned the gammadion to its own world. The enemy forces had splintered with the loss of the malacostracan demon. The hypnotizing power that had bound the armies of Sephis together had vanished in an instant, leaving its victims confused, witless, and wandering. The siege of Ourdh was over.

Kesepton and Relkin went down to the harbor and started a fire to signal to the *Nutbrown,* waiting out below the horizon on the great river.

Relkin automatically collected wood from here and there, twigs and brush for the most part. They piled them high on what had once been the dockside of ancient Dzu, and Relkin tore a piece off his shirt and shredded it on the point of his knife to make some tinder. Kesepton watched him work and marveled at the boy's ability to survive. Dragonboys were tough— if he'd ever doubted it, this campaign had convinced him.

The fire took quickly, and they started two more and completed the prearranged signal for the *Nutbrown.*

After a minute's wait, they saw two lights out upon the river and they knew the ship was coming.

An hour later, the *Nutbrown* boats came cautiously into the old, ruined dockside of Dzu. Kesepton gave them the news, and a great shout went up from the men in the boats. A moment later, it was echoed by the crew of the ship.

Quickly they worked to move Vlok and Chektor aboard, lashing together three boats to make a raft and hauling the wounded dragons up onto the deck with block and tackle.

Wandering through the Temple, a little later, Swane and Relkin heard noises from behind a locked door. They pried the door open and released Banwi Shogemessar, the Fedafer of the well-watered land, emperor of Ourdh, master of the great river, etc., etc.

He babbled at them in Uld, which they could not understand, so they lead him down to the dock.

At the sight of Ribela, the little Fedafer gave an inarticulate cry and tried to run. Relkin collared him and with the aid of some seamen, they pushed him into a boat and rowed him out to the ship.

It was near dawn. The wounded dragons were aboard, the *Nutbrown* was raising her anchor while the crew set sail. Ribela stood on the forecastle alone. The witch gazed back at the ruined city as it started to recede behind them, her thoughts filled with wonder and concern.

A nearby sound startled her. She looked over her shoulder. The dragonboy Relkin and the leatherback from Quosh were there. Ribela started to say something, but was preempted by the boy who pointed back to the city.

"Look, lady."

She caught a movement in the air above the city, something huge, as big as a dragon. It wheeled there, circling over the Temple.

"The rukhbat," she murmured. Ribela realized with a chill how close she had come to being taken forever into the grip of the Masters.

The rukhbat gave a wailing cry, then turned and flew away into the north.

"What is it?" said Bazil.

"A thing of the enemy. It was to take me to Padmasa."

"Too late for that."

"Indeed, Sir Dragon, too late and all thanks to you."

Baz grunted and hefted Ecator in its scabbard. "Too late thanks to this sword!"

EPILOGUE

Far away in the chill catacombs of Padmasa, the news of the destruction of Sephis and the demise of the Mesomaster Gog Zagozt provoked rage among the High Ones.

An unusual meeting was held. In a single chamber, the Masters congregated. The psychic power in the room was so intense that even Mesomasters could stand it for no more than a few minutes at a time.

The problem in the East had grown worse. First at Tummuz Orgmeen and now in Ourdh, they had been defeated. The arrogant little city-states on the littoral of Argonath had become a menace. It was time that the Masters turned their resources to the task. It was time for the utter destruction of the Argonath.